OCTOBER 6, 1906: OMEN OF DISASTER

Young Tracey Whiteside joined her lover on the terrace of the little house on Russian Hill. They'd spent a passionate "honeymoon" the night before, and this morning they were to be married at City Hall. From the highest point in San Francisco, arms about each other, they looked out toward the bay; the air seemed to be unnaturally still.

At that very moment, one hundred and fifty miles due West of where Tracey stood enraptured, the old merchant ship, *Carrie*, skippered by Otis Whiteside, moving slowly on a quiet sea, suddenly suddenly shuddered and rose out of the water as though flung by a giant hand. Otis was unaware that a huge fissure had opened in the San Andreas Fault, many fathoms beneath the ocean, and was moving relentlessly toward San Francisco . . .

THE SCARLET SISTERS

Lee Davis Willoughby

A DELL/JAMES A. BRYANS BOOK

Published by
Dell Publishing Co., Inc.
1 Dag Hammarskjold Plaza
New York, New York 10017

ISBN: 0-440-07640-4

Printed in the United States of America

First printing—1985

Chapter 1

The girl awakened abruptly, disdaining any ritual yawning or stretching. She made the transition as if turning a silver dollar from its reverse side, *sleep*, to the obverse, *awake*. In the dry heat of her cotton chemise, the dawn sun piercing the railroad car blinds with golden spears, she remained motionless on the blanket roll bed, feeling the wheels speed over the rails of the Great Plains. Lillian Whiteside knew they were the Great Plains, because Clara Clayton had told her so and Clara had become her best friend in the past two weeks—a friend who didn't tease her about being the youngest of the group of thirty-two prospective brides, or steal her ration of food or squeeze her out of her turn to sleep on the railroad car floor. And Clara was her window to this world west of Boston, for she and Clara were a little different from the other thirty girls.

At twenty-four, the buxom and rotund Clara Clayton was the eldest of the group, an orphan and yet not in the sense of the others. Clara was already a rural New England school teacher when she lost her parents, while the other girls had spent the majority of their young lives in an orphanage.

Not Lillian Whiteside. Only with Clara had she shared the secret of how she came to be on this journey. Even the semi-educated Clara was aghast that a father and brother could be heartless enough to sell her to the McHenry Mail-Order Bride Service. Her chagrin was tempered when she learned the various orphanages had received a "fee" for the other girls. Clara's situation was different. She was a contract bride on a "match." Her prospective husband was a school teacher who required a bride with a similar background, and who would pay her fee to Thomas McHenry.

Lillian bounced purposefully from the bedroll and dressed swiftly, with a deftness remarkable in the swaying vehicle. In one quick motion, she pulled a petticoat to her waist and thrust over her slim seventeen year old body a dull brown cotton dress, coarse brown stockings and six button shoes. Then she squinted at her head in the midget mirror between each railcar window, fingering her long chestnut hair with angry strokes and proclaiming in a harsh, loud voice: ''The only thing of value and love my mother could give me was a hair brush. When I find out who stole it, there'll be a widower at the end of the line.''

She was met by angry grunts and groans from one end of the railcar to the other. Delighted that she had given them all a rude awakening, she kicked aside the rolled blanket between the seats and raised the window blind.

She smiled, bringing a sparkle to her dark green eyes. The Whiteside men were ocean-going seamen and she had been raised in a Boston house that looked upon the Atlantic. Before her was another sea that stretched to the horizon. A brown sea of waving terrain, the rock outcroppings the masts of ships and fishing trawlers.

Then, she saw something that had nothing to do with the sea. Flanking the train, but rapidly gaining, were a group of horseback riders. Yet, unlike any riders she had ever seen before. They and their mounts were like one, as though someone had glued these men to their saddles.

As she looked up the rail line to the west she beheld the grandest, wildest sight—such as few wagon train people were permitted to see and live to tell about. Many hundreds of Indians in full war paraphernalia, riding their splendid war ponies, rushed the train *en masse*. Some were galloping in one direction, others cantering in another, their lances topped with many-colored streamers, the fantastic Indian costumes lending an awful charm to the whole.

''Indians!'' Lillian gasped, as if not quite sure.

In equal portions she was awed and scared. Looking from west to east she perceived nothing but danger, which only increased her agitation; so she naturally turned to Clara as a protector, as a young chick espying the hawk in the air flutters toward the mother wing.

Lillian blinked her dark eyes as she crossed the aisle to a pretzel like form curled on the car seat.

"Clara, I have something to ask you."

The woman, vengefully seeking sleep beneath one twisted blanket, did not stir.

"Are the Indians here friendly or not?"

The sleeper snapped her head away from the whispered voice. "Lillian, please let me sleep a little longer. You know how hard it is for me to get any rest in these seats."

"I just wanted to tell you that there are a great many Indians riding along with the train."

The woman's head, shoulders and fleshy arms jerked upward from the seat as if propelled by a spring. She seized the pull cord of the blind and yanked. On the south side of the train was nothing but barren plain. "Good God. Is this one of your pranks? The sun is hardly up."

Lillian pointed. She whispered again—the breathy sounds almost tormented.

"On my side."

Wrenching her head around from the unnatural sleeping position, the woman could now see for herself. "If memory serves me correct, we would be in the land of the Cheyenne. But, sweetheart, we should be quite safe here in the train. If there was danger the conductor would have been through the car already."

Lillian was reassured by Clara's remarkable self-possessions and coolness.

Then, above the clatter of the wheels there arose a sound that brought Clara to her feet. As though on a given signal several hundred Indian voices broke into a cry so shrill and penetrating that only the dead could have slept through it. Both were aware that the sound also came from the south side of the train, where a score of braves were now racing along.

"You might go wake up Mr. McHenry. I'll see to the rest of the girls."

Lillian departed in brisk, quick steps—not the sullen

shuffle common when being sent to see Thomas McHenry in the next car.

Since they had left St. Louis the man's personality had changed as quickly as the travel arrangements. The journey had been accomplished in easy stages from Boston, with lay-overs and comfortable nights in inns and hotels. For that week and a half the fifty year old man had been father, mother and guardian of his angels. Then the train became their home and would remain their home until California. Even though the girls had a car to themselves, Thomas McHenry had made it like a prison. The car to the rear was a private car, which no one was allowed to enter. McHenry had purchased a quarter of the car next so the girls couldn't get by him to mingle with the passengers of the other four cars—and especially the first car after the locomotive.

McHenry, as though he had known the woman all his life, had informed his charges in St. Louis that the fashionable private car was especially designed by George Pullman for it's owner, Mrs. Liberty Wells O'Lee. whose husband had been one of the instrumental builders of the Central Pacific Railroad they would be riding into California. A woman, according to McHenry, who had become vastly rich and had been a personal friend of President Lincoln.

After the stuffy car, with night body odors, Lillian sampled the fresh morning air as though that were her only mission at hand. She put aside her normal fear of having to step from one platform to another. The first time she had looked down at the coupling device, she had been nearly mesmerized by the pattern of the parallel railroad ties. For a second it had seemed like the ties were rushing backward while the railroad car was stationary.

But for a moment she did glance down again. But in that same moment a shadow pattern began to wave among the rapidly moving ties. It made her jerk her head up and to the side.

Their heads were no more than twenty feet apart. It was as though they were stationary, as well, the Indian's pony already lathered keeping at a dead heat with the train.

Oddly, she thought only that they were about of an

equal age, this first Indian she had ever seen so close. Perhaps she was also his first sighting of a white girl, for his red and yellow painted face seemed momentarily puzzled and his bow arm frozen in place. Then it began to draw back.

Lillian halted all fears of crossing above the coupling. In one bound she was across and reaching to open the car door. Just as she began to push it open she heard something whistle by her head and imbed itself in wood. The natural reaction of curiosity made her look back and up. Had she jumped a split second later the arrow would have gone right through her head and not into the railroad car.

Lillian squeezed through the door and then fell back against it. Shivers ran up and down her back. At the far end of the car she saw the conductor enter and begin to pound on the doors of this Pullman sleeping car unit. At another time she might have laughed that he was attired only in long red underwear, but still had his round hat perched on his head as a badge of authority.

Then his repeated growl brought her back to reality.

"Get down on the floor and stay away from the windows."

The car had been designed to sleep twenty-two in their own right side of the car cubicles. However, Thomas McHenry had purchased the two four person roomettes—one for his private bedroom and one for a quasi office.

Lillian had been in the office unit, so assumed the man would be in the first door on the right. Abruptly, she opened the door and stepped in.

Thomas McHenry stood in a nightgown peeking out of a corner of the window blinds.

"The conductor is telling everyone to stay away from the windows."

"Good morning, Lillian," McHenry answered, as though a formal greeting was necessary, and without turning. "I think they are just putting on a boyish show for us. I've made the trip by wagon train, you know, and don't hear gunfire as yet."

Lillian swallowed hard. The man always tried to sound like the last authority on any given subject.

"I was almost just shot by an arrow." Even to herself her voice had a hysterical ring.

"To be sure," he said, turning, as though passing the time of day.

Then she did almost laugh. The pale blue one-piece nightgown came to just below his knees. His bare legs were almost laughably skinny and bowed and the nightcap seemed out of place above his moon face with its steely grey eyes and carefully clipped black mustache.

"I assume the girls are all safe," he went on, going to where his attire for that day was hung on a wall peg.

"Clara is getting them up."

McHenry studied his clothing, more attentively than her information. A man of meticulous schedules, he was momentarily loath to don fresh clothing until he had gone through his morning ritual of sponging off in the tiny lavatory.

Just then the conductor pounded on the door and Lillian swung it open.

"You both stay down on the floor," he rasped. "I'll go see to your young ladies, Mr. McHenry."

"Dressed like that?" McHenry snorted. "I forbid it!"

Charley Skopas blinked in disbelief. "Gotta go through that car to warn Mrs. Roach and her nieces."

"I am quite sure," McHenry uttered, in his insufferable manner, "that the sharp-tongued Mrs. Roach is capable of handling all of these savages by herself. Now, would you be good enough to fetch me my morning ration of hot water. I wish to bathe and shave before dressing."

Lillian could read in Charley's dropped jaw and flared eyes what he was thinking. The gentle old man's feelings toward Thomas McHenry were well known to all of the girls. It had been quite a burden for Charley and the dining car porter to haul food back to the girl's car three times a day, but McHenry had paid a special fee to the rail company to have it done that way. Charley, who had raised four daughters and had three granddaughters, knew that a proper young lady was the best protector of her treasures before marriage. Not a man who normally had beastly thoughts about any other man, but he had strong suspicions as to what manner of marriage preparation talks McHenry had with his girls individually in his "office."

Having been in the railroad business for four decades, he touched the brim of his cap with a finger, as though accepting McHenry's words as an order and quietly closed the door. Then he continued on toward the rear of the train. His main objective was the caboose and the rifle chest. He couldn't understand why the brakeman was not firing already.

"That was the outside rear door," McHenry gasped. "I'll have that man's job for disobeying me."

"He has his job to do as he sees it," Lillian muttered.

"Shut up!" McHenry growled, pulling off his nightcap and starting to raise the gown over his head. Lillian instantly turned away. "And look at me when I am speaking to you, young lady!"

"You are undressing, sir," she gulped.

"Don't give me that *innocent* nonsense! Your brother Karl was quite explicit in explaining how he had introduced you to the difference between male and female."

Lillian was aghast. "That is a horrible and wicked lie. I have never looked upon a man, including my brother, in my life."

McHenry's laugh was cruel. "Does your father also lie? He sold you to me because he feared you would turn out to be nothing but a little tramp and a sailor's whore. *I* am the one who has had to lie to your prospective groom. And you are still down on my schedule for this afternoon. I know a few tricks that will make your young man think you are still a virgin on your wedding night."

"But I am," Lillian cried, unable to stop the instant flow of tears.

"Very good, my dear," McHenry simpered. "Repeat this same act to convince the groom. You really have been a very difficult client. The other girls have been far more cooperative and appreciative of my training. Now, now, dry up the false tears. As long as you are here, and we really shouldn't leave, we might as well have the lesson now. Give me your hand."

Lillian was momentarily confused, but did not turn or offer her hand to him.

"I am not going to stand for one more second of your insolent ways," he barked, grabbing her by the wrist and pulling her arm backward. She tried to pull away, but his grip was like a vise. With a savage jerk he tugged her hand to his groin, but when it came in contact with thigh skin she drew her hand into a fist. And as though a twin reaction, her other hand also formed a fist, even as her body began to turn.

Her mother was a tiny, shy creature who never talked back or crossed Tracey Whiteside, but Lillian had seen her give her brother, Karl Whiteside a few belts that made him cry in pain. That was the image she had in mind when she brought her fist in contact with McKenry's belly.

The cubicle was filled with the sound of a scream and air being let out of a bellows, but her wrist was instantly released. She didn't wait for any other reaction. She was out both doors, as though they were one, jumped the platforms and tore into the next car.

She was met with pandemonium. Because the girls would not heed the warning of Clara or Charley they had raised every blind in the car. That many young white women in night dress had delighted the Indians. Almost every window, or each side, had been broken by arrows or expertly tossed tomahawks. Now, they were riding in close, making obscene gestures as to the girls' fate when the Iron Horse was captured.

Clara came down the aisle on the run. "Thank God, you're back. I can't make these ninnies listen."

Nor could Lillian barely hear her over the screams and wailings of thirty females gone hysterical.

"Then forget them!" Lillian shouted back over the din. "Let's get down and save ourselves."

From the rear of the train they heard the bark of rifle fire. Why the Cheyenne had not used their carbines up to the moment would remain a puzzlement. Meantime a fresh band of Indians were taking up the chase and were not remiss in using their shooting sticks. The two women were just crouching down when the first shot from the Cheyenne came flying over their heads.

It was too much for Karen Smothers. As though she had been hit, her scream went an octave higher than any other and she began to race up the aisle.

"Get down, you silly goose," Clara screamed, "get down!"

The girl's eyes told them that she was not hearing Clara. The scream turned into a mournful chant.

"They're going to rape us and kill us! All of us! I'll kill myself first!"

Clara jumped up to capture the willowy girl in her arms and try to soothe her. As soon as Clara was up, Lillian heard her growl and mutter. She looked up and saw that Clara was hit, an arrow coming from a front window struck her in the back, with the arrowhead coming out her left shoulder blade. Clara sank to her knees and then sat back against the aisle section of a seat. If nothing more it stilled Karen. As though ordered she sank down beside Clara and stared at both ends of the arrow as though it had pierced her body.

"Stay with her, Karen," Lillian soothed, "I'm going to go get Charley."

Karen nodded dully. Lillian sensed that the responsibility would keep her mind just as dulled.

Lillian got around them, creeping on hands and knees toward the far end of the car. Crouched between the last row of seats were the "trio."

Amy Forsyth, Beth Mooers and Carol Wilson had been dubbed the "trio" long before this journey. "A", "B" and "C" nameless arrivals at the orphanage on the same day, they had been inseparable friends for eighteen years.

Next to Clara, Lillian liked them best of the whole lot. They were honest, straightforward girls. Each knew, without saying it out loud, that they were very plain females of face and body. All reared in a Catholic orphanage, they had been given the option of becoming "mail-order brides" or taking the veil. None had the true calling for the latter and made a unanimous vote for the former.

"How is Clara?" Amy asked, who was always the spokeswoman for the trio.

"I couldn't help her, but am going to find Charley."

"We aren't allowed into the next car," Beth Mooers said, as though repeating someone else's words. Beth was always the negative for anything Amy would say positive, leaving Carol Wilson to jump one way or the other.

"I don't think it applies right now," Carol said, in her husky voice that always sounded like she didn't want to get caught talking during the "silent hour" of prayer. "We'll see to Clara until you get back."

It gave Lillian comfort in knowing she was not alone in handling a situation she had never faced before.

Life was like a series of constant headaches, Charmayne Roach maintained. No woman, she would say, can ever articulate fully to a man her sentiments about the reasons behind female headaches. And the average women—and she was not average as a veteran of a thousand such blinding headaches—could convey the irrational reason behind them to the non-sufferer. The headache of not wishing to have a man was one thing, but bearable. It was the cursed sense of disorientation, of distortion, when having been without a man for two months, as she had been, that brought on the other level of pain. It had come on that morning—a few minutes after the conductor had awakened her—with a palpable click, as if the Indian attack were responsible. Fighting the onset, she dressed quickly in the closest garment at hand and waited. There was another facet of this manner of headache that defied definition: the magnification of the petty annoyance of waiting.

Because she could only sleep in total blackness, the windows in her bedroom of the private Pullman car had been sealed over and draped for this journey. In the next compartment she could hear the muted, wispy sound of two of her four *nieces* wondering what she had gotten them into. She offered a silent prayer they would not storm in on her for help or inspiration. Her mirrored face was haggard, the clean beauty filmed with worry. For a month she had had no pride of the flesh, but her distrait appearance irked her less because she did not look attractive than as a cruel reminder of a month of failures and shortcomings, a month of things done badly, mishandled. Through the veil of pain, she thought of only four "nieces" recruited through her carelessness, a mother in St Louis she had insulted, her San Francisco career, unfulfilled and half-hearted— and, now, the real wreckage of her marriage.

She tried to submerge the past. It reminded her of the endless arguments she and her husband had engaged in over the past several weeks. It were as though two decades had never been lived. When he had been injured in a wagon train accident in 1849, she had no choice but to leave him and her mother in St. Louis, going on to the gold fields of California with her brother. She had won; he had sulked; now she wondered if perhaps he had been right. The first time, not this time.

The first time had been a living hell. After three days in the gold fields her brother had been killed by a claim jumper and she was left to search for a means of survival. She had used her beauty, wits and talents to make more gold than panning for it. In time, as the gold fields petered out, she found herself in San Francisco and in time the madam of a house. The substantive basis for the endless arguing for the past weeks. Neither Fritz Roach, nor her mother, would return with her as long as she remained what she was, even though her profession had paid for their food, clothing and lodging for twenty-one years. It was like attempting to untangle the backlash of a fishing line; eventually one got disgusted and snipped away the impossibly snarled knots with a knife.

She had departed with her creel filled with only four fish, when she desperately needed a good dozen replacement girls for the house. But she had to admit the true reason for her headache. Never once in those weeks had her husband even tried to take her hand or kiss her or even suggest she might lie beside him in bed after he had been lifted from his wheelchair. She had been treated like a leper, although the doctor had told her that Fritz was fully capable of being a full man, except for his legs, crippled below the knees. Therein lay the insult to her mother, to care for Fritz as she had done for two decades. Both women understood the underlying meaning of the outburst, even though both knew in their heart it was unfounded. But the stinging words could not be taken back or immediately forgiven.

Footsteps outside her door were halted by a rude female voice.

"But I must go through this car to find the conductor," she heard a voice demand.

The negative was even ruder and Charmayne slid back her door, which was on a sliding track.

"What seems to be the problem?" Charmayne asked, in the melodious alto she had learned to use only on male clients when they seemed too boisterous.

"Little slut wants to go through the car," Babe Ebersold answered, red-eyed, her nose covered with beauty cream.

Lillian didn't need to be told she was looking upon Mrs. Charmayne Roach. She had watched the elegantly attired lady alight from her coach in St. Louis before boarding the train. At that moment she did not see the haggard look, but only recalled the classically beautiful face under the heavily feathered hat, the high, proudly-carried breasts, hourglass waist and elegant carriage.

Nor did Charmayne need to be told that this was one of McHenry's girls. At various water and fuel stops she had seen them stretching their legs on the siding. And this one she had noted every time. Lillian was her ideal as the perfect recruit. Fresh, with a body still youthful enough to suggest the marvelous female lines it would have in two to three years. Which also applied to the hair and face. The chestnut hair Charmayne would have shortened to shoulder length and used a hot curling iron upon. Although the girl was slim, the face still retained too much baby fat. Once it was outgrown, it would be a perfect heart shape of creamy complexion, with those marvelous dark green eyes making it exquisite.

"Of course you must go through," Charmayne said, "and I shall escort you."

Babe sniffed and flounced back into her cubicle in her

wretched cotton wrapper, knowing she had made a mistake signing up with this madam. She knew she should have stayed working the riverboats between St. Louis and New Orleans.

Lillian couldn't help but note the condition of the cubicle as she passed. The floor was littered with newspapers and dime novels, opened clothing boxes, an antipasto of dirty dresses, odd shoes and lingerie. The Roach *nieces* seemed to shed clothing like molting pigeons. And the next cubicle was little different. These two *nieces* stood in the door and eyed Lillian as though she were one of the savages. Oddly, Lillian could not help but think that the *nieces* looked somewhat older than their aunt and hardly measured up to her elegant, cultured self.

"This is most kind of you . . ." Lillian started to say, as they rounded the corner into the main portion of the private car, whose sight stopped her words short.

Never had she seen such beauty. A round dining room table, with four Queen Ann petite-point chairs sat to the right, with a high-boy of crystal and China to the left. The rest of the car was set out as a living room, in a simple color scheme of deep rose and ivory. The chairs and divan were plush velvet over cherry wood frames and arms. Half-way down the right side was a Franklin stove the porcelain front in rose and ivory, flanked by floor to ceiling book racks.

Other than a hair brush, Lillian's mother had given her one other great gift—the training to read. It was another secret she and Clara shared in common, and now Lillian felt envy. When she had seen the dime novels in the cubicles she had desired them to read on the long journey. Now she envied Mrs. Roach such a library.

She hesitated and let her eyes wander over them just long enough for the wise woman to pick up her cue for an opening gambit in getting to know her.

"Do you read, my dear?"

"Some," Lillian stammered.

"Then feel free to come and select whenever books you desire."

"Oh, my, we are forbidden . . ."

Charmayne stopped her short with a smile that was sweet, inviting and asking for forgiveness. "That was my rule, dear girl, to keep the curious passengers from turning this into a tour stop. So, if I made the rule, I can break it on your account. But, we can get to that matter later. Our concern right now is the care of your wounded friend."

Her compassion warmed Lillian deeply. Only at a distance had she seen the women of "class" in Boston and they had all seemed so cold and aloof, as if they couldn't be bothered lowering their eyes to the common trash they saw on the streets. Mrs. Roach hardly fit that mold.

Nor did she let the coupling bother her. She stepped across without looking down and sailed right into the caboose.

Charley was racing from right windows to left windows, firing rifles he had set out by each. The brakeman laid sprawled in the open door at the end of the caboose. No one needed to announce he was dead, his posture clearly indicated his fate.

Wagon train instinct motivated Charmayne to begin to reload Charley's rifles as she called over his shots.

"How many more rifles?"

"These six and four up in the cab of the engine."

"I'll take two to my car and send you back someone to reload."

"But . . ." Lillian started, stopped and then went on. "What about Clara with the arrow through her shoulder?"

Charmayne began to thrust boxes of cartridges at her to carry. "Don't worry Charley with that, I'll see to it. I came West the first time on a wagon train, my dear."

It was the second time she had heard that phrase in the past hour, and as if by magic the first speaker of the phrase appeared.

"How dare she bother you, Mrs. Roach!" McHenry gasped, in mock shock. "Lillian, return to our car immediately."

"She shall," Carmayne said coldly, "to fetch the wounded woman to my car."

"Oh?" he blinked, and saw his own opening wedge to

get to know the woman and her nieces. "I would be most happy to be of service, Mrs. Roach."

She picked up a rifle, shot back the bolt, inserted a cartridge and pushed the bolt back home. "Did you follow that action?"

"My dear woman, I have been on buffalo hunts with some of the great scouts of the west."

"Then help Charley reload for a savage hunt."

"No need," Charley carped. "They'll start pulling back in a second or two."

"Why?" It was like a soprano, alto and baritone trio response.

Charley was consulting his pocket watch. "Close to twenty minutes to Cheyenne. They didn't get us, but they don't want to cut it short and have us get in and warn the pony soldiers to give them chase. I'll fire after them for another two minutes and then give it up."

"Why two minutes," McHenry demanded.

Charley chuckled. "Ain't due to start delivering hot shaving water for another two minutes, sir."

And the first hot water was delivered to the private car of Charmayne Roach. It was for medical and not shaving purposes. The trio, with a fluttering Karen in the wake, had helped guide Clara to the dining room of the private car, while Charmayne had ordered a clean up of one of the cubicles. She had an immediate rebellion on her hands.

"So," she said, in a voice so low and menacing that they immediately got her measure as a leader, "you refuse to go into a roomette that normally sleeps four. At the next stop, ladies, is the Cheyenne Social Club. I bought you in St. Louis and I have about fifteen minutes to decide which of you slovenly creatures to sell to them."

Then she went and took one look at the arrow and at Clara. Amazingly, here was the second of McHenry's brood who had caught her attention. Experience had taught her that a certain percentage of men came into a brothel on a wave of fantasy. They wanted the most exemplary female available to fulfill their expectations. Others were downright homesick, needing a countryfied woman with meat on her bones.

Clara was all of that. Even with a burning pain in her shoulder she held her head high.

Charmayne was simple in words and deed. "Clara, and I hope you don't mind my calling you Clara, I am going to grasp the arrow and break off the arrowhead end. Then, with one quick thrust, I will pull it out from the back. I won't lie to you. This is going to hurt. Frankly, it is going to hurt like hell, so scream if you wish. Then I will pour some brandy into each side of the wound." Then she laughed. "That's when I shall scream, for it is imported brandy."

"Then let's each have a swig of it first, dearie." A faint smile appeared on Clara's pained face. All of the woman's features had an off-center quality. One hazel eye seemed fractionally higher than the other and her nose had nostrils at a slant. Even her ears, with the brown hair pulled back into a bun, were out of whack.

The deed was done swiftly, without a single flinch. Charmayne studied her patient warmly, wishing she had two dozen like her.

A glance from the corner of her eyes told her that Lillian was no longer alone.

"Well," McHenry snorted, "glad to see that over. Come, Clara, back to *our* car!"

"You just wait!" Charmayne shouted. She poured a dram more brandy into each side of the wound. "She is going nowhere until a doctor sees her in Cheyenne. And after that I shall go by his orders."

"If they are necessary," he shrugged.

"If?" She eyed him with amused wariness. Was he also going to do some selling in Cheyenne? For a moment her fine features revived and she was an adolescent beauty—so young, so fair—who had been secured into the business by a man just like this. She would never have a chance to get even with the original, but McHenry would make a marvelous substitute.

* * *

There was to be a six hour delay in Cheyenne, while these three special cars were switched over to Central Pacific from Union Pacific. Time enough for Charmayne to commerce a trade, if not a sale, with Bill McFarlan at the Cheyenne Social Club. He was ready for new stock, but not extra girls. Times were not like they used to be. A wagon train might linger for days, a train for hours. Times were just getting too fast and complicated.

But for the local cowhands, four new girls would increase his business fourfold and he thought the same would apply for Charmayne.

Actually, she didn't care. She just wanted four new bodies who knew nothing of the past few hours. Her sights were now set higher. The challenge of recruiting the best had stirred her again. The headaches were gone.

They might have returned if she had seen Thomas McHenry sighting her coming out of the Cheyenne Social Club. His every intention had been to rid himself of Lillian Whiteside and Clara Clayton, no matter the loss.

Now he saw another buyer, who would pay the cold, hard cash.

Chapter 2

It was cold and hard, but hardly cash. The Central Pacific train sat motionless in the high Sierra's, a spring snow storm holding it fore and aft.

The fireman made a tepee out of his finger tips and lifted the peak to his tiny mouth. "Bet we are able to break through before they can get here to dig us out."

"You're on," murmured the engineer.

They did not take into consideration that the melting condition was vanishing as rapidly as the sun into the Pacific west.

Charmayne dusted away the condition as if she were chasing a fruit fly off a piece of fruit. "It happens every May. One train or another always gets bogged down in a spring storm."

"I'm certainly glad you have the stove," Lillian enthused. "The rest of the train is like an iceberg."

"Then why not stay here to read your book."

"I wouldn't want to disturb your nieces."

Charmayne nodded compassionately. The four new girls had been given strict orders to stay within the roomette so that no one would know of the switch. "They all have a touch of the sniffles and are staying in their compartment."

"I would love to stay, Mrs. Roach. I feel so different in these surroundings, but would feel guilty being warm and cozy while the other girls were huddled together under their blankets."

"Then invite *some* of them to join you, especially Clara. I want to examine the wound and see if the dressing needs changing."

Charmayne had come to the conclusion that Lillian was smart as a raccoon on most matters and innocent as a lamb in all others. She knew that the girl would bring along only those who had helped with Clara.

The *some* were easy to invite, the trio segregated from the rest, as usual, with Karen huddled nearby waiting for inclusion.

"You four go on in and tell Mrs. Roach that I am waiting for Clara."

Lillian frowned. Ever since her episode with Mr. McHenry, he had had little to do with either of them. It now puzzled Lillian that he had sent for Clara the moment she had left to go borrow a book. The normal session with McHenry ran for an hour or two. She was debating whether to leave word with one of the other girls when Clara entered the other end of the car.

Even when Clara approached, there was a moment of hypnotic silence. Clara was immobilized by McHenry's effrontery, clutching something to her breast.

"How dare he!" Clara screamed. "How dare he show me this picture now! I should have been told the truth right at the start!"

Her high voice liquefied; she was sobbing. Lost in unreasoning tears, she fled through the door to the platform. Lillian, shaken, but always compassionate, sped after the plumpish figure.

The low lying snow clouds neutralized the late afternoon sunlight. Clara presented only her back to Lillian, although she had lifted her fevered face to let the snow flakes melt upon it.

"Go on through to the next car," Lillian ordered. "Mrs. Roach wants to see your wound."

"No," she said hoarsely. "I now wish the Indian would have killed me." She lifted what had been clutched against her breast and held it up at arm's length. "That's my future! The man has already outlived four wives in fifty years. How does McHenry have the gall to compare me with what the man requested in his letter. 'A strong, work-horse woman under thirty with a command of reading and writing to help teach in our farm school.' Oh,

Lillian, that doesn't hurt as much as the fact that the man demanded someone plain at the cheapest fee McHenry had available. I feel . . . I feel . . ."

Lillian had been staring over her shoulder at the tintype. It was hideous—three inches wide, a green-velvet frame, and, within, a stern faced man of seventy with a long straggly beard and a toothless grin. Then, in a swift, angry motion, Lillian tore the tin-type from Clara's hand, glared at it and tossed it out into the snowbank.

"I don't know how we are going to do it, Clara, but you will never have to marry that man. Now, come inside before we both freeze to death!"

Charmayne sensed that some great drama had just been played out, but was adroit enough to keep from prying too quickly. Instead, she became the charming hostess in the salon of the private car, regaling them with stories of San Francisco. She gave them a sense of the splendor of her house on the Barbary Coast, without letting them know the true nature of the house.

"I made my money out of the gold fields and now mainly out of the shipping. San Francisco has become the biggest port on the west coast."

Lillian drew in a breath. "Do you then, by chance, know a sailor by the name of Otis Whiteside?"

"I would hardly call him a sailor, my dear. He is the captain of one of the finest ships in the Lee Line. Lee, of course, being the line owned by Mrs. Liberty Wells O'Lee, the lady in the first car of the train—" She stopped. Charmayne afforded herself a secret sign of the cross. Was this the wedge she was looking for to get Lillian away from McHenry? "Do you know him, my dear?"

Lillian had shut her eyes. Her bloodless fists were pressing at her throat. Then Charmayne, cursing her own obviousness, recalled Lillian's last name. But it just couldn't be, she told herself. The big, lumbering Swede with near-white blond hair and muttonchop whiskers could not be related to Lillian. He was a regular customer when in port and she'd thought she knew his history well. He had been at sea since he was twelve years old and had come off a Swedish ship three years before to go to work for Liberty.

She also knew, that even though his face was still boyish and the light blue eyes were full of the desire for adventure, that he was quite a man. But, she reminded herself, that was beside the point. "What is it, Lillian? Do you feel sick?"

Lillian shook her head and opened her eyes. "I'm fine. It was just a bit of a shock to learn that you knew him. Just a very distant relative, that's all."

It was Clara's turn to frown. She wondered why Lillian had lied. This had to be her brother they were talking about; the one whose service Lillian's father, Tracey Whiteside had sold for three years to a ship so he could have more rum money to drink away.

Then, when it was obvious that the train would not be moving on that night, and they were bedded down in their blankets and bedrolls, Clara reflected on what they had told her.

For warmth they had all remained fully dressed, but Lillian's motive was two-fold. She waited until the car was filled with the sound of sleeping women and quietly unwrapped herself from the blankets.

"Where are you going?" Clara whispered.

Lillian motioned her to silence and put her mouth close to Clara's ear. "Mrs. Roach may know my brother, but I can learn more from the woman he works for."

Clara looked at her challengingly: that car was strictly off limits. But she couldn't deny the glint in Lillian's eyes. She had to let her try.

Lillian went down the aisle slowly and calmly. She only had the memory of a two-year-old to go on, and even that was a bit confused. Her brother Otis had not been mentioned in the household for fifteen years and her young memory of him became blurred with that of her brother Karl. Then, the night her father sold her as a mail-order bride, her mother had gone to pieces.

Trying to repress the feeling that she would never again see this child, as well, Maureen Whiteside had shared her broken heart with her daughter. For two years she had been able to keep track of her son's ship, without letting her husband know. Then, when Otis went to the Pacific she had no way of keeping track of him. And then came a truth that was shattering. Tracey Whiteside was not Otis's father. His father had been a tall, blond Swedish sailor who had swept Maureen off her feet. They were to have been married on his return from Cuba. The ship was caught in a hurricane and went down with all hands on board. Only then did she learn she was with child. Tracey Whiteside was a sailor on her father's fishing trawler. He was quite willing to marry her to take a step up in life and she had no choice but to accept the drab man, but Tracey had hated Otis from the day he was born; giving all his love and attention to Karl, who came a year later.

And, continuing to be quite frank, Maureen let Lillian know why she wasn't fully loved by her father. He had not wanted the burden of more children and Maureen had been grateful that he had more desire for rum and other women then her bed. Then, one drunken night, he must have thought she was one of his other women. She had tried to reason and resist him, but he took her by force. She was then blamed for getting pregnant again and for giving him a girl instead of another boy.

Lillian's only delight in hearing the story was that Otis was only her half-brother—there was no Tracey Whiteside blood in him. She had promised her mother to try to find him and to try to make her marriage a loving one, even if she didn't know the man Thomas McHenry had selected for her.

But going through the cold railroad cars, she couldn't help but wonder if McHenry's selection for her was as disasterous as his selection for Clara. She shivered, more on that thought than the cold.

This private car was totally different from Mrs. Roach's. Through the platform door window Lillian could view the whole salon end of the car. A fire blazed in a pink marble manteled hearth. Royal blue velvet was draped at each window, with crystal gaslight sconces between each. The plush furniture were in various hues of blue velvet, set upon a carpet as pink as the marble fireplace. At the far end, before the entryway to the sleeping compartments was a massive teakwood desk of oriental design, illuminated by a crystal desk lamp.

A woman stood beside the desk, with her back to Lillian, saying goodnight to three stair-step children in night clothes in the charge of a Chinese maid. And when the woman turned, Lillian saw that the women, like her private car, was in a class by herself.

Liberty Lee, because most in California had started to drop the O, was as slender as a willow branch and hardly looked like the mother of three. Her gown of rose moire gave a sparkle to her green eyes and was expertly draped to set off her rounded bosom, slim waist and full hips. A band of the moire sat upon her brown curly hair, holding it back away from the classic contours of her face.

Still, in Lillian's view, she did not look as formidable and unapproachable as the off limits warning suggested. So, mustering her courage, Lillian turned the handle and ventured in.

Immediately a barrier arose before her that she had not been able to see from the door window.

Li-Tan kowtowed, but more to stop her advance than in greeting.

"Private car, missy. No allow."

"I wonder if I might have a word with Mrs. O'Lee," Lillian stammered. She had never seen a Chinaman before and was suddenly more fascinated by his pigtail then her mission.

Li-Tan was old and tough and posed as stupid to throw occidental people off guard. He had been a gift, through the House of Soong, from the Emperor P'u Yi to Chu-chee, the Chinese name given to Liberty O'Lee by her old friend the powerful merchant, Kai Soong. A slow speaker of English, because Liberty always conversed with him in Mandarin dialect, he chewed each word in his mind before answering.

"Perhaps no. Mistress busy with other matters."

Lillian could see that the woman had taken a seat at the desk and was ignoring them as though they were not a mere twenty feet away.

Lillian would not be put off. "I have just come from the

private car of Mrs. Charmayne Roach. I have been informed that a certain Otis Whiteside works for Mrs. Lee. I wish only information as to his whereabouts."

The man shook his head. "Mistress busy, I think."

With that Liberty did shuffle the papers in front of her on a pretext, her face immobilized. She wouldn't let this girl see the rage she felt at the mention of Charmayne Roach and Otis Whiteside.

It had been almost, learning in St. Louis that Charmayne had a car on the train: using her influence, she had kept the two private cars a part. Now she felt threatened, reinforcing her conviction that they were plotting against her because she had been fighting hard to get rid of the Barbary Coast district. Sure, it was a sexual haven for her own sailors, but she felt they could be just as well serviced by the bordellos of Oakland.

"I have a very personal reason for wishing to know about him," Lillian pleaded.

Liberty, without looking up, spoke in crisp Chinese. "Send her away," she said hoarsely. "I have nothing to say to her." For Liberty thought she now saw Charmayne's gambit. She regarded Lillian as one of Charmayne's girls and this as a ruse to prove to her that one of her sea captains, and the best of her sea captains, was involved with one of Charmayne's little sluts.

"Please," Lillian begged, ignoring the woman speaking only in Chinese. "It is a family matter I need to discuss with Otis Whiteside."

Because her mind was centered on her conflict with Charmayne, Liberty made a rare error—she misinterpreted Lillian's words, taking 'family matter' to mean the noose of a bastard child that this girl intended to hang around Otis Whiteside's neck.

"Inform her," she said, speaking in cold, harsh English, "that his ship is in the Orient and will not return for three to four months."

Li-Tan smiled indulgently and opened the door for Lillian's exit.

Lillian knew it would do no good to argue further, although she could not understand her rude treatment.

Still, she had information she hadn't had before. But it dashed one hope that had been building in her mind—throwing herself on the mercy of her half-brother to save her from the marriage McHenry had in store for her. She would just have to come up with a different solution to save herself and Clara.

Chapter 3

No solution to the dilemma came to her the next day after the train was plowed out and made its way down into a different world. The fertile valley along the American River was abloom with spring.

The Lee car was uncoupled in Sacramento and Lillian felt a strange relief. Whatever she was going to do at the end of the line, she somehow didn't want that woman knowing about it.

Then they rode through farmland ablaze with color, making Clara wonder if her lot in such an area would be too bad. It was hardly like the harsh New England farms with their long, hard winters.

It hardly seemed possible that they had been nearly frozen to death the night before and were now sweltering in heavy, humid heat.

Nor had anything come to Lillian yet when they detrained at the Oakland railhead. But, again, her mind was swayed by the apparent wealth of Charmayne Roach. Two magnificent coaches were there to take Charmayne and her *nieces* the rest of the way to San Francisco.

But the motivator for Lillian's plan came when they reached their destination—in the form of Charmayne Roach's *nephew*.

Johnny Lord was an emotional chameleon. His happy tears in greeting "Aunt Charmayne" soon gave way to "counsinly" largesse with the four from the Cheyenne Social Club, so long of leg, so high of breast. He discussed their ambitions—where they had "studied" before Cheyenne, who their "teachers" had been, and what each thought was her special "technique." They matched his mimicry with an aura that suggested they were all from Swiss boarding schools.

As the "czar" of Barbary Coast prostitution, Johnny Lord was far from impressed by the quartet and miffed that Charmayne had not done better.

"Oh, dear Johnny," Charmayne simpered, "I do want you to meet some of my other travelling companions."

He had spotted Lillian the moment she had detrained and had immediately assumed she was one of Charmayne's picks. When it proved out that she was not one of the selection, the chameleon had turned moodily brown. Now, getting a chance to at least meet her, he was rosy red again.

But first he was gentleman enough to meet Amy, Beth and Carol—weighing Charmayne's words. Then Karen and Clara—bringing Charmayne's words into balance, so he was amply prepared for the last introduction.

"Charmed, Miss Whiteside," he murmured in a voice that made her quiver, then made her quiver again when he gently took her hand and touched it lightly to his lips.

Instinctively, they knew they were star-crossed and never meant for each other, but that first touching of flesh had generated an electricity between them that was an undeniable force.

His first sighting was now reinforced. He had his choice of a hundred different women, of all varieties, on any given night of the week. But no woman, ever before, had created such instant desire as had this one. As a connoisseur of women, he did not see her as a seventeen year old ingenue, but as the epitome of womanhood she would become in the next decade or two.

Lillian was carefully sizing Johnny Lord up as he stood before her. First, because she really only knew Boston fishermen type sailors, she pegged him as a gentleman. It wasn't just his stylish dress or contintental style of kissing her hand, or even the genteel manner in which he had greeted and talked to his aunt and female cousins.

Nor was it his looks—although she had to admit that his coal black hair, with diamond sparkles, his lake blue eyes, lantern chin and perfect smile made him one of the handsomest men she had ever seen. These were all the externals. It was the interior being that she somehow sensed that made her quake. The touch of his hand had been almost like a vow that committed her to no other man but him. It was almost frightening. She didn't even know what love meant, for in seventeen years she had never even experienced family love. She stood with weak knees and shaken emotions.

"I have told Lillian and the other girls, that they must come visit us in the Barbary Coast," Charmayne gushed.

"I think that would be delightful," Johnny answered, picking up his cue. "The house is spacious and can always take in additional guests. Where will you be staying?"

McHenry intruded suddenly into the group. "That hardly concerns you," he said. "You are, sir, speaking with ladies whose hands have been asked in marriage. Ladies, those are the carriages you will now enter to go to our hotel."

"We're well aware of their intent upon arrival, Mr. McHenry," Charmayne said. She smiled indulgently and her tongue flicked suggestively over her lips. "Because I hear you have trained some of them quite well for their fate—"

McHenry turned scarlet, inflamed with memories of that harrowing punch from Lillian, who he now blamed for this degrading comment. "There was a time, *madam*," he snarled, putting unmistakable meaning into the word "madam," "when I considered discussing a business arrangement for a couple of my charges. I now plan on going ahead with my original contracts for them."

Charmayne leaned close, so only McHenry could hear her. "It all boils down to the same thing, McHenry. We are both in the business of selling flesh."

The color spread upward on McHenry's face, reds and purples rising from his choking white collar. "Get to those carriages and join the other girls!"

He stormed away and began to direct the departure. He did not see that Johnny Lord had divorced himself from the group to talk with the second carriage driver.

Lord was still there to help Lillian up into the coach. "I was hoping your hotel would be in San Francisco."

"I, too," she said ruefully.

Her tone stirred in him a hope. "Ours will be the last ferry departure for the night, but some fishing trawlers come over after that."

Lillian laughed, drawing on a memory. "I'm well aware of that, sir. My family are fisherfolk and often have to ferry people across the St. Charles to Boston."

He smiled, having left her with the promise of a rendezvous.

Then the carriage rolled away. Lillian looked at the other girls—six women unsure of their future. "Do we really want to let McHenry make the choice of our future?" she asked.

Clara exchanged a startled look with Lillian, as though she'd revealed their secret to the others. Lillian had seemed her only ally, but she sat back to let the others communicate their feelings.

"I'm suddenly very afraid," Karen whined.

"However you want to look at it," Amy said for the trio, "we are bound by the signed contracts."

"True," said Beth, being positive instead of negative to the spokeswoman's first words.

For once Carol Wilson could make it unanimous or stand on her own.

"What makes you think he will keep his word about the men we are to marry? He has tried, with each of us, to take our virginity for himself. Doesn't that tell us something about the men he has contracted us to? Our whole lives we have been told when to kneel, when to pray and when to yield. We've heard what he has saddled poor Clara with: when to get up, when to pull the plow horse, when to teach. We just went through a Civil War over slavery. Perhaps it was the wrong one. We are the real slaves! The black people now have more rights than we have as women. Frankly, I don't feel obligated to a contract that was signed by the Mother Superior."

Lillian's eyes were opaque, haunted. She had absorbed Carol's words only in part. Her own mind had been made up with the last words from Johnny Lord. She would find him again, even if she had to swim the bay. But, foolishly, she had raised the question among the rest, never expecting this outburst from Carol.

Suddenly, she shouted at Clara. "And you—why don't you speak. You are the one who wants out of this the most."

Clara appeared temporarily shamed by the serenity she felt. Wiping her eyes on her sleeve, she sat forward on the coach seat. "Because my decision is made," she announced simply. "I shall vanish and you will never know where I've gone."

"We vanish together or we don't vanish at all," Lillian said sternly.

"Agreed," four voices echoed.

"Agreed," Clara said wanly.

And suddenly Lillian was puzzled. She had somehow made herself general without a battle plan. She rapped on the roof and told the carriage driver to take them back to the wharf. He smiled. He had already been paid handsomely by Mr. Lord to do that very thing.

Charmayne stood at the rail of the ferry, looking at the San Francisco skyline, and took Johnny Lord's hand.

"It's so good to be home. I'm sorry the four are such lightweights."

"The six to follow are not bad, however."

Charmayne laughed. "They will never break away from McHenry. I've tried every ruse in the book."

"I don't know," he mused. "From what you say, I would put my money on Clara to make the break, and then for Lillian to follow. If the others follow, fine; I've left a solid trail for them to follow."

"Yes," she agreed, "Clara is the oldest and the most logical one to break them away . . . but, Lillian has something gnawing at her that I wish I could pin down."

"Another man?" Johnny asked in alarm.

"Yes," she said very, very slowly, because she suddenly wanted Johnny to have something to stew over.

* * *

Johnny Lord's solid trail was muddied right from the start. The greedy cabbie indeed delivered them back to the ferry wharf and immediately departed, calmly forgetting that part of the fee from Johnny was for the hiring of a boat.

The ticket clerk waggled a pink hand. "Now, miss, I can only say it one more time. There is no more ferry service until tomorrow morning and I don't know of another boat for hire."

Clara turned away and looked at the startled faces, then had a moment of alarm. "Where's Lillian!"

"Wandering down the wharf," Amy said, as though it would get Lillian into trouble.

But Lillian was looking for a way out of trouble. She cursed herself for not remembering the location of a wharf she had seen from the train window. It had so reminded her of a section of the Charles River that she had grown momentarily homesick. Then Johnny Lord had taken away all thoughts of homesickness. The harbor was festooned with the lanterns of many vessels, but none of the silhouettes seemed to have the size and shape she was looking for. For a moment, she feared the fleet she sought was too great a distance away. Then she let her nostrils take charge. She turned to a secondary wharf and at the far end could see the bobbing and weaving of familiar masts.

Her heart sang when she looked down at the fishing vessels. These sailors were also following an age old law of the sea and lighting their lanterns a half-hour before sundown, while others were folding and mending their nets for the next day.

She studied them carefully until spotting one that was built along the same lines as the Whiteside trawler.

At first the old fisherman hardly acknowledged the young lady sitting on the wharf and calling down comments to him about his boat.

"Yep!" he muttered. But his eyes were blossoming at her knowledge.

"You can make sure that net never breaks in that manner again by using a knot my grandfather created years ago."

"To be sure. What sort of knot?"

"Do I have permission to come aboard and show you."

"Granted," he chuckled, and then became a little dismayed when five other young ladies appeared on the wharf as Lillian scrambled down the ladder to the deck.

The knot instruction quickly over, Lillian prolonged her stay by making him try it several times while she continued to ask questions about the length of time to get to San Francisco, the cost of the ferry ride and how one got across without the ferry.

Thomas Feeley grew impatient with her probing. "Am I taking it that you young ladies missed the last ferry."

"Yes, sir." Lillian gulped. She had never lied before and had to think the words out carefully. "We were travelling with a Mrs. Charmayne Roach and were to be her guests at her home on the Barbary Coast, but after leaving the train we got separated."

Feeley's slanted eyes betrayed nothing. There wasn't a man alive in the bay area that didn't know the Barbary Coast and had at least heard of 'Lady Charmayne', but his poor fisherman's pocketbook had never been full enough to see the inside of her establishment, let alone afford its pleasures.

"Heard tell of Lady . . . the lady."

"Oh, isn't that marvelous. Now, if we could only get to her."

Feeley fussed something over in his mind. Just once in his life he would love to have an evening in such a house, but this bevy of young chicks puzzled him. They seemed too pure and innocent to be the creatures of such a notorious madam.

"It occurs to me, Miss Whiteside, that I haven't dropped in to see my daughter and grandchildren for a spell, they be living in San Francisco. Wind seems fair enough and it costs no more to take six extras across if I be deciding to go."

"That's generous of you, Mr. Feeley," Lillian exalted.

" 'Cept my crew's already gone for the night."

Lillian laughed, only she was the only one who knew how rueful it sounded. "I guess my father always wanted another boy, for I had to work some each summer on my grandfather's trawler. I'll do everything you tell me to do."

Feeley blew warm breath through his blunt teeth. "Then tell the ladies to get themselves and their luggage onboard. I'd like to be out of this harbor before we've lost all of the sunset light." His request for payment he would make at the end of the line.

It was an enthralling sight, the lights of the city coming to life on its many hills like a swarm of fireflies going about their nightly chore. Lillian had seen a similar sight, coming into Boston at night on the trawler, but for the others it was a brand new adventure. Except for Karen. Feeley's fishing boat had hardly left the mouth of the Oakland inlet before the choppy bay water turned her stomach.

But Feeley soon found that his request left a gaping unanswered question.

"You might mention my kindness to Mrs. Roach."

"Oh, that we certainly shall do, but how do we find this Barbary Coast and her house?"

He dared not tell them that the notorious district started right at the wharf at which they had docked, went left and right and stretched inland to California and Kearney Streets. A crowded district of unlit muddy streets that were hardly wider than alleyways.

"Most big houses like that are on Pacific Avenue, Miss Whiteside. That's about five blocks that-a-way!"

With heartfelt thanks they scampered onto the wharf and departed with glowing pride that they had put the bay between themselves and Thomas McHenry.

But they soon found that the unlit streets provided more fear than they had ever known before. Drunken sailors fell in the streets and slept where they dropped. And those with enough sobriety left to remind them of lust tried to reach up and grab at the skirts and ankles of these unexpected intruders.

Trying to stay together they dodged and whirled, and used their small round travelling cases as weapons to fend them off.

"Oh, no!" Lillian cried, when Karen began to retch again. "Duck into this alley, but don't be long. We're safe if we keep moving."

It sounded like good logic, but she wondered, catching a sideway glance at Clara. She was the oldest and should have been the strength for them to lean upon. But she had no strength even for herself. It was all such a horrible nightmare that she was having trouble keeping from going over the cliff to full hysteria. She dared not look at the trio. Their constant whimpering was unnerving enough.

The scream from the alley shattered their last thread with sanity. For a moment, all appeared frozen, divested of will and purpose. Then Lillian and Clara acted.

It was so dark in the alley that they couldn't see, but only feel the flaying arms and legs. Using their own fists and feet they tried to aim them at trousered legs and sweatered arms. Adding their own screams to Karen's they tried to free her.

But it was the sailor who broke from their attack and did the running.

"Your shawl!" Lillian cried at Amy as they came from the alley.

"I'm cold," Amy wailed.

Lillian didn't have time to argue the point. She snatched it away and wrapped it around Karen's shoulders to cover her bare breasts. Then she signalled for them to march along behind her.

Finding the house, in Lillian's eyes, appeared hopeless. There was no end to this jungle of taverns, drunkenness and depravity. Where did civilization begin again? Where was this fashionable Barbary Coast with the big houses such as they'd seen from the trawler? They had all seemed high up on the hills, like floating castles of light in the air.

Suddenly, the street ahead was filled with a horde of men on horseback with pistols raised in the air. In that moment the street turned deadly silent, followed by volley after volley of pistol shots.

Panic-stricken, the drunken sailors began to scream and run away from the horsemen.

"*Vigilantes! Vigilantes!*"

As though it were the most dreaded cry in the world, the taverns began to empty, and even more sailors poured onto the street. In terror, some ran toward the horsemen, who were now riding forward, grim-faced and swinging clubs with deadly accuracy.

Above the screams of the men were the scream of five females whose minds had dropped to the unthinking pit of total fear. They had not understood the meaning of the word or what was happening. They only knew they were caught in the middle of complete bedlam.

Only Lillian sensed—and she didn't know why she sensed it—that the hostile men would not be hostile toward them.

She tried to move toward them, pushing through the crowd of shouting, scrambling, screaming men. She felt a jolt as a sailor tried to rip her travelling case out of her grip. She was not sure if it was intended robbery or his desire to get his hands on a weapon to fight back with, but she kept her grip firm.

"Let go of that, you beast!"

But the burly sailor held firm until a club grazed his head and he went sprawling.

"Help us out of here!" she shouted up at the horseman. He looked down as though not believing his eyes.

"How'd you get here?" he stammered inanely.

"Boat . . . let us off . . . Been wandering . . . Looking for the house of Mrs. Roach."

Now his eyes turned to complete disbelief, but he couldn't just leave them in the middle of what would turn even bloodier. His men were all private citizens bent on cleaning up that pest hole of their city, but these women seemed so totally out of place. He turned horse around and used his club to make a path.

"Go down this alley to Broadway, the next street. Her house is the largest one in that block. Now, go!"

They didn't need encouragement. They ran the length of the alley and pounded on the door of the largest house they could find.

With friends in high places Charmayne and Johnny had been forwarned of the vigilante attack. Johnny had not even opened his lesser houses that night and Charmayne's clients had departed an hour before.

Therefore, the commotion in the foyer took them by surprise.

"What is the meaning of this?" Charmayne demanded in a high-pitched voice. "I thought you'd paid off the vigilantes not to bother us."

Johnny cast her a sidelong glance filled with contempt. "Must you always jump to conclusion before you ascertain the facts. Those are female voices I hear."

The third person in Charmayne's spacious office-parlor arched his eyebrows in surprise as he turned to stare at Charmayne. "I should think," he snapped, "as the woman of the house, you would go to look into the matter."

"My servants shall inform me," she replied coolly.

But before he could state his thoughts further a maid was at the door with an explanation of the commotion.

Johnny Lord burst into peals of laughter, which did not amuse Charmayne and brought a troubled frown to the other man.

"I shall place myself behind the screen for your meeting with them," he said, with pointed meaning.

Kai Soong positioned himself behind the screen he had presented as a gift to Charmayne. A gift of his own oriental cunning design, allowing him, as the silent money and land partner behind Johnny Lord and Charmayne, to be invisible at a meeting, but to be able to see all that transpired in the room.

They had often wondered why a man of such power would want to keep his business operation with them such a secret. His House of Soong had been the main supplier of coolie labor to build the Central Pacific; he had waged a great "tong" battle here and in China to become the master of the House of Soong in China—only to give it all up and retire to San Francisco three years before. But one never questioned the full motives of this Chinaman. Nor did they question the disguise he had fashioned to come into the Barbary Coast unnoticed. Nearly everyone had Chinese servants and he liked to think he looked like the poorest old man of the lot—which he did.

Johnny, leaning against the black marble mantle, agitating his bourbon in small circular motions, spoke now with disgust. "We are going to have to handle them like any other new recruits, Charmayne. That's the sad fact."

"With you giving each their first tryout?" she questioned acidly.

"I was thinking of the seclusion period for their sake. You know McHenry will hit you first thing in the morning on their whereabouts."

Charmayne paced, having asked the maid to stall them a moment, and now hearing Johnny's *sotto voce* advisory: "Here they are." Pivoting, she smiled faintly at them. Then her face fell.

"My dears, what has happened?"

As though she had suddenly regained the position of spokesman Any began to spew forth the story of their ordeal: the missed ferry boat, the fishing boat arrival and then the trauma of their journey to Charmayne's house.

Charmayne was aghast, Johnny highly amused and Kai Soong greatly troubled. He studied the faces of each of the six as though they were each a cup of tea leaves that would divine past, present and future. Each presented a different problem to him, that he did not want to prejudge too quickly, and especially not that night.

"Well—" Charmayne paused, then resumed rapidly, knowing that she could never lie well. "I hardly feel at fault. The ferry wharf is but a few blocks of safe walking. Still . . . Why are you here?"

"Why?" Lillian's voice was like the rising notes for an aria introduction. "You encouraged us all to get away from McHenry. We have!"

"I encouraged nothing, my dear," Charmayne simpered, fluttering her fan. "I merely invited you to come and visit."

"Isn't that one and the same?" Lillian shouted. "And you!" she turned to Johnny. "You said there was always room for more guests."

Johnny Lord didn't budge. He played with his bourbon and then laughed. "That I did. I was the one who encouraged and still encourage. You are the most exciting little baggage to hit town in my memory. Oh, you need some filling out—another inch or two on the bosom. And you all could do with clothes. You all look like you were meant to be let off in Salt Lake to join the Mormons."

Charmayne darted an angry look at Johnny, as though he had gone too far too fast.

"Perhaps we would have been better off," Clara said, her voice still dulled from the experience.

"That's beside the point," Lillian persisted, still unsure of what Johnny fully meant. "Yes, I admit we may have taken your words too much too heart. But, please, grant us hospitality for the night."

A signal was flashed through the screen. "But, of course." She went to pull the bell cord for the maid. "However, you shall have to bunk in together."

"After the train, anything will be heaven," Karen murmured, beginning to feel a bit safer.

"This is hardly a heaven," Johnny said softly. "It's a house with a certain function in life."

Charmayne turned her back on him. "That doesn't concern them right now."

"I think it does!" His voice had turned hard and cold. "We've never pussy-footed with the others and they are no different. It's not a hotel. We put things right on the line and then let them have a night to think about it."

Charmayne was in a quandry, but the signal said Johnny was right.

"But they are different," she insisted.

Johnny bit her words off. "They are women, which makes them no different than the women we have upstairs. Except those are trained to make us a profit. Save for being fresh meat, I frankly don't see much profit here, with the exception of Lillian."

Clara Clayton, her face contorted, cried at Charmayne: "What is he talking about?"

"I'm talking," he broke right in, "about the oldest profession known to man. *Ergo,* the highly sophisticated art of woman pleasuring man for the turn of a profit." He halted. He found revulsion in Lillian's bright eyes. Momentarily it shamed him, wishing he could have brought her along in a gentler manner. "Granted, tonight you came through one of the hardest neighborhoods in this land. You, Karen, were nearly raped by one of those thugs. Yes, thugs. Low creatures who are never allowed to darken these doors." Johnny shook his head very slowly. "There are houses down there to cater to that manner of man. Here, it is quite different." Then he let his voice fill with compassion. "Look, you have been through one hell of an evening. You need to bathe, relax and get some sleep. But, never, ever do I want it said that Johnny Lord lied to you. They call this the House of Peony. Please don't judge it, or us, until you get to know all that it stands for. Oh, Helen, we shall have six guests for the evening. Have some of the girls help you get hot water for them. Goodnight, dear ladies."

"Are we going to stay here?" Karen sounded faintly hysterical again.

"It's one step up from where we have been for the past few hours," Lillian said acidly. "And, at least, we know the truth about where we are."

They plodded away, really wanting to think about nothing more than the bath and bed.

"Well," Charmayne snarled, even before Kai Soong could step out from behind the screen. "You certainly left me with egg on my face."

"You brought it on yourself," Johnny said earnestly. "You would have coddled them until tomorrow and then lost them. You're losing your grip. Look what you brought back! Four cowboy saddle tramps. Hell, they are hardly worth putting in my lowest dive."

Charmayne looked appealingly at Kai Soong. The Chinaman's sure grasp of any event always cast him as a mediator between the two.

"Johnny makes many good points. On the other hand, I can understand Charmayne's hesitancy. I'd suggest this." He folded his arms and his long fingers with their polished nails tapped on his biceps. "Let us look at them not as six, but as individuals."

Johnny shook his head. "We're looking for trouble.

When they come in as a group, they act like a group. Pick a leader and handle them all through her.''

''They seem to have their leader,'' Kai Soong shrugged.

Charmayne made no comment. She was still smarting from Johnny's words.

''I think that was just for tonight. She had the wit to go for the fishing vessel, and enough spunk to stand up to us. She doesn't have it in her to lead them all into prostitution.''

''You say this thing because you have personal desires for her, my young accomplice.''

''You're damn right I do,'' he cried exuberantly. ''She's the most exciting female I can remember.''

''And shall never become a true prostitute—even for you.'' It was said in such a prophetic tone that they looked at him oddly. Sometimes he was just too mysterious for them. ''Nor the big one, although she shall serve us well. The other four shall also serve us—profitably, of course. In the morning this man McHenry shall come to you. Put the oldest one and the young one behind my screen. Let them see the protection you can offer. Let them see the workings of this house. Then I shall give you instruction on the other four.''

He rose, smiling to himself. He felt pity for Johnny and Charmayne. They thought in days and he thought in decades. For each of these six, in his intricate way, he had charted a path—not centered for all around the 'House of Peony.'

It had been their first real bath and bed in days. They slept like babies, except for one.

At dawn Clara found Lillian still sitting in the window seat of the bay window. She crawled in beside her and offered motherly arms.

''Not sleeping won't help, dear.''

''I couldn't turn my brain off, Clara. I watched all the lights twinkle out in those houses and have now let the sun show me what manner of city this is for us. Look! Gingerbread houses crawling up the hills and those mansions. I particularly like that one with the widow's walk. That's what I thought we were coming to.''

''Your main upset is over this Johnny Lord, isn't it?''

Lillian's eyebrows arched; her face flushed. Groggy with fatigue, fearful that they were in over their head, she had considered that deeply. "I don't know what to think of him, other than that he was honest. I thought he had a personal interest in me. I . . . I've never had a man interested in me. I don't know what love is."

Clara nodded. "I've never had to give it much thought either, dear. Oh, I've had the adoration of schoolboys who always get a crush on their teacher. That's a warm, wonderful feeling. I always thought it would be the same with a man, for they never really stop being little boys."

"Clara," Lillian said softly, on a long note. "Is there love in this other thing?"

Clara touched her ruby cheeks. Hot salty tears brimmed in her eyes. "What almost happened to Karen last night I know well, Lillian. I was fifteen and he was a live-in teacher who worked for my father. He was well educated and used all the right words to make me think it was just a learning thing, a part of my education. The horrors came after my mother caught him half-way through the act. They made me feel the shamed party, and as though I would never be able to wash away that sinful act. I can't even remember what it was like, because of those shameful memories. What I'm saying is, yes I think people do it without love being connected to the act, just like that teacher. He didn't love me."

"I don't even know what the act is about," Lillian stammered, "except that it somehow makes babies."

Clara frowned. "That depends upon the cycle of our womanly curse, Lillian, but it just gave me pause to wonder how women in a house like this avoid it."

"I'm not sure I know what you mean."

Clara, not far beyond Lillian's own innocence, still had some womanly knowledge to share. But after sharing it, she ended on a strange note. "Did you ever stop to think that we were about ready to give ourselves to men without love, even though some preacher might call us man and wife?"

Lillian gasped. "Clara—you make it sound like one and the same. That's dreadful!"

"Is it? Didn't McHenry try to do it with each and everyone of us? Why doesn't that make him a whoremaster? And isn't he in a way selling our bodies to those men?"

"Are you saying we would be better off here than going back?"

"I'm scared stiff on either course, but what other choice do we have."

"We can hear you!" Karen cried. "We are human and a part of this, too. I don't think I want a man to touch me ever again."

Clara searched her vocabulary for diplomatic words. "Karen, dear, the whole world is not made up of men like that or places like that. Nor, were we excluding you. We thought you four to still be asleep. So, do we crawl back to McHenry or do we find out exactly what it is Mrs. Roach has to offer us?"

An ashamed silence settled over the group. The rock of truth was hard to turn over as a full group. They could share a common fear of the unknown, but a step in either direction almost had to be of individual choice.

Lillian touched her forehead; a nudge of guilt bothered her—*she* knew her choice and it was colored by Johnny Lord.

The maid entered the room. Their groggy minds had paid little attention to her the night before. She was a bright, jolly girl of about their own age.

"Cheers! Glad to see you all up and about. In case you've forgotten, I'm Laura. Laura Kahler. Lady Charmayne would like to see Miss Clara and Miss Lillian in her office."

"Lady Charmayne?" Amy interrupted. "I thought in places like this they called them madams!"

Laura tried to ignore the rudeness. "No. And in this house you won't be called a whore, either."

Embarrassment colored Amy's face and Beth jumped to her rescue. "And what do they call maids in a *house* like this?"

Laura laughed. "If the truth be known we are apprentices with maid duties."

It was Carol who cut through her meaning. "You mean

you are learning to be one of them, but you don't have to do what they do each night?''

''I should be letting Lady Charmayne explain this to you,'' Laura whispered, ''but she probably thinks I'm having to wake you up. You are right, miss. For six weeks you are just a part of the household staff to learn how it functions by a strict set of rules. You never get your first client until Johnny Lord thinks you are lady enough, for we only have the finest gentlemen coming here.''

''Then we insist upon seeing her as a group!'' Amy announced regally.

''Oh, this isn't that kind of a meeting, miss. There's one difficult gentleman stewing in the foyer to see her. She's not about to see him without two of you present to hear his words.''

They all knew it had to be McHenry, but were amazed he had found them so quickly.

''But, then he will know that we are here!'' Lillian gasped.

''You just leave that to Lady Charmayne and follow me.''

They were escorted down a backstairs way, through the hustle and bustle of a kitchen staff preparing for breakfast and into the office by a back door.

They were greatly amused by the screen device, and Lillian had the oddest notion that it had been used on them in the same way the night before.

Charmayne sailed into the office on a cloud of pink chiffon and feathers, followed by a thunder storm.

''I'm puzzled, Mr. McHenry,'' she cooed. ''I'm not clear on why you would come directly to me. Please sit down.''

''Listen, lady,'' McHenry barked, accepting the invitation as though it were his due, ''Don't try to suppress anything, my men will get wind of it. Six of them! I've never lost a girl before and they were right cozy with you. I'll have printed posters all over this town by noon offering a reward for their return.''

''What in the world would I want to suppress?''

''I saw you make the switch in Cheyenne. I was even

going to offer to sell you my two trouble makers—Clara and Lillian."

Charmayne laughed lightly. "That would have been a mistake." A note of nastiness crept into her voice. "I don't buy my girls, Mr. McHenry, and they are on a 50-30-20 basis after they start making a profit."

"I don't understand those figures."

"They are fair business figures, sir. Fifty percent for the house, thirty for themselves and twenty for their food, lodging, medical care, transportation here and clothing. The last is major. A product well presented makes it sell at a better price. It's a lesson you could learn for your business."

"I didn't come here for advice," he snarled.

"Nor did I ask you to explain your business figures to me."

"Well, here is a bit of information about my business. I have contracts covering each of those girls and if I find out you are involved in their disappearance I might consider using the word kidnapping."

"Kidnapping!" Charmayne exclaimed.

"That's why you'd better open up with me and keep clean with me. If not, every newspaper and every vigilante will be on your back. I'll make them see that you stole those girls away from the husbands they're intended for to turn them into whores!"

"There are some in this area," she answered sweetly, "who have come to question enterprises such as yours. Almost a form of white slavery. If push comes to shove, Mr. McHenry, make sure you don't push me too far. Now, I think you know the way to the door."

McHenry gulped down his retort, realizing it would be useless, fully aware he had lied. He had lost several girls before this and the law would not help him. The girls were free human being who had the right to change their mind. Out of fear he could make them feel his contract was fully binding, which was why he usually picked orphans and stupid girls. Still, he was going to keep a watchful eye on this house.

* * *

Charmayne, as cool as she had been in the office, was standing anxiously at the head of a large U shaped table in the dining room when Laura escorted Clara and Lillian in and showed them to their seats. The other four were already at the table with ten other women of various ages and in various types of morning wrappers. Against each wall were another half dozen women in maid's and cook's uniforms, as clean and crisp as if they were servants in one of the millionaire mansions on Nob Hill.

"Ladies, just because we closed early last night does not change our normal Sunday schedule. I understand things have been very lax around here during my absence. Well, the 'dragon' is back.

"We have some guests with us. Clara, Lillian, Karen, Amy, Beth, and Carol. And I underscore the word guest. I hope you six will forgive me if I stay with my regular schedule. We are a very large family here and only survive through one voice of authority. I will meet with the six of you right after breakfast. Now, ladies you may begin to eat while I continue."

Charmayne raised a lorgnette to her eyes and scanned the sheaf of papers in her hand.

The six wolfed down their food, the finest they had had in almost three weeks. They paid little attention to Charmayne, for it did not concern them.

But Lillian listened with growing fascination. Some time between when they went to bed and this morning, the matriarch of this female clan had done a very careful inspection. She knew where every speck of dust lay, what garments had not been mended, what food was going to waste. That day the house would be cleaned from top to bottom with all hands at work.

From a chart Charmayne was able to tell that one girl had missed her bi-monthly appointment with the doctor, another had allowed a gentleman to stay in the house until half-past midnight.

"That is a rule I will not allow to be broken by anyone at any time. Which is just as strong as no overnight gentlemen. Ladies, if we send our clients away by midnight, it is for their own protection. Because the private clubs close at midnight, their wives never suspect they were not there. The next time it happens, the girl will be fired on the spot and the gentleman never allowed back into this house."

Charmayne then got specific on certain acts that the girls were being asked to be performed. So specific that Lillian's ears turned red upon hearing the exact manner of things Charmayne would allow and not allow.

"We are a house of pleasure and not depravity. You are each talented enough in your own right without having to be humiliated by these uncommon requests. I understand these things happened while I was gone. I am back and will again take charge of matching the taste of the gentleman to your special art."

And, whether for the ears of the six, or just to refresh the memory of the ten, she went over the ritual schedule of a normal day.

"Breakfast is at 8 am with everyone in attendance. If you are sick you will have a maid call me to your room, so I can ascertain if you need the doctor. From nine to ten you will clean your room and prepare your clothes for that night. The maids, as usual, will be responsible for cleaning the rest of the house during the morning. Remember, this house must be as clean and fashionable as the one the gentlemen leave behind—their home away from home. On Tuesday and Thursdays you will spend the rest of the morning with the seamstress on new outfits and alterations. They may see their wives in the same dress twice, but never here.

"Some of you have been skipping lunch because you think you are getting too fat. Then you will spend that hour in the garden pulling weeds. But you will be one place or the other. Just as you all shall rest from one to four, unless you have been granted permission to go shopping. *And,* you always go shopping in no less than a party of two, *dressed as ladies*. You all know what happens when I catch a single girl going out for a matinee with a client."

Then she got fretful. "Our apprentice maids work very hard to fill and refill those tubs for your bath. It's not because I believe 'cleanliness is next to Godliness' but because I don't want your garments ruined and a client complaining to me about your aroma. If they wanted that kind of woman they would go to one of Johnny's lesser houses. You will bathe daily and be properly dressed for my formal dinner each evening.

"Come on, girls, look at the record. I know I have harped on the clients with wives, but that's to set a hallmark. You've been to three marriages this year, and one right here in our own parlor. Isn't that the dream of every girl who prostitutes herself—to find that special man? I don't want you working for me forever. I love giving away the bride! In this field there is nothing worse than a woman who has been in the business too long. That means she has given up hope.

"Now, for the benefit of our guests, that is the end of my Sunday sermon, other than to tell them that Sunday is different here. We follow our same work schedule, but are not open for business. Our dinner is a marvelous buffet and we relax for the rest of the evening as family."

"She makes it sound exciting," Amy said.

"With undertones of the nunnery," Beth corrected.

"But with better prospects for husbands," Carol mused.

"She didn't say anything different in our meeting than at breakfast," Karen reflected.

"I read it differently," Clara muttered. "But, then, I heard her with McHenry. She's giving us a sanctuary out of his grasp. Really, a bit like Laura. For six weeks we work for our room and board, learning her system, but free to leave it if we don't want to . . . you know what. But, I'm also pracical. Those ten, and the apprentice maids, are extremely comely women—and, amazingly, quite nice. There is not a one among us who can hold a candle to them."

"Speak for yourself," Amy simpered.

"Right!" Beth echoed.

"A lot of it is cosmetics, training and dress," Carol reflected.

"I think I could stand it here six weeks just to stay away from McHenry," Karen murmured.

"Why don't we take it a step at a time," Lillian said, with simple logic. "She mentioned the six weeks as her standard rule. But, all she said to us was to enjoy this day and evening, then see what McHenry did on the first of the week. That's all we've really been offered."

"That's hardly the way I see it," Amy snorted.

"Nor me!" came Beth's echoing snort.

Carol sighed. "Lillian's right. Everyone else is busy with their chores and here we sit. Nothing would make me happier than to have something to do. This is worse than sitting on that damn train."

"Why, Carol," Karen giggled, "you cursed!"

"I have it!" Amy chirped, as though not prompted by Carol on this original thought. "Let us show our gratitute by going to offer our help. As a trio we always made points with the Sisters by volunteering."

"Always," said Beth.

"But we're no longer a trio," Carol corrected.

"But surely we've become sisters," Karen timidly suggested.

For once it was Beth who giggled and took the lead away from Amy. "And soon to become 'scarlet sisters.' "

It reduced the four to giggling co-conspirators as they left to go volunteer.

"Do you feel excluded?" Clara asked.

"Hardly," Lillian sighed. "Although it is almost laughable. They seem to have forgotten the basis for their histrionics."

"If they even know what the word means. You know, our 'scarlet sisters,' do have a point. This morning, going through that spotless kitchen gave me a start. It was as though I had been there before and knew where everything was. When I was growing up, my mother was not like other mothers. Her kitchen was her crowning glory in life and I was not allowed to enter, or learn from her. I would sneak away to a neighbor's house and delight in being able to share her cooking arts. I would then daydream of the day I would have my own kitchen. Don't laugh, when I say it is the kitchen down below in this house."

Lillian smiled, her love for this girl growing constantly. "Then go, Clara. I've never known a kitchen in my life that couldn't use an extra pair of hands."

"What about you?"

"Me?" Lillian laughed. "I burn water bringing it to a boil, and leave more dust on the furniture than I take off. I make lumpy beds and always forget when to push the yeast dough down. Now, get along with you, before you learn all my faults."

Clara hugged her warmly and raced away, almost colliding with Laura in the door.

"Where's she off to? Where's the others?"

"Off to the wars of dust and scullery slavery."

Laura interrupted. "Get them back here at once. I've got to take them to the locker."

"Locker?"

"Breakfast was fine, according to the Queen Bee, but she insists upon formal dinners, espcailly Sunday. They've got to be properly dressed."

"We are all nearly the same size, save for Clara."

"That's some help, but the seamstress will kill me calling her out on a Sunday."

"Perhaps that won't be necessary, Laura. I've always made my own clothes. What do we have to work with?"

It proved to be a room larger than the bedroom the six shared, with rows upon rows of dresses dating back to a decade or more.

"Break them away from their duties one at a time and I'll handle this, Laura."

Unfortunately, Amy was the first to arrive and the most difficult to handle. She changed her mind a dozen times and still was not pleased. Thereafter Lillian got smart. She selected an echo of a dress for Beth, a contrast for Carol and simplicity for Karen. They accepted without challenge and she was able to do their alterations in no time.

Clara was a challenge, until she got into Charmayne's private area. Clara almost rebelled, until Lillian put her foot down.

"All right, miss smarty," Clara stormed, "And what might you have picked for yourself?"

"Haven't given it a thought."

"Then fair is fair. I'll do one up on you." She went through rack after rack, while Lillian let out seams, added panels and turned a Charmayne into a Clara size.

"There!" Clara exulted.

Lillian gasped.

"Don't you go changing on me. It's the perfect addition to round off the 'scarlet sisters.' And, my dear, I know you've worked harder on mine, than the rest, to make me look good. I'll wear it with pride."

The coolie made his delivery to the kitchen of the sweetmeats and disappeared. Kai Soong never put his finger between the squabbles of women, but he smiled to himself. In a private room, which few knew about, the coolie began to change into a peacock.

The other male guest, amazed at his first Sunday night invitation ever, arrived in elegant evening attire of black and white.

His hostess, and some of her girls, were already in the parlor. For a moment Johnny Lord thought he had overdressed. Charmayne and the girls were formal, but hardly up to their standard of evening elegance. Within moments the other girls and Kai Soong had arrived. Only then did Charmayne send Laura to fetch the other guests.

Their approach down the circular staircase and into the parlor had not been planned. It was just a pattern that had been forming of late: Amy considering herself the natural leader and spokesperson, echoed by Beth and rebutted by Carol. The first two looked nice, with Carol a little more stylish. Then, the wispy Karen, in simplicity that made her a little princess of charm.

But then came a gasp. Clara was too large to ignore, too queenly to overlook. For once clothing had made her handsome and she swept down the stairs in regal splendor.

Lillian felt stupid. She had spent the entire day on the other dresses and hardly any on her own. Her dress felt baggy, too long and cumbersome. "And who," she had wondered, putting it on, "wore solid white with funny little green stones sewn onto it?"

Charmayne, upon seeing it, had nearly cried out in terror. That was her emerald dress worth nearly $10,000. Then she calmed, having to admit she had never received a single comment on it. And now, as Lillian carefully came down the stairs, to keep the long train from falling forward and tripping her, it was receiving applause from all those below.

"My dear," Kai Soong said to Charmayne, gesturing toward Lillian, "before you is the one person capable of stepping into your shoes. She is a seed, of special quality. The ground must be the finest to plant her in for the seed to grow. We may never see the flower of the seed we plant, old friend, but the responsibility is ours."

Rather than feel resentment, Charmayne was imbued with pride. If only Kai Soong were correct, and she had never found him wrong, then it would be like having the child she had always longed for and had never possessed.

"I feel," she gulped, "as though all six of these young women were brought to me for a reason. Today was most rare. Without being asked, they took over chores."

"Last night you looked at frightened creatures," he said softly. "Oh, what I saw of their stars in consulting the heavens! Four who form the cup that holds life and the handle to support it. They are special coins for us to handle wisely. The sixth, shines in a part of heaven all her own. What you considered as failure last night, I foresee as ultimate success for us all. May I escort you in to dinner?"

"That has always been Johnny's chore," she laughed.

Kai Soong did not laugh. His sternness came near rudeness. "He will escort you no more."

Charmayne accepted it with a shrug, recalling that she did work *for* Kai Soong.

Johnny Lord was the least insultable of men. In his youth he had yearned to be a riverboat captain, but his knack for cards landed him more often in the gambling casino of the Mississippi boats he worked on. By the time he was eighteen he found himself in California and in ten years his understanding of men's desire for gambling and women had rocketed him to the top. Everyone on Barbary Coast deferred to him willingly, fearfully. They realized that his mastery over them was honestly earned. The bald truth was that the vigilante attacks in those ten years had made the area shaky, in a state of financial disrepair. Merger of houses, financial arrangements with Kai Soong, wholesale firings of 'card shark' dealers—all were part of the pattern of existence in the past two years. It was a tribute to Johnny's vigor that his business sense had dispelled the odor of decay.

Still, he would have traded his $70,000 annual earnings to be accepted back on the riverboats. He was too decent to be a gambler. If a man were honest with Johnny Lord, then they knew that subterfuge and sneaky tricks were alien to him. But once crossed, the twenty-eight year old 'czar' could be quietly forceful.

"Do you hate me?" he asked quietly, as he escorted Lillian in for dinner.

"Hate is a wasted emotion," she mumbled.

"You don't even hate your parents?"

"What do you know of them?"

"Don't you think McHenry contacted me, as well? Don't you think I've learned more from him than he from me?" The rhetorical question, self-answering, was part of Johnny's arsenal. "I also learned the name and whereabouts of the man he had you slated to marry. I could make arrangements for you to see him, to size him up on your own, if you wish."

"Why do you think I would wish that?"

"Isn't that what you came here for?"

Lillian started to answer and paused. In view of the circumstances, the answer should have been an unequivocal yes. But that, after all, was before her meeting with Johnny Lord.

"Why do this for me and not the others?" she asked instead.

"Who said it was just for you?" he laughed. "Unbeknownst to McHenry, I obtained the names of the other five prospects, as well. It wasn't difficult getting a line on each of them. The man for Clara already has one foot in the grave and the other four prospects don't strike me right for your friends."

"You hardly know them."

He laughed again. "You forget I'm in the business of knowing women, all kinds of women. Those four are suited for marriage, children and clucking to each other over a back fence. Shall I tell you what I think about you?"

A blush rose to Lillian's face. "I would rather not hear."

She was saved, for the moment, from hearing, by Charmayne ringing the little silver dinner bell. She would love to hear what Johnny Lord thought of her, but not for another—what Johnny thought of her for himself.

Their intimate chat on the way to the dining room had gotten under Charmayne's skin. Her face was intense and set the mood for the first part of dinner. Kai Soong sensed imminent disaster and quietly replaced her as host. By the time the entree was served, Charmayne felt a little sorry over her attitude. From time to time she wished she were still one of the girls.

For Lillian there seemed no way to avoid Johnny—not tonight; not tomorrow. The dinner party ended in the garden, with coffee and liqueurs under a starry canopy. The regular girls made their exit as quickly as possible, wanting their free evening to be more or less away from Charmayne. Even when her friends wanted to retire, Lillian was reluctant to leave and was given an opportunity to stay by Kai Soong.

"Charmayne, would you see me out? I believe Johnny learned some information today that would be of great interest to Miss Whiteside."

Good-nights said, Lillian and Johnny were left alone.

"You didn't tell me all?"

"Everything, except that the man you are contracted to marry is fairly well-to-do, a widower in his early thirties with two young children to raise. For reasons known only to him, he did not seek out one of the local girls as a second wife."

"Must we discuss it tonight?"

"No. Come, I must also say good-night. This house may be closed on Sunday, but I have other business to attend to. Let's go in this way."

They took a side door into a section of the main floor Lillian had never seen. The lights were low, and Johnny in his dark evening attire strode along the shadowed halls without speaking, a circumstance that intensified Lillian's sense of unreality in being alone with him. They passed a large room with green felt-topped billard tables, a marble bar and massive fireplace. Because he assumed she had been part of the cleaning crew, he did not break the silence to explain that this was the gaming room. At the end of the hall he stood aside for Lillian to enter the room.

In this sunken central room, under a domed ceiling, gaslights played on a carp pool, and inlaid marble floors gleamed with a soft pink warmth. Rosewood tables of various sizes were scattered about, bordered by intimate groupings of rose damask-covered chairs. Here, too, was a marble topped bar and an even more massive fireplace.

"How beautiful," breathed Lillian, breaking the silence "It's so—breathtaking!"

"Oh?" Johnny gave a soft laugh, slightly cynical and curiously disturbing to Lillian. "It's the greeting room, where the men are matched up with their lady of the night. I have always found it cold and impersonal, but Charmayne prefers to keep this phase of the business a little cold and impersonal. I know you would add a warmth and a charm that is needed in the room."

The words were emphasized by the hand that now came up beneath her elbow, touching her through the sensuous cloth of the evening gown. Johnny guided her down the three steps, across the room and up three more steps to an archway. His touch, though light, sent electric messages throughout her nervous system.

"I would never want to be in charge of such a room," she said, attempting to put an icy tone in her voice. At the same time, she disengaged her arm from Johnny's and went through the arch and found herself in an alcove that opened onto the main foyer.

"I wasn't really casting you in that role," Johnny replied in a voice vibrant with meaning, "although . . ." He let his words trail off as he stared at her under the glow of the large foyer chandelier.

Lillian could think of nothing to say to fill in the void he had created, and she became uncomfortably aware of her own heartbeat.

"Are you afraid of me?" he whispered.

"Afraid . . . ? Of course I'm not afraid." But once uttered, she knew she was afraid. Not afraid of him, but of her own suddenly turbulent emotions. Tremblingly aware of his proximity and his good clean male odor—with a sweetness she had never smelled in a man before.

"You can't fib to me," he said in a voice that had gone as quiet as sin. "You know that I want to kiss more than just your hand in saying goodnight."

"Please don't," she gasped, fighting the shivering sensations that were taking command of her body as he gently took her hand.

"I said I want to. Did I say I would? You don't know me very well, little sparrow. You will have to be the one to invite me for that first kiss."

Now his dark head moved down to meet the uplifted hand, until she could feel the warmth of his breath on her skin. She was mesmerised by his hand where it revealed curling black hairs protruding from the white shirt sleeve. Then her hand was turned and his soft lips pressed into her palm, again and again.

"This will serve as a memory," murmured Johnny, "until your lips invite. Such lovely lips . . ." He kissed her palm one more time and then without another word he turned and departed.

It seemed her palm and taken on a life of its own. She raised it to her lips, thrilling her as though it had become his lips. She closed her eyes against the unsettling images it was creating.

Then, cuddling her chin in that palm, she turned to cross the foyer and go up the stairs to her room. Something made her look up.

Never had she seen such a hateful face glowering down

at her. Panic replaced the warm glow. She felt like a child being caught with her hand in the cookie jar.

"How dare you . . . how *dare* you!" Charmayne's whole body trembled with an indignation that was not entirely righteous. "You will live by the rules if you intend to stay under my roof and my protection. I want you out of *my* dress in five minutes' time."

Rage gave Lillian strength, and she began to undo the eyelets from armpit to waist as she ascended the stairs.

"I was not told it was your dress," she murmured on reaching the landing. "Thank you for its use." She pulled her arms free, let the bodice and skirt fall to her ankles, stepped briskly out and left the disheveled mass at Charmayne's feet. She almost stumbled with faintness as she started up the next flight of stairs, expecting a harsh order to bring her back to pick up the dress. With relief she made it to the third floor, then fled to her room.

Chapter 4

For the time being Lillian was outvoted. The other five lived as though wearing horse blinders. Clara had found a haven in the kitchen, even though her eyes blazed defiance at how the cook could demand a clean kitchen and still be so lax in her food preparation. "Sweet Karen," as the regular girls came to call her, because she would do their every bidding, was being very politic. "The Drudges," as the regular girls came to call "the trio", could not help but feel their exclusion and pulled farther into their three-way sisterhood, thus excluding Karen, Clara and Lillian. Starved for inclusion, Karen buttered her bread on the side of the regulars, while Amy, Beth and Carol seemed quite content in helping the maids.

For a week Lillian was left to fend for herself, growing more and more distracted, as though Charmayne was punishing her with silence and keeping her from Johnny Lord. Although in truth she preferred dealing with her own unruly emotions without him there to ruffle them again. She, at least, had a means of escape, as soon as her half-brother returned from sea. But three to four months seemed an eternity.

At the beginning of their second week, Kai Soong and Charmayne got together with each of the girls to discuss the problems at the House of the Peony.

"I do love the kitchen," said Clara with real conviction, "but it has certain faults."

Although Charmayne scoffed, Kai Soong listened to her analysis of its problems, and its potential.

Likewise, when Kai Soong had concluded a meeting

with Karen, and then one with "the trio", he sat quietly in the office trying to formulate his thoughts. Johnny and Charmayne sat with him. Because they did not speak out, he assumed they had no comment.

"Perhaps I was listening to my stomach, not her words," he said. "Your meals are bland and overcooked, Charmayne. This fly will stick to our spider's web if we give her control of the kitchen. Plus, I like her idea—offer our gentlemen dinner with their lady of the evening. It is charming and profit-making."

"Done," Johnny said, seeing the protest forming on Charmayne's lips.

"Now." Kai Soong paused in mid-tour of his thoughts. "I have made a discreet visit to Robert Duocoming. He tried to avoid his dealings with McHenry, but leapt at my suggestion of being a private marriage broker. A man very long on cash, desperately short on the social graces. He felt, by bringing in an Eastern bride, he could aspire to a higher social status."

"Lillian is hardly godlified," Charmayne scoffed, to get her dig in at Johnny.

"I'm not thinking of Lillian," Kai Soong said shortly. "Duocoming is better suited to a shy, young person—with the drive to get him accepted, as she wishes to be accepted."

"Karen," Johnny and Charmayne echoed as one.

"That's right. Who else? Now, for the other three." He laughed self-mockingly. "I could ruin the whole social structure by their placement, but sniff enough brimstone surrounding us. Certain families are in my debt and I wish them further under my grasp. You two, at this time, do not need to know how I shall bring about those three marriage contracts, but it shall be done—and making the girls and the families beholden to us. Now, I have made arrangements for tutors to come here each day for the next five weeks. They will become proper ladies before I start to introduce them into certain circles."

"One little, two little, three little Indians," Charmayne chanted, "but what do I do with the sixth little Indian maid?"

"For the next five weeks she shall become your personal maid."

"Sorry." She paused before she uttered her pure hatred for Lillian and how the presence of the girl had turned her unrequited love for Johnny to contempt for both. "I'm not blessed with your staggering capacity for control. I can now see why McHenry had such a problem with the girl. I can't stomach her."

"Good Christ in heaven," Johnny stormed, "stop this act! Why aren't you being truthful? Act like a normal woman! Cry! Shriek! Scream! Roll on the floor and admit you are jealous! But stop these damn dramatics and remember the rules we started under. You're a married woman, Charmayne. This may be an amoral business, but I told you right from the start I had certain principles I would not forego—and one was never becoming the lover of a married woman. We've been friends, but don't ruin that friendship by this petty little game you've been playing."

"Johnny," she soothed, as though he had everything wrong, "whatever do you mean? Must you always paint everything in extremes? I am only making her live under the house rules that you helped to establish, and I can't help it if the girl doesn't like me. But, I see that you two see something in her that I don't. Personal maid? What a joke."

"Go on, go on," Johnny said. "We need the catharsis. Let's assume I have bedtime plans for her . . . even though you know she's a bit skinny for my taste. Ah, hell, you know I try to bed every new one that comes along. Why are you, suddenly, making her special? She's just another dame, right?"

"May I quote you?" she sneered. He nodded. "I should be more tolerant."

He wanted to remind her that tolerance was not her strongest suit, but a look from Kai Soong stopped him. Feeling she had gained a cutting edge again, she said: "Then you shouldn't begrudge me this request. Keep out of her sight and mind while she stays here the next few weeks. Let me handle matters in the way that I know best."

The next five weeks were like living in a prison, although only Lillian seemed to notice it. Clara was content in her kitchen, the five with their studies and lessons. There was a certain satisfaction among them that Lillian had been excluded. Lillian, however, was not ever aware.

Charmayne had her constantly on the go. After breakfast at seven-thirty, she followed the madam during inspection of the girls and their rooms, frantically taking notes. From that point on, she was constantly at Charmayne's side, observing and assisting in the parlor and gaming room, until closing time at midnight.

But Lillian's heart was not in her job, that was clear. During the breakfast meeting her mouth would tremble a little, when she knew that Charmayne was being overly unjust toward one girl or another. Charmayne would rant on and on about "Setting an example"—her most famous phrase and excuse. The examples, in Lillian's opinion only brought about glares of hatred. But the embarrassing moments that Lillian was forced to experience, were Charmayne's unannounced visits to the rooms when the girls were entertaining their clients. The "madam" would charge in, no matter what was in progress and depart unabashed and unaware of the glimmer of resentment left behind in her wake. Resentment that even Lillian could not conceal.

"I've been going over the reservation book, Mrs. Roach," observed Lillian politely, putting the ledger on Charmayne's desk. "Some of the gentlemen who were coming weekly, have not returned in two to three weeks."

"I can hardly control their sexual drives. And won't you call me Charmayne."

"If you wish, madam." Lillian, taking the hint she might go on about business matters if not the name. "It is not a question of their control, but our barging in upon them. They don't seem to come back after that."

The pencil going down the income column skipped a beat, but the answer came steadily enough. "They are also a party to my rules. They only get what they pay for."

"Can't you let your girls see to that?" Lillian persisted. "And let the gentleman have the privacy they've paid for?"

"The girls would steal me blind with added favors," came the reply, and this time the pencil went back to its arithmetrical work.

"Is that a greater loss than the men never returning again?"

"In my opinion, yes." Again, the pencil, like a measure of truth, moved erratically down the column. "But, you don't seem to agree."

"Perhaps, I don't," replied, Lillian, carefully respectful.

Charmayne sighed, this time out loud. "You claim to be the innocent virgin and still give me lessons in prostitution. What is on your mind, really?"

There was a moment's hesitation in Lillian's reply. It would have been so easy to blurt that she was no fool—she was aware of the favorable treatment being given to the others while she paid her way as a personal maid and slave. She had accepted it, because they needed the help and she knew she had a half-brother who would soon be able to help her—but she still needed a roof over her head until that time. And, she could have blurted out her own resentment, blaming Charmayne for keeping Johnny away from her, but her answer came levelly enough.

"Not a lesson in prostitution, for I have known no man. I'm citing the rule you set down for me as your maid."

"Rule? What rule?" Charmayne suddenly flared.

"If I saw error, I was to correct it in your sight."

"In others!" she screamed. "I never make errors. What time is it?"

"Nearly ten o'clock," she sighed, knowing whatever she said would be fruitless.

"Then, I have a few errands for you to run. Here is the list and the money."

Curiosity impelled a sudden decision on Lillian's part. Surely, there would be ample time to run the errands' and check on her half-brother's ship.

Within seconds, led on by her thought, Lillian was in the sunshine, on the dusty street that led to the real streets and hills of a city she had not yet seen. Above her, on the summer-green hills, the mansions stood out like jewels in a crown. In the nearer distance, a hodgepodge of row houses lined the twisting streets.

Amazingly, within two blocks, she was off of dirt streets and onto cobblestone and then brick sidewalks. It was like leaving night and entering day.

Enamored, she wandered, until totally lost. Then she laughed at her own foolishness. She had accepted the shopping list without a question as to the location of each merchant.

Then a man emerged from a shipping company office. His tall powerful build was accentuated by the working clothes he wore—The white pants and jacket of a naval officer, with gold embroidered epaulets and cap.

She felt, in an odd way, that she should know the man. But, she put it down to wishful thinking and entered the building.

The cavernous office was a bee-hive of activity. One whole wall was a floor to ceiling chalkboard lined off in sections to note the names of ships, their departure or arrival, cargo and passengers on board. Every bit of information was there but the name of the ship's captain. Facing that wall was a glass fronted balcony, beneath which was a series of desks behind a railing.

Liberty Lee turned from the balcony window and scurried to her desk. She picked up the ship's horn and blew into it to summon her general manager.

"There's a young lady who just entered in a maid's uniform," she told Deckler crisply. "She will ask for information on Otis. Tell her nothing, but find out where she is employed."

"You say it's a matter of tracing a relative?" Deckler asked a moment later with a crisp, professional tone.

"I believe one of your captains might be my half-brother, but I can't be sure."

"Really?" Deckler jiggled his pince-nez. In defiance of California heat and summer wear, he wore a navy-blue suit, black high-top shoes, a stiff white shirt and navy string tie. Deckler's head was so hairless as to suggest he shaved it once a week with the same straight razor that made his pink face hairless. Because his eyebrows and lashes were so blonde, they added to the impression of a skull covered with skin, with the only contrast being his steely gray eyes. He was a peeled, hard-boiled egg.

"If I could just learn when Captain Whiteside's ship might return."

"That is always hard to say, miss. If you would care to leave your name and address, I shall put it in his letter box and have him contact you."

Lillian felt impatient over the lack of information, but took the offered pen and paper and prayed he would not recognize the address.

Deckler's eyes blossomed. He made short work of getting rid of her and went upstairs to report to Liberty.

"Fascinating," Liberty murmured. "She does live at Charmayne Roach's house, but the maid's rig confuses me. Dick, as a single man of forty, I think you need a night on the town."

"Are you suggesting . . . ?' he gulped, as though the mere thought of entering such an establishment would mar his perfection.

"I am," she laughed, "but don't go into a snit. I had a business dinner with Kai Soong last night. He was probing me for possible men of import for a certain project he is working upon. You will be going to her house to meet with Kai Soong. I know what you are going to say, but I have my own reasons for not wishing to ask Kai Soong direct questions about this Lillian Whiteside. You will do the snooping for me. Now, send a runner down to Otis's ship. I shall expect him for dinner at eight and will keep him in conversation until after midnight. That will keep him away from Charmayne's his first night back in port."

Lillian recognized the carriage and her heart skipped a beat. Now she knew why Charmayne had gotten her out of the way, but even with her stop at the Lee Shipping building she had been able to run the errands in less than two hours.

Then as she approached the house, the front door opened and Johnny emerged with a slender, well-dressed man. At closer range, Lillian saw the face—aged, cruel and bitter—giving the lie to what appeared as a youthful body.

"Hello, Lillian," Johnny beamed. "You weren't supposed to be back so soon."

"Was there a reason I wasn't supposed to be here?"

"Not really. Oh, may I present Harrison Andrus. Harrison, this is Miss Lillian, one of Miss Karen's friends."

The man nodded a greeting, looked swiftly at the quiet street, stared for a moment at the maid carrying the bulky packages, then scurried into the carriage and leaned back into its shadows.

"He was nervous about coming," Johnny whispered, "but is quite taken with Karen. You will hear more about it tonight."

"Tonight?"

"I'll let Karen tell you about it. I want to get him out of the district before he backs out on the deal."

The miraculous circumstances of timing, of sheer good luck that had brought her home at the precise moment of their leaving did not set well with Charmayne.

The moment Lillian was in the foyer she motioned her into the office and found fault with each and every purchase. Then Lillian was curtly dismissed.

In the foyer Lillian was hissed at from the alcove leading into the greeting room.

"You silly goose," she laughed, seeing Karen peeking around at her, "what game are you playing?"

"A heavenly one. Oh, Lillian, I've met the most marvelous man. We are to meet with him tonight to make the final arrangements for the marriage."

"We?"

"I hope you don't mind, but I felt I had to have someone with me. You don't mind, do you?"

"I'm very honored, Karen. But what am I supposed to do?"

Karen shrugged. "I'm not sure, but it was Johnny's suggestion that I should have a woman along with me."

With a shiver of delight, it dawned on Lillian that Johnny knew Karen would pick her over the others. It got them both away from Charmayne.

Throughout the rest of the afternoon and early evening Charmayne was a tyrant. In her stubborn pride, she was bound and determined to keep Lillian away from Johnny at the expense of everything else.

During the dinner hour, Clara came and whispered to Charmayne. Per her custom of the afternoon she ignored the report that a carriage awaited Miss Lillian. Her jealousy of the girl had crowded everything else—the business, the rules—out of her head. She considered herself a tenacious woman, zealous of her own status as the finest madam in San Francisco. She felt she knew exactly what she was doing.

"I have marvelous news," Charmayne chirped, as though she were still the master of proper timing. "A carriage awaits our dear house guest Karen. We may soon be hearing wedding bells." She laughed—the sharp edge of her voice had vanished. "Lillian, dear, you are to escort her. As they are waiting, you had best go as you are."

Lillian found herself begrudging Charmayne everything—her position, her power, her clothes, her contact with Johnny Lord. Then she put it aside, to escape for one night.

It was not until shortly after midnight that Lillian was returned to the house. The customers had left and Lillian was amazed to find the regular girls still in the greeting room, along with Clara, Amy, Beth and Carol.

"Well . . . ?" Charmayne said, on a long note; as though chiding a child arriving after curfew.

Lillian looked at the expectant faces eyeing her and the empty doorway behind her in a little puzzlement. In that instant, from every woman, prostitute or virgin, she felt a universal bond.

"I came back alone," Lillian stammered, a little unsure of how to start.

A note of curiosity crept into Charmayne's voice. "That is obvious. Kai Soong said nothing of what was happening when he came back to meet with that . . . Oh, what was his name?"

"Deckler," Clara prompted. "Mister Richard Deckler."

Charmayne beamed. "Very good, Clara. You pick up on names quickly, all the way back in the kitchen."

That night, with Lillian absent, Clara has made sure to identify all of the visitors to Kai Soong. To make sure, she had taken over the serving of Kai Soong and his guests with her specialty dishes. What Clara had learned she signaled Lillian they would discuss privately.

"Kai Soong certainly had a busy evening," Lillian laughed, getting Clara's signal.

"Lady Charmayne," Lillian said, using the title for the first time, as though in disgust, "you sent me from here as Karen's escort, without knowing where I was escorting her. Mr. Andrus seems a man of quick decisions. His mind made up, he had a minister there to marry them. Karen's things are to be sent to her tomorrow."

Charmayne opened her mouth and closed it. She had been about to inquire why Lillian's absence had been over five hours, but did not want to raise the point in front of so many.

Lillian hid her relief. "And now, I would like to be excused."

Charmayne waved her away and Clara was quick to follow.

"Kai Soong does work quickly," Lillian said, as they climbed the stairs. "I heard him discussing the girls with Johnny. For reasons that those two seemed to understand, he switched Karen to this Harrison Andrus—and if the house is any indication, she married money. *Big money!* And now Amy for this Richard Deckler. I met him today, and don't ask how, but they will make a perfect pair. Thus Beth will go to Robert Duocoming and Carol to one Basil Meeks."

Clara had met them all that evening and had heard much the same, but it still left her questioning.

"I thought he still wanted you for Mr. Duocoming."

"I wasn't mentioned," Lillian said, as though in great relief, "nor were you."

"Which suits me!" Clara boomed with laughter. "Kai Soong has offered me something greater than a husband. He was so taken with my cooking tonight that he will see to my becoming the main cook. I love the idea, I really do!'' Then she felt guilty over her own happiness. ''But what of you?''

Lillian shrugged, as though quite indifferent to the whole matter. She stilled her trembling heart until she was snuggled in her bed. Then she let her emotions soar, reliving every dreamlike second of that marvelous evening.

During the wedding ceremony Johnny's eyes had burned into her like living coals. He had hardly left her side during the reception, making sure that their hands met each time he handed her a glass of champagne or a plate of the excellent food.

And she knew, when his carriage departed the Andrus mansion, that the driver had been ordered to take the long way back to Lady Charmayne's.

''Do you know what my mind was doing as they were being married?'' he asked casually.

''No.''

''It was pretending that it was you and I taking those vows Lillian. Lillian! I don't like the name, nor do I like Lil, which I have tried in my mind.''

''I enjoy Lily,'' she observed, with a breathless catch to her voice, wanting to return to the first part of his statement. Deliberately, she laid a slender hand on Johnny's arm. ''Only my mother ever called me Lily. You may, also, if you like.''

''I am honored,'' answered Johnny, his eyes sliding downward from her face to the shadowed swell of her bosom. The look was like the touching of their hands, tingling Lillian's skin, reminding her of what he was. At the same time the sinews of his arm tensed beneath her touch and she instinctively knew that she could hold dominion over this arrogant man from this moment on.

''I'm inviting,'' she murmured in low disturbing voice, to make him see that the offered kiss was a giant step for her.

And a single kiss would have been a devastating insult to such lips, in his opinion. He felt a thrill of expectation coursing through his veins like wildfire—a sensation that made him wonder, for one more moment, if indeed he shouldn't marry this one.

They rode in silence, slowly, through the hills of San Francisco without seeing them. They forgot who they were or where they were—and only the horse seemed to care, for the driver had long since fallen asleep on his perch.

Lillian was aware and yet not fully aware of all that was happening with his hands and the expert way in which he was undressing her. To cover her embarrassment, Lillian started to shed a portion of her innocence. "I want to see the wicked side of my nature and his nature," she told herself lamely.

Then came the shock of sensation. His hands turning every nerve end of her body to quivering response. Their contact so slow and sensuous that her voice had to express thought: "I'm glad you didn't wait for me to ask for this!"

Lillian became unbearably conscious of the fact that they were performing in a rolling carriage what the girls at Charmayne's performed in a bed; which posed a startling question. Why were the girls being paid to receive such liquid-fire pleasure?

For one marvelous moment while the world stood still, the answer seemed utterly unimportant. All that mattered was the feel of his virile body pressing her hard against the leather carriage seat; his mouth that continued to kiss her with tender love; the erotic thoughts she had of when they could share a real bed together.

And that, she felt, answered Clara's question. She had been left aside, because she was earmarked for Johnny Lord.

She slept, dreaming of the lips that closed over her with hunger, the hands that molded her breasts gently, the masculinity that had aroused and awakened her feminitity. Awakened it to a fever pitch that had burned away any thought of it having been a wicked act. She felt with all her young heart, that she had experienced love.

For her, that answered everything.

Chapter 5

"A woman can only give away her innocence but once," Lillian said sternly. She looked at the four new girls through narrowing eyes, with an expression they could not read. The line of her mouth grew cruel, drawing itself into a sardonic twist. "None of you probably remember your first time, but don't ever let the customer know that. By fair means or foul, make him think he is the first." She paused.

She had lost her innocence, to a man who had given her nothing in return for eighteen years—not passion, as she wanted passion to be; not compassion, except in a business sense; not love, in terms of a wedding vow; or ever a commitment. There were times she hated Johnny Lord for what he had taken so casually—so cruelly. She had first hated him for the child he had put in her womb and would not accept, nor would she destroy. She hated him for the coldblooded relief she had shown when the child was still-born. But each new hatred was only an arousal of her feelings of love. Her emotions were too forgiving—time after time. And because he had always dangled a carrot, she had chased it for eighteen years; and for that she hated him most of all.

"Now, you will be shown to your rooms and will begin a six weeks' course on the rules and manner of this house."

"Wait a minute!" The girl's faded eyes gave her a searching look, as though she had seen few daylight hours. "I'm here to start clamping them on tonight and make some hard cash that I desperately need. I don't need no lessons on how to make a stud feels he's in the right pasture."

"I'm sure," Lillian said coldly. "You, my dear, by my leave may go to the front door. Henry will see that the carriage takes you wherever you wish to go." She stood, regal and unwilling to back down on that decision. The still-born child had years ago added to her breasts, while a dye from China kept her hair a sunburst red to give an added sparkle to her green eyes. At thirty-five her face had become a classic of pink marble beauty—haughty and self-assured.

For ten years, because she held out hope of marriage, she had suffered under Charmayne Roach. Then, when Charmayne retired, she saw her advancement to madam as a business working partnership between herself and Johnny. He was humiliated by such a thought and avoided her.

Then the 'House of Peony' closed, to the loud cheers of the Vigilantes. For six months the 'elite' gentlemen had a choice of Johnny Lord's flea-infested houses or nothing.

The majority elected for nothing.

"What's she up to?" Johnny stormed at Kai Soong. "I know she has been recruiting new girls, but where's she going to put them. The old house is gone! Torn down!"

The eighteen years had turned Kai Soong into a wizened old man. He cloaked his sickness from the world and his friends. He could calmly accept death whenever it approached him, except for one small matter that was still held in secret.

"Perhaps," he wheezed, fighting the constant congestion in his lungs, "she tired of one of your diseases."

"What are you talking about? I have no ailments."

Kai Soong laughed drily, like corn husks being peeled. "I will not expound on them all, but only a single one. Fear is a disease and you suffer from the worst kind—fear of marriage."

To avoid comment on that subject, he growled: "Are you backing her in a new house?"

"The money was borrowed from me, but I have had no other say in the matter. I would gather," Kai Soong continued, almost on a sneer, "that you have not received an invitation to her grand opening—this evening."

"I certainly did not!" Johnny growled through clenched teeth. "What opening? Where?"

"An oversight, I am sure," Kai Soong said, in an even tone, baiting a pre-set trap. "Then you must go as my guest. I tire these days of the old rickshaw. Have your carriage call for me at eight."

Johnny Lord, his hair flecked with silver, could not refuse his major financial and land backer. Besides, he was totally curious.

He knew that 'Peony House' was gone, but as Kai Soong had owned that land he had paid no attention to the razing of the entire block. He assumed, as San Francisco had been led to believe, that a private school was being erected by the Catholics on the old ground.

The entire block had first been closed off by a ten foot high adobe brick wall, with massive iron gates opening onto two streets. For the next two months a steady caravan of supply wagons disappeared behind the wall. No one asked about them, for they were the supply wagons of Nathan Tedder, and the Tedder family were only commissioned to build the finest of buildings.

And, this too, was a mark of Lillian's growth over the eighteen years. Shunned by Liberty Lee, denied the truth by Otis Whiteside when they finally met, never a real part of Charmayne's house, because Johnny did not want to share her with any other man, Lillian had been able to develop two strong talents of her own: an astute business sense and an in-depth knowledge of every San Francisco family. She knew, even before she approached them as builders that the Tedder family had built the Lee mansion on Nob Hill, that Selena Tedder loathed Liberty Lee and that Nathan Tedder had once had an affair with Liberty. That he was a customer of Charmayne, was only secondary. Like *Casa Lily,* she was building her revenge brick by brick, board by board, with each old scandal stored away in her arsenal.

The carriage crawled to a halt, dozens of other carriages preceding it into the grounds. In that moment between dusk and dark the Spanish style structure seemed to be all white and old gold. Through the open window of the carriage, scents of the flower bordered drive breathed a freshness into the foul-smelling streets nearby.

Duplicates of ancient lamp standards were now being lit along the curving drive to the front portico; from the interior patio—which was the centerpiece of the square building—the plaintive twang of guitar music mingled a bubble of voices.

"Who are these people?" questioned Johnny, as they reached their goal. Kai Soong shrugged and smiled, as if he knew little more than that he had been invited.

Their carriage door was smartly opened by a young Chinese lad in a simple, but effective, costume of white with gold trim.

Inside the portico another young Oriental man bowed and escorted them through an arch to the patio, were clusters of tables covered in bright cloths, were rapidly being filled by people in elegant evening attire. In the center of the patio was a rippling water fountain with flowers and candle molds floating in its base pool. Against the house walls were two dozen enormous earthenware wine vats, each twelve feet tall with vines and flowers growing out of the top and cascading down over the sides. From the second and third floor balconies, which wrapped around three sides of the patio were strung colored lanterns. A small army of other Chinese boys, in the same white and gold uniform, roamed about with trays food, wines and fruit.

"I don't believe this!" Johnny's attention focussed immediately on a table of recognizable faces. That Karen, Amy, Beth and Carol would come to wish Lillian well was not surprising. But for their husbands to attend was almost shocking. Each, in their field, were among the most influential men in the city. Then he began to recognize other faces that shocked him even more. "How in the hell did she get them here?"

"Ah, curiosity is not just for the young."

"But Lily led me to believe she gave her farewell to the

business when we decided to close down and raze the old house.''

''Her first farewell.''

''Her *first* farewell? I'm not sure what you mean.''

The usual slow smile played over Kai Soong's face, adding further wrinkles to those already there. ''When a madam announces she is going to retire there is always a big fuss to gain her girls—at least, if she is a young woman, in her prime and successful. In a way, Lillian got rid of the old stock, wanting girls who will look right for such an elegant setting.''

''And where does that leave me?'' Johnny scowled.

Kai Soong shrugged. ''That is up to Lillian.''

The remark made Johnny Lord feel ill at ease. Not because of his attire. In his formal tailcoat he could have been considered the handsomest and best dressed man in the dazzling array that Lillian had assembled. He saw Tedders, Havens and even a Lee—although a quick scanning did not reveal the presence of Liberty Lee.

Then his feeling of discomfort deepened; he felt like an intruder as Lillian swept down the curving white wrought iron stairway from the first balcony. The women stared with frank envy at the gown of white moire with pearl embroidery, at the white ostrich tips and aigrettes in her sunburst chestnut hair, and at the deep blaze of the massive emerald necklace and matching earrings to set off her eyes. She greeted each table of guests as though she had been the queen of society for years.

A tall, middle-aged man in formal black, approached them.

''Good evening Master Soong.''

''Good evening Henry. Your staff seems quite prepared for the event.''

''Thank you,'' he said, his long horsey face showing no expression. A butler by training, he had doubted the wisdom of using Chinese boys. He had even doubted the wisdom of his taking on the position in such a mansion. ''They have been very willing learners of my methods. Ah, Mr. Lord. Miss McHenry is most pleased to learn you have come along with Master Soong.''

Johnny was baffled. "Miss McHenry?"

Kai Soong chuckled. "For personal and professional reasons Lillian decided not to use the Whiteside name. She thinks its a laugh to tie the McHenry name to the business."

Henry Muffler, even after hearing the story of her arrival in California, did not think it so amusing. But at the wage he was being paid, he kept his silence.

"Miss McHenry," he said, addressing Johnny only, "would like you to follow me, sir. She will give you a personal tour of the house before the other guests are offered the privilege."

Johnny now went through a third emotion. It was all a set up. Lillian and Kai Soong had cooked the whole thing up to get him there. He didn't know whether to be angry or pleased.

Lillian, who was a little nervous with the man she had purposely avoided for a little over a year, personally conducted Johnny through the vast, rambling structure. Johnny was overwhelmed by the master plan of the four connecting wings with the patio center.

To the left of the arching entry was the new greeting room, almost barbaric in its splendor. It opened into the next wing's first floor, which was a dining room with bas-relief covered walls, massive chandeliers and dining room chairs in red plush.

It, in turn, opened onto the back wing, which was Clara's kitchen. But Johnny, who was a man of simple food tastes, thought wryly, What good is all this?

Clara, who had rounded out considerably in eighteen years of sampling her own cooking, nearly squeezed him to death in a bear-hug.

"I'm being spoiled," she boomed. "I have a chef for every department and they all have private living accommodations on the next floor."

It was the living accomodations that Johnny felt was the most outrageous waste of space. Above the greeting room and dining room were twelve bedrooms, each with a private bath. The beds were enormous, the rugs ankle deep and each bath had a gigantic porcelain-lined tub. But, according to Lillian, these rooms would be used only for the entertaining of the customers. The girls each had their own private bedroom on the third floor of those two wings.

When they reached the fourth wing, Johnny's jaw dropped. It was Lillian's private world. Then, despite himself, he began to laugh. Here, on a smaller scale, was a duplication of the mansion the Tedder family had built for Liberty Lee.

Hearing his laughter, Lillian grew angry.

"You don't like it?"

"It's not that," he chuckled. "Do you know what Nathan Tedder has designed this from?"

"Of course! On my orders!"

"Oh, Lily, Lily, why do you let that woman get to you?"

"I ordered this in an angry mood," she said truthfully. "She tried her best to get Kai Soong and Nathan to talk me out of this scheme. That's why I even enlarged on my original idea. This is going to be the most elegant house of assignation the world has ever known. Look at those people down there. They are still too much involved in making their money grow to give a damn for real class, but they crave it."

"I see," Johnny said thoughtfully. "Go on!"

"By the end of this week, I will have the first group of six girls ready to go. Ladies, Johnny. Trained like you've never seen prostitutes trained before. Polished, cultured, refined. If they don't like my way, out they go."

"And where does that leave me?" Johnny mused.

He still had not seen that portion of the front wing that opened to the left of the entry arch. It was a gambling casino like none he'd ever seen before.

"It will be run by the same rules of dress and conduct as the rest of the house," she said sternly. "With one difference. Just as it will now be with the girls, they must have a dinner reservation before they can gamble."

"What if they want both?" he asked firmly.

"Then we realize a double profit. I'm a businesswoman, Johnny. I don't intend to run a charitable institution."

"I agree. And you want me to handle this end of the business?"

"I trust no other."

"Good!" Then he added gloomily. "And what of us?"

For all her scheming to get him there, she knew when to keep her mouth shut.

"Please, Johnny—we settled that long ago."

"I know, I know. I know I have been the only one. Likewise, I never bedded a single girl after you took over the house. It was my way of showing my respect—how much you meant to me. Oh, damn! What's the use of talking about it?"

"Absolutely none," Lillian said gently. "I have my own self-respect to think about, too. darling. I am still a madam who has known only one man."

After she sent him back to join Kai Soong she went to the dining room thinking. Why am I opening this old wound? she wondered. It was a recurrent dream that some day she would get him to consent to marriage. But at thirty-five it was growing almost too late to bring another child into the world.

Well, she mused, it would be a form of love just to have him around as a business partner. And I hope I am strong enough to keep him out of my bed.

Then she pushed all those thoughts aside. The "regrets" had far out numbered the acceptances, but she still had eighty guests to seat for dinner. And she had planned no surprises for them. The girls were forbidden to venture down from their private bedrooms that night. This was Miss Lily McHenry's night to show off her new home and not what business would be conducted in it henceforth.

She gave a signal to the stringed quartet to begin playing and went back to the patio.

If there was a single regret over the evening, it was of her own making. Even though she knew that the President of the Pleasant, Lee, Whiteside Steamship Line was at sea on the flagship "Carrie," she still tried to get Amy Deckler to bring along Mrs. Otis Whiteside. But even though Dick Deckler was general manager of the PLW Line, Amy claimed not to know the woman.

Lillian had taken it as another slap in the face from Otis Whiteside. Still, she felt he had little room to be so uppity. Everyone knew that his wife Carrie was the ''pass for white'' daughter of Mammy Pleasant. Nor did Lillian really have any feelings about color lines. It just irked her that Otis Whiteside would flatly deny he was who he was and make jest to Charmayne Roach that he would not think kindly of a half-sister, who had entered such a trade. Hadn't he, before he married Carrie, been one of Charmayne's customers? Well, there would come a day, she vowed, when Otis Whiteside would regret that statement.

Chapter 6

On that same evening, Daniel Lee came into his mother's home office, his thin face gray with misery. Liberty took one look at him and jumped from her seat.

"Don't tell me something has happened to Mick!" she roared.

"It is not your grandson," Daniel whispered. "He is quite safe and at home asleep."

"Then what the devil is it?"

There were times Daniel Lee could hate his mother. At twenty-eight he had many duties in the far-flung business ventures his mother had invested in, but no responsibilities without her approval. The only thing he had done to please her was to produce a son who reminded her of his grandfather. At least, that was more than his brother and sister had done. Alexander Grace Wells O'Lee, at twenty-five, could do no wrong in his mother's eyes. Although Daniel saw everything he did as a wrong. His twenty-three year old sister, Miranda Lee Buford, he considered a snob, her husband Will Buford as a leech and their desire not to have children as yet an insult.

"Well . . ." Liberty demanded.

"It's this telegraph report on Monsieur de Lesseps and the Panama canal. He has admitted that he is nearly bankrupt."

It was no news to Liberty. She had received private dispatches from the man from whom she had accepted shares, instead of cash, for her interest in the Panama Railroad. As she had helped link America by a transcontinental rail line, she had dreamed of cutting ocean travel time by that central canal through the Isthmus of Panama. Now, it seemed doomed to failure and a new canal route was being considered by Eastern money.

"I am aware," she said crisply, "of his financial problems, but think it time to cut ourselves free of him and still keep an interest in that canal. I have made arrangements to go east. Where is your brother? I thought he was having dinner with you and Helen this evening."

Daniel stood up and faced her soberly.

"Damn him!" he growled. "I will not be a party to his lie! He went to *that* dinner party."

"Oh, no," Liberty said sorrowfully. "All right, I'll handle A.G. when he gets home. Goodnight."

Then she sat down again behind her desk and stared moodily out into space. How the years had fled by. It was a fact that she had been the first to learn that Lillian was not after Otis in the "family way" she'd thought. She might have then acted differently if her information had not come from Kai Soong. Then she didn't care how Otis handled the matter, but was secretly thrilled that he denied any family connection. But it was also a fact that her hatred of Lillian became a personal thing. A jealous thing. Wrongly, because for once in her life she didn't have the guts to ask for the full truth, she saw Lillian as the young version of herself in Kai Soong's eyes. The love and respect she had for him began to wither and die because of what she assumed in her mind. It didn't take much imaginetion on her part to picture the two of them together; Lillian as she had once been. It hurt!

"And why are you hurt?" she asked herself aloud. But she didn't want to face her own answer. After Dan O'lee had been killed building the Central Pacific Railroad, Kai Soong had taught her how to be a goddess; how to use men for her financial and political advancement. He had been a magical teacher and partner and then his duties had called him back to China and the House of Soong.

Upon his return, for the linking of the Central Pacific and Union Pacific, there had been the joy of old friends reunited.

But to her utter amazement he stayed in San Francisco

and allowed his son to become the Master of the House of Soong in China. It was difficult for her to imagine anyone giving up so much power, while she was striving to gain a power of her own.

He was still the same old Kai Soong, but confidence in him melted like snow in a noonday sun. He was secretive to the point of being curt. The private life inside the walls of his home became a mystery. Although the Chinese servants were prone to gossip, they feared to gossip about old Master Kai Soong.

Liberty thought she knew the answer to his secret, and therein lay the first hurt. Her old friend, who knew her heart like an open book, would not reveal his heart to her. Then, for a brief span of time in the fall of 1873 they were forced to join forces again. The fortunes of Liberty Lee and Kai Soong survived that panic, but only their business fortunes. She had gained no more information on his personal life than before.

Then, although they lived within a mile of each other, they drifted apart and seldom saw each other. Only when one or the other needed business advice did they communicate, and Liberty did not think well of Kai Soong's arrangements with Johnny Lord.

Soft footfalls across the foyer brought her out of her reverie. She moved with quick determination, well aware of who she would be confronting. At another time she might have laughed, looking out her office door.

"Does your lack of shoes mean you were trying to sneak in without saying goodnight?"

"Good evening, mother," Alexander Grace Wells Lee slurred, his tongue thick from champagne. But in answer to her question he just shrugged.

As always, Liberty felt a pang of pity looking upon this son. At twenty-five A.G. was uncommonly unhandsome, with a head that was too large for his body that was still of boyish frame. His sandy hair was thin, near to balding and his face seemed in a perennial pout. He, of all the children, had needed a father to help in his rearing. Many times Liberty had wracked her brain to pinpoint an O'Lee or Wells relative he reminded her of. She always came up with a zero. He neither looked nor acted like any of them. And the love that she felt for him always seemed overshadowed by her pity.

"I want to speak to you," she said sternly, "concerning your whereabouts this evening!"

"Jehosaphat!" A.G. exploded. "Mother! . . . When, will you stop treating me like a ten year old?"

"When you start treating our family name with the respect it is due."

He squared his shoulders and faced her soberly.

"Respect," he growled, "be damned. It's my business what I do with my life."

"Like hell it is! We have business and social obligations of which you're a part. How in hellfire do you think it looks for you to associate with all the wrong people?"

A.G.'s face paled, then his cheeks mottled red.

"There was hardly a person there who has not been in this house. It's a very beautiful building, the dinner was excellent and the hostess charming."

"I am well aware of her clever maneuver designed to make her socially acceptable," Liberty said. "But what of tomorrow night and the nights after that. It will be business as usual. I am not a naive woman, son. I have seen her type of business from both the oriental and occidental point of view. If your male needs have become so strong . . . I would suggest you quietly take a mistress."

A.G. grinned. He was quite aware of what looked back at him from his shaving mirror. He wondered how shocked his mother would be if she knew he had to pay extra and loathed the houses of Johnny Lord. Charmayne Roach had always treated him in a kindly way. He felt Lillian would tender him the same courtesy. It was not that he desired a woman each time he had gone to the old house. It had been a place of relaxation and comfortable surroundings. Many times he had paid for nothing more than another person to have conversation with. His mother, brother and sister seemed to have only one topic that interested them—business—and he always seemed excluded.

Even though he had spent four years in an Eastern college, having been back home less than a year, he was no more included in decision making than before. He felt of no use to anyone and pouted over his bleak and unhappy life. Several times in college, unable to really make any friends, he had thought the long sleep of death would be more enjoyable than living. He had considered himself too weak to even take him own life. And for once in his life he pushed aside his weakness to talk back to his mother.

"Don't you ever get tired of playing God, mother? You say a mistress? Shall it be Chinese like the woman father had?"

Liberty stepped forward slowly, her breath making a warning sound like a coiled rattlesnake.

"Mention that matter again," she said quietly, "and you will find yourself ousted from this house and family!"

"What family?" he roared. "You pull all the strings. It's bad enough for Danny and Miranda. It's worse for me, because I'm really no use to anyone. Just because a person is ugly doesn't mean they don't have a brain."

The peal of the doorbell kept Liberty from having to answer that charge. She turned and marched to the door, her mind filled with guilt.

A.G. could hear her answer the caller in Chinese. It put another arrow into his heart. In his youth and teens he had been surrounded by Chinese servants and nurse-maids. His mother had kept them under control with the Chinese she had learned from Kai Soong and the servants, but the children had been forbidden to learn the tongue. He had always regarded it as one more way his mother had of excluding them and retaining a certain power all her own. Perhaps to spite her he had secretly taken four years of Chinese in college, passing himself off as a potential missionary to the heathens.

At that moment he wished he had never taken the studies. The caller was a servant from the House of Soong and the message seemed unbelievable. No more than a half hour before he had seen Kai Soong laughing and joking as he departed in Johnny Lord's carriage. How could the old Chinaman be dying? He had to have heard wrong.

"Put on your shoes," his mother ordered, upon returning.

"Kai Soong has sent for me and I would like you as an escort."

He looked at the stricken face of his mother and the anger left him. Her voice had conveyed a desperate need. He had never seen his mother afraid before and it made him feel more of a man than he had ever felt before.

Chapter 7

Liberty stood in the doorway a long time, feeling the room take on a gradual chill from her arrival. The servant had not bothered to tell her who else Kai Soong had called to his deathbed.

Two of the women she knew quite well from the past. The third only from a distance. Still, she marvelled at the change in each and had to reflect on when she had last seen them.

Even though Mammy Pleasant was a director of the shipping line, it had been years since she had attended a meeting—always giving her proxy to her son-in-law. Liberty could well recall the reason for her non-attendance. She had been the one to slyly get Mammy to invest in Otis Whiteside's flagship, with every intention of getting out of the shipping business. But then, as her interest grew in the canal scheme, she saw the importance of keeping the Lee Line and used her money and power to convince Otis that a merger was the answer. Mammy had fought the idea, for reasons she would not give to her son-in-law, but Liberty knew.

There was still too much Southern thinking in Liberty O'Lee. Even though she had helped, in a way, to see that Otis and Carrie were married, her mind could never fully forget that Carrie was Mammy's daughter. As long as Carrie went to sea with her husband, Liberty regarded it as a perfect marriage. But after their third child was born, and Carrie stayed more and more at home, Liberty's attitude changed.

She had always felt herself without prejudice, but when

she had seen what had been done to her part of the South during Reconstruction it had gnawed at her and without fully realizing it had taken her spite out on Carrie. Whenever she could she had excluded the wife of the President of the line and just had Otis for dinner 'business meetings.' In her mind she had a womanly excuse for the reasoning.

Carrie, now the mother of six, had let herself go. Once a striking beauty, slim and fashionable, she had given up her figure more and more after each birth until she was dowdy in Liberty's opinion. More of a drawback to Otis's social standing than an asset.

And that night was no different. Carrie looked like she had been pulled from bed, which she had. With six children, even with servants, her day was from dawn to dusk. Still, if there was a really happy person in that room, it was Carrie Whiteside. She was constantly surrounded by the love of her husband and children and thrived on giving them happiness in return.

Carrie could not help but wonder at this summons. There had been times when she had feared and loathed Kai Soong. She knew how close Mammy had been to the man, but she had always tried to keep her distance. And looking at Mammy Pleasant, with the Angel of Death hovering over that house, she feared for her as well.

No one knew, not even Mammy, her true age. White-haired and shrunken in size, she had in the last few years begun to confuse the dates of important events in her life, nor did she really care if they got confused. Her life was now centered on her little house, her garden and the visits from her grandchildren. Weekly, one of Carrie's kitchen servants would come to restock her larder and do the major cleaning. All other days seemed to melt together.

But, at that moment, her mind was lucid and sharp as a tack.

"You age most gracefully, Liberty," she said, her wrinkled mouth breaking into a friendly smile.

"Thank you, Mammy." As though they had each put aside bitterness for the moment, Liberty sailed into the room, took the wrinkled brown hand and pressed it to her cheek.

''I never thought we would see this moment.''

''I should have been the first to go,'' Manny said sadly, putting her own hand over Liberty's and giving it a gentle squeeze. ''But then, I don't think I've seen the man more than once or twice in the past several years.''

''The same here,'' Liberty grinned, ''then it was only for business. Hello, Carrie.''

Carrie's eyes, looking at her mother and Liberty, were sad. Poor women, she thought, who should have remarried after the deaths of their husbands, instead of wasting their womanhood in the business world of men. In her opinion that was where each of their hardness had sprung. Still, because the woman had made her husband a very rich man, she really didn't dislike Liberty. For that matter, she had had her fill of society in her youth and cared nothing about being excluded now. Her idea of a perfect social evening was being with her children.

''Hello, Liberty. Do you know Miss McHenry? We have just met. Lillian McHenry, this is Mrs. Lee. Liberty Lee.''

Liberty looked at Lillian with grim amusement. ''We have never formally met.'' Liberty was tempted to call her Miss Whiteside, but knew that was not the time to turn over that rock in front of Mammy and Carrie.

''How do you do,'' Lillian said formally, but did not rise or offer her hand.

How she has changed, Liberty thought bitterly. Strange that she has none of the hard look of the prostitutes that used to follow along with the building of the railroads. This woman was regal, elegant and soft-spoken. She remembered her only as a child in a maid's outfit. They were two totally different people.

The arrival of a houseboy brought all their thoughts back to the present.

''He wishes,'' the boy spluttered, tears brimming his oval eyes, ''you come now——''

They followed, as though it were a nightmare that wasn't really happening.

Kai Soong was sitting in his big chair, four lesser chairs in a semi-circle in front of him. He was dressed quite elegantly, in the attire he had long ago selected for his burial. He hardly looked like a man about to die.

They stood there foolishly awaiting his command. To their surprise he motioned only with a slightly trembling hand, seating Lillian first.

Because she was the last seated Liberty's mouth tightened slowly into a hard line. It just helped to underscore what she thought about the relationship between Kai Soong and Lillian.

"It is true," he began slowly, his voice the only hint that he suffered internal pain. "That my hours are few. I could have spoken to each of you separately, but I wanted you all to hear what I have to say to each. The spider of life so many times wove us into his web. My dear Liberty, how I envied your remarkable husband. I have had two wives in this life, but only one woman I really loved. For a brief moment we were like two moths too close to the same flame. We cavorted, but knew it meant death for each if we continued on. I thought I could forget you by returning to China . . . to my duties . . . to my family obligations. I could not forget, but you were a different woman upon my return. Your star was as I long ago foretold . . . A woman of great power and means. My continued love for you would have meant your ruination. That I could not do, no matter the hunger in my heart."

Liberty sat livid with rage. He may have been dying, but she would have to live on with these women knowing that they had once been intimate.

"Mammy," he went on hoarsely, "I have never respected a business mind, man or woman, more than I have your very own. Had fate not planted our ancestor seeds on different earthly ground we could have been the most forceful couple known to man, but we each learned to live in our world, although forced to live our lives in the world of a race that not only does not understand our black or yellow skins, but understandably fears them. Which brings me to Carrie. A product of one world who has been capable of living in the other, but still knows the stings of being looked upon as a half-caste."

"But no more," Carrie said simply.

Kai Soong smiled. When he returned to her for his final request, he would remind her of those words.

"Lillian is almost a stranger to all, but myself. For eighteen years I have watched this flower bloom into maturity. There are those who would malign her, but without cause. She, too, has my respect for her business mind and she, too, also knows what it is like to be sold into a form of slavery."

It was Lillian's turn to shudder. That part of her life she did not want exposed to these women—especially Liberty.

"Which," he continued, "is the base upon which I have brought you together. Knowing that my number one wife was content to stay in China as a maternal grandmother for the House of Soong next generation; knowing that I could never possess the only love of my life, I took unto myself a secret number two wife here in America. To cast out all others in my mind, I selected a young girl of Norwegian birth.

He sighed, "It is a cruel form of slavery, the buying of a woman for a wife. The girl had been told nothing of me and her eyes mirrored hate from the first meeting. That is why, dear Lillian, I was so careful to place your friends. Life is too short without a few grain of happiness sprinkled upon the surface. But eighteen years ago I was not thinking of the girl, only that she was a replacement for Liberty. Still, I felt a new joy in my heart when I later learned she was with child. That is the key many times to make a union complete. But, no. It—it was not to be. Twice she tried to take her life and that of the child. Then she was not left alone day or night until the coming of the child. That night, seventeen years ago, an error was made by the mid-wives. In bathing the new-born infant they turned their backs on her for just a few minutes. Instantly, she used their knives to leave this world."

He paused, letting each person form his own mental image of that scene.

"My late-in-life son was most healthy," he said, running his tongue over dry lips, "but already of great concern to the mid-wives. He was obviously half-caste and would become an object of great scorn in the House of

Soong. That night they were paid handsomely for the deed they must do. The next day my second wife and still-born son were buried with enough pomp to make sure the message got back to Master Soong in China."

"How could you?" Mammy gasped. "You let them kill that innocent little baby?"

Kai Soong smiled. "That has been my reason for such a private life, dear Mammy." He clapped his hands and a section of the wall opened. Behind it stood a six foot young man of seventeen. He was a striking admixture of East and West. Coal black hair and fair complexion, with the slightest oriental slant to his deep blue eyes.

Liberty saw at once the cut of Kai Soong in his face, although it had been chiseled finer by his Nordic blood. She had seen many children over the years born of the mixture of Oriental and Occidental blood, but never like this. This young male was different—his beauty was haunting.

"May I present Eric Soong. Since birth I have maintained a separate house and servants for him. Not a single Tong agent in this city knows that he lives. It must remain that way or the House of Soong would order his immediate death after my own." He lifted a scroll from the table beside his chair. "I wrote down my wishes for Eric in case I went forever to sleep one night. Now, I shall speak them—with some changes—and then destroy my writings. You four I name as his trustees until age twenty-one. You all, except Lillian of late, have been linked with him since birth. Every business venture we have enjoyed has put profits into his private trust and cannot be touched by my son in China.

"Liberty, he has been sheltered and tutored for seventeen years. In time he shall need to know the social graces of the East, where I wish him schooled. As well, I wish for him the business sense of Mammy, you and Lillian. Carrie, not only does he need the guidance of a mother to a child, but what he must expect as a half-caste in this world. Lillian, the bulk of his trust is invested with you and Johnny Lord. You may all hate me for this, but you are all now connected together to protect his trust."

Liberty didn't comment at once. Then, ever so slowly, she stood up. With deliberate grace she walked forward and bent down to kiss him on the cheek.

"You old humbug. You are not about to die, but just want to prepare us for this new obligation. I think it would be wise if we discussed this in full with a lawyer—say tomorrow."

"Goodbye, Liberty," Kai Soong said simply.

"What time tomorrow?" she demanded. "I was planning on leaving for the East."

"I know," he said sagely. "If that earth is to be moved, you will see to it. But, you have another who could see to this matter." He turned and looked A.G. full in the face, where he had been standing quietly by the door. "I trust your second born fully," he added softly.

A.G. stood there foolishly waiting comment from his mother. Liberty only sniffed, as though it were a senile suggestion and swept from the room. Before he could turn to follow her, A.G.'s eyes locked with Kai Soong. He felt the strangest surge pass through his body, as though the man commanded him without a word being spoken. He had been given a moral obligation that could not be refused. And he sensed, even though his mother did not, that he was looking upon the man for the last time. But it was odd following his mother out. There was now no sadness in his heart. For the second time that night he had been made to feel like a needed person. And somehow he knew that one of the remaining would let him know his needs.

Soon after, Mammy and Carrie left. Lillian started to leave with them, but Kai Soong held her back.

"They do not believe, because they do not wish to believe," he said. "You have only known me as an old man, so you will be the least shocked by the final moment. Eric will need someone. Will you stay?"

How could she refuse, either of them. It had been a shock that he had tied her hands in a business sense not only to the youth but to those three women. She returned to the anteroom outside his bedroom and waited.

It was almost morning before she realized what she should have done. But once the idea came to her, she acted immediately. She walked back into his bed chamber, ready to give him a resounding no.

No one sat in the seats, but in an alcove beyond the screen Kai Soong lay atop a four-poster bed. Eric stood beside the bed, looking tall and pale in his Mandarin gown, and absurdly boyish for all his seventeen year old six-foot frame. When he turned, it was with calm adulthood.

"Thank you for waiting, Miss McHenry," he said.

"Is he gone?" she demanded.

"Moments after we put him upon his bed. It was peaceful. It is I who have taken so long to wish him goodbye. He was a great father to me, although at time I hated him like he was my prison guard. We could not part with that feeling between us."

"What now?"

"The arrangements are made," he said. "Don't worry, I'll take care of them. I am well-schooled in the Chinese ways. Three days will pass before the world is told of his passing. It is a time for the family to overcome their grief. In this case, his family is his old and faithful servants."

"And you? Shall I stay for your sake?"

"I appreciate that," he smiled, "but his wishes at the end were plain. He wished you, above the others, not to be concerned with his passing, for you must now concern yourself with the new life put in your care."

"I see," she said dully, knowing that the decision she had made in the ante-room was now null and void. She was linked with Eric Soong and couldn't beckon Kai Soong back to change matters.

Three days. She would grant Eric and the old servants their three days of private mourning. It also gave her three days to figure out what she would do. She already sensed the power struggle it would pose between Johnny Lord and herself. She didn't want to think about how the other women would handle that business portion of the trusteeship.

She did feel one decision was hers alone to make, although not sure how to properly bring it about. Out of respect to Kai Soong, without letting anyone know he was dead, she had to keep the house closed for the next three days—or longer.

Henry, who had insisted upon driving her one-horse chaise into Chinatown, was puzzled by the blaze of lights in the kitchen wing. Because they had left by the back entrance, he pulled the chaise back around to that entrance.

"A moment, Henry," she said, jumping down. "I will see you inside and then see to putting the horse away."

Lillian now saw all the kitchen windows aglow, but saw them differently than Henry. "Put the horse to stable," she said. "It's only Clara playing motherly and waiting up for us."

Once inside the kitchen she wished she'd listened to Henry. A burly man sat at the kitchen serving table, his back to her, stuffing food into his mouth. On the table, within his reach, sat a pistol.

It gleamed dully in the light of the gas jets, next to the polished silver he ignored while using his hands to eat. At the stove stood a terrified Clara.

"Appreciate the food," the man growled, "and now no more lies. You go wake up Lillian for me. It's very important."

Lillian's heart turned as cold as steel. She would have known the voice anywhere.

"She's awake and standing behind you."

Karl Whiteside turned. His face was sooty from too many days riding behind a steam engine, and his eyes were red from lack of sleep.

"Hello Lillian-girl," he rumbled, "how nice you are looking."

"What brings you here?" she snapped.

Karl's jaw dropped a little. "Is that anyway to greet kin after so many years."

"Kin?" she said grimly. "Only savages sell their kin into bondage."

"Damn good point," he said calmly. "Paw and I had to work our butts off to pay back McHenry after you skipped out on him. Nasty bastard charged us interest to boot. You did us real dirt, girl. It put Paw into his grave, that's what it did."

Somehow the news did not move or shock her. That

night she felt more grief over the death of Kai Soong than over her own father.

"And Maw?" she asked.

"You ain't seen her?" he asked, somewhat surprised. "She took off West right after he kicked the bucket. Well, she might have had trouble finding you, what with the name change and all."

"You didn't seem to have any trouble," she said coldly.

"Hell of a lot of trouble," he said gruffly, as though it were all her fault. "Went first to that mansion Otis lives in and got short answers from some maid."

"Otis? Otis who?" she asked blankly.

"Your half-brother," he smirked. "That's what gave me the clue to find you out here. Sailor buddy of mine told me about this steamship line trying to get a canal built for ships. Name was right, so I figured I'd find you and Maw with that big-cheese."

"You figured wrong," Lillian forced a laugh. "It seems he is not the same Otis Whiteside. I found that out years ago. But that still doesn't explain how you traced me here."

He seethed at her even asking. "I have ways of jesting information out of stable boys. Had me the address in Chinktown and the name of the driver in no time. But for a moment thought I'd been had until I started thinking upon the names. McHenry sure stuck in my craw. Then he told me your carriage had just left and how I could find you. Had to pull a gun on an old moose face to let me in and feed me. Where the hell you been?"

"I hardly see that as any of your business."

"I'm making it my business."

She stood there brooding, remembering. There had been a day when she was small—eight, she was, she thought—that he had used that tone of voice on her before. He had made her stand for hours gilling fish onto a line for hanging and drying. That old hatred came surging back.

"No, I'm afraid you are not," she said sternly. "And don't reach for that gun. It frightens me not. Now, why did you come?"

Karl looked at her, and smiled with grim mockery.

"Money! You owe me for what I had to pay back to McHenry. Looking at this place I don't think that's a problem."

It wasn't a problem, even though she thought he was slightly twisted in his mind. She owed him nothing, not even the food he was eating off her table. She wanted to be rid of him and was now thankful she had lied about Otis, even though she owed him less than Karl.

"I'll pay you, but not because I owe. You and Paw spent that blood money and should have repaid it. I'm going to pay you for the peace and happiness I have known because you sold me away. That's eighteen years. I'm setting a price of a hundred dollars a year, with one condition. You will take that money and never let me set eyes on you in this town ever again. Looking at this place, as you said, it must give you the idea that I have not done it on my own. I have friends, Karl. Powerful friends. Return and I shall just give them a nod to make sure I never have to see you again."

Karl sank back in his chair as she stormed from the kitchen to her office, his face ashen, his mouth working, shaping words that never came out.

"It's not enough!" Karl finally bellowed on her return, then his voice broke. "I got a family now, Lillian," he got out. "Had to sell Paw's boat to get here for help. What help is this?"

"Triple what most *honest* men earn in a year," she said, giving no quarter. "However, I have in my other hand an additional two hundred. A very handsome price for that pistol, if you let Clara come and take it from the table at once."

"Take it," he laughed. "Best money I ever made on stolen property."

Clara came and snatched it up while Lillian counted out the money. Karl bent over the stacked gold pieces, his thin lips smiling.

"Now I need a bed for the night. You can't deny me that."

Clara's fear had vanished, once she had the gun in her hands. She held and cocked it like an expert.

"You heard Miss Lillian's deal," she said clearly. "It did not include a bed—now or ever. Let's just see your backside going out that door."

Karl roared with delighted glee. "Ain't no bullets in the damn thing, you pea-hen. I could take it away and smash you silly with it."

"You would never get a foot out of the chair alive," a quavering voice said behind him.

He spun in the chair and sat looking at Henry, the butler's stoic face as cold and still as death. In his hand was a deringer, pointed right at Karl's heart.

"Well—" Karl said heavily, "I know when to say goodnight."

"You mean goodbye," Lillian said coolly. "Take your money and go."

As though she would snatch it back he scraped it off the table and into his hat. Then he spun on his heel and marched through the door.

The trio stood silent, not wishing to voice aloud what each thought. They didn't trust the man to depart forever.

"I'm very tired," Lillian finally said. "Let's all call it a night. Oh, I've decided not to open for a few days. I just think the girls need a little more training."

They had no reason to question her, but did wonder. Each, to get her off to bed, made an excuse to linger.

"Goodnight, m'um. I have yet to put the horse fully away."

"Goodnight, Lillian. I never leave a dirty dish for the mice to lick clean."

Lillian nodded and went to her apartment. It seemed as stuffy as her mind. She pushed open the casement windows and looked across her grounds. In that year of planning and building it had become her little world. It had now been invaded—twice that night. Mentally by learning she had a new seventeen-year-old partner and physically by an old brother.

Each element was disturbing. God knew, Kai Soong had poured a small fortune into the block, telling her not to worry. She had not worried, because she had never given a single moment's thought to his death. But now there would have to be an accounting. She prayed that Nathan Tedder knew all the figures—what was paid and what was still owed. After paying off Karl too handsomely, her cash reserve was not that great. And now that she had decided not to open for a few more days, it might become nip and tuck.

Dawn was painting the garden with a pink glow. Her hand reached out to close the casement, but the motion was arrested abruptly, as she peered toward the curving drive to the back of the house. A shadow had darted from the side of the stable and across the road. A wild surge of rage overcame her, thinking that Karl was still upon the property.

Cursing, she scurried from her apartment to stop him short at the back door. But before she got to the kitchen she heard a great hue and cry from the back porch. By the time she was in the kitchen she was greeted by an unusual scene. Henry had a nondescript form in his arms, which was hammering at his face with considerable force.

The stoic butler paid no heed to the blows but strode to the center table, with a screaming Clara running at his heels.

''What is it?'' Lillian shouted over her.

''Thought it was himself returned, m'um,'' Henry breathed, dropping the rag-tag bundle as though a sack of cloth on the floor.

''Nothing but a street urchin trying to steal the garbage,'' Clara insisted.

Lillian couldn't tell if the mass was male, female or even human. Then, the creature lifted its head, a mass of soot grimed hair tumbled down, and Lillian could see that it was a girl. Then a snarling face peered up at her and her mind whirled with *déjà vu*. It was entirely too young to be her mother's face and yet it was. Cramped into a constant fearful scowl of unhappiness.

''Who are you?'' Lillian gasped.

''Tracey,'' the child blurterd belligerently, as though they were supposed to know.

Lillian was taken aback. Not only did the child look like her mother, it bore her father's name.

"I see," she finally said, regaining her senses. "We now know your name is Tracey, but why are you here?"

"You know! My Paw was here!" The child had recovered and stared at her with cunning eyes. "He brought me out West to live with my Aunt Lillian. Does she live here?"

"Yes, she does," Lillian whispered. "But what of your own mommy?"

"She's dead," she said calmly. "Died with the baby in her last child-birthing. Got two older brothers who are at sea."

Lillian didn't need to ask how they were put to sea, but her heart could not help but go out to this niece she did not know she had, even though Karl had said he had a family. "How old are you Tracey?"

"I be twelve my last birthday." Then she studied Lillian carefully. "You must be the mistress of this house."

"Why do you say that?"

"You're dressed pretty and she smells like a kitchen cook. I know 'cause I worked awhile as a scullery girl in a nice house in Boston. Got the sack 'cause Paw made me steal food for him. They didn't mind if I took the leftovers, but Paw wouldn't eat the leavings of others. Wanted me to take only the fresh stuff for him. Don't know why. My Maw never made anything but fish stew or baked beans for us. Say, this is some kitchen. Does my Aunt Lillian work here or as a maid?"

Lillian had let her rattle on, learning much, but was now stopped short.

"No, honey," she said gently, "I am your Aunt Lillian. Where did your father go?"

Tracey gasped and looked at the fashionable woman in alarm. "Went to catch the boat back across to the train. Said I was to sneak in, 'cause you were only a servant and were to get me a scullery job."

"Lord knows I could use something other than Chinese help," Clara extolled.

Lillian frowned, unsure what she should do. But first things had to be first. "When did you eat last, Tracey?"

"Or have a bath?" Henry sniffed.

"Can't rightly put a time on either," Tracey giggled, "but know that both have been a long time ago."

"Henry draw a bath in the guest room of my apartment," Lillian ordered, "and, Clara, the sun is high enough to consider breakfast, even though we haven't been to bed."

Henry was a little shaken, but not Clara. She had come, during their eighteen year association, to understand Lillian fully. What the Whiteside family had done to Lillian, was nearly being repeated with this generation.

Lillian's thoughts were less kind. She felt duped and $1,800 poorer for the honor of being saddled with a twelve year old. Saddled was the only word she could muster. How could she, as fashionable as the house may be, take into it an innocent twelve year old as a resident?

A half hour later, fascinated, she watched the frail little girl put away a farmer-sized breakfast. Tracey ate as though it were the only meal she had consumed from one coast to the other. At last she looked up and said:

"I slept last night in a boxcar. I can really sleep anywhere, but I am really very tired."

"I turned down your bed, after your bath," Henry said tenderly, which made Clara and Lillian exchange a glance.

"Thank you, Henry," Tracey beamed. "I know the way. And thank you Aunt Lillian for letting me stay the night."

"The night?"

"I'm a little ashamed that Paw got it all wrong, which he does all the time. You've got the finest luxury house I've ever seen and I don't want your husband embarrassed tomorrow with you having to explain me."

Lillian stammered and Henry came to her rescue. "Off to bed with you, girl. We'll worry over that when you are rested."

"Well," Lillian breathed, when the girl was out of earshot, "what got into you?"

"Only a statement, m'um," he said, trying to return to his insufferable tone. "The lass equated me to the butler in the establishment she briefly worked, when I brought her some of your night things after her bath. She's precocious, and quite charming."

"Precocious? Charming?" Clara could not help but giggle, which was more of a booming roar. "I think the old fart is human after all."

"Really!" Henry was aghast. He had stood somewhat in fear of the cook since his arrival, but he would not be called names. "That child has a spark of lady in her. More than I can say for some in this room."

In a huff he departed, leaving Lillian and Clara to break into laughter.

"The old goat," Clara chuckled. "You know he meant me."

"You needled him into it. You sweet on him, Clara?"

Now Clara turned huffy on her. "Farthest thing from my mind," she insisted. "Stuffed shirt of a man if I ever saw one."

Lillian wondered on that as she returned to her apartment. She knew she should stay up, but knew that Clara would break the news when the girls came down for breakfast.

Even though it had been a night of triumph and then turmoil, she was glad for this excuse to postpone the opening. It would give her three more days, or so, to smooth out a few of the rougher girls—and come to grips with the problem of Tracey.

She peeked into the guest bedroom and her heart melted. The child was like a doll upon the huge bed. The grime washed away, the honey blond hair cascaded over the downy pillow. As though painted in Dresden, the face was serenely asleep.

The sight tugged at Lillian's heart. For the first time she realized how beautiful her mother must have been in her youth. For that sleeping face was her mother's sweet face. And that brought another tug to her heart. If she could believe Karl, which was questionable, then her mother might be right in the same city.

But that was insane, she told herself. Her mother had been harbor wise and would have traced down Otis Whiteside, if not herself. No, she instinctively knew her mother had not reached that far west. But how far west had she gotten? It began to gnaw at her. For eighteen years, thinking her mother back home, she had given her little thought. Now, not knowing where she was became a nagging worry.

Lillian gasped and wondered how this phantom had suddenly appeared in her sitting room.

"I didn't mean to frighten you," Eric grinned.

"How did you get in?"

"I am my father's son," he said timidly, almost apologetically, "and often had a chance to study the drawings of this house. I came by the secret passage through the west garden and wall. No one saw me, I'm sure."

"But why did you come?"

"I'm not sure," he said sadly. "My house was lonely after I left the house of my father. I suddenly wished him back desperately."

"So do I," Lillian said fervently. "God knows, I could use his sage advice!"

She noticed that he seemed different, awkwardly shifting from foot to foot.

"You notice my difference, dear trustee. My legs are not used to being clothed in the pants of a Western man. But I thought it wise to borrow a Western suit from the wardrobe of my father. I am not very happy in it."

To mention his discomfort turned his handsome face bleak and she pushed aside her distress over his sudden appearance on the scene.

"It is a rather horrible fit and please don't call me 'dear trustee.' I am Lillian and nothing more."

Now he was pumping Lillian's hand, as though he would break it off.

"Thank you! Thank you!" he repeated, as though greatly relieved. "I wish your friendship greatly."

Lillian stood a little stunned. The touching of their hands, excluding the pumping motion, had been a moment of discovery. It had sent a quaking thrill through her like never before. She didn't understand it and cursed her mind for seeking an excuse to touch him again.

"You know that your father kept a secret room and wardrobe here?" She hesitated, a little unsure of what she should or should not say. "It is now yours, if you would care to see it."

"I would! I would!" he thundered.

He seems, Lillian thought, incapable of speaking quietly in English. She wished very much at that moment to be able to speak Chinese. "Follow me—please," she stammered.

Beneath the West garden, with an entrance off the secret tunnel was a windowless chamber she had never entered. It had been designed by Kai Soong, furnished by Kai Soong and only seen by Kai Soong.

"This I do not believe!" Eric gasped. "In my father's house is a painting of the Master's court. I feel as if I stand in China at this moment."

"It is marvelous," she gasped with him in response.

The teakwood furniture was heavily inlaid with gold and jewels, with padding tapestry of purest silk and silver thread. Rugs of ancient pattern were scattered upon marble floors. Although a single cellar cavern, it was divided into separate areas by latticework screens of ivory imbedded with pearls.

"I will be honest . . . Lillian," he said fervently. "For my father has been honest with me the eighteen years of my life. His son shall fight me more than Wang Soong fought Kai Soong for the control of the House of Soong. It is tradition for Soong men to fight each other for the Master's seat. But the blood of my mother would not be accepted. Now, we are in the days of mourning for this man who legend will be forced to remember as the Soong who brought us to these shores. During mourning I do not fear, but after the days of respect every Tong agent will await word from my worthy half-brother as to the price for my death."

"Why?" she gasped again. "You are no threat to them."

He smiled. His Nordic-Oriental face was a work of wisdom as well as beauty. She suddenly felt him the elder.

"I have been well versed in his business affairs," he laughed. Lillian could tell by his tone that he meant no offense as to those business affairs. "Of the hundred-odd 'flower houses' in this area, he owned three-quarters of the property on which they stand. My father, being a respectful man, sent a portion of that profit home monthly to my

Uncle Ta. I, with your approval shall do the same. But, dear new friend, that money is like a grain of sand on a wide beach. They shall wish me dead for another matter. During the great Tong Wars my Great Uncle Wang Soong stole millions from the House of Soong. When I was with my eighth year my father learned the secret of how Wang Soong had hidden that money in America. On each of my last ten birthdays my father gave me a clue word, but not in order, as to that secret." He hesitated and frowned. "During his final hours, when words came to him with great difficulty, I was given the other words in rambling sentences. That is my fear. I now know what the House of Soong and the Tong agents would love to get from me before my death."

"They, as I understand, are already rich and powerful. Why would this money be worth taking your life over?"

"The amount," he said soberly and patiently, "is somewhere in the realm of thirty-two millions of dollars. I have trouble thinking in hundreds."

"And I in thousands," Lillian said soberly, seeing the vastness of the situation at once. "I wonder if Kai Soong revealed any of this to the others?"

"I think not. He said to you that a new life would come into your own. He said this not to the others."

Lillian checked her tongue. After eighteen year she fully believed in Kai Soong's all seeing vision of the future. For the moment she was thinking more of the new life of Tracey than the new life of Eric, but to say so might form a wedge between them. At that point she was thinking all business. She was a trustee of one of the richest young men in California, and perhaps the only one who would really understand the measure of his business properties.

"And you are that new life," she sighed.

Suddenly he was on his knees, grasping her about the waist and pressing himself close.

"Those are the words I sought to hear," he breathed deeply. "I am sorry. At times he was very close and mainly so distant. But I loved him, for I knew no other to love. I must be weak, for rivers want to flow from my eyes."

"I wouldn't call that weakness," she intoned solemnly. "You have lost a mother and father, as I have lost a mother and father. Yet, I can shed tears over the loss of your father before my own. Why? Because I lost a being I respected."

"Did you love him," he gulped. "I mean . . . did you . . . two . . . together."

"No! But, honestly, now that you raise the subject I think I would have been honored by the asking." Again she hesitated, weighing her words. "I used the word respected, but I guess that also means love. He was so special to me."

His head pressed into her lap, his body shaking with powerful sobs. She reacted to her instincts without questioning where they might lead. She stroked his head and nestled him close.

"Let it all out," she soothed. "Let the rivers run until they're dry."

He held her for a long time and then looked up half guilty and half defiant. His eyes were heavy, and his mouth wore the unused look of a boy who had never been kissed. He muttered a silent phrase in Mandarin and vanished with a little sob.

"I wish," he said, "to stay this night in my father's old room, which shall become my room."

"You may do as you wish, Eric."

In that moment she became conscious of what Eric was wearing—a moire silk single garment, unfastened to the waist and molded to his hips and legs—with nothing underneath, she suspected. The realization made her suddenly, overwhelmingly conscious of his youthful sexuality. Not even with Johnny Lord had she played this game. She found herself unfamiliar with what she so expertly taught others. For a moment she was afraid to be alone with him.

"You look very attractive," she told Eric in as steady a voice as possible." She remained standing several feet away from him, in neutral territory, her arms around her own waist as if for protection.

"The words I wanted to say to you," he retorted.

Lillian's face betrayed her concern. "Thank you, but do you realize I am old enough to be your mother?"

"The Chinese look upon age as the most beautiful part of life," he said, his eyes sliding down her low-cut gown.

"But you are so young—"

"My own experience with myself tells me I am fully a man. Would you wish me first with one of the girls that I now co-own?"

"We do not own them! They are employees to perform . . . you know what they perform."

"No, as a son of the House of Soong I am untouched merchandise—knowing the meaning of the words and not the actions that go with them. How am I to know this business unless given a taste of it?"

His words were mocking—another effort, it seemed, to taunt her into something she thought she would never desire. She wanted to fight him, to resist the feelings in her own body. Instead she said: "Shall I send one of the girls to you?"

He raised a quizzical eyebrow and she loathed herself for having made the offer. She knew at that very moment that even if he said he would accept one of them she would stall and fight him. She wanted him. She wanted him in the green state that he was—a male virgin.

"I don't believe that you would allow that. My father didn't approve of whores, you know."

"Only the profit they brought him," observed Lillian rather cynically. "Are you suggesting I find you a young mistress for your training?"

"I suggest only someone who will protect my virtue so that I can still be married without shame."

"That's a large order. You're a tall, healthy male. If I find such a girl, what of the strong risk of her becoming pregnant."

He smiled, bitterly, without humor. "That is why I am discussing the matter with you as my trustee. Do you know what it's like in Chinatown for a girl to find herself with the child of a white man? The Tong agents do not like mixed blood. I, therefore cannot have a China girl, because they always seem to have a child. I would be ostracized even more completely. The child would be dead at the hands of the mid-wives."

"What do you want, then?" Lillian strained for patience.

"Can you not read my heart?" he asked sardonically, "or see what is in my eyes?"

Lillian tightened her fists and fought against the answer on the tip of her tongue.

"Your heart and eyes are Chinese and I do not understand the language."

"I was under the impression that male needs had a universal language." A ghost of a smile turned up the corners of his soft lips as he issued the taunt. "Is it too much to hope that a trustee is also capable of teaching?"

"Eric—" She took a step forward, involuntarily, and her eyes searched his face. Never had she seen such open lust and it was unwise that it now matched the lust in her own heart.

"Is that what you wish?"

There was a moment's hesitation in his answer? Then he said, softly, "Did it ever occur to you that except for one man you are as virginal as I?"

Lillian's heart contracted; her palms grew damp. "How were you aware of that?" she asked, her heart in her throat.

"I am my father's son," he answered quietly.

"I see," Her eyes narrowed, and there was a moment of fright. He stood there, seeming to possess all the powers of Kai Soong. Then, suddenly, she was angry with herself. Realization flooded through her, and with it, once again, the knowledge she had never let Kai Soong get to her with his mystical powers. Why, then, let Eric!

"I've decided to put an end to this conversation and I don't want a repetition of it at a later date. For a while, I was captivated by the idea of seducing you as a male virgin. Perhaps that is what you wanted, as well. It would have been very exciting to make love to a man who knew not its thrills." She forced her eyes upward, to meet his, and in them she found a dark enigma that made the next words impossible to say. "I do not think it is best for us," she said softly. Her heart rebelled to the point where she thought it would suffocate her. "But, Eric, a lesson on this business. I am a female who must always make male business decisions . . . I don't want to make the decision regarding us . . ."

Like a panther he was beside her. He captured her chin with one hand, and forced her face upward to meet him. His eyes then showed panic as to his next move and she helped his hand to slid around her waist to support her. She was thankful for it, for his inexperienced kiss was like an explosion, and the force of it bent her backward against his arm.

This time there was male gentleness in his touch, not like Johnny Lord's greedy aggressiveness. Still it was a driving, instrusive kiss that demanded the parting of her lips. This time was not like with Johnny. Here was a gentleness with the possession and yet a youthful animal hunger that could not be denied. Her arms stole around his neck and clung. Then she knew she was lost. His hands, moving like a serpant in the grass, molded about her buttocks, and brought the length of her against his strong body. Through the thin cloth of each garment she could feel their body fires mix.

"I am most guilty. If some knew I was not mourning, I would be cast out as a nothing. But only now do I feel the ache inside me easing since first I saw you . . . and knew that this moment would someday be . . ." And, as though sure of his next moves, he played his hands intimately over her hips, and his lips lightly touched her hair. He led her toward a screen behind which he had seen a canopied bed.

And for the moment she put everything else from her mind. Wordlessly, she allowed Eric to unsnap the back of the gown and let it fall in a rumpled mass at her feet. It had been designed to be worn without undergarments. His rush of heavy breathing brought her eyes to his face. His eyes were lidded smoky, heavy with desire.

"Now let me undo your buttons," she murmured, starting with the Mandarin collar and let her fingers make erotic touchings on his long, lithe frame as she peeled away the silk.

Beneath the cloth his skin was smooth and hairless, like that of a baby. The word 'baby' was like a trigger, and her hands came away from his waist and he had to complete the removal of the garment.

His youth almost made her stop such foolishness. But his excitement had been real during the undressing. It was a gambit she might educate all the girls upon. It had, she would have to admit, been a real source for her own arousal.

Before she could think further he was lowering her to the bed and in a rather clumsy manner trying to take a position over her.

The discomfort of not knowing grew in his eyes, and the pout to his mouth was evident. "Have you not taught many others on their first time?"

"No, I haven't," she protested breathlessly, as his eyes flared in disbelief. "I have known only one man in my life."

"Then how can you be a madam?" asked Eric cynically.

She laughed mirthlessly. "Your father didn't have to be a madam to know the proper running of this manner of business." She added softly. "Besides, you are not a client."

"But you will still have to be my teacher," he retorted.

"Then, shall we start over?" she whispered, and lifting her head upward from the pillow, she invited a kiss. With the tip of her tongue she drew the shape of his mouth, pulling them both back upon the pillow.

Gradually, she worked his body into a proper position. As his knowledge increased so did the point of her pain. She tried to push it from her mind, as she had always been forced to do with Johnny, without success.

No, she mentally screamed, don't let it be the same. I don't want to spend my whole life in fear of this pain that all others see as pleasurable.

When she heard his muffled gasp and felt the warmth of heavier breathing against her face, she swiftly relaxed. Always before that had been the sign that Johnny had sated himself and would momentarily jerk away. But her body remained pinioned. Eric's movements began again slowly and she was quite aware that there had been no lessening of his desire.

A warmth spread through her like a brushfire. It overcame the pain. From her toes to her fingertips she began to tingle. For the first time she began to make demands of her partner, desiring her own fullfillment. It was not that she had never experienced a climactic moment; it had never been a thing of real joy.

She took her time savoring her new-found senses. For some reason this realization left her with a tiny kernel of revenge. She could not resist a small secret smile of utter amusement. Her love, she thought, was no less for Johnny Lord; but she might have just gained a new tool to make his love for her a surer thing. The next time Johnny wanted physical love, she would handle him as she had just handled Eric.

There was a very long silence, as if they would never, ever, breath again. But at last Eric whispered. "What are you thinking?"

"What a good student you are." They were the first words she could muster.

"And will there be further lessons?"

It was a matter she knew had to be dealt with immediately. She knew she should deny him utterly—but did she want to deny him?

"I think that is something to be discussed at a later time, Eric. However, I think we should keep this our secret."

"I agree," promised Eric, with a heavy sigh.

"Why don't you sleep now. I will send word to your housekeeper that you are safe in Kai Soong's quarters here."

"I think I would like to sleep," he yawned, stretching like a contented cat.

Lillian rose, but was still very much aware of him as she stepped into her gown. The honey gold of his body would stir any woman, she reasoned, and to feel its nudity made the world stop. Then there was a lurching sensation; she felt her sensual desires already back at a peak for him.

Noticing that he was asleep, she fled the chamber. She knew her thought was entirely unappropriate, but another moment in Kai Soong's room and she would have been right back in bed beside him.

Chapter 8

She took her time bathing, considering as she soaked what she might wear that night. Her head swarmed for a moment. For the past several days she had been like a person divided into four separate parts. A portion trying to play the role of an aunt and keeping Tracey from learning the manner of her new home. She still had obligations to get her girls ready for this opening night of business and again keep Tracey from overhearing or coming into sections of the house which had been forbidden her. Two of those sections were the other divided sections she had lived.

Purposely she had kept Johnny from meeting Tracey and Tracey from entering the casino rooms. Johnny's reaction had given her her only laugh during those days. He verbally assumed, and she did not correct him, that he was being denied an invitation to her apartment because of the past. She knew now that even if Eric had not come into her life she would have acted the same toward Johnny. As business partners they meshed well, but as lovers they still faced problems.

One problem was of her own making. Her heart loved Johnny Lord, would always love Johnny Lord. But her body was now enamored of the sensations created by Eric Soong. Nor was it just the physical pleasure, because even though she had returned to Kai Soong's room four nights running, not every night had ended in love making.

For hours each night they had sat and talked and she had burned his image onto her brain as though etching it with acid. Just having him around made her tingle with a youthful vitality. Twice, during the days before the funeral, they had met with the other trustees. In those meetings Lillian had tried to remain aloof and fully businesslike. Purposely, she had let Liberty be the dominant voice at each meeting, even though Liberty constantly reminded one and all that this added burden was greatly delaying her own business.

Only once, when Liberty had rather rudely sent Eric from the room, had Lillian almost blasted back at all three women. Without having solid reasons to back up her feeling, Liberty candidly told the gathering that she saw the young man as naive and unable to handle his own affairs now or after he was twenty-one. Carrie had then added her feelings about Eric, in her eyes seeing him as arrogant and snobbish. Mammy saw him in a different light. She thought his manner was a sly pretext at stupidity to throw them all off course.

Lillian felt she was the only one who had really gotten to know the real Eric Soong. In their long talks, the sheltered shyness vanished. He had been tutored by the finest Chinese and American scholars that Kai Soong could obtain. He was a storehouse of cultural and business knowledge that had never been put to use. She found his mind bright and alert, while still being very much Kai Soong secretive.

And in knowing him so intimately it gave her a secret power over the other three woman. She had a control over him that they did not share and she would keep it as a hole card to someday use as she saw fit. For some reason this realization left her with a tiny tinge of doubt.

Frankly, she had to admit that she was coming to admire the business minds of Liberty and Mammy. Carrie she would still hold at arm's length, but the other two she wanted to get to know a lot better.

The clock chimes told her she had soaked and thought quite enough. Because she had not really considered attire she made an imoulsive decision. It would be a new crepe de chine that was cut with deceptive simplicity to look like it had been poured over her body. A single piece that had been smartly shaped to the swell of her breasts beneath a high neckline in front, draped into a cowl at the back. She felt as soft in the gown as it looked against her ivory skin. On her left shoulder she pinned a cluster of rubies set in gold. That night she would wear no other jewels. She took great care with her hair, piling it high upon her head to give her an added four inches of stature. She pinched her cheeks and lips, wanting no false makeup to distract from her natural beauty.

Johnny Lord was already waiting in the casino, tall and smartly handsome in maroon velvet dinner jacket and narrow black trousers that emphasized the virile thrust of his legs. A maroon tie was knotted over the elaborate silk ruffled shirt.

No doubt for the eyes of the dealers who stood waiting at the tables, he moved quickly to greet her and brushed a light kiss against Lillian's forehead. "You look ravishing, Lily," he murmured. "More a virgin than a madam."

Lillian smiled as brightly as she felt, and pulled away, not too swiftly, for she knew that six male's eyes were devouring her and making their own judgement. "You also look quite chic," she remarked. "More a patron of the opera than a gambler."

"Your guest list also looks like the opera crowd," he said negligently. "I don't think there is a person there who has gambled with me before. Are you sure they are here to fornicate, as well?"

"Matters not," she said dryly, and when he laughed despite himself, she explained. "They now must pay a full fee for the evening when they make their reservation, excluding their gambling, of course."

"What an unusual system. What if they desire something different after they get here?"

"I have just one standard price now, Johnny. The one thing I always hated about this business was the haggling over what sexual desire should have as a price tag. We all know why our guests are here, so why have to use all the crude words. Once they are in their rooms, the girls know how I want them handled. They are all trained in every manner to please, except I will not allow anything bizarre or out of keeping."

* * *

"I've always agreed with that," he admitted. "But we do cater to lust and—" But then, memories of what he had demanded when each girl was new intruded and he did not want Lillian throwing that in his face, and he stopped.

"And we cater to their money," she replied, and turned to inspect the tables for black jack, poker and the long, new table she had ordered from France. "I still don't understand roulette, but I'll look forward to you teaching me." Then she found herself uttering words she had not intended. "On our first evening I don't think I should dine alone. Will you join me? Henry is trained to know which guests have time to gamble before dinner and their other pleasures." And almost at once she wanted to take back the invitation, but he was too quick to accept.

The hour and a half passed more pleasantly than Lillian expected. For the first time in their relationship they could stand as equals in neutral territory. Johnny's fund of gambling knowledge, together with his depth of experience in prostitution, and a thousand other details of history on the men in the area, benefited her greatly.

It was Johnny at his most urbane, and for a time Lillian almost forgot all the pain of the unfinished love affair between them. Time now to just concentrate on business, she decided. For the moment, she allowed herself the pleasure of seeing her careful planning come to fruition—and found, strangely, that she had so well orchestrated the operation that she had little to do.

At eleven o'clock Johnny tactfully closed the casino, leaving those gentlemen who had paid for further pleasure only an hour for fullfillment. Those who had come only for dinner and gambling seemed contented with the closing time.

"It's really quite remarkable," Johnny told her, easing the money trays into the casino office safe. "These tables made more in four hours than some of my others will net with all night sessions."

"And not a single fight or knifing," she snidely reminded him.

As he laughed his arm rested lightly on her shoulder,

quite like in the old days. Even through the velvet sleeve she could feel the warmth of him seep through the folds of her dress. The nearness of him, the maleness of him, the mixed scents of alcohol and cigar were like aphrodisiacs to her senses. Aphrodisiacs that, tonight, she did not want to stir her. In two hours she would be meeting Eric in Kai Soong's room.

And as though reading her mind Johnny raised a ghost.

"Speaking of those business establishments, I got a letter from Liberty Lee. I've been given a week to present my account books on the businesses I shared with Kai Soong. Quite a committee of trustees. Were you as shocked as I over his having this well hidden son?"

She licked her lips nervously and nodded.

"Which one of the children was he at the funeral? All of the people from Chinatown were dressed as though they were personal family members."

"I thought that was quite touching," she said breathlessly, wanting to avoid direct comment on Eric, "and was told it was a mark of great respect that they all considered Kai Soong as the elder of all family groups here."

"Well, I certainly would like to meet him. I don't mind discussing my business ties with you, but there are aspects that I will feel right strange discussing with Liberty, Carrie Whiteside and Mammy Pleasant."

"I am in much the same boat," she said, again being able to avoid the main issue, "but Liberty seems to have a good sense of getting all the affairs ironed out. Kai Soong may have thought he was doing things to help his son, but a lot of it is like a spider's web, with only the spider knowing the exact pattern of weaving."

"I guess I just thought the old coot would never die." His voice was roughened in texture, peculiar in timbre, almost aching in grief. "Lily, you've got to make arrangements for me to meet the kid. How old is he? How long before I can deal with him directly and not through the trustees?"

"Not until he is twenty-one," she said unevely, cursing the weakness that made her breath come and go so rapidly. Then she knew it was not weakness but fear. She did not want those two men close to each other, but knew it had to happen sooner or later. "Give me some time to get things settled down and then I will set it up. But, for right now, I really should go upstairs and check on things."

"I thought that was a chapter you tore out of Charmayne's rule book."

"I don't go into the rooms, if that is what you mean. But I have worked out a system with the girls so that they know I am close at hand if they should need me. Kai Soong had those hallway floors imported from Japan. As I walk along they sing like nightingales and the sound penetrates into the rooms. If a girl is having trouble with a customer there is a button cleverly designed into each headboard. When pushed it makes the wall sconce nearest that bedroom door flicker."

He shrugged as though it was a system that would go to waste. "Go do what you must. I'll finish up my bookwork. Shall I wait to have a night-cap with you?"

That had also been a ritual in the old days. A ritual she had planned on bringing back, until Eric Soong came into her life. Now she had to handle it carefully

"Yes, but it will not end up with you going to bed with me, Johnny," she said, with soft deliberation. Before he could make an issue she quickly left the office.

As she came into the softly lit corridor of the guest bedrooms she had made a determination. She would have a quick drink with Johnny Lord after all the guests had departed, but on a totally different matter. He, too, had to be set straight on the rule governing her private apartment now that Tracey was residing there. She was surprised that Clara or Henry had not informed him as yet.

And as the Nightingale floor began to sing her thoughts went to Tracey. She did not want the business touching the child in any way, but she couldn't keep her a prisoner in the apartment wing.

Then all thoughts were shut out. Three doors down, a flicker of light warned her of a problem Luann was having. Lillian turned the knob slowly to make a quiet entrance into the room and was shocked at what she saw.

Luann sat cowering on the bed, her back pressed against

the secret button. Her pale face had been smeared wildly with makeup, rouge rings painted around her nipples and a whole box of powder sprinkled over her from head to foot. But the real shock for Lillian was the man in the room. Luann had been matched up with Neil Fletcher, the son of the Oakland shipbuilder. She found herself staring at one of the largest uncouth men she had seen in her life. The man's girth alone frightened her. Not only was he well over six feet tall, his shoulders and chest were like a massive barrel. His horsey face and eyes were reddened from excessive drink.

"Good evening, madam," he said smoothly. "I've been waiting your arrival, as Luann told me you would."

"Who are you and where is Mr. Fletcher?"

His voice had a nasty edge to it, as if he considered her worse than dirt.

"My name wouldn't mean anything to you, but you will never forget my visit."

Grinning with mean intent, he put a massive hand over his genitals and began to massage. Lillian ignored him.

"Luann," she said firmly, "how did he get in here?"

"All I know," the girl whimpered, "is that Mr. Fletcher said he had left something in the casino. He was gone so long that I went ahead and got undressed. When the door opened he had this brute with him and then left."

When Lillian turned back she saw brutality come into the man's face. "So, it would seem Neil Fletcher put you up to this. Might I be told why?"

"Fancy clothes don't change your business none!" he croaked. "I got me the sickness from whores like you two. The Vigilantes are paying me well to get a bit of revenge and make you think twice about opening again tomorrow night." Then he mumbled, "If you don't start getting out of that dress, I'll enjoy shredding it off you."

Lillian started to back away, as though in fright. "If you rape me, you will be the loser. I'll have the police onto you within the hour."

"Bull!" he roared, picking up a chair and tossing it at the fireplace. Even as it shattered his voice rose over the splintering wood. "Fletcher has me protected with them. You ain't going to do a thing."

"He's sold you a bill of goods," she said as evenly as possible, feeling the wall become a barrier for her back, "or else he forgot to tell you all the facts. This house is partially owned by the Chinaman who just died. The House of Soong will have their own ways of finding you, with or without the police."

He grew instantly silent, staring at her and pondering. Then his dull brain considered it was all a lie and the next chair was lifted like a toy and aimed at the large mirror over the fireplace.

Lillian saw that her gambit was starting to work. The noise he was creating was bound to be heard by the other girls, but she would have herself well protected before they had been able to bring Henry on the run.

Nervously, she put her hand behind her back and started to feel along the wall until her fingers came to a rosette of wood carved into the wainscoating. It took the least amount of pressure to make the secret little door slide silently open. Her fingers closed over the hidden derringer and she pulled it out.

Because she had not batted an eye at the shattering of the mirror he began to move towards her, his massive hands clenched into threatening fists.

The scream escaped Luann like a knife cutting through the room. It spun the man and he charged the bed. Luann tried to cower further into the headboard out of his reach, but he made a single leap onto the bed and began to use his hands and feet to kick at her body and pound down upon her head and face. As Lillian added her own scream of warning to Luann's shrieks, the bed collapsed with a thunderous roar.

"Leave her alone!" Lillian shouted again, bringing the derringer from behind her back and pointing it at him. "Leave her alone or I'll fire!"

The ape lumbered around on the fallen bed to face her. He grinned at the weapon as though it were a toy that would hardly phase him. And then, suddenly, he leaped like his burly legs were taut springs released.

Lillian's impetus to scream again was gone. The arch of his leap was going to crash him right down on top of her. Without giving it a second thought she squeezed the trigger. For so small a gun its report was like a cannon blast that echoed and reechoed around the four walls.

Then he did crash into her, pinning her against the wall and making her collapse from his weight. As he rolled away she saw the neat little hole between his eyebrows and a fraction of a second later she was drenched with a spray of hot sticky blood.

To escape it she turned her head in time to see the door come flying open. Standing in the doorway, their faces filled with fear, were Johnny and Henry. She fought down a faint of relief.

"He hurt me bad," she heard Luann whimper softly.

"Get the guests out of here," she ordered Henry. Her voice had gone throaty. She licked her lips, tasted blood, and spat in disgust. She got to her feet and, as the two men watched in wonderment and doubt, shakily went to Luann.

Her movement set the men in motion. Johnny stepped into the room and closed the door behind him. No need for anyone in the quickly filling corridor to look in upon the grisly scene.

Lillian sat down upon the broken bed and cradled Luann in her arms. It no longer mattered that Luann's blood was now also drenching her. "Hush, Luann. Let me see what damage has been done."

Luann raised her head but could not stop the tears of pain and fright.

One eye was already beginning to swell shut and the largest flow of blood was coming from a badly broken nose. The fair skinned girl was already showing bruise marks on her-thighs and breasts, but Lillian's quick examination didn't suggest that anything was broken.

"I want to get her out of this room," she said to Johnny. "Get the hall clear so we can take her around to my wing."

"What about you? Are you hurt?"

"Hardly," she said shortly. "It's his blood. Somehow

he was smuggled into this house by Neil Fletcher. I now look at it as attempted murder."

"Lily, you can't be serious!"

"Damn serious," she said, eyeing Johnny steadily. "To kill may not have been his primary orders, but if I had not fired I would be in worse shape than poor Luann. I'm not about to let the Vigilantes get away with this."

Johnny immediately saw great trouble ahead for every house. With Kai Soong dead the Vigilantes were showing their muscle again. By striking in this manner at the premier house, it would send shock tremors out to the other houses. He feared that this man had so stupidly bungled his job that it would create a scandal to come back and haunt them all.

"Are you absolutely positive, Lillian? This hardly sounds like Fletcher."

Calmly, she told him what the man and Luann had said step by step, then, without mincing words, told him everything that had transpired in the room since her arrival.

"Now, let's get her away from this room and that corpse," she finished.

Johnny turned strangely silent as he went to look out into the hall. It was not that he did not believe her story, but that the hired stooge was dead at her hands. The Fletcher family were rich and powerful. He was already anticipating the various ways Neil Fletcher would lie his way out of ever having been there.

"There are just a few of your girls in the hall," he called back over his shoulder.

"Then let's go," Lillian said sweetly, helping Luann to her feet. "Your nudity isn't going to shock them."

A moment later she cursed not having at least thrown a sheet around Luann.

"What are you doing here?" Lillian glowered at the nightgown clad little figure shivering the hall.

Tracey's eyes were like saucers. The glowering question froze her answer on her lips. After so long a time of a near starvation diet, the quantities of food in Clara's kitchen made her insatiable. She had been on her way to the kitchen when she heard the frantic calls arousing Henry.

Like a magnet, her curious mind suggested it as an opportunity to see a portion of the house she had never seen before. But once in that hall, the talk among the girls had turned her into near panic.

Tracey's silence angered Lillian. "Get back to your room!"

Before Tracey could move, Lillian had swung down the hall with Luann under her arm. But the anger Lillian felt was now directed back to herself. She had not even thought of Tracey being there when she had decided to take Luann back to her wing. Now she was unsure in her own mind how she was going to explain this event to the child.

Johnny Lord stepped up to the child as if he didn't have a problem in the world, although he somehow felt she was going to be a problem.

"Well, my little pretty," he soothed, "who might you be?"

Tracey studied him carefully, wishing to ask the question in return. "Tracey," she faltered. "Tracey Whiteside."

"Whiteside," he mused, then his heart turned a little cold. He took the frail girl to be about ten or twelve. His mind could not help but revert back to the still-born child that he and Lillian had shared in common. Had Lillian, like Kai Soong, kept a secret child from his knowledge?

"Yes, Whiteside," Tracey went on, as though he had asked a question. "I came to live with my Aunt Lillian, but don't understand why she is called Miss McHenry."

Johnny chuckled, almost with relief. "That is a very very long story, my dear. Come, I'll see you back to Lillian's apartment."

Walking along in her bare feet Tracey had a chance to study the man. Her young mind immediately decided he was quite handsome and had to be a gentleman because of his dress. "You didn't tell me who you are."

He chuckled again, this time out of pleasure. "I am Johnny Lord. I've known your aunt for about eighteen years."

"Eighteen years," Tracey repeated softly. "Then you would be the one that Aunt Clara says is 'a damn fool who doesn't know quality when he sees it.' What did she mean?''

He sighed. ''Because I didn't marry her.''

''Don't you love her?''

Johnny's stomach churned. He resented being put on such a spot by a child. ''Love has nothing to do with it.''

''I suppose not,'' she said drily. ''I know for a fact that my mother didn't love my father, yet they were married.''

Johnny blushed deeply, having faced that argument many years before. ''I didn't say that I didn't love her,'' he mumbled.

Tracey smiled up at him, sweet and innocent. ''I think I know your feeling. I don't know what love is, either.''

Johnny stared at the small honey-haired, pale-faced girl. It was not the family resemblance that brought him up short, but the same innocent simplicity that once had been Lillian. Instantly, he recognized the feeling that came over him. He had never felt guilt in his life and now tried to shove it aside. A moment later his guilt turned back to anger.

In the hall outside Lillian's apartment stood a young Chinese man, nervous and unsure as to whether he should discreetly knock on the door.

Instantly, Eric Soong recognized the gambler. Many times in the past several years he had sat behind a secret screen while his father held business talks with this partner. Then, as now, there was a sleekness to Johnny Lord that Eric did not like.

''Good evening, Master Lord,'' he said smoothly. ''I am Eric Soong and have much knowledge of you from my father.''

''Good evening,'' Johnny growled. ''What in the hell are you doing here?''

''I wanted to learn if the opening night was a rousing success—in which I have an intimate interest,'' he said.

Johnny eyed him. This was not the mere child he expected to meet as Kai Soong's heir. This was a male as tall and virile as himself. He felt duped and didn't know why.

''You know about the operation of this house?''

Despite his young years, Eric saw his answer as inappropriate at that moment, viewing who Johnny was escorting.

"Perhaps my answer can wait," he shrugged, "until you are finished with Mistress Tracey."

Johnny seemed to warm to him for having said that. He had nearly forgotten the girl stood beside him and had no need to hear the hard questions he wanted to raise. "Run along, Tracey. I'll see you again very soon."

Tracey went along to her room without comment to either man.

"Thank you for reminding me that she was here," Johnny said, a bit less coldly. "I was not aware that she was here until tonight."

"Nor I."

Johnny started. "But you called her by name."

Eric smiled enigmatically. "I am my father's son. Just as I learned from him the manner of his business activities, if not their actual performance. Lillian has helped explain a great deal of that to me."

Johnny's heart began to ache in a way never before experienced. He tried to sort out his earlier conversation with Lillian. She had not corrected his assumtion that Kai Soong's son was still a child. Child? Standing before him was a young man in his late teens. At that age Johnny had already become an independent gambler and had known every prostitute on every river boat he had worked. Lillian? More calmly than he would have thought possible Johnny said, "Do you call all your trustees by their first name?"

"No. My father instructed me about each of them and the respect that must be shown, even though they be all women. With Lillian it was different. Our friendship bloomed as a fresh flower from the first meeting."

Johnny could not help but wonder what else had bloomed between them. But he put that aside for a new hurt that Eric's words had uncovered.

"I can't help but wonder at your father's choices for trustees. There is not a man in the group."

"You are thinking of yourself, of course, sir?"

"That's obvious, and for damn good reason. He has an interest in seventy-four of my houses and gambling dens.

I'm not about to run them through a committee of pea-hens.'' His tone was not defiant, just firm. ''You're old enough to work with me man-to-man. Why did he put them in charge until you are twenty-one?''

Eric nodded sadly. ''Were I full Chinese I would have been a part of the House of Soong at any age on the date of my father's passing. He has tried to protect me under American law—my Norwegian mother was an American citizen. You were not fully excluded, Mr. Lord. You alone, of all his various business partners, were given free rein to run your establishments without control from the trustees.''

Johnny blinked. ''What . . . that's not the way Liberty put it to me in her letter.''

Eric smiled. ''My impression, sir, is that she will do everything in her power to run you and Lillian out of business and out of town.''

''What is the meaning of this?'' Lillian demanded harshly, stepping into the corridor with a bathed and dressed Luann.

Johnny looked into the glowering eye of Lillian McHenry and was stunned by what he read in them. She desperately feared the two of them being together. For the moment, Johnny decided to fall back on the sage advise Kai Soong had given him when he first coveted Lillian—'A wise man does not mix love and business in the same cup or he might find himself drinking a bitter brew.'

''Oh, we just bumped into each other while waiting for you to clean up Luann,'' he laughed. ''I was learning some things I didn't know before.''

Lillian's heart nearly stopped, his words suggesting her worst fear. ''Run along to your own room, Luann,'' she said weakly. ''I will have a doctor look at your nose in the morning.''

Eric looked from the battered girl to the strained face of Lillian and was perplexed. ''Has something gone amiss here tonight?''

''Slightly,'' Lillian laughed drily.

It was only then that Eric noted that the pattern of her dress was not red and white, but that it was blood stained. ''Are you all right?'' he gasped.

"Other than the fact that I have just killed a man, I am in fairly good shape. Eric, you might as well come along and join Johnny and me in a night-cap. We have to wait for Henry to return with the police to remove the corpse and get their report."

Eric looked at her with loving tenderness, which made Johnny cringe. "I should have been here to protect you, my dear friend."

"Oh, Lillian is quite capable of protecting herself," Johnny laughed. "She's been doing it without a man for the eighteen years that I have known her."

Lillian spun and strode back into her apartment in a cold fury at the double implication of his words. She went directly to the bar and without thinking automatically poured three drinks: Johnny's favorite, her favorite and a glass of the Chinese wine that she knew Eric was partial too.

When she turned back to the sitting room, with the tray of glasses, she had calmed herself with a firm determination. It was her life and she would not allow either one of them to outstep the bounds she had set for them.

But even as they accepted their drinks, they each reminded her of a greater problem—Tracey.

Reluctantly, she had to leave them alone again. She went quickly along the inner hall to the pink and blue bedroom, which Tracey had fallen in love with. She found the small girl curled in a chair before the unlit marble fireplace.

"Tracey," she said proudly, "I'm sorry you saw what you saw, but I admire the way you kept calm."

Tracey's eyes misted with tears. She refused to look up. "They say you killed a man," she whispered miserably.

"To put it in it's logical order, Tracey, I killed the man before he had the chance to kill me. You saw what he did to Luann." She put up a hand to stop the question that was forming on the young lips. She had a knack learned from Kai Soong of anticipating quite quickly what was on another's mind, and she instinctively knew all of the questions Tracey was about to throw at her.

Slowly, because she was dealing with a quite innocent mind, she began with a rather simple sexual education explanation, knowing that at twelve years of age it was not too soon for Tracey to learn the basics of life and its functions.

Never having had anything explained to her by her mother or father, Tracey was thoroughly enjoying being treated in such a forthright manner. Because Lillian was keeping it all quite simple, she could understand and follow along.

"So that's how babies are made," she mused. "I guess this is kinda like going to school."

"Quite," Lillian said simply, then was taken aback. "What schooling have you had, Tracey?"

"None," she shrugged. "Paw said it would be a waste and I'd be better off learning to be a maid."

"Yes," she sighed, "that's the Whiteside theory. Put the boys to sea and the girls anywhere you can stick them out of sight. Would you like to go to school?"

"I would love to, but I know from the house I worked in that it costs money and takes nice clothes. I ain't got either."

Lillian decided quickly that the sharp-minded child had to be told the rest of the truth. She minced no words in explaining the world's oldest profession, the various types of houses in the business and how her house was unique and different.

"Tracey," she concluded, "this apartment is a world set aside from that other world. I don't want you to become a part of it anyway. I want you to become a lady as I always hoped I would someday become."

"But you are the grandest lady I have ever met, Aunt Lillian. Besides, you said you didn't do the things your other girls do for men. Didn't you become one because of your love for that Johnny Lord?"

"Where did you get such a notion?"

"From something Aunt Clara said to Henry while I was having lunch in the kitchen today. Said she was glad you two would be working together again and that it might take away each of your stubborn blindness and get you to the altar. Why haven't you two gotten married? I think he is a very nice man."

Lillian's face stung from the question as much as it might from a direct slap. "Honey," she soothed, "as you grow older you will learn that there are just certain men in this world who are scared stiff of the responsibilities in a marriage. I guess you could say that Johnny is one of them."

Because he came charging into the bedroom indignantly, Lillian was aware that he had heard.

"Mortimer came himself," he declared icily to Lillian. "The corpse has been gone for a half-hour and he is waiting to talk to you."

"Johnny," she scolded, "where's your urbane touch from earlier this evening? Can't you see that there were more important matters to clarify with Tracey?"

"Lillian, I am not fully aware of who Tracey is!"

"Quite true," she said simply on a shrug. "She is my brother Karl's daughter. She has come to live with me."

"Fine," he scowled, "but why was my name brought into the conversation?"

"Why not?" Lillian snorted. "Had you been a moment sooner in arriving you would have heard her call you a very nice man. Don't ruin her image of you." She winked at Tracey. "Some day I'll find just as nice a man for you to marry. In the meantime, I plan to be completely honest with you. But promise me right now one thing. You will forever put out of your mind what goes on in the rest of this house and never associate yourself with those who live in that wing."

"I'll do whatever you wish, Aunt Lillian."

"Good!" Lillian sighed. "Now I can go and beard Mortimer in his den."

In the hall Johnny chuckled and then roared with delight. "You really are some kind of a woman. In one night you handle a brute animal and a wondering child with equal ease. I do gather from what was just said that you were honest as rain with her."

"Why not," she said pointedly. "I have an opportunity with her to correct the mistakes my family and others made with my youthful life. I want her to be able to hold her head high above the gutter business we are in and realize that there is a life for women other than this and what the Whiteside men wish for their female children. If you want the straight truth, Johnny, she was all but sold to me by my own brother.'' Then she added, firmly ''but you are never to breath that truth to her.''

''I'll agree on one condition.''

''What is that?''

''That you don't cut me out of her life. She will need a male ''uncle'' around just as much as an aunt.''

Her first instinct was to chide him on how near that came to sounding like a marriage proposal. Her second instinct was to be cruel and say that Henry would be around for any male influence and guidance needed. But without hesitation she went by her third instinct. She stepped forward and kissed him on the lips. The kiss did not call forth an embrace from Johnny Lord, although his arms were greatly tempted. He accepted it for what it was—an expression of deep-seated gratitude for his understanding and offer of help.

And he glowed with the sense of advantage it gave him over Eric Soong. He was the mature male Lillian would need in the raising of Tracey—not the boyish Eric. Although he had to admit, in getting to know Eric further during Lillian's absence, he could find no fault in the lad. In fact, he would even take Eric's suggestion on how to get around Liberty's letter of demand on the books.

Only one thing still troubled him. No matter how sly he had been in the questioning of Eric, he was still unsure as to whether Eric and Lillian were having an affair. The boy was too much like his father—tell you everything you wanted to know and still not reveal a damn thing.

Johnny Lord decided to let it ride. Businesswise he was too greatly involved with both to make an unnecessary wave.

Then, following Lillian back to the sitting room, he came to a profound truth about himself. He had never been a lonely person, even in being alone. But the years were slipping away and no longer could an all-night poker game sate him. He was rich enough, for a man in his early forties, to retire comfortably. But that would be real loneliness. Tracey Whiteside, even though she was just twelve, was the first female he had looked upon as something other than a sexual challenge. And it made him cringe to think of the number of twelve to fifteen-year-old young females he had seduced in his life time to bring them into the field of prostitution. In the other seventy-four houses under his name he was laughingly called the "Cherry Picker."

But like Lillian, he felt like a white knight to protect Tracey from such a life. It was quite a new experience for Johnny Lord. Then an acid thought came in to ruin his glow. Lillian's still-born child would have been the same age as Eric Soong. If there was a God, which he often doubted, that Being had added a wry touch to his life. *Sans* marriage, he was being coupled with a young man the age of his still-born son, and a girl-child like a little sister.

He burned away the acid thought to get back to the glow. Each child he would accept in the measure that they accepted him.

Mortimer Stern wished only to deal with those crises he could handle. He knew, because San Francisco was a town of loose tongues, that he was considered a misfit, a lazy bastard, and a wry joke as Chief of Police. He disregarded their comments without comment in return.

"His name was Hank Tremble," he announced, casting his bulging eyes heavenward, "may his soul rest in peace." Then he laughed, a very vindictive sound. "The bastard will never get to Heaven, Lillian. I don't think the devil will even want his likes in hell. You've done me a great service by getting him out of my hair, but it will stir up a hornet's nest with some. The Bible thumpers will have him a martyr in no time. Are you prepared for the heat Fletcher will cause as a result of this?"

Lillian gasped in disbelief. "He was the one who brought the beast into my house."

"Can you prove it?"

Lillian laughed derisively. "In the old days, Mortimer, I didn't give a damn who had been here or not. That's what the Vigilantes were counting upon. Fletcher's a damn ignorant fool. Thank God I didn't have time to do the banking today. I am sitting with his registration card and check for this evening. Is that proof?''

Stern frowned. ''It's proof that he intended to be here, but was he?''

''I have knowledge of that,'' Johnny said firmly. ''He lost over $3,000 at the gaming table and signed a marker with me before going into dinner.''

Stern sniffed with pleasure. He resented the Vigilantes forever mixing into his business and making him look like a an ineffective fool. ''Who did he gamble with and who did he have dinner with before he went upstairs to the girl.''

''Let me set you straight,'' Lillian said coolly, ''about the operation of this house. Mr. Neil Fletcher was assigned to Luann right from the start. She joined him for cocktails, gambled with him in the casino and had a candlelight dinner with the so-called gentleman. Once they were upstairs he began to play his little game. He claimed to have left something in the casino and the next Luann knew he was letting the ape into her room.'' She paused. ''Forget it, Mortimer. I know what happened and Luann knows what happened. Book me, if you think you can make it stick. If not, then I'd like to call it a night.''

''I'm trying to do my duty, Lillian!'' he grumbled.

''Poppycock. I said I was tired.''

Stern shrugged. ''No reason we can't leave it until tomorrow.''

Suddenly, Lillian wanted them all gone—*all*. No Eric, no Johnnie, no Moritmer Stern.

After she saw them out she turned and noticed a clean-cut young man who hadn't departed.

''The exit line was for everyone, buster!''

''Shall I quote you on that,'' the young man said, steering her into his path, ''I'm Carl Howard of the *Chronicle*. You're not quite the woman I expected to meet tonight.''

''You expected to meet me?''

''I was given a tip on what would happen here tonight,''

he chuckled. "There is a lot of Fletcher money in our newspaper."

"Don't make for very honest reporting, does it?"

"*Doesn't* make," he corrected, with a grin. "I'm sorry. I had no right to correct you, but it's just in my nature."

She studied him a little closer. In a rather chubby way he was quite a sexual being. She almost laughed. Until Eric came into her life she looked on no man as sexual except Johnny. "Correct all you like, but let's get down to the basics. Go talk to Stern."

"That won't get me the story of what Neil Fletcher was doing here tonight."

Now she laughed. "And what could you do with the real story? If the Fletchers have money in that paper the truth would never be printed."

"Trust me," he pleaded.

An hour later as she crawled into bed, she was not aware she had given an interview to a very honest reporter. The morning *Chronicle* banner headlined:

SHIPPING HEIR SCANDAL
N. Fletcher tied to Murder
in House of Lily. Vigilante
Group involved.

The news was immediately the scandal of the entire bay area. Neil Fletcher was not the kind of man who blithely took such abuse and ordered Carl Howard fired and a retraction printed. Just as immediately, Carl Howard walked two blocks to the *EXAMINER* and laid his cards on the table. Publisher David Bryson was fighting to keep his head above water, but was astute enough to ascertain the truth in the reporter's story. He made news by hiring the reporter that Fletcher had fired, which raised eyebrows as to who was telling the whole truth.

Lillian had ignored the morning and afternoon papers, her mind divorced for the moment from the events of the evening before. That day she had a single goal.

Amy stood between the fluted columns of her central foyer, flanked by a maid in a starchy uniform and a butler starched by time. It had amazed her when the messenger had come from Lillian that morning requesting an afternoon visit. It amazed her even more to learn Beth and Carol were to be invited. She feared accepting a 'murderess' in the home of her husband, but how could she deny Lillian anything.

Like errant children Beth and Carol had been taken in tow to be ushered quickly up the sweeping staircase of the Nob Hill home to Amy's private rooms. And equally like an errant child Lillian was greeted and led quickly up to the room.

Lillian, still a little stiff and sore from the night before, clung to Amy's arm as they ascended. A sly smirk played at the corners of Amy's mouth.

"It is not by accident that Mortimer Stern was here for breakfast this morning," she whispered. "My husband Richard is on the Police Commission, you know?"

"I didn't know," Lillian whispered back, but questioned the need for whispering. "But I am not here to discuss the events of last night."

Amy chuckled. "You don't have to mince words with us, Lillian. You are among friends."

In the hall Lillian heard the giggles of Beth and Carol, and it angered her. They thought this was going to be a gossip session for her to bare her soul, same as she was aware that they had attended her open house out of curiosity.

In eighteen years she had come to look upon them as three foolish women: selfish, avaricious, greedy, and self-indulgent, obsessed only with the status they acquired through their husbands. She almost wished that Liberty Wells O'Lee was in town. As much as she was incapable of liking that woman, she knew that Liberty would look on this problem with keen intelligence and give her sound advice. But the "Trio" were her only available source of support. She put on a sweet face to greet them and take command from the start.

"To explain this emergency meeting," she said in the soft voice she would use in training her girls, "I must start with a bit of background history. I can't recall if you were aware that my father and brother Karl in a manner sold me to McHenry as a mail-order bride. I only mention that to give you a clearer picture of a recent visit I have had from that brother. He's not a very nice man, but that is beside the point. Thinking to get rid of him, I bought him off by repaying the money he claimed they had to repay to Thomas McHenry. I now see it as money spent to buy his daughter, who he more or less left on my doorstep. In his perverseness, he told the child he was bringing her West to live with her Aunt Lillian."

"Was he aware it was a whore house?" Amy asked.

Lillian sighed. "I don't think it would have mattered to his kind if I had been only one of the girls. Whiteside men have never had much use for their females."

"Whiteside?" Beth said peevishly, settling her plump frame onto the settee. "That was your name before you started calling yourself McHenry. You were always short with us when we'd ask why you were changing it."

"My reasons were sound then," she said irritably, "but they matter no longer. Even though he denies it, I am still convinced that Otis Whiteside is my older half-brother. But that also has little to do with this and yet, in a way, it does. Tracey is an innocent twelve-year-old with no education whatsoever. She is a sweet, bright child who I was determined was to learn nothing about my business. Last night rather ruined that plan for me. She saw and heard too much and I had to have a serious talk with her. She took it, I must say, with almost adult sensibility. More so than some snob hill residents I could name."

"Don't include us," Carol corrected. "We know what you have been through during these years. If the paper is correct, you protected yourself like any other woman would have protected herself. We all know you never became like the girls you have working for you."

"Except," Amy said slyly, "you have opened yourself to another little bit of scandal."

"How is that?"

"My dear," she simpered, "my kitchen staff are all Chinese and it is the talk of Chinatown that Kai Soong's half-caste son sneaks away at night and does not return until morning. It takes very little imagination to know where he spends his nights.''

Lillian blinked angrily. ''Kai Soong was my business partner and had private rooms in my new home. Eric is now my business partner and those rooms are his. It is also a matter of protection. The House of Soong in China are bound to move against him and rid themselves of the so-called disgrace of his half-caste state. As one of his trustees, I felt my house safer from attack than his in Chinatown.''

''Do you still feel that way after last night?'' Amy asked.

''That attack had nothing to do with Eric Soong. You all know why the Vigilantes directed it at me.''

Amy shook her head sadly. ''My husband says that part of San Francisco has become coarser than ever, in spite of the charm and beauty of the rest of the city.''

''Our husbands agree,'' the other two echoed.

Lillian was silent, but wanted to laugh aloud. She had often wondered why this troika of women, when hitched together, never seemed to refer to their husbands by name. They were still the orphaned trio band together against the world. But this was not the time to point out their vanities.

''I could not agree with them more,'' Lillian shrewdly observed, sensing the need to make their husbands important. ''Why do you think I built elegant splendor? I could make just as much money down further in Barbary Coast, but I would not be happy. Let's face it. This is a seaport town and will never be fully rid of prostitution. However, if I can clean up my act, so could they. Perhaps I can have some influence in that quarter being one of Eric's trustees. And I think you will all agree, especially your husband, Amy who makes his livelihood from the sailors and shipping, that this is a matter for the police and not the Vigilantes.''

They all nodded.

''Now back to my main point,'' said Lillian with an unusual softness in her voice. ''We all have come a long way in these eighteen years. Much farther than any of us dreamed possible when we first arrived. We now have the opportunity to give that same advantage to Tracey. I want her schooled. I want her properly clothed. I want her associated with the best of this town and not connected to my house. You all saw how my apartment is separate from the rest of the house. It's something like the stack houses that climb the hills. They have common center walls, but the lives on either side of that wall do not have to be the same. Tracey is going to be brought up to be a real lady, with your help."

Now that a touch of glamour had come into the request, Amy was slightly soothed over the meeting. She sighed, heavily, putting aside the fear that Lillian was going to ask for their husbands to step into her war with the Vigilantes.

"That's no problem," Beth said expansively. "Carol and I each have twelve-year-old daughters in school."

"Be that as it may," Amy sniffed, ascerting her normal leadership role, "you heard what Lillian said. Tracey has had no schooling whatsoever. The poor child would be totally lost being thrown right in with them. I would suggest that she be given a year or two with the tutor that we retain for my Bobbie."

Her offer registered very clearly with all of them. Her fifteen-year-old son was a topic that they all avoided, because Amy very seldom discussed the child that was kept separate from her other children.

Bobbie had been nearly three before he uttered his first words and then they were always a jumble. He was still backward and babyish by the time he was old enough for school. It had put Amy into a dark and troubled mood. She loved that child as much as the others, but his constant tantrums were making her less of a mother and wife.

Then Daniel Fetterson, publisher of the *Chronicle*, introduced her to a young visitor from Denver. Carrie Robb had just made quite a hit on San Francisco as an educator and woman of letters. As a schoolteacher she had seen other backward children and prevailed upon Amy to let her visit with little Bobbie.

Carrie had fully expected the woman to balk at her findings. The child was greatly retarded and even with proper training might never gain more than a six to ten year old maturity of mind. She was amazed that Amy requested her help in securing a teacher to at least try to train her child. But all was to be done secretly and quietly so that it would not become a blemish on the rising career of her husband in Liberty's shipping company.

And even though it was never discussed among them, they all had shared Amy's heartache over the years.

Lillian looked at the woman that she sometimes didn't fully understand, her eyes electric with excitement and gratitude.

"That is a very sweet and generous offer, Amy. On behalf of Tracey, I thank you."

"Nonsense," said Amy preening with pride that she had the courage to make the offer. "Miss Phillips has scolded me the last couple of years for not allowing her to have another child or two present for her sessions with Bobbie. She feels he needs the challenge of competition. Although, I must be quite honest. He has a very mean jealous streak toward the woman and hates it when I try to impose upon their time together. I think we should make arrangements for Tracey to meet Miss Phillips alone the first time. And there is the problem of clothing. Bobbie would be a slovenly little pig if it were not for her rule that he must be properly dressed for her school sessions. I will leave the clothing matter to Beth and Carol. Having had only boys, I am not much of an expert on little-girl attire."

"She must think I have Tracey in tatters and rags," Lillian laughed when the three women were on the street awaiting their carriages. "Clara has been able to find some things for Tracey, but you both know Clara's taste in clothing, even for herself. Likewise, I can dress all my girls quite stunningly, but that's not proper for Tracey, either."

"When can we meet her and get started?" Beth enthused.

"No time like the present," Lillian said.

"Then let's do it!" Carol said with hearty laughter. "Beth, I'll go directly to Augusta Cramer's shop and shoo away all the other customers for the rest of the afternoon. You go and pick up Tracey and bring her right back. This will have to be a complete outfitting, right Lillian?"

For a moment Lillian felt a little miffed having been excluded from the shopping spree. Then she saw a certain advantage in being excluded. From the very first she had wanted Tracey to learn the style of these women and the way that they shopped. It would have been very easy for her dressmaker to handle everything, but that would have been a tie to the business side of her life and that she did not want.

"Complete," she answered, "and hang the expense. I want her dressed properly for this Miss Phillips and the rest of the town."

Chapter 9

Lillian took one look at all the garments and held her tongue. Tracey felt slightly guilty in having acquired such a vast wardrobe, but was exultant over the fine-quality goods. Even though Lillian considered only half of them of a utilitarian nature, she had been assured by Beth and Carol that they were exactly what schoolgirls were wearing. Lillian knew that if she put her girls in such garments they would take to their beds with the vapors.

But there was a consolation. Beth and Carol had fallen madly in love with Tracey and she thought of them as two of the grandest ladies she had ever met.

The next day Tracey's judgement of Amy was a little more reserved and she stood in awed fright of the dour Helene Phillips.

During the feverish tumult of those two days the absence of Johnny Lord passed unnoticed by all save Lillian. The first night she recognized his need to be down in his own district in case trouble arose. She also accepted the fact that it was safer for Eric to stay away. But the scandal did not result in a single cancellation. In fact she had to turn down request after request for reservations.

But the next day had been strangely lonely for her. Bright and early Henry had taken Tracey to the home of Miss Phillips and waited to transport them both to Amy's. To get Clara over her hurt feelings of not being invited to the meeting with the other 'Scarlet Sisters', the two women shared a simple lunch together in Lillian's apartment.

"I do hope we can keep her divorced from that side of the house," Clara said with genuine concern.

Lillian eyed her for a moment and then threw back her head and laughed. "I'm sorry," she said, "but we are forgetting that we have never let the house get in our way of living a life separate from it. Nor do we see Henry lusting after any of the girls. Let's just keep it on that plane."

"And . . . Johnny . . ." Clara hesitated.

Lillian began to fret. How did she keep Johnny away from Tracey without being downright rude? And that night, when Johnny didn't arrive again, a loneliness such as she had never before experienced seized her. With Eric absent as well, she felt cut off from all knowledge of them.

An hour before closing, a troubled Henry came to tell her of a messenger at the back door. Lillian had not been aware of the fever she was running until she stepped out into the breezeway between the kitchen and carriage house.

"Oh, that feels marvelous," she enthused to no one in particular and then saw Eric's houseboy. "You have a message for me?"

"No, missy," he replied. "I was sent by the old lady housekeeper to keep an eye on Master Eric."

"Where is he?"

"With Master Lord."

She frowned and he laughed.

"With him last night, too. They go from house to house to house. Of course, leaving Ling outside each time. Tonight much different. They stay whole night in one house."

Lillian was peeved and it showed in her voice. "Why come and bother me with this?"

Flushing deeply and hastily crossing his arms in front of his face, as though she would strike him over his answer, he selected his words carefully.

"Ling see many white men and Chinamen come into the streets. A man known to Ling tells Ling to go home quickly. I tell him I must warn Master Eric and he forbids me such, chasing Ling away with swings of his Tong axe. I fear I have no one to tell but you."

Her heart began to beat with great rapidity. She was intensely aware of Henry's closeness. "Get me a cloak, Henry."

"I'll get the carriage instead."

Lillian could barely get out a weak "no." Then she calmed her fears. "I can go quicker and safer by foot."

"You are not going alone?" Henry gasped.

In spite of herself, Lillian had to smile. "I've come to know the district quite well in eighteen years, Henry. I'll keep to the alleyways that even a Vigilante would fear to enter. Now, quickly, just grab me one of Clara's shopping cloaks."

As he entered the house to do her bidding, she began to remove her jewels, let down her hair, and strip away the train of her gown. There was no time to change, but she didn't need those yards of cloth weighing down the speed she desired.

"Ling go with missy?" he asked with genuine fright.

"I have another job for you. Go back to the house and warn Master Eric's servants to go to the homes of relatives for the rest of the night."

"I go at once," he sighed.

Henry handed her a plain brown cloak. The stony face froze for a second, then a sly grin played on his thin lips.

"I think you are an expert in the use of this," he chuckled, handing her a derringer.

She shuddered, but accepted it and tucked it deep into the slanted pocket of the cloak. As she hurried after the fleeing houseboy, she prayed it would not have to be used.

The alleyways were dark and appeared almost deserted. Lillian slid from one to the other and was careful to note each street that she crossed. They, too, seemed deserted, but in nearly every doorway shadowy figures seemed to lurk.

Oddly enough, without having asked Ling, she knew exactly where she was going to find Johnny Lord and took her shortcuts accordingly.

But Barbary Coast was different that night. There was no sound of drunken sailors and music bombarding the street. The gambling houses, saloons, poolrooms, dance halls, theaters, and brothels were all deadly silent.

It was then rather surprising to see the last street operating as usual. Every window ablaze with lights, with many brothel girls still hanging out their windows and calling down prices and specialties to the men in the street.

But the men in that street gave Lillian her greatest fear. They appeared to stagger drunkenly from building to building, but she knew at once that they were not drunk and were not sailors, although dressed as such. She almost had to admire someone in the Vigilante group for coming up with such a ruse. They had frightened the other streets into silence by appearing in their normal garb.

Without being seen she was able to dart into the ally behind the *Golden State Saloon* and make it unseen to the back door.

Once inside came her first challenge. The hulking black man jumped up to block her entrance.

"It's only me, Big John," Lillian laughed, throwing back the cloak hood. Then with a wicked smile she added: "I've come to catch Johnnie in an embarrassing moment."

"And so you has," he chuckled. "Got us two new little girls in today and he gave one to the young Chink and been with the other all night long."

"How lucky for each of them," she said, then turned serious. "Big John, there's trouble on the street. Bar this door and don't let anyone in."

Big John respected two people in life, because Johnnie Lord and Lillian McHenry were the only two who ever showed him respect in return. The madam who ran the rooms above the *Golden State Saloon* and her girls treated him worse than they would a cur dog. The dealers in the gambling portion of the saloon looked on him as a 'fetch-me' boy. He would bar the door, as Miss Lillian asked, but because he wasn't told to, he wouldn't warn anyone out front that there was trouble in the street.

The fourteen-year-old girl had animalized Johnnie. He thought he was going to train her, and time after time had to resist her from bringing on another arousal.

He lay spent atop her, measuring what an artful addition she would make to Luella's bevy of overused old whores. She was pretty enough, but too young, to work in Lillian's house. That thought was on his mind as he regained enough strength to get to his knees and get out of the bed.

The inward crash of the door startled him, but he didn't have time to turn.

The full force of a snapping bull whip cut into his neck and shoulders. The impact knocked out his breath and half collapsed him to the floor.

"Son of the devil!" the attacker, dressed as a sailor, bellowed as he raced in to snatch up a kerosene lamp and throw it through the window to the street below.

The girl began to moan and cry.

In the street the lamp exploded like a signal bomb. Johnnie tried to get his head up and was met with a rain of viscious stinging cracks from the whip. He rolled away and tried to protect his face and head from the blows, only to find them now directed to his genitals.

"I'll shred that goddamn thing to ribbons," the man cursed.

Johnnie moved his hands to protect such from happening.

"Drop that whip," Lillian screamed, "or I'll squeeze this damn trigger."

"You already are a murdering whore bitch," the man swore, recognizing her.

"Then you know I have no fear of kiling again," she muttered fiercely.

That message he would not ignore. He turned and jumped right out of the window he had broken with the lamp.

Johnnie paled when Lillian then aimed the derringer in his direction. "Now listen," he quavered, "you know I always break in new girls."

Lillian scoffed. "I don't give a shit what you do, Johnnie Lord. Just get your pants on and take me to Eric."

That steadied his nerve like a dash of cold water. "I should have known that it was only that Chink you were after. I don't know if you have had him yet, but I think you'll find him sissified. He was right timid about taking on one of my new girls."

"Why shouldn't he be?" she said, her voice trembling. "He's probably as innocent as the girl you put him with."

"You speak from experience, of course," he sneered.

"Stop it," she growled. "While you have been screwing your brains out the Vigilantes and Tong agents have moved into the whole Coast."

"Nonsense," he scoffed.

Lillian glowered at him. Her regard for him at that moment was nil. "Take him back to bed," she ordered the girl. "And when the next Vigilante comes through this door be prepared to die."

Johnnie started to protest and then realized she might be telling the truth. Just then the street below exploded with angry voices and gunshots. He asked no further questions but quickly found his clothing and began to dress.

"Eric?" she barked.

"Next room!"

Swiftly, she turned and marched down the hall to the next door. It already stood open, a frightened young girl peering around its frame. Lillian shoved her aside and glared into the room.

"No one makes a fool of me," she chortled. "I don't know why I am saving your stupid self, but the Tong agents are out to kill you tonight. Follow me!"

Eric Soong had never before known such embarrassment. Try as he might, he had been unable to get aroused by the young girl. He had become an instant object for her abuse and defilement at his inability. She had even at one time gone to the next room to complain to Johnny Lord. And the suggestions that Johnny had given the girl to arouse him had only made him feel greater guilt.

And to be caught this way by Lillian was cruel and brutal. He felt marked for the rest of his life by this horrible shame. He followed her like a scolded puppy.

In the hall Johnny grunted at him. "She is just vicious with jealousy. You must have pleased her very much."

"I don't think I have pleased her at all." There was an edge of sarcasm in his voice. Just enough of an edge to make Johnny wonder if he had been wrong.

The hall suddenly acted as if it had a life of its own. The explosion came as a part of the swaying boards they stood upon. It did not collapse, but below they could hear the screams of pain mixed with the crackle of fire.

"We've got to get out of here," he said matter-of-factly.

Lillian didn't reply, not wishing to waste energy with talk. They were instantly surrounded by acrid smoke. If there was hope of survival, it lay with Big John still guarding the back door. She moved cautiously along the swaying floor to the back staircase. There was an updraught for smoke, but no fire as yet.

A step at a time she started down. After seven steps her lungs were like molten fire, the pain in her chest excruciating. She pulled the hood of the cloak over her head and took several deep breaths. For a moment her head got so light so had to fight against a full faint. Her legs quivered but she would not give up.

"You'll kill us going this way," Johnny cried. "Let's go back to the main staircase."

"She won't listen," Eric croaked.

Nor did she. Not out of stubborness, but because her mind was locked onto another sound. It was the re-experiencing of a long-ago-memory. Suddenly, she knew why she had always been afraid of fire. Once the Whiteside family had been burned out of their home, crawling down a smoke filled stairwell was a mind-stunning *déjà vu*.

She would not think on it. She dared not think on it. She fought to get a foot at a time from one step to the next and then the next. Eighteen of them seemed like eighteen thousand.

But coming into the lower hall she sank onto her knees, gasping. There were silver flashes in front of her eyes, and her head was ringing. For a moment she forgot who she was or where she was.

Big John sprang forward, effortlessly taking her up into his huge arms, and starting toward the back door. Johnny came running alongside. His heart was thundering and his breathing was harsh and unsteady.

"Now here is an amazing sight," he said cynically. "I thought you hated all women."

Big John smiled weakly, blinking the smoke from his big brown eyes. "She ain't no woman, massa Johnnie. She am da Angel of Life that came tah warn us about da Angel of Death."

Once in the alley Johnny wondered if that spirit did not

hover over all of them. The night sky had been turned into an undulating bright orange and every clapboard building seemed to be gushing forth flame and smoke. Each street crossing was dangerous, for the shadowy figures Lillian had seen in the doorways were now hoodlum street gangs burning and looting at will.

There was one oddity that Johnnie noted, that Lillian might have been able to explain. Side by side the Vigilantes and Tong warriors seemed mutually bent on destruction of the area. He had wanted to scream out at them. He and Kai Soong paid a handsome yearly fee for their protection, but he did not want any attention drawn to their flight.

Whether by these sights or the inner sense gained from his father, Eric's knew the answer. ''This is the night the Tong people have selected for my death. I am sorry to pull you into the same boat, Johnny.''

But even as Johnny realized two separate forces had selected the same night for revenge, they were confronted with a nightmare scene right out of hell. A band of men approached half bent over and breathing like animals. Because their attire was not of the district, Johnny took a wild chance with them.

''Thank God!'' he cried. ''At last, men of reason. Kind sirs, please help us.''

''Who are you?'' the apparent leader snarled.

Johnny blinked at him foolishly.

''Oh, forgive me,'' he answered dutifully. ''I am John Smith and this is my wife Jane. Our coachman John and house servant Soong. We came by boat from Oakland, only to encounter a brutal attack. Gentlemen, look at my wife. She is in total shock from the experience. Please, is there no civilization here?''

The first man blinked at him in drunken confusion.

''That's why we're here, mister. To bring law and order to this hell hole of our town.''

''Bless you,'' Johnny simpered. ''Then kindly direct us out of here.''

''You're already out,'' the man replied simply. ''The main trouble was only designed for a three block area down in the Barbary Coast. You're safe.''

Lillian had heard all, but had kept her eyes tightly closed. Her mind whirled with the answers to a million questions. The three-block-area strike was designed against the 'Czar' and his gambling world.

"I can get down now," she said simply to Big John.

"I can carry you all the way!"

Lillian couldn't help it. She began to giggle. "I know you could, Big John, but we need all of our feet to get us fully out of danger."

"We are out of it," Johnny snorted.

Lillian took a breath. "And Eric?"

"He is as safe as we are," he scoffed.

"Is he?" she replied simply. "I would have known nothing about the Vigilante attack if his houseboy had not warned me about a Tong attack against him. An attack that has not as yet come about."

"And you still expect it?" Johnny asked in wonderment.

"He is no good to them alive."

Eric looked at her startled and anxious. "But what good am I to them dead?"

"Everything," she said simply. "It would be impossible to keep them from taking over everything with you dead. You are a minor without a will."

"How did you come to be involved in my problems, dear friend?"

"I'll make a guess, if you like," Johnny sneered.

"No need," Eric laughed, "for it was a stupid question. My father put me in most remarkable hands. He knew each of the trustees for their kindness and expertise."

"And I am sure he was well aware first-hand of their expertise," Johnny said.

"He would hardly have been practical otherwise," Lillian said.

Ahead lay the gates to her home and security. But the gates stood open and unguarded. They could, she suddenly realized be closed and opened only on command.

"Big John," she mused, "that explosion put you out of a job, didn't it?"

"Hum? I guess it did, at that."

"I need a gatekeeper, which includes room and board. It's yours if you want it."

"Jesus!" Johnny barked. "Don't you think I am capable of putting him back to work?"

"Are you capable of putting yourself back to work?"

"What in the hell is that supposed to mean?" he bellowed.

Lillian's eyes began to water. "Everyone forgets that I am still a woman. They look on me as the strong and determined Lillian McHenry—the madam of all madams. But I still have feelings and responsibilities. Still, I will steel myself against my personal feelings about this evening. But I cannot overlook my responsibilities to this house and to Eric. You failed to show up for two nights and I find out they were spent showing Eric the district. I almost feel that it was done behind my back."

Johnny laughed. "He is part owner of everything he was inspecting."

"Which might become nothing more than a bunch of burnt-out buildings."

As Henry was at the front door anxiously awaiting them, Johnny put that thought from his mind until he could discuss it privately with Lillian.

"Dear lady," Henry sighed, taking her by the arm. "I am that relieved to see you. I took the liberty to invite the guests to leave early and Clara has the girls and staff awaiting you in the dining room."

"You anticipate me, as usual," she murmured. "Thank you."

Without invitation or command the four men followed in her wake. Everyone stood as she entered, a little disconcerted, as she advanced on them as though with a vengeful purpose in mind. Without hesitation she threw off the cloak and eyed every person gathered as though measuring their worth to her.

"You may all be seated," she barked in the firm voice that announced she was in full command. "The *Golden State* is ablaze from an explosion and others are bound to be set afire. We are, if we look at the matter realistically, in a state of war. In my opinion it will matter not to the Vigilantes that we are the finest house with the finest clientele. They will still make us a target. Clara, I want our larder kept fully stocked at all times. Also, I want a list of our suppliers so I can ascertain if they are also clients. If they cut off our supplies then we will cut them off. Everyone, this is Big John. Henry, I want you to find a proper uniform for him. Big John is going to live in the gate house and keep the gate closed. No one goes in or out of that gate, including me, without his approval. Until we can find someone for the back gate it will be bolted shut.''

''But it is the closest gate to town for shopping,'' Polly protested.

''There will be no shopping,'' Lillian said softly, but firmly. ''If you have simple needs give your list to Clara or Henry. If they are major needs Henry will take three or four of you at a time in the carriage. I will have no girl walking the streets alone, even in broad daylight. I know I'm sounding harsh, but I am trying to think as the enemy might think. It takes evil minds to throw explosives into a building with no regard for the human lives within. And that, as I see it, is the tenor of their thinking. We are not human beings to them. We are dirty, evil, scum that must be driven from their pristine world.''

''I hope you don't mind,'' Emmy Lou broke in, ''if I impose myself with a personal question.''

Lillian stiffened. ''Not at all,'' she said coolly.

''No one has thought this, of course, but aren't you frightened?''

Lillian nearly laughed aloud from her feeling of relief. ''I wouldn't be human if I wasn't scared stiff, Emmy Lou.''

''Well, then . . .'' Emmy Lou hesitated. ''What if a body was frightened enough to want to leave?''

Lillian's back now went rigid. If one ran it might turn into a panic. ''That's what they will count on,'' she said icily. ''I bet that every fishing boat at the Barbary Coast wharves are busy right now taking the burned-out and the frightened across to Oakland. We are different. We cater to the elite and influential. Over cocktails. Over dinner. Even in bed you are going to become your own best agent. I want to know every man's feelings about the Vigilantes. Who they know as Vigilantes. How they feel about us and what help and protection they might give if we are equally attacked. We won't win this war by sitting back and doing knitting. I want to know the names and faces of this enemy. Then I will know how to strike back."

"That's fine for this house," Johnny said. "But shouldn't we offer some help to those poor creatures down in the district."

"On the contrary. I offered you financial help years ago to clean up those pig-sty houses and your madams talked you out of it. Perhaps this is the best thing that could happen down there. Am I not right?"

Johnny took it personally, something he might never have done before. He rose slowly from the chair, his eyes flashing lightning bolts. "A moment ago you considered them humans," he sneered. "How could you possibly know the lives that they lead and the type of men they must put up with night after night?"

A stunned silence filled the dining room as she stormed from the room.

"There I go again," Johnny gasped. "I am forever saying the wrong things to that woman."

Everyone, including Big John, was too embarrassed to comment. They began to drift away and to mull over everything Lillian had said.

Henry, to make his escape, used the excuse of escorting Big John to the gate house. Unseen, Eric slipped away to hide himself in Kai Soong's rooms. He was too embarrassed to face Lillian after his adventures of the past two nights.

When he was alone Johnny shivered. He had a horrible feeling that he had made an enemy of Lillian and the next few days would be a bigger disaster than that night.

Chapter 10

Johnny was right, on all scores.

The fires raged on through the next day. Normally, the volunteer fire companies were in violent competition to see who could get to the fire first and put it out. The Howard 3, the Knickerbocker 5, the Manhattan 2 and the Tiger 14 all seemed to be fighting to stay away.

They winked at each other and made excuses. "The hoodlums have been trying to burn each other out for thirty years. Let them."

That afternoon when a fire broke out in Chinatown they turned it into a social affair. Tong agents served the volunteers on the Howard 3 champagne as they watched the house of Eric Soong turn into embers.

By nightfall three full blocks in the Barbary Coast had been gutted. That night another block was quietly set to the torch, and another on the third night.

"You say it has nothing to do with me," Lillian said sweetly to the fuzzy haired city official with the walrus mustache, "but it does, Abe. Look, the Vigilantes in their original form were good for this town. This group is making a mockery of that good name."

Abe Ruef shrugged. He was still just a voice and not a power, in his opinion, at city hall. He was amazed that Lillian McHenry had even approached him on the subject.

"That might be true," he said finally, in his heavy French accent.

Lillian played dumb. She knew him to be wily, accomodating and politically ambitious. "If you know any of these men, you might let them know that I will not surrender.

Oh, look at that! I kept you from bidding properly. Mark, Mr. Ruef had the winning hand. The house will stand the loss and pay both winners."

He had been trapped and owed her a favor in return. On a marker pad he wrote out a name.

Even though it was already ten o'clock, Lillian didn't hesitate in having Henry drive her to the distinguished mansion of Lillie Hithcock Coit.

A puzzled maid, who had first been rude, came back to escort Lillian into a sitting room so elaborate with fretwork and hand-painted wall panels to be overpowering. Massive French doors opened onto a balcony, which looked out over the city and the bay. They stood fully open and the room reeked with the smoke stench from the Barbary Coast. Above the fireplace was an eight foot tall portrait of the woman she had come to see.

And when that same woman came off the balcony, Lillian smiled to herself.

Madcap Lillie was barely five feet tall, still prone to wear hats, even when at home, to add to her small stature.

And as in the portrait she entered with the ever present bottle of booze in her left hand.

"At last we meet!" Her voice was like a bird attempting it's first peep. "I've been told that we are the two most infamous Lillies in the West, although you do spell yours Lily."

"I'm flattered to be compared with you, Miss Coit."

The woman laughed and took a swig from the open bottle. "Don't be. You, as the legend goes, cotton after no man. I, in turn am the despair of several dozen beaux and find comfort in only one form of stud—my horses." Then she laughed again. "How wicked that sounds."

"I understand fully. There are few who do not realize that you are the finest horsewoman in California."

Lillie Coit shrugged, as though it were unnecessary to add to the truth of the statement. "What is it I can do for you, Miss McHenry?"

"I'm beginning to fear the spread of the fires in the Barbary Coast. It is almost as if certain people are holding the fire companies back from controlling them. You do have a great deal of influence in that quarter.''

''The clucking tongues do call me 'the darling of the firemen,' and I, too, am beginning to have my concerns. My first you will laugh at. The Fireman's Ball, which I chair, is but a month away. Many notables who support that cause are already making rude comments about my boys. These are men of reason who are pondering what might happen if the city is visited by one of our infamous windy cycles. In my lifetime this town has been razed by six fires and each time rebuilt. That was when Claus Spreckels and I started the volunteer companies. Rest assured, my dear, I do not want to rebuild again.''

Lillian was assured. Returning to the carriage she had to speak twice to Henry before he turned. Nor had he been looking down on the inferno.

''What is it?''

He pointed toward Point Lobos and the wall of grey billowing in from the ocean. At any other time she would have welcomed fog. She found in it a form of cloaking out the ugly and turning it to beauty. But there were times when it became unplesant mixed with too much wood and coal smoke.

''Let's go home. Nothing we can do about it.''

Nor was there sun enough to burn it off by noon the next day. It hung heavy, holding the acrid smoke from the fire in its grip and spreading a sooty blanket over the whole bay. Every eye was red and a person could not talk without coughing and choking.

Lillie Coit accomplished her task through threat. But there was a price. The outer blocks around the fire had to be evacuated and dynamited to rubble to contain the fire.

It took six weeks before people and their clothing didn't smell of smoke. Six weeks in which the fire companies were still kept busy each night with one or two flash fires. The Vigilantes were quick to deny any knowledge of those fires, but men of reason began to wonder in private and aloud why each establishment singled out for burning belonged to Johnny Lord.

''It's good to see you back, Mr. Howard,'' Daniel

Fetterson said crisply. "I'm sorry I was in the East when you were fired. This paper will always stand behind the truth."

"Are you willing to stand behind another truth in this matter, sir?" asked young Carl Howard, the reporter.

"I'm willing to sit here and listen, and then comment."

Carl Howard did not want to divulge the source of his information, but the information Lillian and her girls were gathering in bits and pieces he could see as a whole frightening canvas. He saw it as the beginning of a power struggle to control the whole city.

"Fascinating," Fetterson mused, "but we can't print just theory."

Carl Howard smiled and outlined what they could do daily to raise the rancor of the saner people against the Vigilante group.

The next day the *Chronicle* was bordered in black and listed those who had lost their lives in the fire. And daily, each time a fire took a new life, it was added to the box score on the front page. Without saying it, they were shaming the city into questioning who had blood on their hands and who kept adding more blood.

It was six weeks before the devastated area was cleaned of debris and left like a blackened wasteland. Many could not look upon it without feeling shame.

It was six weeks in which Lillian's quiet detective work through the girls paid handsomely. Not even Mortimer Stern was fully aware of who belonged or gave support to the Vigilante group. Many, who felt the motives of the group were the same as these of the first committee of 1851, shuddered at how it had gotten out of hand. In certain quarters it was hard to keep the news of Lillian's growing list quiet.

Three men on the list asked for private meetings with Lillian, but for different reasons.

Richard Deckler had always been uncomfortable around the woman and beads of dew formed all over his totally bald head.

"I will be frank and to the point Lillian, as usual. Even though I do not condone your business, it serves a purpose for my business. After weeks and months at sea our sailors do require dens of pleasure, what? It is a point on which Daniel Lee does not agree and that's why I found myself having to give the support of the company to change the Barbary Coast. However, you must also face another problem. You have put your place out of the price range for our sailors.''

Lillian held his gaze with icy disdain, if only for a moment. Deckler had all but accused her of being responsible for what had happened.

''This house never serviced them in the days of Charmayne Roach,'' she answered simply.

''I did put that badly,'' he admitted. ''Still, you do have a power in your hands through Eric Soong and Johnny Lord. I would be fired if Liberty or Daniel knew what I am about to propose. Might I add, that I have the blessing of Mr. Whiteside to make this suggestion. We do need houses for the sailors, but couldn't they be similar to your own? These are clean, hardworking men. After a night in that blight they are not allowed back on board until hosed down.''

''For once, Richard, we agree on something. It is a cesspool and I will do something, although I don't know quite what at this moment.''

Robert Duocoming and Basil Meeks arranged to meet with her together.

''Yes,'' she admitted, ''both of your names have cropped up as being supportive of the Vigilantes. So we don't have to bandy words about, I, too, sympathize with some of their motives. Am I being hypocritical in wanting some of the scum of my business chased out of town?''

Robert Duocoming cleared his throat and turned restlessly in his seat. ''No, because you are a practical woman, Lillian, and as a banker I look at your statement as practical. I am not a betting man, but I would bet that you have already ascertained why my name and that of Basil were listed as supporters. There are some very wealthy men on that list and neither my bank nor Basil's stock brokerage could afford to lose them as clients. But I was taken up short at the dinner table last night. My eldest daughter,

Elaine, suddenly broke into tears. She is engaged, as you know, to Hudson Potter. It seems that young daredevil admitted to her the setting of some of the fires. In her eyes he now has blood on his hands, thanks to the *Chronicle*. But it was devastating when she turned to me and said, 'Pappa, if I find out you are also with that horrible group, I'll just kill myself.' Lillian, I have a marvelous wife in Beth and beautiful children. I beg of you, as does Basil, to forget that we are on that list.''

''Thank you, both,'' she said slowly, ''for feeling you had to come and ask this of me. But we are old friends and to a degree business associates. I would have come and discussed why you were on the list.''

Basil Meeks rose. Eighteen years before he had been told he was dying and wanted a child to carry on his name. Carol had given him two boys and two girls and much more. Thin, bent, prematurely aging, he fought off death and lived for his family and a dream.

''Lillian, you are right. You bank with Robert and allowed me, before you poured so much money into your house, to handle your investments. That's a point Robert and I were discussing on the way over. You are the only 'madam', if you will excuse the term, who runs your business like a business. None of the others have a bank account or a single stock with me. Now you have an even greater responsibility as a trustee for Eric Soong.'' He held up his hand. ''We are well aware of the others involved, but want this conversation kept well away from their ears—especially Liberty.''

''That could be difficult.''

Duocoming injected, ''Liberty Lee is not playing fair with you! Ta Soong has arrived from China, Kai Soong's first born son and Master of the House of Soong. My bank has been holding Kai Soong's other assets in escrow for him. Liberty has advised the man that she would look favorably, as a trustee, on turning certain of Eric's affairs over to him.''

''But that would mean Eric's death,'' she gasped.

''You can prevent it, of course,'' he said with pure, cold business logic. ''Liberty has a single vote and power only over the produce industries she and Kai Soong shared in common in the American River valley. Mammy Pleasant and Carrie Whiteside, with Otis, are only involved with the shipping company. If I read the agreement correctly, you and you alone are tied to the most important thing Kai Soong left to his son."

"The land," Lillian said drily. "Six blocks of it stand burned out and the rest, frankly, makes me a little unhappy. The city is rapidly growing. From my front gate to the Embarcadero is valuable property going to waste."

"Excellent point," Basil enthused. "Through Eric you control almost a twenty-block square area. If you move too fast, it will not be profitable. But, Lillian, look at us. Where did the majority of our gold and silver go? Where do all of our stock transactions go? East! Always east to Chicago and New York. In the financial world we are a tarnished city because all they ever see or hear about is the Barbary Coast."

She laughed. "And yet, Richard Deckler advises me that it is a necessary evil."

"Granted," Duocoming sighed, as though preparing to lecture a child, "but must it cover such a vast area? Could it not be squeezed into a more controllable three block area on the fringe of Chinatown below Columbus Avenue?"

"It could," she murmured.

"And then," Basil declared vehemently, "we could take a large section over here on California Street and turn it into the Wall Street of the West."

"That would take a lot of money."

"We have the money," Duocoming jumped in quickly, "to buy or lease the ground." He paused. "You don't want to stay in this business forever, Lillian. You also now have the responsibility of Tracey. Whatever you do for Eric Soong, make sure you don't do it for free. Liberty would love to get her hands on all that money to plow into that damn canal project of hers. Don't let her do it! Let's keep California money in California!"

There was an embarrassed silence as they waited for her to comment. These two financial wizards kept staring in wonderment at the woman who was a madam in a call house. Did she fully realize that she had the power over land that could be worth multi-millions?

Lillian began to sense the magnitude of what Kai Soong had saddled her with. She was in a position of having to walk the Nightingale floor and not making it sing. She respected these two men for their honesty in wanting to protect her. She valued their judgement and business sense. She was also excited over what they wished for the district. But, as though Kai Soong stood at her side, she had to be practical.

"Robert," she said at last, "as you are handling the banking affairs of Kai Soong, could you arrange a meeting, very private, with a Ta Soong? Until I safeguard the life of Eric, everything else is moot."

He smiled. "It shall be done."

Eric smiled at her quietly, coolly. "I was beginning to feel you hated me. The rooms of my father are nice, but so lonely. Will I ever see daylight again, I ask myself? I also ask myself if my father was mean and sadistic and will I always have to fear death at the hands of Ta Soong."

"You know his name?"

"Why should I not? He is still my master, even though I be a half-caste and half-brother."

"He is in town."

A feeling of utter defeat overcame Eric. He visualized his life now being over.

"I am planning to meet with him," she went on. "However, I shall do nothing without your approval."

"What of the others?"

"The bankers have given me a very clear picture of what business and land arrangements they have, Eric. To a degree, it is you and I who have to make the big decisions." She was about to continue but stopped her next words in mid-flight.

Eric's face was puzzled and then it cleared.

"What must we offer Ta Soong for my life?"

Lillian stood for a moment staring at him. She rushed and collapsed at his feet, burying her head in his lap. "All that even I owned with Kai Soong, if he will just give you back your freedom."

"No, dear friend," he gasped, and hesitantly began to stroke her hair. "Never that."

"There is the land. I've looked at the financial figures. Plenty to buy out Liberty Lee."

"I think that is wise, although I am unsure what the business entailed."

"Leave that to me . . . and Johnny Lord."

"Shall we not do business with him?"

"I think not," she said gravelly. "But I have to think that out carefully."

"You cannot do all of this for me without gaining back something for yourself."

"That's what the banker said, as well," she laughed.

"The man is wise." He pondered. "My father would charge people ten percent to handle their affairs of business. You shall get the same."

Lillian managed a dignified nod of her head, but once it was done she began to have doubts. Had she twisted him into a position of having to offer such a fee. For the first time ever she felt like a true whore in having profited from him through womanly wiles.

She looked up, wanting to explain herself fully. Charmayne had taught her too well to read men's eyes. Eric's eyes burned with lustful desire. Nor did the Mandarin gown conceal her effect upon him.

She longed so desperately for him that she stared. Because of her stare his arousal increased. Involuntarily his length stiffened more and jumped beneath the silk cloth.

Lillian felt suddenly, deliciously vengeful. As much as she desired the feel of his youthfullness filling her, she knew it could never be again. She had to disgust him, as he had been disgusted by the young prostitute or he would gain control over her.

She moved her cheek and rubbed it temptingly over the tented cloth and than ran her teeth seductively up and down the length of the turgid shaft.

Eric's face went ashen. "I told you my feeling on that."

Wildly Lillian shook her head, lifting the gown up to his waist and exposing him.

Lillian nearly laughed. Eighteen years in the business as a successful madam who could explain this act with careful deliberation without experience—it was absurd. She put her lips over the torrid, rigid flesh and shuddered. It was soft, youthful and wicked. Surprisingly, as she moved it further into her mouth she felt as though it were entering between her legs as well.

"Oh, no," he whispered.

Eric's mind exploded. Disgust turned to lust. Because the administrator was different so was his response. In an instant he was built to his peak. He had never felt anything so exciting and pushed forward, forcing full entry. Lillian gasped and gulped. His charge went deep into her throat just as the storm brewing in his loins reached its volcanic eruption.

"Anything," he gasped. "Anything you now wish, I am your servant."

Lillian could not blame him. She could only blame herself. Now she did feel the whore. She had not put a stop to something, but only opened a new door and a new problem. And a problem for herself. She had played a wickedly dangerous game and come away with the strangest feeling of enjoyment and fullfillment.

In that moment Lillian saw crystal-clear what she must do with Eric Soong.

Fright as well as fire helped reduce the ladies of the night by some 1,500 and the number of houses to just over thirty. Many long-standing madams kept their girls in the Oakland area, but the majority vanished to parts unknown.

In silence Ta Soong absorbed all of Lillian's remarks. It was strange being back in America and dealing with a woman who reminded him of the Liberty Lee of his youth. More and more he was sensing that he was again thinking American Chinese and not Old World. He wished that Kai Soong had not left him with such a burden. Even though he was now Old Master Soong he still wanted to be fair and just out of respect for his father's wishes.

Lillian did not fear Ta Soong, feeling that dealing with the man was very nearly like talking to Kai Soong. All in all he seemed to find all of her suggestions very reasonable and fair.

Now, she had only a few days to start bringing all her plans together.

Chapter 11

Then, through the *Chronicle*, Lillian published a full page ad. At first glance it was made to appear as though she was listing the names of her clients, which brought hearty chuckles. But a closer reading revealed that she was exposing all the members of the Vigilante society. Many men found themselves in greater disfavor with their wives than had they been caught as one of her clients. Deny as they might what little part they had played with the group, it fell on deaf ears. They were being likened to the Tong agents and San Francisco wanted law and order in the sole hands of the police. Exposed, the Vigilantes quietly disbanded.

Johnny Lord greeted Lillian the afternoon of the ad as though he had just seen her the previous day, although carefully not bringing up the subject of their last meeting.

She stepped backward and blocked him with outstretched hands. "No," she said unevenly, cursing the way his sudden reappearance made her breath come and go so rapidly.

His eyes darkened and his body went quite still. "Why are you trying to keep me out of your life?"

"Because you can't use it like a swinging saloon door, Johnny."

"What would you say if I was here to propose marriage?"

"By the tone of your voice I would know that you were lying."

He spoke quietly, after a moment's silence. "Yes, I would be lying. But you knew I was never cut out for marriage, right from the start. But we have always made great business partners, haven't we?''

''Damn! I am also a woman with desires other than business!'' she cried out so suddenly that it made Johnny start and her voice echo and recho throughout the office. ''So out with your reason for being here!''

His face froze. ''I've just come from Liberty Lee. She is not in too good a frame of mind, seeing as how you placed Daniel Lee's name in your ad.''

''I should have exposed him as one of the main ring leaders of that little group.''

If her thrust had hit home, nothing in his face betrayed it.

''But I would have had to expose my source of information,'' she went on. ''Thanks to you, I've learned how to be sly and devious. I should have known you'd go to Liberty and warned you that it would be a wasted trip. We had a meeting of the minds and she sold back to the trust what connections she had with Kai Soong. The same will be true with the Whitesides and Mammy Pleasant by the end of the week.''

''Where does that leave me?'' he gritted through his teeth.

''I will put it simply,'' she said, quelling the disorders that always resulted from his being near. ''Kai Soong always owned the land and you the buildings. For that he was given a twenty percent cut. Since the fires, that is rather slim pickings. Eric, on my advise, wants to be fair. You are reduced to fourteen houses, two saloons and one gambling hall, right?''

''I plan on rebuilding,'' he snorted.

''I hope you do,'' she said, as though he hadn't spoken. ''But Eric has decided that he wants nothing to do with that business. Your little tour convinced him of that. He is a very sensitive person, Johnny, and you sealed your own fate by trying to get him to take on that young prostitute. He didn't touch her, you know?''

''How was I supposed to know that! Hell, I thought you had already taken away his innocence!''

Lillian's insides curled into a tight ball. She had determined not to let the conversation drop to that level. It would be hard to make Johnny understand, but after she had accepted Eric's explanation as truth, she had been denying him as well. She could not be trustee and mistress at one and the same time.

"Here is his offer," she said calmly as possible, ignoring his charge. "He will deed you the property rights to the land those seventeen buildings stand upon for a full dissolution of the partnership."

He blinked. "Hell, a man would be a fool not to jump at such an offer. Where's the catch."

She sensed, rather than saw, the change that had overcome him the past few weeks. The jolly, kidding 'czar' had been replaced by a sober-minded adult unsure of his future. To this Johnny Lord she could not lie.

"There is no catch, except his regard for you. Although, it ties in with the agreement I had to make with the agents from China. They wish nothing material from him, for they gained handsomely from Kai Soong's other enterprises in Chinatown. But they want him divorced from Chinatown and the House of Soong. Lawyers are drawing up papers for him to take his mother's maiden name. As soon as that is done he will leave for Europe to study and find out what career he wishes in life. That also divorces him from this business, in case you are interested. I have bought out Kai Soong's shares and this property. I also have set aside money to buy out your interest in this casino."

"You certainly have been busy," he shrugged.

His words and calm manner rankled Lillian rather than soothed her. "I have had to keep busy so I wouldn't think too much. Well, do you agree to everything?"

"Everything," he said just as calmly as he had said before. "But in spite of that, I have one other vital question for you."

"Well?" she demanded, hotly.

He looked at her and smiled on a slow grin.

"I'm still going to need you, Lillian."

"Johnny!" she stormed, but the stern look on his face kept her from raving on.

''Lillian,'' he said heavily, ''please let me have my full say. I've made two mistakes in my life and both of them concern you. We both agree that the first was in not marrying you right off the bat. The second is scoffing at your suggestion about cleaning up the Coast. There is hardly anything left to clean up, but I can do it with the resources I have. Will you give me advice on that if I have to come and ask?''

''Without question,'' she smiled and was grateful for the asking. She was starting to close many doors in her life, but wanted to leave a few of them ajar. This was one of them.

Chapter 12

Lillian's eyes misted with double pleasure.

The Palace Hotel courtyard was the perfect setting to show off her new Victorian carriage. Big John looked so proudly important as he pranced the twin white horses through the tunnel and circled the maroon coach around the interior courtyard to the columned entrance.

Lillian stood back, as though just one more of the hotel guests gaping at this show of elegance and class. The carriage boy was quick to spring forward and help the young lady alight. His glowing face and the murmur of two fancily dressed woman near Lillian nearly brought her to full tears.

Tracey came out of the carriage with the regal grace of a princess. With ladylike calm she collapsed her parasol and used it as a walking stick. Four years of proper diet and care had turned her hair into a luxurious mass of glittering honey-gold that she wore in massive curls that cascaded over slender shoulders and rested on her high pointed breasts. She would never grow beyond her four feet ten inches, but had been trained by Miss Phillips to carry herself as though she were four inches taller. There was the sparkle of the joy of living in her clear blue eyes and the hint of laughter always played at the corners of her rose-bud mouth. Because she seldom had reason to frown, her creamy skin was a taut mask over the finely chiseled cheekbones and delicate nose. Her sixteen inch waist was the envy of every girl at school, as were the clothing usually worn to accent her perfect young adult figure.

Because this day was special for her she had selected a

linen gown of lemon yellow with burnt orange accents, that matched her gloves, parasol and pill box hat. She looked around until she picked out Lillian and burst into a radiant smile.

"Hello, Aunt Lillian," she bubbled.

"Hello, darling," Lillian smiled, knowing she was now the envy of the other women, and kissed Tracey on each cheek. "I see you had no trouble getting out of school on time."

Tracey laughed, locking her arm through Lillian's. The sound was like silver bells on a winter sleigh. "Mr. Marchbanks was delighted to be rid of me for the afternoon. He says that I am so far ahead of the other girls that he is thinking of putting me into the next level."

"Well, we'll talk about that later."

"Oh, this is going to be so much fun!"

"A young lady only gets to celebrate her sixteenth birthday once."

"But I get to celebrate mine twice," she corrected with glee.

Lillian frowned and chose not to comment. Had she known that the trio had planned a birthday party for Tracey's school friends that evening she would have made this luncheon a private affair, but months before Amy had come up with the idea for this lunch and Lillian had agreed. She always seemed to be sharing Tracey with one or the other for this holiday or that event or just because they all loved her as dearly as Lillian and wanted her sparkle in their home.

She had become very special to Amy and Richard Deckler. The two years she had spent with Miss Phillips had been the turning point for Bobbie. He had advanced to such a degree that he was again a part of their family life, even though he would never ever be more than twelve years old in mentality. And when Tracey was around him he showed traces of being even older.

A stir of excitement thrilled Tracey's heart as they entered the ornate splendor of the lobby and were approached by a tall and imposing gentleman.

"Welcome to the Palace, Miss Whiteside," he said,

being courteous to bow to the guest of honor first and then to Lillian. "Miss Lillian, what an honor to have you with us today. I have already escorted the other birthday guests up to the Garden Terrace. This way to the elevator."

Tracey's sensuous mouth made an "O" in her creamy face.

"You should feel honored," Lillian chuckled. "Felix seldom leaves his seventh floor world to greet guests in the lobby."

"Is that where we are going?" Tracey gasped. "That highest balcony that's enclosed by the huge skylight?"

"That's it. You don't get by the elevator boy unless he knows you have a reservation. But what I love about it are the windows. Every table looks out over some part of the city." Then she almost laughed on a thought. She wondered in which direction Felix Hanover had seated this little group.

The elevator opened right onto the balcony—was a jungle of rubber plants and hanging baskets of fern. The window table Felix had selected looked east towards the Cliffhouse and Seal Rocks.

The Mesdames Duocoming, Deckler and Meeks anxiously awaited them, each bedecked in a hat that rivaled the fresh flower arrangement on the table.

It had first been planned as a party of seven, but Clara and Henry had presented Tracey with a private birthday dinner the evening before. Tracey had accepted that as an excuse, but not Lillian. With each passing year Clara had divorced herself more and more from any gathering with the 'trio.' She found them frumpy, self-centered and snooty. "All they can do is brag about their brats," she would grumble. Lillian had learned to leave well enough alone. Clara was the one becoming a crank in the years since she passed forty. There were times only Tracey could get a civil word out of her.

Now she was glad Clara was not in attendance. The trio greeted Tracey with giggles and kisses as though they were her school chums and not matronly women who were all becoming overweight.

Tracey saw nothing wrong with the greetings and accepted it with the relish of attention it brought to her from the other guests. It was all so overwhelming. It was her first 'adult' luncheon out. Her first visit to that swank hotel and the first time she had been this high in a building looking over the city.

"Perhaps," Felix said smoothly, seeing the desire in her eyes, "while the ladies have a pre-luncheon cocktail, you would care to walk around the entire terrace."

"I would love to," she bubbled and was off.

Amy inhaled as though caught in an act of mischief. "Cocktails?" she whispered. "Is it allowed?"

Lillian laughed. "At the Palace it is considered the chic thing to do. I bet there are some Nob Hill battle axes who nip here when they wouldn't at home. Might I suggest, it being a party, we let Felix serve us his famous champagne cocktail."

They all nodded immediate agreement.

As Tracey continued her waltz around the balcony she could not help but appraise the other diners. She had never, in one place, seen so many elegant and finely dressed ladies and gentlemen. She was not aware that they were thinking much the same of her.

One young man followed her with his eyes until the regal woman sitting opposite him soundly scolded him for being rude.

Tracey was used to such looks. The school had a separate section for girls and for boys, but once a week they all gathered together in the music room for formal dance class. The older boys always fought over her as a partner, on the excuse that she was the only girl who didn't have two left feet. The other girls were always pea-green with jealousy that she was so popular with the boys, but Tracey always treated all the boys the same—with cool indifference.

She got back to the table just in time to hear Beth give out a querulous gasp:

"Lillian, I just noticed! You are not wearing hat or gloves!"

"I've never worn a hat in my life and why put on gloves that you just have to take off to eat?"

Beth had no intention of dropping the subject. "It's an almost unwritten code for San Francisco women these days."

"Then Liberty Lee and I must both be outside the code," she snickered. "I failed to see any evidence of hat or gloves on her person when we passed her table on entering."

Beth timidly glanced around the terrace until she spotted the imposing woman. Liberty sat in animated conversation with a ruggedly handsome youth in his teens. In reality her attire was the simplest in the room and Beth dropped the subject. Robert Duocoming was in the process of refinancing several businesses in the Lee empire for Daniel Lee and she dared not be overheard making any negative comment about the man's mother.

Tracey had followed Beth's eyes and was surprised that this Liberty person was the same woman who had scolded the young man. One could not live in San Francisco for four years without having heard of Liberty Lee and the Lee family. But this was the first time Tracey had ever seen the woman.

Two years before, on a trip to Panama, Liberty had grown deathly ill with yellow fever. Many had feared that she would never survive. Once the fever had been broken and she had gained enough strength to return home, the effects of the fever were obvious. Her hair had turned to a pure white and she had to now use powder to hide the faint yellow tinge to her skin. The classic face and neck had started to wrinkle and there was a squint to her eyes because she was too vain to wear her glasses in public. She had grown a little too thin and never seemed to be able to regain her proper weight. The thinness, however, only seemed to add to the queenly way she held her head and body.

As though the name Lee was imposing itself on the party, another Lee came out of the elevator and glided directly toward their table.

"Miss High and Mighty," A.G. W. Lee chided, with a chuckle. "Now I know why you turned me down for a business lunch today. Girls day out, huh?"

"I take it you know everyone," she said.

"With the exception of one," he answered truthfully. "Hello, Amy. That was a marvelous roast beef dinner the other night. What a grand boy Bobbie is becoming. I'm sorry my sister-in-law made him feel uncomfortable. Ah, dear Beth. Tell Robert that I have just come from a meeting with my cold-blooded brother and the percentage figures sound all right. Now, don't scold me, Carol. I promised your girls that lace I brought back from Switzerland and I haven't forgotten. I have been so busy since my return trying to become a self-employed businessman that everything else has been put aside. Which brings me to you, Lillian. I am scheduled for dinner in your apartment tonight, right? Have you received an answer from Eric on the land?" He waved his hands as though to shoo away his own questions. "Enough of that later. I am still waiting to be introduced to this unknown young beauty."

Lillian laughed, relishing the moment. She had dreamed and schemed for the past four years over the day she could properly introduce them. Even though A.G. had become an exception, a dinner guest in her apartment when they had private business to discuss, she had always planned it on the nights that Tracey was with one of the trio. From the corner of her eye she could see Liberty squinting in their direction. Lillian could not have hoped for a more triumphant moment.

"A.G. may I present my niece, Tracey Whiteside. Tracey, Mr. Alexander Grace Wells Lee."

"Charmed," he said, with a slight bow. "I have always been aware of the mystery niece in Lillian life, but would it embarrass you if I said you are one of the most beautiful young creatures I have ever seen in this town of beauties."

"You've already said it," Tracey laughed, "so don't embarrass me by repeating it."

"You younger generation," he smiled. "You are like my nephew Mick. You always have a clever comeback for your elders."

"Really," Lillian corrected him with a nervous laugh. "Don't make yourself sound so old. There is really not that many years separating you and Tracey."

"Really?"

Lillian smiled knowingly. To the day she knew it was only eleven years. "But to answer your other questions. Yes, you are my dinner guest this evening in the apartment and I do have a reply from Eric in Austria."

"How nice," he said. "Ladies, it has been my pleasure. How nice to meet you, Miss Tracey. I'd best join mother before she comes and treats me like Mick. That grandson is her pride and joy. She has a charcoal drawing of my father when he was seventeen and a soldier at the Battle of Shiloh. It is utter remarkable. Mick is the spitting image of father."

"Your father must have been a powerfully handsome man," Beth said, "if that boy is his image."

"He was," he scoffed, "but none of his looks seemed to pass my way. I think they found me under a rock."

Beth blushed deeply. She had not meant it in that way at all. Because of his sparkling personality and dapper dress, no one who knew him well ever thought of A.G. as rather homely. Still, she was grateful to Tracey for jumping in quickly.

"It was delightful to meet you, Mr. Lee. Thank you for stopping by my birthday table."

He bowed again and left. Around the table each had their unuttered thoughts as the appetizer was served.

Lillian felt elated and comfortable. She could sense that A.G. was taken with Tracey and that Tracey was not repulsed by him. It was a very nice beginning and she still had two years to work upon her plan.

In the past four years she had been a very careful real estate salesman for Eric Larson Enterprises. Parcel by parcel, lot by lot, she had been able to surround her home with shops and offices of newness and vitality. The Wall Street of the West was four solid blocks of banks, stock brokerages, a stock exchange, insurance companies and lawyers offices.

As though it were a fence of her own design, she had built and leased business offices around the three block Barbary Coast area so that it could never again expand. But only Johnny Lord had been wise. His establishments were now clean and well run, but the rest of the Coast was perhaps even trashier than before the fire.

Eric was now twenty-two, but the year before had given her full power of attorney. He had finished his studies in Paris and had come to the determination that he wanted to go to Austria and study to become a doctor. He was quite willing to go along with A.G.'s business proposal, without knowing that Lillian would only offer it on her own terms. She was determined, in two years time, that on Tracey's wedding day she would become Mrs. Alexander Grace Wells O'Lee.

Beth sat back during the delightful lunch and took more note of the events transpiring at the Lee table. After A.G. made pantomimed excuses as to why the conversation had taken so long at the birthday table, she could tell by Liberty's face that she was not pleased with her son associating with Lillian in public. And she could tell the moment that the explanation about Tracey was given, for the grandson slyly peeked around to get another look at her. Nor did Beth miss the fact that Tracey caught that look and sent glances in return.

Mentally Beth shrugged. For a moment she had looked on him as a good prospect for her sixteen-year-old Ester, but she could be a matchmaker for Tracey just as well. When she saw Mick excuse himself from the table, she made her own excuses, praying that none of the others would join her. Afraid that she might miss him, she tarried in the little foyer of the rest room alcove until he emerged from the men's wash room. She made sure they both tried to go through the archway at the same moment.

As a young gentleman he stepped back and waved her to precede him.

"How kind," she said with a gracious smile. "Oh, I am sorry. I didn't recognize you, Mick."

"You know me?"

"Well, I know your parents and uncle quite well. They have been dinner guests at my house. I am Mrs. Robert Duocoming. Which reminds me. We've had no reply from your parents on your attendance for the birthday party this evening."

"Party? . . ." he stammered and stopped. "I'm afraid I know nothing of a party."

"Strange," she said, not wishing to let him know there never had been an invitation. "It is my honor to act as hostess at the sixteenth birthday party for Miss Tracey Whiteside, the young lady we honor at lunch today. I was most careful with the invitations to her school friends."

"There's the error," he laughed with casual aplomb. "My grandmother has had me privately tutored for the past three years. I really don't belong to any school."

"Oh, my!" Beth gasped, feeling her opportunity slipping away. Then, as had been her stock in life, an utterance of truthfulness saved her. "I saw the looks pass between you two during lunch and thought surely that was a sign you knew each other and would be at the party."

He smiled sheepishly. Seldom had he looked upon a girl as he had looked upon this one. The girls he did know, which were few, he had always regarded as little more than friends. Still, he had been wracking his brain during lunch to figure out a way to pick the brain of his Uncle Alex to learn more about her. Then the sheepishness vanished and it was pure grin. Beth was suddenly aware why a beautiful woman like his grandmother had fallen so madly in love with his grandfather. He may have been but seventeen and she a shade over forty, but she would have traded places immediately with Tracey to capture that fine male gleam in his eyes. "Is it possible for me to still be included?"

"But, of course," she said, then caught his eye sternly. "I hope you will make your parents understand my utter embarrassment that the initial invitation went astray. I don't know how I shall explain this to my husband."

Mick cast her a most knowing grin. "Then why explain, to either of them? My parents are going out for dinner this evening, so there is no reason why I can't attend, provided I am given time and place."

She gave him the information and he etched it on his mind and stalled for a few moments before returning to the terrace.

Mick E. Lee wanted to let all of this slowly filter down

through his lanky six foot frame. His seventeen years had been a strange mixture of the mundane life in his parents home, although he respected them dearly; a world set apart, when his grandmother had him in tow, making sure that the tutors were the finest and his studies proper. He hated it, but loved her too much to rebel. He could never be the same type engineer and draftsman as his grandfather. The only splashes of color in his life, which thrilled him, were supplied by his Uncle Alex from time to time. A part of him could be as conservative as his father, kindly as his mother, forceful as his grandmother, liberal as his Uncle Alex, and still leave him to be nothing less than Mick E. Lee.

He knew, because of the manner in which they lived, that they were not poor, but had no grasp of the real extent of the family wealth. He had not, up to that point, been included in any family business discussions; although aware that his father and grandmother were involved in many enterprises.

But that day, across the room, he had felt a warmth overcoming him that had turned into a consuming fire. He was sure that he was going to go insane if he didn't get to meet that golden-haired minx, but then, what was he going to say. She was so polished and refined and assured of herself. He was still in knickers! Even though he was now aware that he was a year older, he hardly felt it. He just knew that her first question to him that evening might lead him into an embarrassing *faux pas*. She looked like she knew exactly what she would do with her life and he didn't have the slightest idea.

He was almost tempted to race right by his grandmother's table and tell Mrs. Duocoming that he couldn't attend the party, but suddenly realized he'd become suddenly aroused, and to sit down quickly. He knew Tracey was somehow responsible, but no one had taken the time or trouble to explain his changes from little boy to growing man. Nor, until that moment, had he had reason to ask.

"Really, Mick," Liberty said icily, on his quick seating, "you have been gone forever."

"I was talking with one of the ladies from that table,"

he said honestly. "Seems I was invited to a birthday party I wasn't told about."

"Your parents are probably wise to screen your invitations," she sighed.

"Why, grandmother?" he insisted. "My parents know Mrs. Duocoming, so surely they must know this Miss Tracey Whiteside."

"Hardly," Liberty sneered.

He puzzled a moment. "Is she related to Otis and Carrie?"

"No," she said sternly.

"Still," he said honestly, "I would like to go to that party. It's only a—"

"That's enough!" Liberty growled. "I don't want you associating with them!"

"Why are they any different from us?"

Liberty refused to answer and A.G. chuckled. "The difference, dear boy, is that there is no difference." Then his voice grew gruff. "Your grandmother, if given her druthers, would make each of us male Lees suffer for the things she feels your grandfather did to her. That's why she feels Miss Whiteside's aunt is not worth associating with."

"That is quite enough," Liberty stormed.

"No," A.G. said quietly, "it is only the beginning, mother. Mick, while you were away from the table I outlined to your grandmother a desire I have at the present time in my life. She scoffed at it, just as your father did earlier, because I am supposed to be the stupid dolt of the family. I may not see you for some time, because I have just cut all ties with your grandmother and father."

Liberty rose haughtily. "Come, Mick. We shall leave your uncle to see to the bill, now that he is a free agent from my purse strings."

"Yes, grandmother," he said reluctantly and confused. "It is nearly time for my appointment."

"Appointment? What is this?"

He grinned, giving his face so much the look of Dan O'Lee that it made her wince. "Don't pretend that you didn't know. It's the last fitting at the tailors for my long pants.''

''Bother! Mick, I just have too many other matters on my schedule this afternoon. The tailor will have to be put off!''

His face clouded. ''You don't have to go along, grandmother. I am seventeen and have been there three times alone already.''

''Your father is such a boob,'' she said, as though she could already visualize the outlandish fabrics he would have selected on his own. ''Alexander, what is your schedule?''

When he was called Alexander by his mother he knew it was time to be most careful. ''Little more than a haircut and manicure,'' he lied.

''Good,'' she murmured. ''If nothing more you do have most excellent taste in your attire. You will go with Mick and approve of his selection.''

That, Mick E. Lee could accept with pleasure. Without being told he had already modeled his new attire after styles worn by his Uncle Alex.

A.G. secretly smiled at the command. He had a tendency to classify people in life, with a separate column for male and female. His mother was given a column of her own. He could utterly adore and fear her in the same breath. Well aware that she had spoiled him in his youth, as she tried to do with Mick, he had learned at an early age never to take advantage of the situation. He knew her little games. She felt that this little family chore would bring him back in line and make him forget his silly notion of starting a business of his own.

A similar thought was going through Mick's mind. He was dying to find out what his Uncle Alex meant by having cut his ties with his father and grandmother. He wondered if the man sometimes felt as he felt, suffocated by having to do the wishes of others and never being asked his own desires. Seldom did he ask for anything, for his personal wishes were quite simple. Even as a child, when his nursery would be overcrowded with toys, he would be more impressed with the boxes that the toys came in than the toys themselves.

Perhaps that was why he was so unimpressed with his own mother and father and the life that they led. Neither seemed capable of living from day to day without a battery of servants at hand to keep them going. At times they seemed like grey shadows who filtered in and out of his life. He could not recall a single time he had seen his father touch his mother in love or affection. Equally, on his tenth birthday, his father had announced that the childish goodnight kiss was no longer necessary. As if in relief, his mother let it apply to her, as well. That, in his judgement wasn't living.

For the first time in his life he questioned why A.G. Lee seemed to be the only happy member of the family. He really didn't see his grandmother as happy, or his Aunt Miranda. He wasn't sure why, but he didn't want to spend the rest of his life like them.

A.G. was not only pleased with his selections but flattered.

"However," he told the tailor, "he shall require one outfit for this evening." He paused. "And it should be a little on the formal side. Say, the blue serge."

The tailor sighed, but could not afford to refuse the man. "It will take me another hour or so."

"Fine. Mick and I have a few errands in the neighborhood. Why don't we say three hours, to give you plenty of time."

Mick did not protest until they were on the street. "I don't have three hours, Uncle Alex. I am supposed to be back with the tutor by three-thirty."

"Not everything is learned from books, my boy. Come, I need something a little stronger than those pansy little drinks served up by Felix."

Mick was delighted. He sensed the spirit of adventure and was ready for it. Until he had visited this tailor he had never been below Powell Street except in a carriage. Here the hustle and bustle was an excitement all of its own.

On Montgomery Street, around the corner from the new financial center, A.G. entered a building with an eloquent facade.

"My boy, this is Duncan Nicol's Bank Exchange Saloon. A watering hole strictly for gentlemen of means. The loudest sound you may hear is the clearing of a dry throat."

Mick had been led to believe that a saloon catered to the lowest scum in town. He was amazed to see a very ornate room with a long polished bar, behind which stood sober faced barkeeps in dark suits. And it was quiet. So quiet that the man almost whispered his greeting to A.G. and asked his pleasure.

"My usual," A.G. said softly, "and I think a dram of Duncan's special ale for the lad. This day he is to cast off his knickers and put on the long. We are waiting for the tailor to put in the final stitches."

"Me congratulations," the man beamed, shoving a beefy hand in Mick's direction.

Mick beamed back and shook the hand. Then he realized what his uncle had done. "Do I dare drink?"

"You daren't not," Alexander Grace Wells O'Lee chuckled. "Just as you dare not miss that party."

"I sure want to go," Mick admitted. "I've been waiting to get your advice on that and some other matters."

A.G. was struck with the humor of the situation. He was the last member of the family that anyone ever sought out for advice.

"Well, lad, you have my opinion on that matter. She is quite a looker, isn't she?"

Mick blushed. "I . . . I don't know what to think . . . about her . . . other than . . . well, I don't know."

"I don't want to embarrass you," A.G. said gently, "but the conditions of your knickers was obvious when you quickly sat down. Were you having certain thoughts about her as a young male?"

"I don't know," he said honestly, but really not embarrassed over what his uncle had seen. "It just happened twice. Oh, it's been that way when I wake up in the morning, but never in public like this." He flushed, realizing how badly he was putting it. "I'm pretty stupid about things like that."

"It is not stupidity," A.G. said gently. "It is not that

many years ago that I went through the same period of dumb awareness. I, however, was without a father to guide me from puberty to manhood. Being a homely child, when I admit did not help matters along. In time I stumbled upon those who could help me learn.''

''I am also without a father to guide me,'' Mick said bitterly, ''but I don't like the feeling of stumbling. Who helped you?''

A.G. stood very still, looking at him. It would have been so easy to expose his wounded heart that had been used and abused by the Chinese servants in his mother's household of his youth. Male and female he had been exposed to before he was fifteen. By the time he was Mick's age they would sneak into his room with an opium pipe to so stun his mind that they could talk him into anything, but mainly to take from him anything of value.

Then, one night, the houseboy who had used him time and again as a female in his innocent state, learned that he was to be fired. In vengeful spite he had taken A.G. to a Chinese house of singsong girls. A.G., in an opium stupor was left and a messenger sent to Liberty as to where she might find her son.

He had been mortified, being hauled from the place by his mother and treated as though he were the first male to use his penis in such a disgraceful manner.

For three years, out of fear of his mother, he had been totally celibate. It was also during those three years that he had come to hate his brother with a passion, for Daniel had a way of smiling at him as though to keep his mortification alive. Then he had found Lillian's house. Her girls made him forget he had ever been with a Chinaman or had been caused to have shame.

But to his nephew he could not reveal a single line of his experience or who had helped him. He wanted Mick to walk quite a different path, but still he wanted to give a certain guidance.

''Many helped me, Mick. Some in the wrong way and some in the right way. I really don't wish that for you, but I don't want you stumbling. You had an erection today, which is natural. Until we have a chance to discuss it fully, just put it out of your mind. I need time to find the proper person to help you.''

Almost at once it was out of Mick's mind, because his uncle had never lied to him. If he said he would find someone, then he would find someone.

A.G. began to question the sanity of what he was thinking. What sweet revenge it would be to take Mick to Lillian's and to let his brother Daniel know about it. He chided himself for the thought. The only person who would lose would be Mick.

''Now, while we are in this area, I want to show you what I am considering. You'll be the first in the family to learn.''

''But I thought you said you had discussed it with father and Grandmother?''

''You see, Mick, I said this afternoon would be more learning than from stale books. I knew they would turn a deaf ear to anything I might propose, which they did, so I fed them a lot of malarkey.''

They turned off Montgomery and headed down Washington. Within a block, Mick's skin was crawling. Even though it was mid-afternoon the area seemed held in pertetual gloom of night. The streets were narrow and reeked with the wasted humans who lived in utter degradation.

''I don't like it here, Uncle Alex,'' Mick stammered.

''I didn't think that you would. But you had to see this to know what I dream. Come, within a half block you will be gasping.''

Within that half block they were into the six-block area that had been burned out and rebuilt.

Here the streets conformed to the width of those up town and were alive with pedestrians and carriages going to the shops, home-craft factories and ethnic cafes that had sprouted up.

Mick stood very still, looking at it.

''I don't understand,'' he said sadly. ''Why can't that area be like this?''

A.G. grinned. ''That is my dream. I am about to go into partnership with a Chinaman to improve that land.''

Mick stared at him incredulously. "You'd trust a Chinaman over father and grandmother?"

"Every time," he said, almost angrily. "But you don't have all the facts. The land back there is owned by the Chinaman, but has been under the business control of Lillian McHenry. Ninety percent of the people in there are squatters, but she has said little about rent in four years. You may not know it, Mick, but the produce you eat each day is transported by the people of that area."

"That filthy place?"

"Each morning the barges dock at the Embarcadero and carts, manned by those people you saw, haul them to Drumm Street for the market. It's a filthy, disgusting place."

"How can you change it?"

"By razing it and building anew. Your grandmother and a man named Kai Soong were financial backers for the very productive farms that are today along the American River valley. In those days they needed Chinese labor to grow Chinese foodstuffs for the coolies who were building the Central Pacific Railroad. The majority of those Chinese farmers stayed on their farms and soon adapted to other crops desired by the non-Chinese.

"Four years ago your grandmother sold out her interest to Kai Soong's heir. I learned of it through Lillian McHenry and pleaded for the first time in my life. The only times I feel I was ever happy was spending some of my youthful summers on those farms. Eric Larson allowed me to buy back Liberty's share in the farmlands."

"Who is this Eric Larson?"

A.G. laughed. "He is the Chinaman, but half Norwegian and uses his mother's maiden name. He is studying to be a doctor in Europe. I saw him in Paris and he was greatly impressed with my scheme for the farms. Oh, I left that out, didn't I. I travelled Europe for vegetable strains I feel would do very well here, as well as my other purpose for being there." His eyes glowed with excitement. "Mick, their farmer's markets are gems of cleanliness and artistic arrangement. It is so tastefully done that you want to buy everything in sight. That's what I want for this city! A produce district to rival the best in Europe.''

''Have you money for such a large venture?'' Mick asked logically.

''I will have,'' he smirked, ''As soon as I finish having dinner this evening in that house.''

Mick looked and gaped. He was used to the turrets and towers and baroque balconies in the homes that surrounded those of his father and grandmother. But here through the gate of the high walls was pure Spanish flavor. He saw it at once as one of the grandest buildings he had ever seen.

''You know the people who live here?''

''Intimately. It is the home of Lillian McHenry. I might also add it is the home of her niece, Tracey Whiteside.''

Mick scowled. ''She lives there! Whee! She must be the richest young maiden in town.'' His scowl deepened. ''I bet it will be a party for a bunch of rich snobs. I don't think I should go, Uncle Alex.''

''Why not?''

''Our family doesn't have that kind of money. Pappa says we are just hard working people.''

A.G. was taken aback. He had never had occasion to learn what Mick knew about the family, but surely he didn't think tutors came free.

''Nonsense,'' he said, ''we may be hard working people, but no one, no matter how much money they have is better than the next. Well, we best get to the tailor or you'll have nothing proper to wear this evening.''

Chapter 13

Lillian laughed with uncontrolled mirth. For a Lee to think that she had more money than Liberty was the best laugh she had ever had.

A.G. now felt on safe ground. He related his scheme to her straightforwardly.

"I appreciate your wanting to go it alone on the produce market," Lillian said simply, not wanting to put her own cards on the table quite yet. "The stock you have for sale would more than cover the cost that Eric and I have placed on that land. However, I have tried to keep Eric's money free of entanglements."

"I see this as little different than your arrangements with Basil Meeks and Robert Duocoming," he said, showing that he also had an astute mind for digging out little known business information. "Isn't the entire financial center sitting on little more than leased ground?"

"It is," she said in wonderment, "but for a very good reason. That money goes directly to a bank in Switzerland for Eric's personal living and school expenses. However, I am not closing the door on your proposal, seeing as how it does tie back into your partnership with Eric on the farms. To be frank, and I am speaking more for myself than for Eric, we really don't have that much desire to be involved with the Lee Enterprises with a few stocks here and there. Yes, what you have gained over the years as tokens adds up to a tidy sum and has given you nice little dividend payments. Not to hurt your feelings, dear friend, but they have been, in my opinion, sops to keep you quiet but with no way of having a say in any of the busisness matters.

Eric and I would find ourselves in the same boat—minor stock holders who would be sneered at by Liberty and Daniel.''

A.G. couldn't help it. He began to laugh. ''Exactly the reason I want to be on my own. The only real voting stock I own, which I didn't include in this group, is what I have in the PLW Lines.''

Lillian took a breath. ''Oh?''

''When Otis wanted to build the *Carrie* as a flagship, and took Mammy Pleasant in as a partner, the Lee Lines were not involved. Otis found out he was short of funds and went to Liberty for help. She bought stock from him in my name, because I was still a minor and she would have control of it. She already had merger in the back of her mind, as I see it now. When the merger came I was given equivalent stock in PLW.''

''Which you still have,'' Lillian mused. ''Do you mind if I question its worth.''

He didn't mind at all. Everything he owned was up for barter to get his hands on that property. Lillian fought to keep the excitement from her mind. She had been prepared to lease the land to him in exchange for a marriage commitment. Now she saw where she could gain something of real value and power. How marvelous it would be to have voting rights on the Board of Directors of PLW and to force Otis Whiteside to sit at the same table with her.

''That stock,'' she said slowly, ''would adequately cover a down payment on the property, but still leave you strapped for proper funds for clearing and rebuilding. I propose this, A.G.'' She paused until she saw the eager gleam in his eyes. ''I will buy that stock for cash and Eric and I will give you a workable partnership lease on the land, with one proviso. I am already thinking ahead for Tracey. By the time she marries I want her totally disassociated with this house.''

''Isn't that the way it is now?''

Lillian laughed bitterly. ''You saw your mother today. She loathed every minute of your standing and talking with us. What would she say if Tracey were to marry . . . say, a Lee?''

A.G. roared with delight. "You would never hear the end of her screaming."

"Good! That's the proviso, A.G. I will buy the stock for cash, work with you on developing the land and give you a fifteen year partnership lease, as long as I can look forward with some hope to the time that Tracey becomes a Lee."

A.G. looked startled and anxious, thinking that Lillian was moving quite quickly to marriage before Mick and Tracey had even met. But the offer was too tempting not to play cat and mouse with her.

"I think you used the proper word," he said cautiously. "Time."

"I wasn't speaking of the next five minutes," she cut him short. "I was looking two . . . three, even four years down the road."

"That seems an adequate time," he laughed, still thinking of Mick. "That gives both parties a fair time to get acquainted and a fair time to carefully plot the whole happening so that it isn't a total shock to mother and Daniel."

Lillian sank back without commenting. It had been so easy, she wondered why she had been fearing his reaction. Perhaps, she had to admit, it was the manner in which he used her establishment. He was an excellent customer, always the first to compliment Clara on her dinners and very easy on the girls. Many had been the time, the girls would confess to her, that they did little but have marvelous conversations with Alexander Lee. Still, when his desires were right, she knew she didn't have to fear his being homosexual. Then she sat forward, suddenly.

"The quicker we get started the better. I don't want it to drag out so they can worm that stock away from you. Also, for the moment, I want Tracey to know nothing. Let all of this come upon her quite naturally."

"I agree," A.G. sighed, wishing for it to come upon Mick just as naturally. He felt a little guilty, committing to something just to let him be an individual free from family strings.

* * *

Although it was nestled among turreted castles and structures of granite that looked like museums, the Duocoming home was as much garden as house. The house, to be sure, befitted one of the largest bankers in the city, but the garden was Beth's world of love.

That night it was festooned with Chinese lanterns, brightly colored tents, a dance floor and ten-piece orchestra, tables heaped with food, waiters with trays of drinks and a birthday cake centerpiece of sixteen tiers.

Tracey had expected a small gathering of her school friends. Their two dozen was greatly outnumbered by the over two hundred adults that had crept onto Beth's list.

For the first hour and a half, Tracey wondered if all parties were so boring for the guest of honor. Her hand ached something fierce from the receiving line and after that amount of time she would not have been able to match a single face with a name given her by Beth. Not even the growing table full of presents stunned her as it had in the beginning.

"A breather," she said, when no one stood in the line for a moment. "Was Aunt Lillian aware this was more an adult party?"

"I'm really not sure," Beth said slowly, carefully weighing her words. She wanted to speak the truth, but she knew it was unwise. "I suppose I just assumed that she would be busy working."

"Not tonight. She had a dinner meeting with Mr. Lee and said she would see me later to give me my present."

"Here?" Beth jerked her head around as though Lillian would appear on the scene instantaneously.

"I doubt that," Tracey chuckled. "Oh, here comes another one."

Beth suddenly started shuddering, for she could see the short woman who walked behind the tall man. Robert had insisted that they be on the invitation list, but she never dreamed they would attend.

"Good evening," she gulped. "Mr. and Mrs. Otis Whiteside, may I present you to our birthday girl, Miss Tracey Whiteside."

Tracey felt suddenly ill-at-ease and unsure how she should react.

The big lumbering man stepped back to let his wife come through the line first. Carrie curtsied, smiling weakly and moved on. She had resented Otis insisting that they attend, but for once he had been forceful. He was not attending for the guest of honor, but to get closer to Robert Duocoming. Liberty Lee, in his opinion, had a blind side of late. Every cent she could muster was going into the Panama Canal scheme and it was bringing the PLW Lines to near ruination. He needed the advise of Robert Duocoming without it appearing too obvious.

"Happy birthday," he said, bowing so he would not have to shake her hand. But as he came up from the bow he allowed his eyes to look upon her and his heart nearly broke. Before him, in perfect image, was the face and figure of his mother. But that was another life, a life he had denied for twenty-two years to Lillian. He could not recant now, or ever.

"Captain," she said, holding his light blue eyes in her equally blue eyes, "thank you." Then she had a devilish thought. "It is an honor to bear the same last name as you."

"It is a common name," he said nervously.

"First names aren't so common," she pressed on. "I was named Tracey, after my grandfather, and not Maureen, after my grandmother."

"I suppose Otis came from somewhere," he lamely said. "Good evening."

His massive shoulders seemed to sag as he turned away. He prayed that this Tracey Whiteside was nothing like the father he had known and more like the Maureen Whiteside he still would dream about as a loving mother.

"Is that you, Uncle Otis?"

He turned back to the line and what a second before had been the tired, wrinkled face of a man in his mid-fifties tightened into a boyish grin.

"Mick? Is that you, lad?"

"Please! Please!" Beth begged. "I must do the introductions on the line."

"To be sure," Otis grinned, casting an appraising eye over his favorite youngster in the world next to his own children.

"Mr. Mick E. Lee," Beth said, getting back on track, "may I present our birthday girl, Miss Tracey Whiteside."

Mick put out his hand hesitantly and Tracey accepted it. He did not crush it, as had the hundreds before, but held it as gently as a young kitten's paw.

"Did you have a pleasant lunch?" he gulped, thrilled by her touch.

"It was marvelous," she murmured. "But I was not told you would be a guest." She gulped, her experience with boys being mainly in the dance class, but wanting to speak her truthful mind. "You look quite dapper in that suit, Mr. Lee."

"Thank you," he blushed, then felt truth coming to his lips in return. "It is my first suit of long pants."

"I know the feeling," she giggled. "My skirts have only gone from calf to floor in the last year."

Beth cleared her throat, but only to get attention. "Tracey, my dear, you have been in the receiving line quite long enough. Mr. Lee, could I impose upon you to take Miss Whiteside to the food tables?"

Mick blanched, this really being his first party outside his parents' and grandmother's staid affairs.

Seeing his discomfort over the situation, Otis jumped quickly. "We would be honored to accept the young couple with us, Mrs. Duocoming."

"Thank you, Captain Whiteside."

Tracey was suddenly amused. Here were two men she was intrigued to get to know all at the same time. Carrie Whiteside she thought she would sidestep for the moment. The woman looked like she was going to throw a tantrum at any moment.

Before they were ten feet away from the reception line, a battery of young men came charging from all directions, seeking, demanding and pleading for a dance.

With no dance instructor there to protect her, Tracey very calmly told each when they might come back to ask for a certain dance.

Carrie waited until a table for four was found and the men went for food, before commenting.

"You seem to be quite a favorite with all the boys," she drawled, "but then I suppose you've been well trained by your Aunt Lillian."

Tracey was not dumb. One could not live that close to her aunt's business and not know what it was all about. Still, that statement was so blatant in meaning that it couldn't be overlooked.

"My training comes from the teachers in my school, Mrs. Whiteside. These boys are members of the dance class. I'm not even aware if my Aunt Lillian knows how to dance. Do you know how to dance?"

Carrie averted her eyes. "I was once an excellent dancer. The belle of every ball in this town."

"You are still a very beautiful woman and probably still an excellent dancer."

Carrie looked back. There had been so much warmth and sincerity in the tone that she didn't scoff. "I'm a mother of six who should be home with her children, that's what."

"You can only be a mother a part of the time," Tracey said, "and a woman the rest of the time."

Carrie replied, "My dear young woman I am most happy being a mother and a woman all in one."

"Is that because you fear those who still think of you as black?" Then Tracey blushed, embarrassed, because it had slipped out so easily. "I'm sorry. I am only repeating the words I have heard from others."

There was a long silence and then Carrie looked up beaming. "I haven't feared that in years, dear girl, but it prides me to know that the story is still around. I'm not ashamed of one ounce of black blood in my body, but I can see where my actions have led people to believe so. Well, here's one gal who is going to dance her shoes off tonight at your birthday celebration." Then she smiled sweetly. "Please tell Lillian one thing for me. She should be very proud of you."

Tracey blushed again, but it was only seen by one

person. Carrie, as soon as the men returned, was on her feet and amazed Otis by dragging him to the dance floor.

"What did you do to her?" Mick asked in amazement.

"Reminded her of her youth, I guess," she shrugged.

"Oh, that," he chuckled.

She didn't like the chuckle. "I notice," she said coldly, "that you greeted your Uncle Otis and excluded her."

"I did not," he insisted.

"Just think on it," she stormed. "And what's more, he is not even your uncle."

"Everyone knows that," he shot back and then stopped. "Why are we fighting?"

She giggled. "Because I needed someone to scream at or go mad."

He grinned. "And I am nervous as a pup around all these people."

She hesitated. "Would you like to walk through Beth's gardens?"

It was his turn to hesitate and gulp. "When I walked here tonight," he said slowly, "I suddenly realized that these were the gardens that I stare down upon from time to time while in studies with my tutor. I've seen the children at play here and I envy them their freedom. I would love to see the gardens."

"Then, let's go," she supplied gently. "I see a dance partner coming that I really don't want."

Tracey could see the excitement in his face, but she did not guess its cause. Whatever it was, she was glad of it, because it replaced the little-boy-lost look.

Then, when they were beyond the tents and Chinese lanterns, held under a canopy of stars, his mood changed. He looked up at the lighted turrets of the Mark Hopkins mansion and openly laughed.

"I have never seen that house from this angle," he laughed. "Because Hopkins is known to my grandmother I have seen the insides, but never fully understood her comments on it. It was designed and built, you know, by seven different architects. My grandmother maintains that they each got their own way, wall by wall, wing by wing, even though nothing of the seven matches any of the others."

Tracey had to laugh. "I see what you mean."

"You live in quite a grand house."

"You've seen it?"

"Only from the outside. I was by today with my Uncle Alex." He gulped. "Someday I would love to see the interior, as I have seen all of these."

Tracey held her comment, looking around and up at 'all of these.' He would have laughed to know that her desire was to see the interior of the great mansions he so casually commented upon. "I don't know which one you live in. I'd love to see its interior."

"It's farther up California Street and sits behind my grandmother's place. You can just see the top of her brownstone house with the captain's walk all around the top."

"It must be nice to lavish so much wealth on a building," she said in a dreamy voice.

Mick laughed. "Didn't your Aunt Lillian do much the same?"

She looked at him puzzled, suddenly realizing he was naive to the facts. "The main area of that building, Mr. Lee," she said, never one to fear the truth, "is a place of business. Only one wing is our home."

"I don't find that unusual. My grandmother's main business office is her home, as well."

She laughed, a little nervously. "It's not quite the same thing. Granted, it does house an excellent dining room and well respected casino, but ten of the rooms are for the use of professional ladies."

"Ladies?" Mick said, a note of awe creeping into his voice.

"Ladies of the night."

Mick blushed, then gulped. "It is a subject foreign to me, but I am not totally stupid."

Tracey sensed that the first was truth and the second a form of male coverup. To save him further embarrassment, she wanted to change the subject.

"I should get back to the others. It's about time for me to open the presents."

Mick looked thunderstruck. "I didn't even think to bring you one."

"There are too many there already," Tracey grinned.

"Perhaps you would allow me to be late with my present."

"It really isn't necessary, Mick."

"Well, I was thinking it would give me an opportunity of seeing you again."

The shameless grin widened. "You really don't need a present as an excuse."

He accepted that without comment. Still, as she opened the mounds of brightly wrapped parcels, he felt that everyone in the garden were aware that he was not represented.

Tracey grinned again, but this time only to herself. Throughout the rest of the evening, whether she was dancing, cutting the cake or talking politely to the other guests, Mick E. Lee seemed to hover near by.

He didn't try to impose himself, nor did he ask her for a dance. When the orchestra leader informed her that he had planned the last number as a birthday waltz, she had to make a choice of partners.

Mick gave her a quick refusal and it baffled her. Her second choice looked surprised but, to Tracey's great relief, escorted her onto the wooden platform that had been built for a dance floor.

"Thank you for this marvelous party, Uncle Robert."

"It's Beth you should thank," Robert Duocoming chuckled. "Except for dinner parties, this is the largest bash she has thrown. It pleases me to see her so happy."

In turn Richard Deckler and Basil Meeks came to spin her about the floor and then waltz with their wives. Next to take his turn with her was Otis Whiteside.

Otis was almost smiling over what he had overheard earlier. "Did you consider, Miss Tracey, that the boy may not know how to dance?"

"No."

"I'm delighted we came," he artfully changed the subject. "And now I must turn you over to the stag line."

Before the end of the waltz every young swain fought to get in a twirl or two. Tracey felt her feet were bruised forever, but there was a more important thought on her mind. With every turning, no matter where she was on the floor, her eyes came back to Mick Lee and his eyes never left her for a second.

And yet Mick avoided her eyes in saying goodnight. He did not want to expose the excitement that was mounting in his heart. He had figured out a birthday present and had to keep it as a surprise.

It baffled Tracey. From what had been said before she thought he would at least attempt to feel her out on a date and time for their next meeting. Why raise the subject and then not pursue it?

Tracey was silent on the ride home, and as Big John made several trips to her room with the presents. Like a dream, she was afraid to speak about it and wake up to find it had never happened. As she prepared for bed, she selected the gifts given by Amy, Beth and Carol. Used to cotton nightgowns, the negligee of pink silk was foreign to her bare skin. The matching robe and slippers made her feel quite adult. She stood before the floor length mirror, brushing out her hair and recalling the highlights of the evening. At the stroke of midnight Lillian came bounding into the room and stopped short.

"You look magnificent, Tracey," she cried, her green eyes bright with happy tears. "And look at the loot! How many people did Beth have at the party?"

"I think everyone in town who would say yes," she laughed, "and some of the presents are very strange. Beth kept track of what each person gave so I can send them a thank you note. I'll have to go see Miss Phillips to find out exactly what I must say."

"That sounds like a good idea," Lillian said, picking up a box of lace handkerchiefs and reading the card. Her eyes flared in surprise. "The Whiteside children were there?"

"Not the children," Tracey answered with a wink, going to her bed, "but the parents. I even got to dance with Captain Whiteside, and I have a message for you from his wife."

"Oh?"

"She said to tell you that you should be very proud of me."

"I'll be damned!"

Tracey stretched out on the bed like a very contented cat. "They had Mick Lee sitting at their table. You remember, Mr. Lee's nephew from lunch today."

"Really?"

"He's a very nice, sensitive young man who was embarrassed because he didn't bring me a present. I think I treated him horribly when I asked him to dance the birthday waltz and he turned me down."

"Probably he doesn't dance," Lillian said, taking a seat on the bed and starting to listen more carefully.

"That's the same thing that Captain Whiteside said."

Lillian measured her words carefully. "You seemed to get along very well with Otis."

"I suppose." She hesitated. "He seemed a little bashful at first, but I think you and my father are wrong. He said Whiteside is a very common name."

Lillian breathed a sigh of relief. After twenty-two years of denial, she did not want Tracey being the one to make him suddenly admit the truth. She wanted that pleasure when the man was forced to work with her on his Board of Directors. And, at the moment, she wanted to carefully delve in another direction.

"I wasn't aware that Liberty's grandson was in your school."

"He isn't. He has private tutors. I'm not sure how he came to be invited."

An image suddenly popped into Lillian's brain and she smiled to herself. At the time, no one questioned why Beth Duocoming had been gone so long from the luncheon table, but Lillian now recalled the 'pleased as punch' look on Beth's face when she returned just a few moments before the Lee boy. Well, Lillian thought, it won't do that matchmaker any good. Tracey was now set for a quite different Lee. Still, she had to find out the direction of Tracey's mind.

"He seems to have made an impression on you."

She giggled. "I think I'm the one who made an impression on him. Every time I would turn about there he would be. He's nice, but he's just another boy."

Lillian relaxed. She should have known that Tracey was

too intelligent to go through a 'boy-crazy' stage. Then she put everything out of her mind but the reason for her visit.

"There is something under your pillow," she said coyly.

Tracey turned and dug her hand under the pillow. It closed on a velvet oblong box and she pulled it out puzzled. She turned and sat up as she slowly opened the hinged lid. She gasped as the light caught the glitter of gold and sparkle of the diamond set between three pearls.

"Oh, Aunt Lillian," she cried, "it is the most beautiful thing I have ever seen. It must have cost a fortune."

"You are worth every cent of it, my dear girl. Put it on so I can see the necklace on your throat."

"The best thing that ever happened to me was coming to live with you."

"It was also the best thing for me, Tracey, and the best for you is yet to come. I look forward to the day when you are successfully married and are an important woman in this town."

Tracey looked up from fastening the clasp, meeting Lillian's eyes. They had developed one of those rare friendships between a younger and older women where love and honesty were the cornerstone.

"I don't even want to think about marriage yet, Aunt Lillian. Tonight, brushing my hair, I realized how adult I looked in my new bedroom attire. I also realized how happy I have been being a growing young lady these last four years. Is it selfish to say I want to hold onto being young as long as possible?"

Lillian reached out and took her into her arms. "Not selfish at all," she cooed. "I wasn't rushing you out the door. Besides, it's going to take a long time to find the man who is right for you. Now, give me a goodnight kiss and dream pretty dreams."

After Lillian was gone, Tracey thought her tired body would go immediately to dreamland, but her mind still wanted to savor that special day. And a corner of her mind was playing a strange game. Mick Lee's grin kept popping into her thoughts like a Cheshire cat in the dark. Having just met him that evening, she couldn't rationalize her feeling. It was strange, but she suddenly started to miss him. He had been constantly with her that evening and yet just on the fringes, except in the lower part of the garden. But in the dark her heart started to ache over the subject left dangling between them. When would she see him again, if ever?

In the days that followed, she felt that it might just be never. Then, for a time, she put him out of her thoughts. Lillian had all but refused to let the school advance her and school became tedious. As spring approached, she was all but forgotten. Lillian was very busy overseeing the razing of the land she and A.G. had signed papers on. A.G. had wanted the work to go on immediately. He knew that he had to get his scheme into operation before others found out about it. It took so much of his time and energy that he never did get back to have his talk with Mick.

That might have been difficult, had he known the scene that took place between his mother and brother the morning after the party. The society editor of the *Chronicle* had devoted nearly a full page to report on the party and those in attendance. When Daniel Lee seemed unconcerned with his son having attended, it only increased Liberty's fury. She was determined to keep her grandson from associating with such trash.

Daily, carefully worded instructions came from Liberty to the tutor. His carefully worded reports back made the man cringe. He was a teacher and not the warden of a private prisoner. His reasoning to Mick for the added studies were slim alibis. They seemed preposterous to Mick until he happened upon one of the instructions.

For the first time in his life he resented his grandmother. "I don't know if I ever want to go to college!"

Liberty shook her head, her cheeks a faint yellow.

"It's not what you want that matters, but the hard part— the responsibilities you will have to shoulder in this family when I am gone. I have made arrangements for you to be prepared by fall to enter school in the east. As I shall be in Washington a great deal next winter, I'll get to see you a great deal. Now, the matter is settled, so no more discussion."

It wasn't settled in Mick's mind. He began to play a strange game with the tutor, doing his work so fast and so accurately that the man had no choice but to let him secretly sneak away for a few hours each day and then fib on his reports to Mrs. Lee.

It saddened Mick that he had to be a sneak when his mission was so simple and innocent in his eyes. He had been unable to get Tracey Whiteside out of his mind, although it had nothing to do with love. First, it was a moral obligation he felt. He would not be able to get over his embarrassment until he had presented her with the birthday present he had planned. Secondly, he could not overcome the images he had of her from the party. He had never had a close friend of his own age, male or female. Like an imaginary friend that some lonely children dream up for themselves, he had built Tracey into the greatest friend he could imagine. But what good was a friend unless you got to see her and talk with her. And after two weeks of his own detective work he was ready to put his plan into operation.

Because the term was so near its end and Tracey was doing little more than killing time, she was given out-of-school assignments to perform each Tuesday afternoon. Because it was a different sort of challenge, it brought out a flair she did not know she possessed. To study the history of the city might have been boring had the teachers taken the normal approach of making her dig it out from stale books. Instead, she was given assignments to interview and make reports on the people or their families who had helped shape that history. Her reports, all who read them agreed, were remarkable. At first she had been shy and hesitant, but as her confidence grew so did her special gift of putting on paper what each person shared with her.

Tracey came to look upon her Tuesday afternoon outings as special occassions. But this Tuesday, leaving the school, she was in a foul mood. In all of the requests the school had sent out to set up interviews for her, this had been the first turndown and the messenger had brought it only fifteen minutes before.

"Well," the embarrassed composition teacher advised, "why don't you go spend the afternoon in the library."

Tracey had shrugged. At least she didn't want to spend the afternoon brooding in the classroom.

The day was bright and clear and still that didn't alter her mood. She walked along Larkin Street in a sulk, debating whether it might not be just as wise to hail a hansom cab and go home. She knew she would gain little sitting in the public library.

She turned at the sound of hooves on cobblestone behind her and turned back when it proved to be only a stylish pony cart coming along. She had not even taken time to notice the driver.

"Boy, was that a slap in the face," Mick laughed, pulling the cart up beside her. "Didn't you even recognize me?"

"It has been a long time," she said coolly.

"Don't blame me," he laughed. "They've kept my nose to the grindstone preparing me for college. May I give you a lift?"

She shrugged. "I guess so. I was on my way home."

"Because you were turned down for an interview with my grandmother?"

"How did you know that?" she asked in surprise, as she let him help her into the seat beside him.

"I've been keeping track of you," he told her candidly. "When I found out about your Tuesday afternoon schedule I knew her turn was due to come."

"How could you have known that?"

"Tuesday before last you met with Mr. Crocker and Mr. Hopkins. Last week it it was Mr. Stanford and Mr. Huntington. It stood to reason that you were talking railroad and she had to be included. Frankly, I bribed her butler to find out when she was approached and what her response might be."

"Which was a turn down," Tracey replied, but to her amazement she said it without bitterness.

"I feel responsible," he said sullenly, like a little boy. "I don't think she wants us to become friends. I've had to sneak around to find out your schedule and learn when we might meet. I still owe you a birthday present, you know."

"I told you that was not necessary," she laughed, her mood lifting.

"But it is, to me. Do you have time now for me to take you to my present?"

Tracey shrugged. "I seem to be at loose ends. Why not? Is it far?"

He grinned. "That would give it away."

"Then I am in your hands," she giggled, sitting back relaxed. The mood was gone. She felt so comfortable with him, as though they had seen each other just the day before. Then she was suddenly thrilled by recalling his words. She had not been forgotten if he had gone to so much trouble to learn all about her Tuesday activities. She took off the wide-brimmed hat and let the afternoon sun play on her face. As the pony cart turned and headed out Geary Boulevard she paid no attention to the direction. Like any friend, who had not seen another friend for awhile, she began to inquire into what he had been about.

In turn he probed into her school work and the reasons behind the assignments. It was give and take and brought laughter between them on the manner they each were being treated.

At the end of the boulevard he steered the cart on a winding road that skirted the beach. At one turning Tracey let out a gasp and a thrilled cry.

"I know the surprise! We saw it that night from the Duocoming garden!"

"Does it please you?" he felt obligated to ask, even though her voice should have told him.

"I have never seen it except at a distance. Whose home is it?"

He looked at her quizzically. "You're the historian. Hasn't anyone mentioned that San Franciscans come to the Cliff House to enjoy watching the seals from their spectacular restaurant?"

She shook her head, unable to take her eyes from the castle like structure built upon the cliffs, its front third jutting out over the ocean, supported by massive stilts embedded in the rocks.

Still, she had not guessed his surprise until he escorted her into the restaurant. They were usheered at once to the wide dining porch that looked down on the Seal Rocks and a table in a secluded corner.

"There is nothing in the rule book that says you can't have two birthday lunches. Except, I don't want to share you with anyone else."

Tracey breathed deeply. Through the open windows, the salty tang was laced with the sweetness of spring. Echoing over the crash of the waves upon the rocks was the constant bark of the seals as they played.

"What a bunch of clowns," she laughed. "Oh, Mick, this is the grandest present of all."

"I hope you are hungry. I took the liberty of ordering for us when I made the reservation."

"I'm famished, come to think of it. I do hope you ordered seafood. It's my favorite."

"I'm glad of that. I don't think they have much of anything else on their menu."

She was delighted with every selection he had made. They lingered over coffee, too stuffed to move—nor did they wish to.

Mick gasped and hissed across the table: "I didn't think we would run into anybody we would know."

Across the porch swept a wisp of a woman, her small size emphasized by the immensity of the feathered and beribboned hat. Her beauty was marred by gaudy makeup and a belligerent glare to her eyes.

"Why are you here?" she demanded, and it came out too shrill.

Mick was instantly on his feet. "The same as you Aunt Miranda. We came out for lunch and to watch the seals."

The woman jutted out her cheek to be kissed and then said viciously: "Shouldn't you be hard at your studies?"

"One must eat. Oh, may I present Miss Tracey Whiteside." Then he was left a little puzzled on how to introduce her. The night before, at the dinner table, his mother had gone into near vapors over the woman. Miranda, without consulting anyone in the family, had left her husband and demanded that everyone use her maiden name again. "Tracey, my Aunt Miranda," he finally decided was his best way out.

Miranda ignored the introduction, possibly because she did not want to be forced into making one herself of the suave middle aged gentleman who stood waiting for her.

"Mick," she said, sugar sweetly, "I would rather your grandmother did not learn I was here for lunch today. There was an emergency board meeting this afternoon and I sent word that I was ill."

This brought the first involuntary smile to Tracey's face. She sensed exactly what the Lee board meeting would be about, because Lillian had been scheduled to attend her first PLW Lines board meeting that morning.

"As you wish," Mick shrugged, casting a look at the waiting gentleman. "I won't tell, if you don't tell."

"See that you don't," she hissed through tight lips and marched away.

"What was that all about?" Tracey whispered.

"To put it simply," he giggled, "she's scared to death I would tell her mother that she was here for lunch with a man."

"Isn't that her husband?"

"Hardly," he chortled. "I'm not supposed to understand some things that are discussed in front of me at the dinner table, but it seems my dear, sweet Aunt Miranda has left her husband and wants to be known by her maiden name. She certainly doesn't waste much time, does she?"

"Perhaps it was just her lawyer."

"Very funny," he sneered. "And what is even funnier is that I wouldn't have known she was here if she hadn't made a point of coming to our table. I didn't know anyone was here but you and me."

Tracey blinked, not sure how he meant it.

"In my way of thinking," he went on meditatively, "everyone needs a good friend to share things with, as we have done. I don't think I've told another living soul as much about what I think as I have during this lunch. You are one great person Tracey. May we do this again some time?"

"I would like that." Again came that odd feeling. She didn't want to let him go. It would have been bliss to just sit and talk with him forever.

Chapter 14

Miranda Lee, being Miranda Lee, could not leave well enough alone. When she finally learned the reason for the emergency meeting of the Lee family board she went like an errant child to her mother.

"I thought the only thing he knew how to do was whimper at your knee," she said snidely.

"Don't use him to cover your own shame," Liberty snapped. "Miss McHenry at least keeps her business within four walls."

"Did I say I was with anyone at lunch?" Miranda asked icily.

"Butter won't melt in my mouth," Liberty mocked and mimicked, batting her eyelashes like her daughter. "Don't you dare try your stunts with me, young lady. You have been a troublesome minx ever since you reached puberty. I should make you go back to your husband, but he has been a bitter disappointment to me. So, you might as well tell me. Who do you have on the string?"

"Guido Giannini is his name. His uncle has the Bank of Italy in town. Guido has vineyards and a winery in Mill Valley. He is the perfect continental gentleman."

"It sounds as though you have known him for some time," Liberty said slowly, making mental notes of anything she thought she should be prepared for in the days to come. To her way of thinking, trouble for the family hovered nearer on this score than the problems Alexander was posing.

"We are both unhappy people in our marriage," Miranda intoned darkly, "but his wife is old-school Catholic.

She returned to Italy a year ago and I met him shortly thereafter through mutual friends."

"I want it stopped," Liberty said softly.

"Oh, really!" Miranda flared in total disgust. "I am not Mick, that you can browbeat. You had your way with me, mother, in carefully planning my first marriage. All you did was force me to look upon men who had nothing more in their veins than cold blood."

Liberty's heart nearly stopped beating.

"You're quite right on that score," she admitted, "but where will this lead but to heartbreak? You have all but said that the man's wife is not about to divorce him. That you should even think of him as a prospect for marriage seems futile. I would suggest you give the matter serious thought, or I might just be tempted to treat you as I now intend to treat Alexander."

Miranda blinked, unsure of her mother's meaning.

"Obviously." she pouted, "you will go to your grave still treating us like children who never grew up. Daniel can take it, because he is such a wimp. If Alex has broken away, then I cheer him on. I won't listen, mother, because I am unsure exactly how to answer you. But for once I have a piece of advise for you. Don't become a harridan with Mick or you will drive away his love as you have that of your three children."

Knowing that her mother was growing too incensed to be reasonable, Miranda quietly turned and walked out of her mother's office.

Liberty Lee was not incensed, she was in deep thought. Only to herself would she admit that Miranda would be better off, no matter what man replaced her husband. And, she had to chuckle to herself. Alexander had pulled off quite a coup. She could not fault him for using his PLW stock to gain land for a business she could see would be very profitable in the growing city. Nor could she really fault Lillian McHenry. After the initial shock of Alexander bringing the woman to the PLW Line board meeting and making his stunning announcement, the woman had amazed her. Because she had Alexander's agenda and background papers, she was well versed in the business matters that had to be discussed, but did not impose herself unduly. Even Otis, who felt he had somehow been tricked, began to answer her intelligent questions with respectful answers.

But of all the points Miranda made, Liberty's mind locked out one. Harridan or not, she would handle Mick E. Lee as she saw fit. She pulled pen and paper toward her as her first course of action. She had never fought an enemy unless it was face to face.

Tracey was on time for the Tuesday afternoon appointment, but puzzled by the letter the school had received.

Liberty had been all sweetness in her apology, wanting it clearly known that she had not turned down the interview completely, but only for that certain Tuesday. It had dawned on her later that her letter had not stated such and she wished a new interview, that Tuesday, if possible.

The school had been delighted, but not Tracey. She sensed that she was not going to interview as much as be interviewed about a certain luncheon with a certain grandson. But she had nothing to hide, so she went with no fear.

Liberty could not help herself. She looked across her desk at the girl steadily, almost insultingly.

"It seems like such an enormous task for such a young school girl."

"Everyone has made it quite easy by being very helpful, Mrs. Lee."

"I shall try to do the same," she said coldly. "I know how people love to gossip, so I shall probably have to spend most of the time correcting the errors of others."

Tracey looked at her calmly and would not back off. "I have been careful, Mrs. Lee, not to let personality conflicts get in the way of historical information. Information, Mrs. Lee, about this city and not the building of the railroad or the Herbert and Chinese farms."

"And why did you bring up those last two points?"

"Didn't you bring me hear to pick my brain on what I might know of them and what my aunt and your son are doing with the old L. Lee Produce Company?"

"Hardly!" she snarled. "What gave you such a notion?"

"Perhaps I was mixing apples and oranges. I was recalling Mr. Crocker's story of how they felt they had pulled a fast one on you with your Sacramento Line and how they ended up with egg on their faces.''

''Charley Crocker repembers that?'' Liberty suddenly laughed. ''Oh, those were the good old days, locking horns with those vipers.''

''I'm sorry I mixed the past with the present,'' Tracey temporized. ''I would like to start again, as I have done on the other interviews.''

A scowl crossed Liberty's face, a harsh, belligerent scowl, she must not deceive herself into thinking that she was dealing with a naive mind. If she granted this request, how could she bring it back to the topic of Mick? But she had to wave the girl on or lose this golden opportunity. An opportunity to make this child see that she was totally wrong for her grandson.

To her amazement she found Tracey remarkably prepared for the session. Her questions were intelligent and based upon painstaking historical research. Liberty found herself expanding, rather than holding back on her answers. She forgot that it was Tracey sitting there, for Tracey had suddenly become what Liberty had not expected. This was not a school girl on a school assignment. This was a young lady who knew how to probe at a subject until it was wrung dry of essential facts.

After two hours they stared at each other for some time, and Tracey saw in Liberty's eyes hatred, bitterness, confusion and awareness of what she had revealed.

''It will take me a couple of days to write up the report,'' Tracey said quietly. ''If I get it to you by Friday, might I have it back by class time on Monday?''

''Back?'' Liberty blinked in confusion.

''I don't turn in my report until I let the subject have a chance to read it and edit out what they do not agree with,'' she explained.

Liberty's brain raced. ''Did I say something that you feel I might wish to retract?''

''A couple of points,'' Tracey said as a scholar and not in judgement, ''on the building of this house and your relationship with the Tedder family. As Mr. Nathan Tedder built my Aunt Lillian's house, I didn't fear making him one of the first people to interview on this assignment. He certainly knows the history of most every building in the city."

"I am sure," Liberty gulped, fighting to recall what she might have said about Nathan. "But, yes, I can have it back to you by Monday."

"Thank you, Mrs. Lee. This may be my best report yet." There was true admiration in her eyes. "You certainly are a remarkable woman."

Liberty waved her away, wishing suddenly to be alone. She dared not bring up the subject of Mick at that point, or she would say the wrong things. Tracey had evoked a memory that she feared she might have let slip out.

She sat, letting the memory drift back, Nathan Tedder's youthful craftiness in wanting to kiss her goodnight, and his youthful gentleness vanishing. She could still feel his mouth clinging to her fiercely, fighting for possession, and his big hands, about her waist, like hoops of steel. She had known it was wrong and tried to push him away. He had merely tightened his grip as she hammered away at his shoulders with her fists and slowly, inexorably, felt herself being bent backwards.

Then the words. The words that had haunted her ever afterward and yet always thrilled her.

"I've been with no other," had been his urgent whisper. "Be my teacher."

Now, as then, she trembled, recalling his lowered face to her breasts and sensing his erection as it pressed hard against her groin. Even though it had been near incestuous she had taken his virginal maleness to dispel her own loneliness.

Suddenly, Liberty buried her head in her arms on the desk and wept bitterly. She had failed with Tracey Whiteside, even though the girl had unwittingly made her face a harsh truth. Her incestuous feeling for Mick was the same as it had been for Nathan Tedder. She would not be happy until her grandson uttered the same urgent plea—'Be my teacher.' And she suddenly feared Tracey as she had never feared any other female in life. That she could finally admit her lust for Mick amazed her and gave her a curious thrill. Was it because she was only seeing him as an image of Dan O'Lee? She pushed that aside.

She raised her head and laughed out loud, savoring a new thought warmly and tenderly. She felt liberated, joyous and full of fire.

Tracey had reminded her of the real challenges she had faced in life and won. She was stagnant. She lived in a body that should have died in Panama of yellow fever and came back to a boring round of rituals.

She needed a real challenge to sink her teeth into. Tracey was that challenge and, she thought, a formidable foe. She would allow the girl full rein to be around her grandson and then prove that she was still the ultimate winner when she stakes were high.

Friday morning was dull and gray as Mick obeyed his grandmother and went to answer the door chimes of her mansion. His mood had been somber at being told to show up for breakfast. He had been living in a state of tension for the past week and a half. He had suffered when he'd heard the servant gossip about his Aunt Miranda's fight with his grandmother. Then, to hear that she had granted an interview with Tracey had nearly overcome him with curiosity. Wednesday and Thursday he had been driven to the near-panic state of storming Lillian's house and demanding from Tracey what had transpired. Then, almost as an aside, his father had informed him at the Thursday night dinner table that his grandmother had requested him to have breakfast with her the next morning.

Never had he spent such a sleepless, fretful night. He went over in his mind every tirade his grandmother might be able to throw at him. He had built up an arsenal of words to throw back at her and he was forced to sit with his powder untindered.

Still, he was annoyed that he was sent from the breakfast table to play butler when she had ample servants.

"Yes," he growled, throwing open the door, and suddenly it was like a sun-drenched day. "What are you doing here?"

"I might ask you the same question," Tracey laughed,

letting down her umbrella and stepping into the foyer. "I had an early appointment with your grandmother to drop off my report before school."

"Who is it?" Liberty demanded, storming out of the dining room, still clad in her morning robe. "Oh, Miss Whiteside, I had forgotten you were coming."

A look passed between the two women and Liberty instantly realized she had just lost round one. Tracey saw the lie and recorded it in her keen young mind.

"I have the report," she said, handing Liberty a folder.

Liberty weighed it in her hand, as though having expected a rather thick manuscript, even though she had done very careful detective work in the last two days to learn Tracey's mode of operation with the others. "As brief as this?"

"I've learned to keep my reports concise, Mrs. Lee."

"Then I see no reason to keep you waiting until Monday. I can read this, at once, over a cup of coffee. Mick, as you know Miss Whiteside, why not help with her assignment. She was given architectural information about the house from Nathan Tedder. But as it was actually built by his grandfather, Howard Tedder, she might like to see the real thing. I will be in the dining room reading."

"What is she up to?" Tracey whispered.

"I wish I knew," Mick said quietly. Turning, he started for the stairs that seemed to float unsupported in space. "But for the moment, I don't care. How grand it is to see you and how much I have missed you."

Tracey followed, feeling foolish, as she stared up at the slim, handsome figure going before her. She, too, had missed him and never realized how much until that moment.

"I hate to correct her," he said over his shoulder, "but it was Nazareth Tedder, and not his father, who built the house."

"I was aware of that and did not want to correct her either. Have you heard the story of the building of the Crocker mansion?"

"I don't believe so."

"Mr. Crocker thought he had full title to all his land and only learned after they started to build the mansion that a house on a lot set back off the street was owned by a Chinese undertaker. The man refused to see why he should sell to Mr. Crocker and built a home on his lot. In a fit of pique he ordered Mr. Tedder to build a 40-foot high fence around the Chinaman's house."

"Come on," he said. "That can't be the end of the story. How did he and his family get in and out?"

"That I won't reveal until we can meet again."

"Then, I hope it is very soon."

He leaned forward suddenly and kissed her full on the lips.

"That's to seal the bargain on our meeting again," he quavered, "and because I suddenly wanted to do that very much."

"I liked it," she stammered in surprise. "Now, I think you had better show me the rest of the house."

As he guided her through the vast rooms, Tracey listened to his narrative with only a portion of her brain; the rest was fighting for awareness of what was happening to her. Her will power was vanishing and her eyes were big with wonderment at the fires his touch was stirring. As much as she desired to be with him, she suddenly feared his closeness.

Never before had she been aware of his male aroma. Now it was heady and mystical, a memory she had to fight to recall. It had not been from Mick before. His had always been the wholesome, scrubbed, schoolboy scent. This odor was sweet, pungent and warmly enticing. And when a name came to mind associated with the aroma she tingled and shivered.

On her own she had gone into the Barbary Coast on a Tuesday afternoon to interview Johnny Lord. It was the outside-the-school assignment for that day.

In four years she had almost forgotten what a remarkably handsome man he was—and even more so with age. His hair was now a lustrous salt-and-pepper. The lines of age on his face added to the appeal of the sparkling eyes and chiseled features.

And as they talked, the gleam in his eye growing dangerous, she had first been aware of his scent. It was the same scent she now detected emanating from Mick. A natural instinct, older than man, told her what it was. It was the scent the male kingdom transmitted to the female kingdom as a mating call.

Mick, as is the case with most males, was unaware of the scent he was discharging. He was only aware that once again she was causing a mental and physical arousal. A frightening arousal, in that he had lost control. Always before he had been able to bring it within bounds. But this was like the first earthquake he had experienced while sleeping in his grandmother's house. A shock would come, shaking his bed violently and then diminish; only to be followed by a series of tremors and then another jolting shock.

"I so desire to kiss you again," he murmured.

Tracey sensed that another kiss might increase her temperature to the point that she would burst into flame. But never had she desired anything so much.

She turned to him, rising on tiptoe, and offered her lips. His arms tenderly stole about her waist and their lips came slowly and lovingly together. Clinging in mutual warmth and trembling unsureness.

Shivering and quaking, half-fainting, they stood clutching each other desperately as their individual juices flowed for the first time.

Slowly they backed from each other, strangely aware that this sexual scene had been without sex and yet utterly fulfilling and ultimate in release.

They looked at each other deeply as though they had created something remarkable and unique, which revealed all of the secret marvels that lay ahead for them.

"I don't think . . ."

"I know . . ."

"Was it only . . ."

"In our mind?"

He grinned. "And elsewhere."

"It was so . . ."

"Golden . . ."

"I shall never forget . . ."

"Nor I . . ."

"Tracey . . ."

"Mick . . ."

"We can no longer be friends."

"I know."

"God, I can't stop my heart beating. My skin feels like someone was sticking it with a million pins."

"Hold me—I feel the same."

"Oh, Tracey, I've got to put into words what this means to me. I love . . . you . . . I Love you . . . I LOVE YOU!"

"If the feeling I have is love, Mick, then I could die very happy at this very moment."

"Don't you dare," he warned. "For I suddenly want something in life I thought I would never want. I've beat around the bush, but never said I rather feared marriage as something hateful. But it wouldn't be hateful for us, Tracey. Oh, God, it would be the most beautiful thing in the world. I've got college, of course, and a career to start—" He stopped short on a gasp. "You will wait for me, won't you?"

"Don't be silly. Of course I will, forever if need be."

"Well," he said, "it won't be forever and we'll have our summers together. Oh, God, I have never felt so good in my whole life."

"Hello, you two!" Liberty called up the stairs. "I have quite finished and Miss Whiteside's school hour is near."

"Oh, dear," Tracey cried, rushing down the stairs.

"I must commend you," Liberty beamed, handing her the papers. "I have corrected nothing and find it excellent work. You might consider writing as a career, my dear."

"Thank you," Tracey stammered. "Sorry I must run, but thank you again."

Liberty was impressed as she saw her out, even to the point of softening her hatred toward her. Then as she slowly turned she caught the full image of Mick descending the stairs, grinning sheepishly. He was not aware, but Liberty was instantly aware of the moisture at his crotch.

She began to shake with rage. "I need not ask what you were doing with that little slut," she said accusingly. "But

I can hardly blame a girl that has been raised by a madam in a whorehouse.''

''Nothing happened,'' he said innocently. ''Only a little kiss.''

''Your pants expose that lie,'' she stormed. ''You shall go home at once and pack.''

''I don't wish to pack, Grandmother. I intend to stay here the summer to get to know Tracey better. As I have decided she is to be my wife, I want to get to know her very well.''

''As long as I live she shall never be your wife,'' Liberty said quietly.

Mick said coolly, ''You are an old lady and can't last forever. I can always wait.''

Liberty turned, and she saw nothing but Dan O'Lee. And memory returned. Dan O'Lee had also taken a Chinese whore as his mistress and she had learned to hate him. And that long-ago anger now was centered upon her grandson. She wanted him out of her sight and out of her mind for the present and thought of the perfect ally to help her.

Lillian sank back in her chair, her face ashen, her mouth working to shape words that never came out.

''Marry?'' she finally bellowed, then her voice broke. ''Liberty . . . she is but a sixteen year old child. I don't desire marriage for her . . . for a few years, yet. For the love of God, I have tried to keep her separate from this house and raise her as a lady.''

Gloomily, Liberty shook her head in agreement.

''I think you have done that,'' she said.

''I am sick, tired and growing old, Lillian. Your one meeting on the PLW board should have told you plenty. We, as women, are surrounded by ineffectual men. I have never said you were a bad business woman, just in a bad business. If I am to leave anything, I want it left in strong male hands. I want Mick well schooled and trained for that day.''

''I cannot fault you on that wish,'' Lillian whispered.

"And to put your mind at ease, I also have dreams for Tracey that do not include your grandson."

"Thank you," Liberty said heavily, "that is all I wished to hear. I think, before Mick enters college this fall, a European tour would be good for his education."

Lillian thought a moment. When such was the case with two young lovers it was fatal to make one think they had been spurned. "I want to handle Tracey in a like manner. In the meeting, Captain Whiteside said he was taking his family on the 'Carrie' on its next trip to South America. May I tell him that you agreed to have Tracey to go along to help Mrs. Whiteside with the children?"

Liberty bent her head back a little, hesitating. Lillian had pulled off a clever check-mate, whether intended or not. She could hardly refuse, but it was putting Otis in a touchy position. She finally nodded, it being Otis's problem, after all.

"While I am here," Liberty said, "might I ask after Alexander?"

"He is doing well," she said simply.

She hesitated. "He is special to me, Lillian. If he appears to falter, let me know."

Lillian nodded, even as her mind began to plot. Liberty owed her for helping break up Tracey and Mick. She would never let her forget this day. But, oddly, she began to wonder if she just might rue it. She had set her heart on Alexander Lee for Tracey, but was she being foolish in standing in the way of young love?

Chapter 15

"It's horribly unfair," Tracey flared, pacing the executive office of the *Chronicle*. "Why should the publisher in New York even raise the question of my gender?"

Carl Howard, who was now the managing editor, shrugged the question off to Daniel Fetterson, who was still publisher.

"They are just more comfortable with male novelists," he said weakly.

"Comfortable?" she sneered, making two more turns in front of the conference table at which they sat, kicking the flare of her hobbled skirt behind her with each turn.

"I know I should not be blaming you two, but it was your prodding that made me study writing in school. To be candid, the only time my European instructors brought up my sex was when they sought my favors."

Carl Howard could fully understand that statement. Six years away from San Franscico had transformed her from an energetic child into a complete lady. She was polished, cultured, talented and beneath the tightly fitted dress-suit was a body that made him wish he was ten years younger.

"And," she stormed on, "when they questioned my writing ability it was to compare it with the Brontë sisters. In Europe they are well aware that they have been dead for nearly fifty years. I question if New York is even aware that they ever lived."

Howard laughed. "And there are some in the literary world who would still like to believe that Harriet Beecher Stowe was a man."

"Tracey," Fetterson wheezed, "why let it upset you?"

Her clear blue eyes snapped, a world of reasons ready to spring from her tongue, but not for their ears. For them she would keep it professional.

"Gentlemen, I am twenty-two years old. Because I was encouraged in school to further my literary training, I remained in Paris for two additional years." She laughed bitterly. "Those editors would not publish me because my French was not pure enough. The English would not publish me because my subject matter was America. Now, New York questions my gender. I'm beginning to doubt my talents, if any."

Gloomily, Fetterson shook his head.

"We would not lie to save your pride," he said. "The chapters I've read are of high caliber, but all of your characters seem to lack a compassion for and understanding of living."

"I am back in the classroom," she laughed, brittle and crips. "How often I have heard that phrase. 'Tracey you are an excellent historian of the manners and customs, but history is also people.' Many times, to be candid, I thought it was a ploy on the part of that professor to add another virgin to his celebrated list. Well, from you two I can accept that fact as truth, without doubt of your motives. Why don't we just toss that manuscript into the dust bin and I'll tackle something totally different."

"That is precisely what you will not do, Tracey!" Carl Howard stormed. "The work, which I have read every last sentence, is masterful; except for the points raised by Mr. Fetterson. Put it away! Take up a new project! But, good Lord girl, don't ever throw away a thing you have put upon paper. Some day you will be prepared to revise it."

It helped, but it didn't lift her spirits. She marched out of the office, depressed. After six years of living abroad, San Francisco seemed provincial. Home three months and she felt like a caged animal.

Her palate found Clara's food starchy and heavy. The theater offerings were worse than those put on by third-rate companies in Montmarte. And after having forced herself to like wine, she found everything locally available to taste like vinegar.

"You've just become a little snob," she said, without realizing she had said it aloud.

"But such a pretty one," a voice said behind her.

She blanched, realizing that not only had she spoken aloud, but she had spoken in French and the soft male voice had responded in French.

"My thought was my own, Monsieur," she said crisply, without turning. She had learned how to handle those Frenchmen who lay in wait for every pretty young girl.

"But you shouldn't exclude an old friend," he said in English.

That caused her to turn and stare in surprise at the tall, impressive man who also stood waiting for the elevator.

"Eric?" she whispered. "It can't be you. I thought you were still in Austria."

The gleam of teeth, white against the golden skin, mocked her, while the eyes continued to devour her delectable figure.

"I have been home almost a year," he said, "setting up my practice. Perhaps I should say setting up an office in which to sit. Doctor Eric Larson seems caught between his two worlds. I treated more patients in a day in Austria than I have here in almost a year. The Chinese fear I am too modern and the occidentals take one look at my eyes and fear I shall stick them with pins."

"I know some of that feeling." Then she frowned. "Aunt Lillian didn't mention you had returned."

"Not surprising," he said, and left the thought dangling as the elevator door opened and they were confronted with other passengers and an operator. "I was on my way to lunch, Tracey. If you have no plans, I would love to have you join me."

"And I would love nothing more," she sighed. "I was facing a rather bleak afternoon. Aunt Lillian's habits have certainly changed since I've been gone."

"Perhaps," he said cautiously in French, "that is a luncheon topic."

Tracey compressed her lips, aware that Eric's concern was not ill-founded. Lillian and Johnny Lord were now troubled by something far worse than the Vigilantes. Abe

Ruef had been able to consolidate his political power to the point of controlling Mayor Eugene Schmitz and getting Mortimer Stern replaced in the police department.

"Why does she keep the business going?" Tracey asked, when they were seated at a back table in a little side street restrauant.

"What else does she know?" He sighed and started again. "The money she has made handling my affairs she has very wisely invested. She wants to be as rich as Liberty Lee and with the strings Liberty has pulled in Congress the last couple of years that will never be. Even in Austria the reports of The Spanish-American War quoted her more than the Secretary of State. When the battleship *Oregon* had to sail 13,000 miles to Cuba from San Francisco, when her canal would have made it only a 4,600 mile sail, she made her point. Tracey, this is a new century. Steam is replacing sail on the ocean and on land. I have even seen experimental models of horseless carriages run by steam. Liberty is getting old, but Lillian is young enough still to want to be in on all of what is new and have enough money that people will no longer think of her as a, a . . ."

"Madam?" Tracey sighed, knowing it might take years before local opinion would ever forget that.

"She no longer needs that business," confessed Eric. "Last month her commission on handling my affairs with Alex Lee was equal to what her house made. And frankly, there is the bone of contention between us, Tracey. Since my return she has acted as though I have no business asking questions about my own affairs. I have not needed the money, so have avoided her. But a climax is coming. Alexander Lee, feeling some sort of strain in working with her, has approached me to buy me out of the farm and the land."

Tracey's slender hands stopped midway through tidying her hair, and slowly her eyes came up to meet Eric's.

"I am the reason for that strain, Eric. Four years ago, when Aunt Lillian came to Paris for my graduation, she was bubbling with excitement. Her own excitement, I must say. With my schooling over she all but had me engaged and married to Alexander Lee. I was shocked and mortified and the news probably pushed me to announce that I wanted two more years of study. I like the man, but not as a partner for life.''

An odd look came over Eric's face, worried, yet guarded. ''Were you aware that the man was married about four years ago? I got an announcement some six months later in Austria.''

''He was married while she was in Europe with me that summer, but she didn't find out until her return. You may not recall, but it was one of Lillian's girls, Luann, that he married. I gather that it nearly sent Mrs. Lee into final shock, but it was Lillian who was nearly unhinged. In cables and letters she castigated me for ruining her great plans for the future and for allowing Luann to come in and steal the man away from me. I wasn't even aware he was supposed to be mine for the stealing.''

''Has she dropped the matter since your return?'' he asked in a tight voice.

''No,'' she said darkly. ''As I started to say, her life style has changed. Clara and Henry had been married for about five years, you know, and no longer live in the house. Clara comes in to oversee her staff and leaves at the end of the dinner hour. Henry leaves with her and Aunt Lillian stays up until all hours. It's not my business, but she lets clients stay until all hours, as well. I'm worried, Eric. She never used to drink a great deal and now she drinks herself into oblivion each night and then sleeps through the whole day. When we have had time together it has been the same song and dance. She will never let me forget that I ruined my chances to become Mrs. Alexander Grace Wells Lee.''

''What are you chances of becoming a different Mrs. Lee?'' he asked unexpectedly.

She could only gasp.

''In this case,'' he said softly, ''it was not the wisdom of my ancient father helping me to see such a possibility. Ever since Liberty opened her purse strings to gain admission for Mick to Eton, I have been honored to be in communication with him. Through his Uncle Alex he learned of my medical career and inquired if medicine should be his goal. Such an answer I could not give at once, but we kept up the correspondence. Because he turned homesick, his letters also turned heartsick. Thus it was I learned of you.''

Letters—Tracey's stomach lurched at the thought. ''That must have been some time ago. I have never, ever, received a letter from him.''

''That is the trouble with young boys with their first love. I was the same. In love with the idea of love and not love itself. Once away from it, with the world opening quickly, it became a shadowed memory and then a puff to vanish forever.''

''Ours was not consummated,'' said Tracey, deciding that in this, she would have to trust Eric. ''It was an emotional experience, but I am still a virgin.''

''I've never doubted that,'' returned Eric dryly, although the letters from Mick had been so explicit that one had nearly driven the young medical student to self-indulgence. But as an individual he now desired certain information for himself. ''However, I am still in communication with Mick. I was able to get him into my medical school in Austria. Shall I mention your return home, or not?''

''I think not,'' said Tracey reflectively, ''I'd prefer you to say nothing of me. It was a youthful thing that I have outgrown.''

''As you wish,'' Eric said, and for the first time his mouth twisted into a wry smile. ''Do you miss certain aspects of Europe, as I? Oh, the music and opera in Vienna I shall always miss.''

Tracey laughed. For the first time in three months it sounded like sleigh bells. ''That was the reason for my statement by the elevator. I've become snobbish because of all that was available in Paris.''

''But, my dear young lady, I have uncovered many cultural aspect to compensate. One such is the Chinese theatre here. It does not matter that you do no speak Chinese. I will translate in French and the rest of the audience will be awed. Will you do me the honor of letting me escort you?''

There followed a few uncomfortable moments, in which neither spoke, and each wondered about starting this new friendship.

Tracey needed it to ease the tension of the past few months. As a graduate student, she had accepted the theatre and dinner invitations of gentlemen, because she had acquired a reputation of being a stunning companion and nothing more. Therefore, she determined, that the acceptance of this invitation would be quite proper.

Eric's experience in Austria had been somewhat different. Because of his unusual mixture of Chinese and Norwegian he was the rarity in Austria. He had to curtail his social life to accomplish his studies. Women sought him constantly. When he went to the opera and dinner, he was well aware of what womanly charms were in store for him.

Returning to America he had reasoned that he would also be returning to the rooms of Kai Soong and a reunion with Lillian.

The rooms were no more, the furniture in a warehouse and the space used by Clara for storage of fruits and vegetables.

Nor was there room for him in Lillian's life. She was cool, aloof, businesslike and almost curt with him as a business associate. He was well aware of her accomplishments with his assets while he had been gone, but he still had to resent her subtle attitude that without her he would be penniless.

Nor was there room for her in his sexual life. In the decade that he had been away she had become a character from his memory: the hard, bitter madams who would come to haggle with Kai Soong. He had determined on his first meeting with Lillian that he would not let her haggle with him.

Just as he had determined on seeing Tracey by the elevator door, that this was a woman he would fight to get into his bed.

Lillian sat in a housecoat at her private bar and lit a cigarette, a practice one of the new girls had taught her. It was a habit she had liked at once. It made the drinks throughout the evening seem so much more enjoyable. She had acquired many ways to make the evenings that she had come to detest bearable. To the chagrin of many she had taken up gambling with the clients, keeping the tables open and dealing all night if she was winning. And now, if a man wanted to pay her enough under the table, she might let him stay all night.

She started to take another sip of her bourbon and put it down hearing the hallway door open.

"Tracey," she called, "I'm still up!"

There was nothing Tracey could do. This ritual had been going on for eighteen months, ever since the first night she had gone to the Chinese Theatre with Eric Larson. She had learned to take the offensive and get to bed quickly.

"I smell smoke, Aunt Lillian," she said, coming into the room and taking off her opera cape.

"Really?" Lillian sneered, trailing twin streamers of smoke through her exquisite nostrils. "I think I like the habit."

"It's disgusting."

"No more so than your present habit," Lillian said cruelly.

"What habit?"

"Running all about town with a Chinaman at all hours of the night."

"What we do is quite innocent. He's a fascinating man, and we have many things in common."

"I've spent a small fortune preparing you for a proper marriage and you damage your chances every time you are seen with him."

"Do I detect jealousy? She laughed. "That's it, isn't it, Aunt Lillian. You were the first to have him and now you resent anyone else who goes out with him."

"How dare he tell you such a thing."

"He's too much of a gentleman to even suggest such a thing."

Lillian ground out her cigarette. "Then how dare *you* suggest it?"

"Oh, really, Lillian! It's been common gossip in this house for years. Your little chippies, though, can't quite understand me. Any one of them would pay him to get him into their bed.''

Lillian was aghast. ''Lillian? Chippies? How do you know they have such thoughts?''

Tracey sank into a chair, studying the haggard face apprehensively. ''I will soon be twenty-four and I guess the Lillian, without Aunt, slipped out because you are a topic of conversation between Eric and me a great deal of the time. As well, a topic of conversation in this house between Clara and the girls.''

''No matter your age,'' Lillian demanded. ''Why are you associating with them?''

''Sometimes it can't be helped. When you lie abed all day they go to Clara and Clara comes to me. It's easier to settle their squabbles than wake you and have to put up with your acid tongue. I wish you would let me know what is troubling you. You have Eric greatly concerned. He never gets a chance to talk with you and some things have him puzzled.''

''You can go to bed now, Tracey,'' Lillian said calmly. ''I do not appreciate your sticking your nose into the affairs of this house or into Eric's trust.''

''Good night, Aunt Lillian,'' Tracey said brusquely.

After Tracey's departure, she poured another bourbon, only to let it sit, tormented by the tensions she dared not expose to anyone.

Far off, she heard the peal of the front door chimes. It was a puzzlement. No one could get through the main gate without the gatekeeper giving them entrance, especially at this hour of the morning. She went to the window and was surprised to find that it had been snowing. Tracey had extinguished the porch light on returning and all Lillian could make out was a huddled mass awaiting entry.

She peered toward the front gate, to see if a carriage was waiting, but the snow was like a curtain her eyes could not penetrate. She wracked her brain trying to recall if there were any late staying guests, but her bourbon-fogged mind could remember little of the whole evening.

She opened the sash and gasped at the rush of fresh cold air. ''Just a minute, Charley! I'll be right down.''

She cursed Big John's replacement all the way down the curving stairs to the foyer. Even though Big John had trained his replacement before his death, this burly man was all brawn and no brains. He could not, or would not think for himself.

"When was it I said I was going to replace him?" she asked herself as she slid back the lock and opened the door a crack. A big foot was thrust into the opening and then a stout shoulder rammed into the panel. The force sent Lillian sprawling.

Then the man was inside, grinning a toothless grin, the melting snow making streaks down his dirty face and dew dropping in the scraggly gray beard. She did not recognize the filthy hulk in the great coat and hat so misshapen it could no longer be called a hat.

"Lillian . . . sister—" he began.

She got up suddenly, then drew back.

"How did you get onto this property, Karl Whiteside?"

"Snuck right in when that carriage entered. Hid in the bushes until it made its exit and the gate man went back to bed. Didn't have him twelve years ago, did yah?"

"What are you doing here?" she demanded, seeing no reason to answer his question.

"That's a long story," he declared, wagging his big head. "But it can wait, seeing as how I'm going to be staying with you for some little time."

"That's impossible," she scoffed. "I have no extra rooms here."

"Then you best make one," he said gruffly. "I feel you really owe me this time, Lillian."

Perhaps, Lillian reflected, if I talk gently and humor him . . .

"That makes it sound like a long story," she murmured, "and makes me think I am going to need a drink. I have a bar in my apartment."

"Now, that's more like it. I haven't had a drink since Los Angeles. Damn undertaker down there charged me forty bucks to bury Maw. I only left Boston with fifty after getting the wire that she was dying."

Lillian had to stop on the stairs and grab the rail for support. ‘‘Momma's dead?’’

‘‘No thanks to you,’’ he said with a crafty grin. ‘‘Thought sure that with your money you'd have tried to find her.’’

She stood weak and defenseless against the charge. Years ago it had crossed her mind to try and do something, but a million things had gotten in the way. Then, when it would come to mind again she would feel guilty and in the past few years she had learned how to put guilt out of her mind, as well.

‘‘And then, in Los Angeles,’’ he continued, ‘‘I found out what a sap you had made of me. I needed work to get back home and heard of a company that needed sailors. They didn't like my looks, but while I was waiting I got something better than a job. On the counter they had a nice little brochure about the company—how nice of them to list the members of the Board of Directors. You lying baggage. If Otis Whiteside denied you as a sister before, then how the hell are you reaping big money as one of them directors?’’

Lillian was to the landing and stopped. No words, she might utter, would ever make him understand.

‘‘I am not reaping any big money,’’ she sighed. ‘‘As a matter of fact, I stay awake at night worrying myself sick over the money that I owe.’’

‘‘You're not going to lie to me again,’’ he growled, reaching out and grabbing her arm in his big hand. ‘‘I plan on being just as rich as the two of you from now on. Don't you think I been asking me some questions? You don't lay awake worrying over money when you waste it sending Tracey off to Europe for school. Hell, she should be in this house helping us to make money. That's my first order! Get her back here to get her butt to work.’’

She could at least be thankful that his information was wrong on Tracey, but she knew she had been wrong. She never should have let him come up to this floor. Below, she could have led him into the casino bar, where she had a derringer hidden. At the top of the stairs she was helpless and without any help that could come to her aide.

A scream would only bring Tracey and in no way did she want him to see his daughter.

The struggle to free herself went on in silence. Her free hand came up, reaching for his eyes, but he twisted aside, and her nails dug into scraggly beard hair that did not hurt him. He merely moved until he had both hands captured.

"Ain't no use fighting," he chuckled. "I'm here to stay, so let's go have that drink."

"You win," she murmured, thinking of another ploy. It would be morning soon. If she could just keep him drinking long enough Henry and Clara would arrive and Clara always came to see if she was still awake or asleep.

He stiffened suddenly, hearing the light patter of feet in the hall. Tracey came around the corner of the wing and stood there looking at them, her face suddenly as pale as death.

"Yet another lie . . ." he mumbled.

"Hardly. She has been back from school for some time. So, now that we are gathered . . . get your damn hands off me," she added coldly.

"Tracey—" he said heavily, but only released one of Lillian's wrists. "You really turned out to be quite a looker. Man, you will make us a small fortune."

"Fortune?" Tracey asked in confusion.

"Your *father*," Lillian sneered, "has come back to cut himself in on what he thinks is big money. For those few brief he spent with your mother, he now feels he has the male Whiteside right to put you to work in this house as one of the girls."

"And what a dilly you will make," he grinned. "Hey, come here! Ain't you got a hug and kiss for your ole paw?"

Tracey hesitated, her mind reeling. Like Lillian she was aware that there was no help about and no weapon near at hand. And like Lillian she tried for a stall.

"I'm twenty-four nearly," she said, as though he might just have forgotten. "I don't even hug and kiss Aunt Lillian anymore."

"I said get your ass over here, Miss Smart-pants," he

stormed. "You both better get it through your pea-brain female heads that I am boss around here from now on!"

Tracey walked slowly forward, seeing the terror spring into Lillian's eyes. She tried to control her own fright, measuring what she might be able to do against the man. Oddly she did not look on him as her father, but as a stranger there to do them harm. Therefore, when she stood before him, she stood erect and defiant.

"You can forget the hug and kiss," he sneered. "I've decided to see how much you are really worth."

Without warning his free hand closed over the collar of the silk nightdress. She heard the sound of tearing cloth and felt the night air cool upon her skin, without once taking her eyes from his. For him to see her nude did not shame her, but the look in his eyes sent her blood as cold as death. If she did not resist at that very moment, then she was about to be raped by her own father.

She took in three deep breaths, watching his eyes drop lustfully to the rise and fall of her firm young breasts. Then she jutted out both arms and caught him square in the chest.

It took him by surprise and knocked him off balance. When he tried to regain his footing, his right foot stepped on nothingness and jarred down to the first step of the landing. The bulk of the great coat and his own weight pulled him backward into a fall.

But the scream was not his. Tracey had not taken into consideration that he still held firmly to Lillian's wrist. Lillian was being pulled right after him.

Tracey was not in a good position to reach out and grab onto Lillian, nor was there time. The momentum of their combined weight was like a rock tumbling down a snow covered hill. With each step they were rolling at a faster rate, their bodies crashing into each other, bouncing off the stairwall, cracking and splintering railing posts and leaving a trail of blood in their wake.

Tracey stood stunned and horrified. Even after the two bodies came to rest in the foyer their screams and cries seemed to echo forever.

Ever after, she would never be able to recall how she

got down to them on her trembling legs. The trail of blood led to a twisted heap in a great coat. One look at the glazed eyes and she turned away.

Lillian's entire body was racked with pain. Tracey could see her throat quiver with the wild, sobbing of death gasps.

"Don't move," she said, swallowing hard to control her own panic. "I'm going for help."

She started for the door and turned back, a rash moment returning. She was nearly nude and it was snowing outside. Just as she determined that she would have to go back to her room and dress, she looked up.

Lining the railing of the second and third floor of the girls' wing was a gallery of faces that ran from curious to total fright. Here, at least, was a form of help.

"Margaret—" she began. It was barely a whisper, but in that vast cubicle it seemed louder than the screams that had tumbled them from their beds.

"What's happened?" the girl stammered.

Tracey took a deep breath. "An accident. I'm going to need help."

"Not from us," Nadine shrilled, locking her arm through that of the man who stood by her side with a towel held about his waist. "About time that drunken old bitch got her come-uppance. Look at that, girls. The old dame got caught turning a trick after we were in bed."

There were times, Clara had always said, when Tracey could mimic Lillian's authoritative manner to a fault. It reared up now, but even more brazen and angry.

"To your room, Nadine," she said defiantly. "And if your gentleman caller doesn't want to answer police questions he'll be gone in five minutes. Margaret, get dressed! I want you to go for Mr. Henry and Miss Clara. Clara is to come here and Henry is to go for Dr. Larson. Sue Ann, when you get dressed I want you to go for Johnny Lord. Ask him to go to the police for me. That will give your gentlemen time to get dressed and depart. Lolly, will you throw me down a wrap. No one ogles in this house unless they pay for it. Now, four of you bring me down a mattress. We can at least make Miss Lily comfortable until the doctor gets here. The rest of you, get lost!"

Within seconds, a night wrapper came floating down. Quickly putting it on, she knelt down beside Lillian.

The woman twisted silently, her face purple from lack of breath, so that Tracey was forced to open her jaw and pull her tongue out of her throat; something she had seen Eric do when a man choked in a restaurant one night. It was then that Lillian's eyes opened, and she took a deep breath through bruised and swollen lips.

"Over," she muttered, the last syllable shuddering up from her throat.

"Hush!" Tracey soothed.

"Over," she repeated. "I'm ready to die because I'm ruined." Then she lapsed into a coma.

Tracey put it out of her mind, as it came to bear on a much more pressing thought. She remembered suddenly, blindingly, that she had just killed her own father. In that moment she was not weighed down with any sense of mortal sin. She felt nothing for the man. Nothing.

For Johnny Lord it was *déjà vu*. The second such incident of self-defense in the House of Lily in twelve years.

But the circumstances he could see were quite different, once he had arrived.

"Tracey?"

She turned, with a stateliness totally out of keeping with the scene. Once Eric had arrived, because his new house was only three blocks away, she had been able to get out of the gaudy wrapper and into a dress of her own. Still there was something awful in her quietness.

"Thank you for coming, Uncle Johnny," she said, her voice clear and colorless. "Eric Larson has given me his first finding on Aunt Lillian. He has her in the casino, ironically on a crap table. Both hips and both legs have been broken and badly shattered. He will do what he can, but fears that it may be a long time, if ever, before she can walk again."

"How did it?" he whispered. "Sue Ann was so confusing."

"My father's dead. I pushed him down the stairs and he took Lillian with him."

"Wait," he said, his mind off on an oblique from what Sue Ann had said. "I wasn't even aware you were back in town. I was just told there'd been an accident. Let's get this straight before Fairchild gets here."

There was no time. An ashen-faced Clara came waddling to them as though her stout legs would crumble at any given moment.

"Tracey dear," she began, "there's policemen . . ."

"Waiting for me," Tracey finished for her. "I don't want them up here. Take them into the dining room and kindly ask Henry to offer them drinks, even though it is nearly dawn. Uncle Johnny, I think I am going to need your arm and your knowledge. You'd better fill me in on Fairchild quickly."

He came to her and put his arm about her slim waist.

"I'll make it quick," he said, and together they walked slowly into the hall to let Clara get a good lead on them.

When they entered the ornate dining room, she had a thumbnail sketch of Harlan Fairchild and his association with Abe Ruef.

The chief and his six uniformed officers stood up as they entered—a little slowly perhaps as they were unwilling to make such a gesture for Johnny Lord.

Tracey looked them up and down, her blue eyes picking out the stout man in a suit who had not removed his hat. Her smile was total censure, knowing full well he had to be Harlan Fairchild, who might have been the Chief of Police, but he stood in her home. He glared back, but she gave him no quarter until his hand went up to take off the sleek derby.

Still, he wanted authority from the first. "I don't want you saying anything, lady, until you get that man out of this room."

"Mr. Lord? Why, he is the one I asked to call you here."

"No, not Johnny," he gruffed. "I deal with him almost daily. It's him, over in the corner. Don't like reporters in on investigations."

Carl Howard stood and came forward a little sheepishly. Only then did Lillian realize that he had been the man with only a towel drapped around him up on the balcony. In her panic she had seen only a sea of faces.

"Mr. Howard is hardly a reporter," she laughed. "He and Mr. Fetterson of the *Chronicle* are my literary agents and friends. I felt the need of friends at this time, as you might well imagine."

Harlan Fairchild didn't understand the term 'literary agent' and hardly understood this young lady, who kept them standing as she kept standing. Because Lillian McHenry was usually in bed or dead drunk whenever he had been by, he was used to dealing with Nadine, who he assumed was Miss Lily's assistant madam.

"Gentlemen," she went on quickly, seeing he was confused, "please be seated. Henry is here with your drinks."

"This is not a social affair," Fairchild blurted, wanting to regain authority. "We just took a dead man out of this lobby and the doctor says Miss Lily is still in a coma. This is the second time a dead man has been taken from here and I want some answers."

Tracey inclined her head the briefest of seconds. When she spoke her voice withheld her inner fear.

"As you have been chief for less than a year, please don't confuse events that are twelve years apart. That earlier event, as Mr. Howard can tell you, was my Aunt Lillian acting in self-defense." She hesitated. "She became a victim tonight, when I had to act in the same manner."

Fairchild snorted. "This 'aunt' business. Is that something you dolls call an old madam."

"I wouldn't know, sir," she said quietly. "She was born Lillian Whiteside. I am Tracey Whiteside. She is my natural aunt."

Johnny Lord relaxed. He realized now that he need not have feared her handling of them.

Fairchild was realizing the same. This young woman, even though she couldn't be bullied, was giving him nothing. He couldn't just drink his drink and go away with a dead body. One of the uniformed young men handed him a note and he smiled.

"And," he snarled, "from papers in the man's pockets, we learn that his name was also Whiteside. Karl Whiteside of Boston. Well?"

Tracey raised her eyes to the ceiling and let a grimace of pain cross her face that she didn't feel.

"My father," she sighed, "who brought me west twelve years ago and dropped me on this doorstep. Only later did I find out that he had blackmailed my aunt into taking me, in almost the same way that he and my grandfather had sold her to be a mail-order bride." Then she looked down and smiled softly to herself before continuing. "In the next few years I was not allowed to know what transpired in the rest of this house, outside Lillian's private apartment. I was schooled here and then sent to Europe to further my studies for a writing career. That brings us up to tonight."

"You are saying you haven't seen your father in those years?"

Her glance was candid, even humorous.

"Obviously not! When I came into the hall, after hearing a loud male voice raised, he was a stranger."

"And remained a stranger to you?" Fairchild said brusquely.

Tracey looked at him. Although clean-shaven he reminded her of her father.

"Not for long," she said clearly. "He made it known that he was going to come into this house and become boss, and made it very plain what role he wished for me to play in this house. May I have that parcel, Henry."

She walked to the stoic figure with a fluid grace that was designed to suggest she could play any role that she might desire. She whipped the torn nightdress from the wrapper and held it up to her body so they could not miss the point.

"My father," she said, with deadly calm, "after gloating over how much he would gain by turning me into a prostitute, put his hands on this night gown and tore it from my body. I saw his eyes. You, all being men, can never understand what I saw there. I was a second away, standing nude, from being raped by my own father.'' She paused and only then did her voice begin to break. ''I . . . pushed him away. I . . . didn't see he still had hold of Aunt Lillian. They . . . they both . . .''

''Isn't that enough?'' Carl Howard demanded, having seen pain.

Jeremiah Dinan, the officer who had given the chief the note, understood. Even though they were in a whorehouse, he saw it was a family squabble. His beat was the Tenderloin and Barbary Coast districts. That's why he had been the first officer found by Johnny Lord. On his beat a man could be murdered for the price of a bottle of whiskey. Shanghaiing to serve on an out going ship was commonplace. Only that evening his fellow officers had rescued a fifteen-year-old boy on Dupont Street who had been snatched to force him into male prostitution. He didn't like Lillian McHenry's business, any more than he liked Johnny Lord's business. But he knew truth when he heard it, and the events that evening had nothing, in his opinion, to do with the business.

''It's quite enough,'' he said quietly and, turning, eyed Fairchild dangerously. ''It's my case, Chief. I'll file the report.''

Johnny and Carl Howard, with Dinan's help, led them out—all but the Chief. He walked around, as though seeing the dining room for the first time.

''Nice . . . house,'' he smirked. ''Too bad Miss Lily will be laid up. Still, she ain't been around much, anyway. Nadine's been seeing to things. Nice girl. Knows how to butter hot toast on both sides, if you get my drift.''

''I'm afraid that I don't.''

He came close, his little watery eyes glinting in his moon face.

''You don't fool me, sister,'' he grinned. ''You may have been off to school, but you know this business. Miss Lily's house is kinda set aside for the Chief. I call twice a week for a social visit. Nadine and the pickings under her pillow have not kept me very happy of late. Now, if you would care to socialize, at my next visit, I might just forget to put my hand under the pillow.''

Tracey instinct was to plant a hard, fast palm against his fat jowl, but he had confronted her with a problem as yet unexplored. Who was going to keep the house operational until Lillian was able? She was well determined that it would be anyone but Nadine, even before his comments. But his comments also raised an unknown. He had left no question but that he collected a payoff in money and services.

She smiled weakly. "I am sorry, Chief Fairchild, I heard your words, but my mind is beginning to shatter. Social? Please, spare me a social visit for awhile. Even though I am responsible for my father's death, I also feel obligated to bury him. I also will have to see after my aunt." Then purposely, she tried to appear confused. "The house? Yes, if you have business, check with Nadine, if that is who has handled things for my Aunt. Good night . . . or really, good day."

He smiled, watching her walk from the dinining room. Lillian had always been a tough nut to crack on a shakedown. Nadine had been easier, not only because she would give bedroom rights, but was not afraid to shake down the girls individually behind Lillian's back. But in his opinion, the niece would be the biggest patsy of all. He would only have to make his demand and she would open the purse strings and loosen the strings of her camisole.

No matter what report Dinan submitted, he would tuck it away for his future private use.

Tracey thanked them, one and all for coming to her rescue. Some, who wanted to stay to help, she had to reassure that she was all right.

It was already Sunday morning, so Clara and Henry had no reason to be back. Clara's staff would see to the Sunday evening buffet for the girls. She was tired of Carl Howard's guilty look and cared not when she saw him again.

With Johnny Lord she felt the guilty party.

"I'm sorry you didn't know I was back, but blame myself for not coming to see you. Don't be a stranger."

He went away, his thoughts moved by strange chemistry.

He felt safe leaving Lillian in her capable hands. He could not believe her. She had been able to wind a man like Fairchild around her finger, while even he stood in fear of this man who was squeezing the district to near-starvation. They paid or they were shut down.

He felt comfortable in knowing that if Tracey had a question, she would call on him.

Tracey could feel the tiredness in Eric, even without looking at him. When they had arrived, she did not know, but out of the casino came a battery of four nurses.

"They will be here round the clock," he murmured. "I know—they are Chinese, but I have found no others to train."

"That doesn't matter to me. She is all that matters."

"Please," he begged, "she matters also to me. Still, I do not want you seeing her when we have to move her. It is going to be a slow process, Tracey. I have tried to put all her broken bones back together, but don't want them separating again. An inch at a time, a step at a time, we are going to get her from the casino up to her room. Go to bed, or where ever you can avoid seeing this. I fear we may never get her to her room alive."

"Then why move her?"

"Her demand," he groaned. "She keeps coming out of the coma at the most awkward times and won't even whimper. Still, she can threaten. I am to get her to her room to die, or she will die immediately. Tracey, I have learned that a patient's will to live increases when their demands are met. I will move her, if it takes forever."

"You are holding something back, in not wanting me around."

"I will not lie," he said gently, "although you must remember that her brain is the target of all this pain. She is blaming you for all that has happened to her and although that is quite false, not having you around will be of great help."

Tracey could understand the blame and feel the guilt. "I understand," she said simply, "but to get to her suite of rooms, you have to pass right by my bedroom. If the door is closed she may think I am shunning her. Her office is in the back of the apartment. I'll go there and wait until you have her settled.'' Then for the first time she did break down. ''Oh, God, Eric, I am responsible!''

''Hush!'' he said sternly, putting a hand under her chin and lifting it so their eyes met. Never had she seen his eyes so piercing and fire-bright. ''My love for her must come first, without diminishing my love for you.'' His eyes hardened, as though his Kai Soong power had seen something he did not want to reveal. He turned away without saying more.

Chapter 16

Later that morning Tracey sat at Lillian's desk in a state of shock. The desk was now tidy, but Tracey had been aghast upon first entering. It hardly looked like a room belonging to the meticulous Lillian McHenry. The desk had been a litter of papers and stacks of ledger books. The wastebasket was overflowing and the bookcases deep in dust.

When Clara found her, with a tray of coffee and food, she was deep into straightening it up.

"Ain't been able to send a cleaning girl in here for well over a year," Clara sniffed. "Herself said she didn't want anyone snooping into her affairs."

"Her affairs seem to be in a holy mess. She's let these bills stack up to a point that I'm not sure if they are paid or not."

"Probably aren't," Clara sniffed again. "I have to pay the butcher cash daily and if Mr. Lee wasn't such a long standing friend and client we'd have to get produce the same way."

"Well," Tracey sighed, "to keep out of Eric's way I might as well look into things as I clean. Why are you still here?"

"In case you need me, child."

In a way, she wished she had left the mess and walked away. In the four hours that it took Eric and the nurses to immobilize Lillian and move her, Tracey tried to make the best sense possible out of the ledgers. Only because they had been kept with such exactness for so many years was she able to see how they had begun to be juggled in the past two to three years.

"I'm sorry, Eric," she said with deep compassion, knowing his state of shock was even greater than her own. "I know you are bone-tired, but I thought we had better face this problem at once."

"What vanity," Eric said grimly. "She never should have tried to play in the same league as Liberty. When did it start, did you say?"

Tracey opened a ledger. "1889 is when she first paid money into the building of a canal across Nicaragua. From the reports it appears the Eastern business executives involved soon ran out of money and the work stopped. In the next ten years it appears as though she alone paid the lobbyist to sell the scheme to the government. She, at least, won one battle. Three years ago Congress authorized a commission to survey both the Nicaragua and Panama routes. When the commission favored the Nicaraguan route, because it would require less digging, she seemed to go crazy. Every cent she could get her hands on went to buy up the Nicaraguan property rights."

"It is now so obvious," he sighed, "why she has been in such a stew these last few months. It must have been a great shock to learn that President Roosevelt said he would accept the French offer of $40,000,000 for the Panama rights. Liberty wins again. Well, except for a lot of worthless land in Central America, how bad off are we?"

"Very bad, as I have been able to trace it. Even though you were here, she continued to use your power of attorney to sell and lease. She sold the American River property and produce district property outright to Alexander Lee. She has a very hefty loan with Duocoming's bank, secured by the lease payments from the financial district property until 1906."

"That, then, is not a total loss," he said drily. "It will not be money out of the pocket for four years. What about the scattered pieces of property and minor leases?"

"That is going to take some time to sort out," she said, pointing to a ledger crammed so full of papers that it looked like the mouth of a whale devouring sea-weed.

Eric sat back slowly. "What was remarkable about our association, Tracey, was that I was left free of all of this to pursue my medical career. I still have no taste for business. Would you have time to help me sort it out?"

Tracey glanced at him uneasily. She knew he was being tactful in not asking about Lillian's personal affairs. It was obvious to her that they had to be in the same, or worse shape as the trust accounts. Then she launched into a discussion the project she had been stewing over.

Eric sat there looking at Tracey with a different kind of dawning respect in his eyes. He had been granted the opportunity to read some of her manuscripts and thought she was an exceptional writer. He marveled at her knowledge of opera, music and the theatre. He was always excited in being the escort for the stylish beauty, but had long ago given up any idea of seducing her. And it was now too late for it to happen, because their friendship was too deep and too intimate to be ruined by a sexual encounter.

"I cannot help but wonder," he said thoughtfully, "why you must take over fully for Lillian. Business management of the establishment I can see, to get it back on its feet. But can't one of the girls fill the madam duties?"

"No," she said stoutly. "Therein lies the main problem. Lillian has been so concerned with getting money to put back into the trust accounts that her own affairs are a shambles. The reservation book and nightly tallies are almost laughably counter to each other. The police may have their hand out for graft, but I have a feeling every hand in this place has been in Lillian's till. If I am going to control that, I have to be boss right down the line."

"Which brings me back to my question of business."

"Of course I'll do it," she said drily. "I'm not going to have much time for writing anyway."

"Oh no," he insisted, "you must take time each day for that, even if it is nothing more than a journal of your daily activities."

Tracey frowned and then she laughed. "Mr. Fetterson says the characters in my books lack compassion and an understanding of living. After what has happened, I think I have to agree. They are quite bland when compared with real life."

Eric looked at her and a hard glint appeared in the deep pools of his eyes. From that moment he would regard her as just as much of a patient as Lillian. This was not going to be an easy task for her and he would not allow her to become another hard and bitter Lillian.

Tracey entered the dining room with the same sweeping grace she would have employed attending a formal dinner party. Clara and Henry were only a step behind her.

Reluctantly, they had agreed to stay for the buffet Sunday night dinner, without a clue as to what she was about. But a few feet into the room and Clara stopped dead still. Sunday had become her day to be alone with Henry in their own house. The buffet she left up to her staff and assumed it was the same affair as in the old days. Her anger soared and she wanted to pull Tracey back out of the room and apologize.

Tracey had also stopped and took in the room with cool appraisal. When she had been young and curious, she had many times broken Lillian's rule on a Sunday evening. Quiet as a mouse she would sneak downstairs and peek in on the buffet. The girls were always so elegantly gowned and ladylike in their manners. She had often wondered why she could not associate with them, for they'd all seemed so friendly to each other.

And in the past twenty-one months, when she had had occasion to see them individually during the day, they had been very gracious and warm.

Now she was seeing the other side of the coin. They sat at a table by themselves, loud and boisterous. The rest of the staff sat at separate tables.

Tracey had sent down word that she wanted three extra places set that evening. It had been done, but at a table apart.

She began fuming as she started forward again. The girls' table was like a pig's trough. Nor was there any of the elegance of the past. Each was attired in whatever struck her fancy a moment before coming downstairs. And it was obvious that most had spent too much time at the bar before sitting down to eat.

Tracey needed a target to immediately get the upper hand and Nadine had unwittingly made herself available. She sat at the head of the table, in Lillian's seat, louder than the rest with uncouth stories about the clients.

Even when Tracey stood right beside the chair, Nadine refused to stop her story and recognize her.

"I believe," Tracey said loud enough for her voice to carry over the din. "That you are sitting in Miss Lily's seat!"

Nadine sat bolt upright.

"Like hell it is!" she roared. "As long as I've had to run these Sunday night suppers it's been my seat, deary."

"You've been running them?" Tracey said coolly and paused until every voice had dropped to silence. "Then that would account for why they have fallen into such disgrace. Once they were quite elegant dinner parties."

"Look, honey," Nadine sneered, waving a fork in Tracey's face, "this is 1902 and modern times. The prissy ways of that old dame don't go no more. Hell, if some of us didn't invite men in off the streets some nights we'd go broke under her system."

"Wave that fork in my face one more time," Tracey declared in clipped tones, "and I'll ram it right back between those over-painted lips. Now, move to a different seat. I have some announcements to make."

"But," Nadine spluttered, "I am taking over . . ."

"Never!" Tracey cut her short, and waited for her to move.

Clara motioned for Henry to sit down with her at the table for three. They had been discussing, for well over six months, retiring. Nadine had put her finger on their thoughts on the subject, but for all the wrong reasons. San Francisco and its men were still the same, it was Lillian's lax ways in the past couple of years that had brought about a change in clientele. Once it had been fun to whip her staff into a frenzy to turn out the best gourmet food in town. Now it was a slap in the face when the kitchen turned out more sirloin steaks than veal *cordon bleu*. She was interested to hear what Tracey had to say on the matter.

"First of all," Tracey drawled softly, forcing them to sit forward to hear her, "Doctor Larson says it is going to be a very long recovery period for my aunt. Aunt Lillian's rooms are being changed about now, for she will have to have round the clock nursing care. Those rooms are off limits. The nurses will do the cleaning and will come to the kitchen for food trays. Doctor Larson will give you her menu, Clara, when he looks in on her this evening."

She paused. She felt relaxed in having established several points. Without saying it, she wanted everyone to fully realize that she was a blood relative with every right to do what she was going to do and that Doctor Larson and the nurses were in full charge of Lillian.

"Now, I don't think I need to repeat my disgust over what I am viewing. Regardless of what Nadine just said, we will go back to the old ways in the morning. In Aunt Lillian's office I found an old schedule. We shall follow it until further notice."

"Hell no!" Nadine spluttered. "Go back to that old saw and I for one quit on the spot."

"Thank you," Tracey said sweetly, "you just saved me having to fire you in the next breath. The same applies for anyone else who wishes to leave."

"Honey," Margaret soothed, "if I read you right, are you planning on being the madam of this house?"

"Yes."

"Honey, you'll fall on your keister."

"It's my keister to fall upon. This house has been more than a home to me. Its business has fed me, clothed me and given me a very good education. I will not fail the responsibilities I now take on."

"Well, girls," Nadine growled, "what's the virgin going to sell if she doesn't have our pussies around. Let's get the hell out of here!"

"Wait!" Clara said sharply. "I haven't had my say!"

She got up stiffly, looking at the encouragement she saw gleaming in Henry's eyes.

"You all think of me as the foolish old dame in the

kitchen, who don't know what's going on in this part of the house. Hell, this is the thirty-second year that Miss Lily and I have been associated in this house and the House of Peony. I've seen hundreds of your kind come and go and with a couple of exceptions, I would just as soon see the pack of you go. Now, when you talk about keisters, Henry and I have ourselves a couple of pretty big ones. Miss Tracey ain't about to fall on hers, when she's got the experience of Henry and me to back her up. Tracey, Henry and I are going on into the kitchen. Can't stand to look at this garbage as food another minute. Won't take me but a minute to whip us three up some supper like in the old days."

"I'll be right behind you, for I have nothing more to say here."

She could hear their murmurs start up as she went through the swinging doors.

As she passed the spot where Henry was waiting for her, he put out his arms to her.

"How very proud we are of you," he said.

She nestled into his hug as though she were twelve again and needed his fatherly touch to make the nightmare demons go away.

"I'm really scared stiff. I don't know the first thing about this business. I'm all bluff."

He held her close. She was the only child that he and Clara would ever be able to come near to calling their own. It saddened him that she was going to have to take on this role and yet was proud of her for her courage.

"And since Clara made her little speech," he chuckled, "which was quite a mouthful for that woman of mine, I think I know how we can bluff them even more. If you are going back to Miss Lily's old schedule, we can go back to the old system."

"Oh, no!" Clara scolded from the range. "You know how it used to disgust you to pair up the reservation requests with the proper girl."

"I learned how to turn it into a game, my dear," he answered truthfully, "and this way it will keep Tracey above all of that. All she needs to be is a charming hostess in the casino and the dining room. I assume, of course, that you intend on returning to a prompt midnight closing and no overnight guests?''

''That's for sure!'' she laughed, breaking away to go see what Clara was cooking that smelled so good. But then she suddenly turned back with a frown. ''Henry, what about the casino? I couldn't find any ledger on it in Aunt Lillian's office.''

''Truthfully, I wish I knew the full answer on that one,'' he said. ''Up to three years ago it was the finest casino in town. More gentlemen were coming for dinner and gambling than ever went upstairs. Then one night all the old dealers were gone and replaced by a new lot. Very unfriendly gentlemen, to say the least. Somehow they convinced Lillian that the tables were losing money because the gentlemen had to go in to dinner. She took away that rule and not only did the dining room begin to suffer but the class of gambler changed.'' He sniffed. ''Business suits took the place of formal evening attire. But why there are no books, I don't know. It was an area where Johnny Lord would be better able to answer than I.''

Later that evening, when he came to check on Lillian, she was able to pose the question.

''May I see the casino?''

''Of couse, but how does that answer the question?''

He smiled wickedly. ''Time for a little education?''

''Hardly,'' she snickered. ''Gambling is quite upper class in France. Their casinos make this one look like it is right out of the wild west. If you must know, gambling and wine were the two vices I did acquire abroad.''

My God, Johnny thought, she's still a virgin! Then he laughed aloud.

Tracey turned back on the stairs. ''Are you laughing at my vices, Johnny Lord?''

''Lack of them,'' he chuckled, coming down beside her and taking her arm to guide her down and across the foyer to the casino doors. ''When seven of your little lovelies came looking to me for employment this evening, it never dawned on me that it would be another virginal madam in charge of this house.''

"Well, I am," she pouted.

"And so was Lillian," he teased.

"She was not," she protested. "She had known you."

"How did you know that?"

She shrugged, taking the keys to unlock the casino. "If you don't recall the first night I met you, then I am not going to remind you."

He blushed, possibly for the first time in his life. "I remember." Then to hide his embarrassment he went from table to table examining everything in the room, frowning deeper and deeper. "Do you have keys for the office?"

"It must be the other one on this ring marked 'casino', here."

Even before he tried it, it was obvious that it was not the key for this lock. "That stands to reason. Even though the casino is locked, the real devilment is locked in the office without Lillian having a key. Tracey, how good are you at roulette?"

"I'm a real winner. I always seem to sense how the ball will fall."

"Then let's try you on this table," he said, taking a stack of chips from the rack and handing them to her.

"I'll start with my favorite numbers," she laughed, putting chips down on squares of her choice.

Three times in a row she won. "See," she gloated, "I told you so."

"No," he said sternly. "I made you win. Come here and stand behind me. See that carefully hidden lever at the height of my knee. You call out a number and watch what I do."

"Twenty-two black," she said.

"All right, as the coupe, I am going to place the pea exactly opposite the twenty-two black slot on the wheel and give it a normal spin. The wheel goes one direction and the pea-ball the other, but my eyes will never leave the spot where I first put the pea. Because I will let the pea pass that spot ten times before my knee will touch the lever. On that rotation I will push it a quarter to begin slowing the wheel. Halfway on rotation eleven. Three quarters on twelve and full on thirteen. Watch!"

"It fell into twenty-two black!" she gasped.

"These tables are rigged and I assume that the cards in the office will be marked and the dice for the crap tables loaded."

"Assume comes from a French word," she said slowly, "which they have an old adage about. It makes an 'ass' out of 'u' and 'me.' I now assume that I have a right to see what is inside that office."

He chuckled, very willing to oblige. It only took three jolts from his sturdy shoulder before the metal bar gave way and the door sprang open.

It was all as they assumed and more. Here were the ledger books that Tracey had not been able to find.

"Damn," Johnny growled, "it's just what I feared. She's let that damn Abe Ruef take her to the cleaners. Look at this, two sets of books. His crooked dealers not only have been skimming the customers, but Lillian, as well. Some of these nights they've shown the house pay off to be so high as to hardly pay overhead."

"But wasn't that her policy, 'give the suckers a break at the gaming table', because they were going to spend it on the girls?"

"A policy that Ruef's men interpreted their own way. Hell, look at their books. They took $50,000 out of here last month and Lillian got only a little over $7,000." He laughed bitterly. "I've got two casinos where I charge that much in rent, plus twenty percent of the house take."

"What can I do?" she asked weakly.

"First, buy some black crepe for the front gate."

"Why?"

He smiled. "There has been a death in the family, remember. Need a couple of days for proper mourning and other things. You've got three girls left, right?"

"Yes," she said. "Margaret stayed. She's been here five years and remembers the old days. Also, she is nearly thirty and I think is fearful of moving on. Sue Ann stayed. I think because this was her first house and she is fearful of what the next one might be like. Maddy Lee stayed. Frankly, I think it was only because she hated Nadine so much that she stayed just to spite her. From what you said earlier, I assume you hired them?''

''And make an ass out of both of us?'' he laughed, then turned serious. ''In this business, Tracey, you don't quickly hire a whore who has been fired or quit another establishment, until you check things out with that establishment. Frankly, I think you did well to get rid of that trash. I haven't been able to get close to Lillian in the last few years, but if she thinks those seven are quality, then the worst girls in my ''B'' houses should be working up here.''

''May I come down on a hiring binge?'' she teased.

''Not into the ''B'' houses,'' he scoffed. ''They would think that *triple sec* was something for three to do together. But, honestly, my ''A'' houses are overstaffed. It would help me if you could use about seven of them, but who will train them?''

''Henry?'' she murmured.

He laughed, wickedly again. ''I was not talking about that training. They are highly professional in those arts, but not in the one I remember about this house when it opened.'' His eyes glistened on that memory. ''Oh, Tracey, this was class, even though you think the casino is wild West.''

''Bring them to me,'' she said quietly, ''I'll see to that training. Now, what about the casino?''

She listened carefully to his every instruction and agreed. The timetable was a little tight and somewhat frightening, but she would have to put her faith in Johnny Lord.

Harlan Fairchild raced his horse up to the gate and scowled at the sign draped in crepe.

''Didn't know the funeral was today,'' he growled down at the gatekeeper. ''I'm the Police Chief and have an appointment with Miss Whiteside.''

''Been expecting you, Chief Fairchild,'' Mark Mathews said courteously, opening the gate. It was his first day on the job and he was determined to do everything correctly. After three months of any odd job to keep his family alive, the eighteen-year-old blessed that morning as something special.

The night before he had heard a man carping about the horrible circumstances that had befallen his place of employment and his desire to tell the new young mistress what she might do with the job. Mark drew near to the man, and used some of his last loose money to buy the man a drink in the tavern. It didn't take him long to learn the address of the man's place of employment, and the next morning he was there bright and early to see if the man had indeed quit.

He had come up to the gate, his eyes widening at the mansion beyond and then puzzling over the stern, grey haired gentleman rattling the chain, as though that would loosen the padlock.

"Might I be of service, sir?" he had asked.

"Blitter," Henry had growled. "Oh, not you! What do you want?"

"I came seeking employment, sir."

Henry looked at the husky, blond fresh-faced youth and nearly dismissed him. "What do you know about these new-fangled locks?"

"Have you lost your key, sir?"

"Son," Henry growled, "after our gatekeeper unceremoniously terminated his service, he departed with the keys and left us locked inside. Not only that, but he hoodwinked the coachman into leaving with him."

Mark stepped back, knowing it was time to bargain. "My father, who is also seeking employment, is a two, four and eight hander, having been with the Overland Express."

Henry stopped rattling the chain, understanding the terminology. "Our rigs are mainly one horse, but the Victoria requires two. The stable contains six horses of fine breed. How many in your family?"

Mark didn't see why that was a concern, but he answered. "My mother, father, I and a sister of fourteen."

"Not too many for the coach house," Henry mused. "Well, young man, whatever your name, free us from this prison and I shall take you up to see if the mistress of the house is willing to hire you and your father to fill our two vacancies."

Mark was prepared for the challenge, having seen these locks handled before. He selected two rocks, placing one under the lock and pounding the other into the padlock face. The arm sprang instantly from its shield and Henry was free to open the gate.

Twenty minutes later Mark Mathews was in a state of near shock. Not only did he and his father have jobs, but they had the gate house to live in. And he would follow Tracey Whiteside's orders to the letter, for his eighteen year old heart had so fallen in love with her at first sight that if she asked him to lay down his life for her, he would do so gladly.

Harlan Fairchild pranced his horse up the drive in high spirits. With the gatekeeper indicating he was expected, he had every reason to believe that Tracey would come very quickly to his terms.

He was, therefore, a little miffed to find her awaiting him in the foyer in demure black mourning clothes.

"Thank you for coming on such short notice, Chief Fairchild," she said, putting out a hand to him.

He took it and wasn't quite sure what to do with it. He finally shook it, a little limply.

Sensing she had him off guard again, Tracey determined to keep it that way. "I would like you to come into the casino with me, sir. As you know we are closed on Sunday and yesterday was a most trying day. Still, even though I bury my father within the hour, I have been going full tilt at dealing with my Aunt Lillian's affairs. You may have heard that seven girls left me, including Nadine? That's minor. They were not of the quality that my aunt built the reputation of this house upon. Only girls of real class make the real money for us, right?"

He had to nod in agreement, because he was not sure in what direction she was leading him.

"And this room," she said, taking out her keys, "is our second source of income." She unlocked the casino room door and ushered him in. She looked about and turned on him with the look of a female who needed his masculinity to help her. "Last night, Harlan . . ." and she stopped on a gasp. "I'm so sorry. I did not mean to be so personal."

"You go right ahead," he smiled wolfishly. "It gives me pleasure to know that you wanted to call me by my given name and that you called me because you had a problem you didn't want to disclose to any one else."

"You are so wise," she said, fluttering her eyes and feeling foolish as she did it. "Now, as I was saying, Harlan, last night was not a common one for me. I lay in bed, listening for sounds from Aunt Lillian, even though she had nurses with her all night. But then, far off, I heard this banging and crashing. I got up to investigate, but by the time I had made my way downstairs all I found was the front door and the casino door standing wide open."

"Attempted robbery? What did your gatekeeper say?"

"You may have noticed, sir, that there is a new one there this morning."

She sailed on into the casino and prayed that he would accept that fact and not delve into it at that moment.

"I came in," she rushed on, "and found the office door as you see it. Looking in, I saw the safe door ajar and as you will see, the shelves devoid of any money. I instantly thought robbery, but rushing upstairs to dress and go in search of a policeman, something struck me as strange. How would a robber have been able to get through the front gate, the front door and the casino door without keys?"

She locked her arm into his and led him to the roulette table. "Harlan, they think they are dealing with a naive little girl. Oh, I admit that I am naive when it comes to certain aspects of Aunt Lillian's business, but when it comes to gambling I have been trained by the best in France. Pick a number."

"No," he demurred, "I always lose at this silly game in this house."

"Come here and I'll show you how you have been losing. It's something I picked up from an expert."

He was fascinated and chagrined at her disclosure. Red faced over the marked cards, which turned to purple over the loaded dice. Then he gasped in surprise over the double-entry ledgers.

"What are you suggesting?" he stammered.

"Stupidity," she said with pure acid, so he would not forget to pass this conversation all the way up to the mayor's office. "But not stupidity on my part, which is a mistake they shall rue. They thought I would see the broken door, empty safe, cry 'I've been robbed' to you and that would be that."

"But isn't that what you are crying now?" he demanded.

"No," she simpered, praising Johnny Lord for giving her the wisdom to pull him into her trap, "for neither you nor I can honestly say what was in that safe. That's what they were counting on, for me to make a fool of myself. But they erred, Harlan. The Methodist ministers forced the city fathers a few years back to control the number of casinos in this town by requiring them to be licensed and inspected. Now I defy you to find a casino license for this address under the name of Abe Ruef."

"Oh . . . I . . ." he spluttered. "Surely . . . he isn't?"

"I have the double entry books," she said sternly. "I have also shown the illegal gambling devices to another person, in case your tongue got silenced before I could bring them to court."

"You can't . . ." he started.

"Can't!" she snarled, stopping him short. "I have papers to prove that the equipment is owned by this house. I want—No, I demand that you bring inspectors here to take off the illegal levers and confiscate the cards and dice. I think you will find that the license for this address is still under the House of Lily name. I want that license without blemish before I reopen the casino or I'll just take the whole matter to the newspapers. Now, let's move on to another point. As I said, Nadine is no longer with this house. When we reopen it will be by reservation only. If you feel you have business with this house, my office hours shall be from ten in the morning until two in the afternoon. Now, you must excuse me, I have family business to attend."

"The case isn't closed yet," he growled, as if to show her she couldn't get away with all she was attempting.

"Did I say it was?" she said sweetly. "However, I

hardly am going to stand around wringing my hands waiting for your final verdict.''

She swept out of the room, waited his exit, locked the door and to her relief saw Henry awaiting her with cloak and gloves.

It had been her decision to go alone. The man she was about to bury had given her life and that was all she could thank him for at that moment.

That morning, looking in on Lillian, had been painful. She was crying pitifully and the nurse said it had been going on for hours.

''Is she in that much pain?''

''Shouldn't be,'' the thick-set Chinese woman said. ''She's smoked enough of the opium left by Dr. Larson to give her a million pleasant dreams.''

The sickly sweet odor in the air was not new to Tracey. Her favorite restaurant, which she would drag Eric back to time and again, was frequented by many older Chinese gentlemen who would smoke from the bubbling water pipe before dinner. But Tracey had never considered it as a pain killer.

''There! There!'' she soothed, taking Lillian's hand.

''Don't!'' Lillian sobbed, pulling her hand away.

''I'm sorry. I didn't mean to give you pain.''

''The pain is in my heart,'' Lillian wailed. ''Karl is dead and you killed him.''

Tracey had blanched and the nurse put a comforting hand on her shoulder. ''Don't pay her no mind, Miss Tracey. Opium makes people say weird things.''

''It isn't weird,'' Lillian insisted, through deep sobs. ''He came to tell me that my mother was dead and buried, and now he is dead.''

''And will shortly be buried,'' Tracey said weakly. It was the first she had heard about her grandmother's death. The woman was just a shadowy memory— A portion of her first twelve years that she had been able to push farther and farther into oblivion as she had begun this new life.

''I'm alone,'' Lillian had continued to wail.

The nurse squeezed Tracey's shoulder, as though to say don't argue with her.

And even though it had been her choice, it was Tracey who felt alone driving out Market Street to the Mission Dolores. Granted, Henry had been pressed into service to drive the Victoria, but he was of her present life. She was alone to bury her past life.

Ironically, it had been a member of her present life, Daniel Fetterson, who had moved quietly and efficiently to make all the burial arrangements and then send a messenger for her approval. And, as a friend, he made sure no mention of the incident appeared in the Monday *Chronicle*.

Far behind the Mission, in a weedy and unkempt section of ground were the "unsanctified" burial plots. An expressionless priest stood beside the plain hearse used for paupers. The few words he would say over the casket had been written for him by the Reverend Father Thomas O'Bannon, who was politic enough to know that the ledger books of Mission Dolores would be red and not black without a certain Mr. Daniel Fetterson, who was a gentleman of Jewish faith, and the help of the *Chronicle* on their charity bazaar each year. And what Father O'Bannon knew, and Father Concannon did not, was that the fashionable gowns donated each year, and which brought the best prices at auction, came from the House of Lily.

But Father Concannon's puzzlement, became Tracey's puzzlement, as well. Parked directly behind the plain hearse was an impressive brougham, with a liveried coachman standing beside the closed door with an elaborate funeral spray.

That some one else was attending unnerved her a little. She felt remiss in not having worn a hat and veil. Anticipating being alone, she had felt the hooded cloak would suffice.

She had no choice now, but to let Henry help her down from the Victoria, pull the hood over her head and walk toward the wooden casket, sitting on planks above an open pit.

Before she was five steps from her coach, the door was opened on the Brougham. Amazingly, she was not now surprised at who stepped forth and took the spray from the coachman.

Even in his tallness he seemed slumped and stoop shoulder, his face drawn and haggard. The slight breeze ruffled his almost snow-white hair, but he refrained from covering his head with the top hat he held in his right hand.

Tracey faced Otis Whiteside for a moment, and the two looked at each other tense, erect, unyielding.

"A letter was left at my home Saturday evening," he said in a quiet voice. "I did not open it until I heard of your problems through Daniel Fetterson. If I intrude, send me away."

"He was your brother?"

"He is not my reason for being here," he said, "even though I did go to the funeral home to look into his casket. It's strange, Tracey, but he looked as much a bully as a man as he did as a boy. The look was there that haunted me at sea for many years. He had been spared and I had been sold into ship service."

"Why have you denied all of this for so many years to Aunt Lillian?"

"You will understand in a moment," he said, stepping toward the grave and eyeing the priest warily, and then placing the spray next to the casket.

Tracey was confused and looked to Father Concannon for instruction. He took it as a signal to get the services started.

"Shall we pray? Father, we commend the spirit of your servant Karl Whiteside into your care and bountiful understanding. Amen. You may lower him!" Then he stepped up to Tracey and whispered. "Mr. Fetterson has seen to the fees. Good day."

Tracey's mind was numbed by the brevity of the service. She stood, confused and bewildered. Otis caught her when she almost fell.

The planks were taken from beneath the casket and it was slowly lowered by ropes.

She watched, guilt growing with each inch it fell, and Otis Whiteside took it in with immediate awareness.

"May I now conduct the service I came prepared for?" he asked.

Tracey looked at him as though it were a lunatic suggestion. He had already made his feelings toward the man known. Still, she nodded.

"Gentlemen, do not let us keep you from covering him over. I had thought to delay my comments until you were finished, but now I see it would be too trying for my niece. You see, for us, this is a double service. We have only recently learned that my mother—her grandmother—was recently buried in Los Angeles. Forgive us, if we do her honor now, as well."

He turned and placed the spray at the head of the grave site, stooped to pick up a handful of dirt and looked down into the grave as though it were receiving another.

His eyes so filled with tears that the grave diggers stood in awed silence until his hand released the dirt.

"It is said," he sighed, "that man is born of woman. I was, but only through later rumor learned that I was born from an illicit act of love." He released a few grains of dirt to drop and echo back. "Arrogance made me deny that rumor, even though I should have seen that I was not of the seed of the man who was your husband. I should have known, dear mother, because of reports I had from sailor friends of your constant checking on me. But then I was sold from the Atlantic to the Pacific. Life went on for me at a frantic pace, and I cannot deny that you became but a memory.

"My guilt, which I bear before God, is that when Lillian came west, I stood in fear of her. I did not want any connection, Mother, with the Whiteside leeches. There were those who convinced me that she was only here to use me and to benefit from what I had accomplished." He wiped a tear from his eye and sprinkled some more dirt onto the grave. Nobody moved, not even Tracey. The man, at that moment, was in communication with his mother and it was electrifying.

"How wrong I was and how many years it took me to understand that wrong. Mother, I can only say that you would be proud of Lillian's success. The crowning achievement, perhaps, the raising of your granddaughter."

The final grain fell from his hand. "This is your son's grave, Mother. Your son by Tracey Whiteside, because I am now free and honor only your blood in my life. But I think you need to know, wherever you are, that we bury him without remorse. What shame he brought upon this family is buried with him. It is you we . . . honor." His voice began to break. "Our love for you . . . was not . . . diminished by the miles . . . that separated us. God love you, and keep you."

He took a rose from the spray, kissed it tenderly and threw it into the grave. Then his body seemed to cave inward with convulsive sobs.

Tracey grabbed him, as he had grabbed her before, and helped him back to the brougham. She stood, watching it depart, and then returned to her own coach.

"Poor man," she sighed.

"I heard his words," Henry muttered. "Too bad he couldn't have thought them up years ago for Miss Lilly's benefit."

This brought the first involuntary smile to Tracey's face that day. "They have been said, Henry. Which means they can never be taken back."

"I must say," Henry said quietly, "that I was moved. His love for his mother was most touching."

"Do you recall your mother, Henry?"

"Regularly, although she has been in her grave for years."

"He just put his there," she said. "Until he wants to let Aunt Lillian know the same, I don't think it is our business."

He nodded, as a coachman and butler. But as a friend and surrogate-father he strongly disagreed. But in all roles, he held his silence.

Returning, she looked around the room at the serious faces of the women who had helped raise her. They were frowning, as though having all used the same make-up kit. Clara had already informed her that they had all been up to see Lillian, so she was prepared for whatever they might have believed from that quarter.

"Tracey!" Amy shrieked. "Tell us it isn't true."

"This is harder to understand than you running around with that Chinaman!" Beth snapped.

"Let her explain herself," Carol said sternly.

"Thank you," Tracey smiled. "I appreciate your concern, but feel no need to explain anything."

"We are aware," Beth said indulgently, "of everything."

"Everything!"

"Everything."

It was like a double echo and Tracey smiled.

"And I thank you again."

"Tracey," Amy said uneasily, "perhaps we haven't made ourselves clear. Are you seriously intending to replace Lillian?"

"No one can replace her," she said sternly. "I am but a fill-in until she is back on her feet."

"But it will still damage your reputation," Beth simpered.

"Is it my reputation, or your own you are worried about?" she asked grimly. "I am thinking of neither one. Frankly, I am thinking of survival. If this house doesn't make a financial comeback, then I might be forced to join these girls in selling my body on the street."

"Of course, you jest?" Carol giggled.

Tracey relaxed. "I may have put it a little strongly. Put your worry caps away. If the truth be known, it will be Henry who will be the real madam. I will be like the pink pony on the top of a carousel, to attract attention but never to be ridden."

"I wish there was some other way," Amy sighed.

"Wishing won't change anything," Tracey said realistically.

"Well," Beth now sighed, "you seem to have made up your mind."

"Which means," Carol said, coming to put her arm around Tracey's shoulder, "that we will stand behind you. If you needs us, at any time, for anything, you know that we will be there to help."

"Well," Tracey said slowly, a devilish twinkle in her eye, "I'm really not all that happy with three of the girls."

The trio looked at each other in a moment of confusion

and then broke into peals of laughter over her jest. For the first time in years, and especially in front of Tracey, they began to recall their first days in San Francisco and how close they came to becoming three of Charmayne Roach's girls. Tracey listened with attentive glee and spent an hour that night carefully recording their tales in her journal.

While the trio had helped her with moral support, others quietly came to her aid on other matters.

Johnny Lord chuckled. "You are a natural pit boss, Tracey. For a trial run, that was one of the smoothest nights of gambling I've ever seen."

"You act as though you had nothing to do with it. Thank you. I really do like the young men you picked and helped me train for this type operation. I'm still curious as to how you got Basil involved in this trial run night."

"Easy," he shrugged. "He makes a fair amount of money off the investments I have with him and I just happened to know that he was going to be hosting those Eastern brokers. I just dangled the carrot and you saw how he sliced it."

With political brilliance, Tracey thought. Because she had agreed to make the night a charity event, his guest list for dinner and gambling had included Mayor Eugene Schmitz and Abe Ruef. The police were not about to make trouble with their offical and ex-officio bosses present.

"You know," she said, "without the girls on duty last night, it gave me pause to wonder. The casino and dining room would be just as successful without them."

"Very interesting thought," he mused. "Why don't you take it up with Lillian."

Tracey knew it was a mistake the moment the words were out of her mouth. She stood quite still looking at Lillian, seeing her face go bleak and forbidding over the suggestion.

"So," Lillian said, "Johnny thinks it's a good idea." She cleared her throat noisily. "Why not? Isn't it enough that you've made a cripple of me for life? You seem to have more influence over Johnny than I ever did, but he always did go for the young skirts. I hope you know how to play rough, Tracey. Abe Ruef doesn't like losing money out of his pocket, but no one asked my opinion on the gambling matter. So, why bother me with this. Do away with the girls, for all I care. If you'd wanted to get your hands on *my* business, you should have made sure that I died when you killed your father."

Tracey stiffened, as though she had been struck. Each time they met, Lillian returned to the same attack. No longer could Tracey put it down to opium talk. It was a cancer growing in Lillian that she hoped Eric could solve.

To keep Lillian calm she'd keep the girls, even though she was doing a miserable job of training them. And, as though her thoughts were read by another, a visitor that afternoon offered a different sort of helping hand.

"Hello, dear pupil. Clara said I might find you here in the casino office."

Tracey looked up, startled. Then very slowly she came erect.

"Miss Phillips?" she whispered. "You—you came here? Please, let's go upstairs to the apartment."

"No," the school teacher said sternly. "This is a business call and this is a business office."

"Then let's at least go to the dining room," Tracey said with gently dignity. "It is almost lunch time and I would love to have you join me."

"But it is almost two o'clock," she protested.

"I prefer it this way," Tracey laughed. "The . . . others in this house eat at twelve, but they're uncomfortable with me present. It will be just we two, and Clara always has ample."

"Bless you, child. I'd like that."

Going to the dining room Tracey took note of Helena Phillips. Although still ramrod straight, she seemed terribly thin. Her hair was more silver than black, worry lines gave a pinched look to her face and her clothing, although spotlessly clean, was a little seedy.

On an impulse, Tracey asked Clara and Henry to join them for lunch.

"Excellent!" Miss Phillips said an hour later. "I have never had a better meal in my life, Clara. Of course, you let your young ladies know the preparation of the dishes to pass on to the gentleman diners?''

''No,'' Clara said, ''but it strikes me as an excellent suggestion.''

''And your rhubarb preserve. You really should put some in jars for them to buy and take home.''

''My dear lady,'' Henry chuckled. ''How would they explain such a purchase when they got home?''

''What is there to explain? Could they not have been here just for an excellent dinner and gambling?''

''Miss Phillips!'' Tracey was shocked. ''Where have you gained so much information about this place?''

''Amy Deckler,'' she said without hesitation. ''She knew your situation, my situation, and thought we might be able to help each other. I won't mince words, Tracey. Five years ago I took on another tutoring job, when I was no longer needed for Bobbie. The man, as I understood it, was a widower with four children. As a spinster, I presume it was my time to fall in love. Frankly, he courted me while I tutored his children. Having gone far beyond the forty year mark, I turned girlish and smelled orange blossoms. They became blossoms in the dust. He already had three other wives in three other cities between here and Sacramento. Unfortunately, and in this house I am not embarrassed to bare my soul, I had already given him the virginity I had carefully guarded for over four decades. I left him standing at the altar with egg on his face and he has done everything in his power to ruin my reputation and tutoring assignments ever since.''

''How did Amy feel you could be of help to me?''

''Look, Tracey, I didn't just teach you what was in books. Carriage, deportment, table useage, manners and customs, music, conversation—everything necessary for a young lady of society to know. Isn't that what you want for these young ladies? Quite frankly I'm desperate for a job.''

''I see,'' Tracey said thoughtfully, hiding the excitement she was beginning to feel over the prospects of the offer. ''And the nature of the business of this house won't bother you?''

"My training will be in the daytime. How it is applied in the evening hours is your concern."

"Henry?" Tracey asked.

"An answer to our prayers, I would say. It will take a lady to turn these sow's ears into silk purses. I say hire her before she changes her mind."

"And I agree," Clara echoed.

Tracey wanted to agree, but wondered if she should discuss it with Lillian. A sixth sense told her to agree and let Lillian know later, much later.

"All right," she chuckled, "it's settled. Miss Phillips, let's be very reasonable, which I think Henry will agree upon. You don't have just the new girls. I want all ten, including the older girls trained on an equal par. Therefore, your salary will be based on the tutoring of ten students. Likewise, as you shall be teaching them quality, you should look the part. Clara, give her the address of our dressmaker and hair dresser. Miss Phillips, no less than seven different outfits and those you have always dreamed about but could never afford."

"Thank you, Tracey," she said, with dignity, "but isn't it time you started calling me by my Christian name?"

"Look, Miss Phillips," Tracey said, the thought coming to her suddenly, "you may become Helena to Clara and Henry. But if you remain Miss Phillips to me, with the same awe and respect as ever, it will carry over to the other girls. Do as you did with me. Raise them to your level and never let them pull you down to theirs, or they will con you with every trick in the book. I want them to fear you, respect you and stand in awe that what you have taught them one day is only a sentence out of the chapters you have to offer them. Make them hungry for knowledge."

Being human, Helena Phillips knew certain vanities, but that statement was the culmination of her wildest dreams. Finally, a student grown beyond her limits, was revealing the subtle message she had always taught. She now had no choice but to do for the next ten students exactly what she had done for Tracey Whiteside. And regardless of the manner of students, Tracey had preserved her dignity.

With the letters of appointment tucked in her purse, she

walked swiftly to the gate, her face radiant with the thoughts of the future.

"I shall see you daily," she said gaily to Mark Mathews. Then she saw the man waiting outside the gate.

"What do you think you are about?" Harry Dill demanded.

"Employment," she said, trying to keep her voice from quavering.

"Let me in to see the people of this house," Dill said impulsively. "I wish to inform them about this woman."

Helena bowed her head for an instant and mastered her tears. He had caused her so many defeats in five years that she had ample practice in handling him.

"It will do you no good, Harry," she said gently. "I have told them all and still have the position."

"Then they are fools," he screamed. "Harry Dill has more influence in this town than anybody. Who owns this damn place, anyway?"

Her hesitation gave Mark time to react. As he now kept a log of who entered and made exit, he knew her name.

"Miss Phillips, you should have waited at the house. My father will be here shortly with the coach."

Nor was he lying. A moment later the Victoria came down the curving drive with Luther Mathews in control of a two-up. When it was forced to stop, because Mark would not open the gate and allow Dill to barge in, Tracey leaned out the door to see what was amiss.

"Mark? Miss Phillips? What is—? And this man—?" Her look went from face to face in about the same manner that her sentences had faltered. Each told her volumes of what was happening and yet she felt she had read the last chapter without them knowing it. And she knew this man, Dill.

"Miss Phillips, please get in. I did not know you were afoot. We'll drop you at your appointment. Mark, the gate! Oh, Mr. Dill, I have no time now. I told you yesterday, no more than I will today."

"Why, madam," he called through the gate, "I'm not here about the back leases. I'm just here to warn you about that deceitful woman you just took into your coach. I've spent a goodly portion of my last five years in making sure people such as you knew that she was a liar, cheat and dishonorable woman.''

''Is that a fact, Mr. Dill?''

''Sure as shooting! Boy, am I glad this proved to be your house, Miss Whiteside.''

''Well,'' Tracey said acidly, ''you seems to be leaving out a few major facts and mixing apples and oranges, Mr. Dill. For the moment I shall hold off your charges against Miss Phillips. I will just inform you that she was my tutor and has my respect for the tutoring job that I have now commissioned her. Normally, I would not delve into her personal life, but now that I am aware of certain facts, I cheer her for having left you at the altar. I regret our laws are so lax that you can get away with multiple marriages by claiming your religion to be Mormon. I will henceforth fight for a change of that law in this state. Now, to the three key words. As a lease holder with the Eric Larson trust I find that you have lied about payments in the past, you have cheated on your sub-lease tenants and have been dishonorable about the upkeep of the property according to the contracts. I was just on my way to see you, but you have saved me a trip. You now stand three years in default on your leases. If they are not cleared in forty-eight hours, then the court shall do it for me, and with pleasure.''

''She put you up to this, didn't she,'' he stormed.

''Nonsense,'' she stormed right back. ''This is a grave you dug for yourself over five years. Lillian was forgetful, and you took advantage of her not pressing on lease payments. One year lapsed into another and you thought you could fool her. I cannot be fooled, Mr. Dill. I have the records and know what is due.''

''Do you?'' he sneered. ''I have friends at city hall.''

''Then I suggest you go to them. Mark, the gate. Miss Phillips and I have appointments to keep.''

''Oh, Tracey,'' Helena Phillips gasped, patting her hand. ''Don't do this just for me. He is a man who always ends up getting his own way.''

''Not this time,'' Tracey said firmly. ''Not this time!''

Chapter 17

Within the year many came to learn that they couldn't win against Tracey Whiteside. She turned the protection racket to her advantage, not theirs, paying to keep the riff-raff away from the House of Lily. Under the rakish mantle San Francisco wore, she had given back to those who could afford it uniqueness and a calm atmosphere for their pleasures.

The Eric Larson Trust was back in fair shape, although still saddled with useless land thousands of miles away. Eric shrugged it off, his practice growing to the degree that he was preparing to take on an associate.

If there was a black cloud, it was Lillian. After the casts were removed she took to a wheelchair, claiming no feeling in her legs. She became even more bitter, demanding and fired nurses as fast as Eric could hire them. Finally, he decided to just let nature take its course, knowing that Lillian would walk again when she set her mind to it.

Still, that was no help for Tracey. She was still saddled with the House of Lily, although the duties had been altered again during the year.

The rapport that Helena Phillips gained with the girls was remarkable, mainly because they stood in awe of her. When Tracey was down in bed a couple of days with a cold, Helena stepped right in to take over the hostess duties in the dining room. Because she was near Lillian's size, outfits were borrowed from her wardrobe. The transformation was both mental and physical. The school teacher played her part with the skill of an actress, knowing she could step out of character at the end of each night's performance. But she was so exactly right for the mood and decor of the room that Tracey decided to keep her on. Because she was so well versed in the talents of each girl, she was soon able to help Henry with the reservations and nightly matching. And at her suggestion a string quartet was hired for dinner music. It won immediate approval of the clientele, but gave Lillian one more thing to carp and bitch about.

"There has to be an error here, Helena," Henry was saying, not unkindly, just as Tracey arrived in the foyer. "Don't let one of her spies get wind of this."

"What is it—what's happened?" Tracey looked from Henry's grim face to Helena's defiant one.

"Come in the dining room and I'll explain," said Helena.

"And what was that bit about her spies?" asked Tracey as the duo led her into the dining room.

"First, let me prove there was no error in the reservation book," said Helena in a tight voice. "There is a dinner and gambling reservation under the name of Lee. A messenger came a moment ago and changed it to three, including Dr. Larson. Henry says you are scheduled to dine with Dr. Larson."

"I'm not worried about that. Perhaps he forgot. Still, it is a little odd his having dinner with A.G."

"Most odd indeed," Henry said grimly, "due to the fact the man was told never to return again after he announced his wedding intentions to Miss Lily."

"Which promted your spy comment?"

"I'm sorry you heard that. Of late it has been her little game to bribe the maids to bring her any little fault they can find with anything."

"Well, this isn't a fault. Let's just see how things work out when they get here. Actually, I'm delighted to see the return of Mr. Alexander Grace Wells O'Lee." Mentally she went over the ledger. She had been able to chip away at the Lee Produce Company bill, but it would be nice to have some of the man's own money from gambling to pay him back.

She left them to straighten out the table arrangements and went to see that the casino was properly set up.

It was going to be a hectic evening. Ten men for the ten girls and eighty for dinner and gambling. Again she thought of the imbalance of the operation. The ledgers were proving that the house was better off without the girls, but Lillian would not listen. Again, Tracey pushed it from her mind.

The evening started at a hectic pace and remained that way. The tables remained crowded, a group replacing a group as they were called for dinner and then returning.

Cigar smoke began to hang heavy in the air, the scent of liquor breath mingled in. The first two hours seemed like the entire evening and Tracey was ready for a break when she looked up and saw Eric in the doorway.

As she started forward, he was joined by A.G. Lee. Remarkably, she thought, time had stood still for the man. His dress was still the height of elegance to compensate for his less-than-handsome looks.

Then, stepping next to him was a pure contrast. The third member of the Lee party was only too familiar, and too dreaded. But she had to keep moving forward and noting the change.

Next to his beaming uncle, Mick Lee looked fit and lean, the baby fat gone from his face, leaving it with firm lantern jaw, a carefully clipped mustache over his stern thin lips, a nose that seemed raised in disgust at the smoke, and eyes as cold and calculating as his grandmother's. Nor did the very-English-cut tweed suit fit with the surroundings. It hung on him like he had worn it for the ship's crossing and transcontinental rail ride.

Still, there was a manly magnetism to him, that she'd known he would someday attain. It transcended his arrogant look and country-style attire. It was that inner quality of Mick E. Lee that England, Austria and medical school could never conquer.

But long hidden emotions could not be overlooked—hurt, rejection and the long years of silence on his part. She didn't really hate him, but she'd have been more comfortable had he not been in the group.

Eric, who had instigated the evening, seemed most pleased with himself.

"This is my new assistant. We just barely got him across from Oakland. His grandmother doesn't think he arrives for three more days or she would be furious."

"A fact they kept from me, as well," Mick admitted, and for the first time his mouth twisted into his wry smile. "I've been told of your courage in taking over for Lillian."

There followed a few uncomfortable moments, in which neither spoke, and memories of their youth intruded. Finally, to ease the tension, Tracey said with business calm, "You are already late for the nine o'clock seating, and here is Helena to seat you."

"But, Tracey," Eric protested. "You and I were to have dinner. Word was sent to make it a foursome."

"Quite true," she said, so blame would fall nowhere, "but you've seen the tumult in the casino . . . Perhaps, I can join you later."

Helena took Eric and A.G. on to the dining room, but Mick seemed to hang back, viewing the interior of the House of Lily as might his father or grandmother. It put Tracey's tension right back at fever pitch.

"So, you are to be with Eric?"

"More or less," he replied rather uncommunicatively. "Uncle Alex is all for it, as you can tell by this dinner gathering, but I still have not discussed it with my family."

"Meaning your grandmother?"

"She is a part of my family." Then, he turned quite formal. "I was hoping that you and I could have time for unfinished business this evening."

"I was not aware of any unfinished business," she said, frostily now that talk verged on the personal.

"In case you haven't noticed, I am no longer a youth." There was an awkward pause for her to answer, which she did not. As a Lee it was painful for him to swallow his pride. "I have done very well in college and medical school." Still Tracey kept her silence, doing nothing to make it easier for him. "I wish to return to our friendship and—other things. I did not live in Europe without learning something of life."

"I also lived in Europe." Her eyes were unfriendly. "Oh, I also did well and took graduate work. But beyond that, I saw no reason to learn 'something of life' and therefore think we have nothing in common. Your table is waiting for you to be seated."

If he was surprised or disturbed, his reaction was hidden in the proud bearing of his face, a look she recalled as being very much Liberty Lee. "You will not have time for me then this evening?" he asked distantly.

"I don't know. I said it would depend on the casino, whether I joined you for dinner. Later is out, of course. My duties are many."

"You are angry with me, aren't you?"

"There is no anger left," Tracey replied coldly. "Once there was anger, when Lillian and Liberty tried to rule our lives. Then came despair and hurt in not hearing from you. We were only separated by the English Channel. Whatever unfinished business you feel we may have, could have been handled then by a simple dispatch on the mail boat from England to France. Now, I must get back to my duties."

Yes, thought Mick with a twist of something rather like envy, she had duties to perform. If only he had such duties! What he had said to Tracey was true. Eric wanted him, but the family, mainly his father, thought his medical training rather a joke. Mick had helped make it so. For a year he would be the leading scholar in his class and then miss a whole term because something else of interest had gotten in his way. For a few weeks or few months, he would dabble until it became mundane and uninteresting. Perhaps, he could now reason, was the element that kept him from communicating with Tracey. He had been in a constant flux of floating between school, when he would work so diligently that not even Liberty would hear from him, and his restless urge to find out what he desired in life.

In all the events that had passed, the only thing that caused no regret was his unfailing work after Eric had given him a recommendation to his medical school in Austria. At least he had been able to leave Europe without the burden of having failed Eric on his conscience.

But his conscience was now centered on her charge. He

was a part of the dinner conversation between Eric and his uncle, but couldn't recall any of it. He was too busy molding a memory into a present form. He had been remiss. Too long he had kept her in his mind as she had been, even though that memory had provided his most enjoyable moments over the years.

But now, as he would catch a glimpse of her in the foyer, or in the dining room talking with Helena or a table of guests, he was amazed. She was one of the most beautiful, exotic women he had ever seen. Once he had experienced an arousal over her without realizing why. This time he could put it to adult understanding. The golden crepe clung to her body and the swell of her breasts hinting subtly at the glories underneath—the perfect body of a "pocket Venus".

She had been short with him, but with the other guests her laughter bubbled, her face glowed with genuine warmth at the pleasure of the task she was about. For that reason he was left with doubt and disappointment.

It was noted by one at the table, and when A.G. gleefully left the dinner table to go to the casino, Eric felt duty bound to comment.

"Not a homecoming like you expected?"

"I'm really a bone-head when it comes to her. I thought I could just pick up here where we left off."

"For her that might be hard to do. She has had to put her own career aside to pick up the pieces of Lillian's. That brings a maturity that may be difficult for you to understand. I'll tell you what I have in mind. We, if you are to be my assistant and associate, have a patient in this house. It is Lillian and I shall tell you no more. I want your opinion without background facts. When I examine her late, I stay to give Tracey my latest report. I'll have Henry quietly show you to Lillian's room. If Tracey asks, I will be honest and say I sent you to see a patient."

Later, when Tracey came into the living room of the private apartment, he was amazed that she didn't flare up at him.

"You always did try to get your own way," she said dryly, and when he laughed despite himself, she explained.

"A good madam always knows what is going on in her house. I was aware five minutes after Henry brought you up here. Well, doctor?"

"I'm afraid it was a rather uncomfortable scene," he admitted. "But when you have been trained on Austrian patients, you learn how to handle such situations." Then he frowned. "I frankly found nothing wrong with her legs or hips. In fact the muscle tissue is just too firm for someone confined to a wheelchair. Her legs are getting exercise, Tracey, and that means she must be walking."

"Eric didn't forewarn you that he thinks the same?"

"No," he said thoughtfully and then smiled. "It must be final exam time again. I will discuss it with him and find out if we might be able to trap her in the act."

"Thank you. Now, let me show you out."

That was the last thing he wanted. Having her alone, the woman that she had become, was not like when they were teenagers. He wanted her, and he wanted her tonight.

"Tracey," he said with soft deliberation, "I lied to you. Many opportunities were presented to me in Europe, but I was never able to accept them. I find that I can't act like your customers. I have always wanted it to be an act of love and not paid passion."

She ignored him, but for reasons she did not fully understand herself, took him the long way back around to the main staircase.

When the Nightingale Hall began to sing he stopped short and listened.

"Don't be alarmed, Eric's father had this floor put in. It sings as the madam walks along so the girls know they have help at hand. There is a system so that they can flicker the hall lights if they need her help." She did not tell him that she had never seen them flicker; first, because there had been no reason for them to flicker and, secondly, because it was Henry who patrolled that hall during working hours. But there was growing in her a sense of his powerful desire. How could she deny that she had pushed aside all other men because of the one who now stood beside her? But she had also become an astute investigator of history. She did not want to end up as Lillian had with Johnny Lord. Still . . .

"Would you like to see one of the guest rooms?"

He colored instantly. "Not if . . . they . . . are . . . well, you know."

"The girls have been in their private rooms since midnight," she laughed. "These rooms are only used when they are with a client. However, I was a girl short tonight and the Blue Room was not used."

"Then I would like to see it, as a sort of reprise of the past." Then, in answer to the question marks in her eyes. "The day I showed you grandmother's house. I don't think I shall forget that day as long as I live."

"Nor I," she choked out, all the wonderment of that particular day flooding back in full force. She opened the Blue Room and stepped in.

"I couldn't tell you what happened to me that day because I didn't understand exactly what was happening to me. I was no longer a virgin mentally."

"Nor I," she choked again.

"Oh, God," he said thickly, "how long must I wait for it to become physical?"

"Most men only think of the physical pleasure after marriage," she said, her icy tone returning.

"Perhaps you have already touched on that problem," he muttered, his eyes murky with regret. "I must still solve an overbearing grandmother problem and the two of us, with Eric's help, have to get Lillian on her feet or you will be chained to her forever."

"Not forever?" she said desperately. "I do what I must do out of obligation, and I do it damn well. But at times, I get overly nervous at the time this is stealing away from the things I want to do. Oh, I don't mean just my writing. But the nights when I would love to be at the Opera and am stuck here. And tonight, for an example. After I thought it out, I wanted to come and join you at the table, but my marriage to this place came first."

"Is that an oblique way of saying you might still consider marrying me?"

If his proposal thrust home, nothing in her face betrayed it, except for a cunning glint that came to her eye.

She knew the sexual system that was used in a room such as this, although the training was done by Helena. Still, she walked seductively toward the bed, not letting him see her loosening the clasps to her dress as she walked.

As she turned back to him, letting the dress slip slowly and provocatively off her shoulder, slide down over her up-lifted breasts and slither to the floor she felt her power and passion rising.

"Do I give you passionate thoughts, Mick? We are adults, so let's realize that we must be realistic. With my having served for Lillian in this place, I am poison for your fondest dreams of marriage, when it comes to your parents and your grandmother. And Lillian? She will walk less, not more, now that she thinks I might have an escape route."

"What are you suggesting?" he gasped, unable to take his eyes from the marvelous beauty of her nudity.

"Simple," she said, and in a stride was undoing his clothes as she knew the girls had been trained to do for a man's full arousal. "Tonight, in this room, I shall be a virginal whore for your virginal maleness. Does that trouble your conscience?"

His eyes flamed with years of sensuous desire, and a hand rose to mold her breast. "It only worries me for after tonight. What then?"

"Just kiss me, you fool! In this business one only worries about a night at a time."

His hungry mouth sought hers, mercilessly. The kiss was long and hungry enough for her to work him out of the rest of his clothing.

For each, then, it was like a dream relived. Now the bare flesh could join in physical release. All of those years of pretending were now actual.

Yet, for the first time, each was human. His lust, having built for hours was seconds in duration. Her fear of pain, which some of the girls claimed happened nightly with each new man, was of no longer duration than his quick entrance and departure. Still, her fullfillment had peaked at the same moment as his own.

At length, his lanky body now quiescent, Mick rose and dressed. His voice was coolly controlled. "I never want to do it in this house again."

"Mick—" she started, fully aware that she had been the seducer and thus the whore.

"No," he grated. "I've made two choices in the last ten seconds. I'm going in with Eric, even if it is nothing more than a lab assistant and I'm going to find a house of my own."

After he was gone, and after she was in her own bed, she ironically thought: does the house make a difference? Without marriage she was still his whore, regardless of where they coupled. Mistress she would not consider as a term, because she expected nothing from him in return. And was she prepared to become merely his whore?

In the night, she wrapped her arms about her nakedness like a shield and felt no protection. She recognized his weakness and would not admit it. She would not fight Liberty over him and possibly lose all. She would accept what portion of him she had gained that night and pray for full measure in the future.

Chapter 18

The afternoon and evening of April 17, 1906 had a great deal to do with the cesspools and palaces of San Francisco.

"Another night off?" Lillian sneered, wheeling the chair about with the expertise learned in the many years she had sat upon it.

"Hardly," Tracey said wearily, "last night, which I did take off from work, I was disappointed in that Senor Enrico Caruso did not sing *The Queen of Sheba* at the opera. Tonight, Eric and I do not intend missing him in *Carmen*."

"Why not be honest?" Lillian huffed. "You may hoodwink the cultural snobs by being seen in public with the now fashionable Chinese doctor, but don't fool the rest of us—we know you bed down after the affairs with his assistant."

"And tonight," Tracey went on, ignoring the charge as though it had never been made, "is Tuesday. You were the one, two years ago, that determined we should be closed on Tuesday as well as Sunday. It is therefore my night off. Besides, aren't you having your little clambake tonight?"

"Surprised you remembered," Lillian sniffed.

"How could one forget," Tracey said distantly. "For over a month you have made a point to let us know that we were not invited."

"You might have at least sounded like you wanted to attend," she pouted.

"I'm sorry," Tracey sighed, wanting no tension that day. "When Johnny said you were interested in getting some of your old friends together I thought it best to let you handle it as you saw fit. How many are you expecting?''

Lillian shrugged, as though it were now too late for Tracey to take an interest. She wheeled away and down the hall.

Tracey waited until she heard the whirr of the descending elevator, which she had put in the year before on Lillian's demand. It had brought change and anger to the House of Lily.

Clara had been angry, but long before the installation of the elevator. The anger had been there since Henry had taken ill in the fall and seemed unable to spring back from one cold after another. Finally, just after Christmas, they both retired.

Tracey's anger had in fact been rising and falling since that day, almost as if orchestrated. It rose when Lillian announced that she could perform her old chores from a wheelchair. It fell when she saw that Lillian and Helena worked quite well together with the girls. But in the last month, her anger returned. A house could not have two bosses.

After laying out the gown she would wear for the opera, she packed a lime green suit-dress, blouse and round hat with small brim in a suitcase.

Only then did she realize how important the outfit was to her future. It would be worn at 7 a.m. the next morning when she and Mick had an appointment with a justice of the peace at City Hall. Then she could announce that the only career she wanted was as a wife and mother.

Still, she hated being a sneak, but reality was reality. Her relationship with Liberty, never warm, grew positively icy when Mick had tried to bring the two women together for lunch, six months after his return. Since that time, Mick had watched in awe as a seemingly endless procession of young ladies were thrust before him at every opportunity Liberty or Daniel Lee could muster. But at twenty-nine he had learned to be as bullheaded as his grandmother.

And both Mick and Tracey agreed to keep their plans from Lillian. She would have been even more difficult, even more unappreciative of their personal desires than Liberty. They were exhausted with her selfishness in holding onto Tracey like a child and slave to her every whim. Feeling themselves trapped, they decided this was their only escape.

Clara, who would stand up with Tracey, and Eric, who was honored to be Mick's best man, shared a common thought: Why hadn't they come to this simple solution years before?

About a mile away, as a sea gull would fly, Tracey's secret was well known to another.

Abe Ruef, sitting in a rear cubicle of the Pup Restaurant, smiled with genuine approval on his confidential law clerk, George B. Keane.

"Georgie, that's why you are invaluable to me. No one else would think to keep track of the marriage licenses being issued. This little marriage plays nicely into my hands on two different scores. Go ahead and tell Fazio that I'll grant his two building permits for 'French Restaurants' on Jackson Street. With Tracey Whiteside out of the picture, which I assume will be the case, Lillian will come to see that I have been beating her at her own game."

George Keane smiled knowingly. He knew that as the leader of the Republican party of the city, it was a situation that Abe Ruef loved: both sides against the middle, with Abe pulling all the strings.

The French Restaurants on Jackson were all a part of his scheme to get even with Tracey and Lillian. He controlled building permits for the city and gave them out as favors for due bills at election time. His French Restaurant franchises he thought was classic and another means of augmenting his income. The restaurants, copied after Clara's, were strictly respectable on the ground floor, offering food and wines comparable to the House of Lily. The upper floors were divided into private rooms, each furnished with a dining table, a bed, and an inside door lock. Because the upper rooms were reached by a separate entrance, many gentlemen were beginning to prefer this discreet alternative for a higher price over the House of

Lily. One did not have to be confined to the use of one of Lillian's girls. San Francisco's reputation as a roaring, randy city could now partake of a new vogue. An illicit affair with another man's wife was now possible in the French Restaurant's upper floors.

"Now, let's turn to a serious matter," Abe continued. "The time has come to move in on the Southern Pacific Railroad. The feud between the railroad and the *Examiner* could not be better had we planned it. William Randolph Hearst may have started it to boost circulation, but his paper has started a ground swell that they can't ignore. Now, who makes Charles Crocker quake when she roars?"

Keane smiled. "And the railroad has power which is felt everywhere."

"You're beginning to get my picture. You get to Liberty Lee and have her set up a meeting for me with the railroad. The Southern Pacific can benefit from my advise and she can benefit from my string pulling. I am going to have dinner at home this evening with the family. Let me know her reaction so we can act before morning if need be."

It was after six o'clock before George Keane was able to see Liberty in person. With dinner guests already in her parlor for cocktails she might have refused to see him had not his name and that of Abe Ruef been their topic of conversation. Fearing there had been a leak of her carefully laid plans, Liberty was forced to see him.

"Thank you for seeing me, Mrs. Lee," he oozed with fake charm. "Mr. Ruef thought you would, being a good Republican and him being the leader of the party."

"Is he?" she snapped. "It is my personal opinion that his time is spent mostly on Union Labor Party affairs."

"Now, Mrs. Lee," he said, as though she needed educating on the facts. "That's only a political force for our own city government. He's still Republican for state and national issues."

"Then on with your point for being here," she sniffed.

"It has come to Mr. Ruef's attention that he might be of some service to the Southern Pacific over their fight with

Mr. Hearst. He would like you to set up a meeting for him with Mr. Crocker."

"I see," she said slowly, realizing he was not there about Mayor Eugene Schmitz.

"He is willing to do you a favor in return."

"Such as?"

"I won't beat about the bush," he said. "A marriage license has been issued for Mick E. Lee and Tracey Whiteside. They have an appointment to be married tomorrow morning at City Hall. If he can be certain that you will arrange his meeting, he can well make certain that no justice will be available to perform the service in the morning. Which will give you time to act on the matter as you see fit."

"A very kind offer," Liberty acknowledged, inwardly fuming at their assumption of her stupidity. It was a State license and would be just as good across the bay in Oakland. But she did not want to ruffle George Keane or Abe Ruef at that moment in time. "Tell Mr. Ruef that I shall look into both matters in the morning. Good evening."

She pulled the bell chord and quickly formulated a plan.

"Charles, send a coachman with a message for my grandson. My plans have suddenly changed. I shall leave for Washington tomorrow and not next week. Therefore, I shall expect him to be here for breakfast no later than six-thirty."

She was all smiles when she returned to the parlor.

"They seem to know nothing, Freddie," she exalted.

"I should think not," the short, stocky military man huffed. "My requests to the President have gone through strictly Army channels."

It was a reaction typical of Brigadier General Fredrick Funston, acting commander at the Presidio garrison. He saw things with simple directness as being white or black. This city government, from the Mayor down, was black with corruption.

"So," Liberty said, "now we can get back to the business at hand." She turned to Eda Funston. "Eda, just before I was rudely called away, you were about to make a point."

Eda gave an uncertain laugh. "I'm afraid it slipped my mind," she said; although nothing ever slipped Eda Blankart Funston's mind. She had been an outstanding society belle when Funston passed through the bay area in 1898 on his way to the Philippine war. It had been love at first sight and she had become a very good Army wife.

"Eda," Funston said brusquely, "we were discussing the blight of this city and the carousing sailors who kept us awake last night staggering up Washington Street. As you are nearly our neighbor, Liberty, I am amazed you did not hear it. There is not a night goes by that you can't hear the yelling and gun fire on the Barbary Coast all the way up here."

"There was my point," Eda said on a sigh. And this was typical of Eda Funston. When her husband was brusque and sharp-tongued, she would frequently follow with soothing words and a profound suggestion. "Now that we are assured that President Roosevelt will appoint an investigator to look into this corruption, shouldn't thinking people be looking for a replacement for the Mayor?"

"First we have to make sure we get rid of the wheeling and dealing at City Hall," Liberty said.

"If Freddie ran the city," Eda said quietly, "things would be different."

"I'm an Army officer and not a politician," he fumed.

Liberty was glad that Charles announced dinner at that moment. She could see that Eda showed a degree of skill far beyond her years and Liberty wanted to chew over the bone that had just been tossed out. She had been thinking of Richard Deckler as a possible candidate. But his shyness and old-fashioned courtesy would be no match against Eugene Schmitz, if they were not able to indict him before the May election. "Fearless Freddie" Funston was an alternative. He was not an impressive-looking man; just a little more than five feet tall. But his shock of red hair hinted at the explosive temper concealed by his dapper outward appearance. Yes, she thought, this just might be the 'little giant' she needed to slay the two-headed dragon of Ruef-Schmitz.

She would quietly feel General Funston out during dinner and then send a private message to Rudolph Spreckels. Not even Funston knew that she had carried a secret message, two months before, to Teddy Roosevelt from his old hunting partner. She had carried one hundred thousand dollars of the millionaire's money to Washington to finance an investigation of City Hall. The investigator that the slow-moving Army channels of communication was just now promising, had indeed been in the area for two months. That had been Liberty's real fear with the arrival of George Keane. She was sure that the brilliant Secret Service agent, William J. Burns, had been discovered in his gathering of evidence against Schmitz and Ruef.

She might have feared had she known of another dinner a little way farther down the hill at a "gingerbread house" that was laughingly called by the common working people as the "house built by the Mayor's extra salaries."

"I know you personally appointed me San Francisco's District Attorney," William Landon fumed at Eugene Schmitz, "so don't give me this loyalty nonsense. I'm breaking Federal law coming to you even now! My office and staff have been under Burns's control to help him in the collating of evidence of bribery and corruption of you two. It's been two months of hell, Mr. Mayor."

"You make too much of it," Schmitz chuckled. "It's the voters who will count next month, and as yet I have no opposition. You just tell him to do his investigation among the working class—my people. They love me because I live a scandal free life. I'm married, with two daughters, and don't drink or smoke. What can he uncover on that?"

Landon shook his head. He knew that Schmitz could assume a pretense which covered up all deficiencies. "It might get you through an election by the people, Mr. Mayor, but never through a trial by jury. On the majority of things, I think I can save you—if you cut yourself free from Abe Ruef. I still have time to make it look like he was the king-maker and you just his pawn."

"That would make me look silly," he said, with genuine hurt.

"Do you want to look silly or wear prison stripes?" Landon shouted. "Let's face it, he picked you out of the orchestra pit at the Columbia Theatre, where you were making forty dollars a week, and turned you into the mayor of your native city. In five years he has turned this into a road-comedy version of Tammany Hall in New York. Do you get a cut out of his 'French Restaurant' franchises? No! Are you in on his Chinese brothels? No! You are nothing more than a Trilby to his Svengali. Burns believes that, between the two of you, not only have the coffers of the City Hall been robbed, but the city itself. Burns thinks that I am going to hear that Italian monkey at the opera tonight. Give me the word and I can go back and change the records so it will look like the banditry of till-dipping was all on Abe's part."

The Mayor nodded his weak approval. Never had he thought they would be unmasked in their wholesale grafting. He now sensed that his halcyon days as the genial political figurehead of the city were numbered. Still, his politician's instincts shrewdly assessed that Abe Ruef had learned none of this through his watch-dog George Keane. Even though that utterly amazed him, he would still steer clear of them for the next few days.

Before the tower bell in Old St. Mary's Church chimed midnight, most of sensible San Franciscans were long since in bed.

Liberty slept without a worry in the world. She felt she had her ducks quite in order. Funston she could navigate and Mick she would just plough under, as she had done with Miranda. If they didn't like her playing God, then they could switch to a different family and religion.

Abe Ruef slept with a smile of confidence on his face, as did George Keane.

Mayor Eugene Schmitz slept with a worried frown of apprehension.

Lillian McHenry did not sleep, until just after midnight when her head fell drunkenly forward on the dining room table. Around her sat the unused tables, uneaten food and a bar of unused bottles. She was the only person to come to her own party and it had been devastating to her ego.

On Washington Street, just down from Liberty's house

on Nob Hill, Freddie Funston wanted to sleep, but was kept awake in astonishment by his wife.

"Good God, woman, the Army's my career, I say and say again."

"This is our home, but is it a safe home for anyone?"

"I agree, woman, but don't confuse me with the issues at hand. It needs a strong man to fight the corruption."

"It needs you," she said. "Tomorrow you may see it differently."

On stage at the Grand Opera House Enrico Caruso was seeing the city in a different light than he had upon his arrival and castigation by the press for not having performed the night before.

Nine times the curtain rose and fell as he took the curtain calls and accepted the shower of flowers.

Exultant over his performance, Tracey let Eric escort her out to the hack stands.

"I have a personal invitation for us to join the opera company at Zinkand's, if you would like to meet him personally," Eric grinned.

"No thanks," she grinned back. "The papers make him sound horrible, and I'd rather remember him this way. You go on, if you like. Aren't best men supposed to get drunk the night before the wedding?"

"Only with the groom," he said, as the tower bell in Old St. Mary's church chimed midnight, "and that means the young doctor is quite soundly asleep. Besides, I said I would come back to the clinic tonight after the opera. I have patients, even though Mick doesn't."

Tracey pursed her lips. "Eric, even though I have kept quiet on this subject before, I have kept your account books. Why do you pour your money into that Chinese medical clinic when they treat you like dirt?"

"They are still my people," he said sullenly. "And look how they are treated? When they were needed to build the railroad, act as servants or plant gardens, they were accepted. Now they are not wanted by this city or the warring factions in China. The House of Soong has called home its Tong agents and doctors for their internal battles. These people are scared and the sick must still be tended.

This being the year of the Bull, in the Chinese calendar, I feel I must answer the bull blood in me, which comes from my father. I talk too much."

"But make much sense," she giggled and pulled him into a hug. "I'll see you at the city steps at the stroke of seven. And," she said, turning serious, "I want you to know of the the men I have come to love in life. Mick, we don't need to discuss, for you know. Henry, for the father that any girl would have adored to have. Johnny Lord, because every girl should have such an uncle. And you! Had my heart not been given years ago to Mick, you could have stolen it away. And since his return, you have been the only one to help keep us together. That was an act of love on your part, Eric, that was not overlooked by me or by Mick. Especially me. My love and respect for you is bottomless."

For the moment he accepted her departing kiss as Eric Soong, remembering some of the dying words of his father. Kai Soong had forewarned him that a heart broken by an occidental woman could only be mended by that woman. For years he had thought only in terms of Lillian, until Tracey had come into his life. Never had he known such love for anyone and he had suffered heartbreak over her and had stepped aside in favor of Mick, but hearing her words he felt mended and pure. Each were dear to him and knowing they would be together after the next dawn gave him comfort.

Mick Lee stretched, feeling guilty as he stepped out on the terrace of the little house he had bought at the very peak of Russian Hill. Not guilty because it could only be reached by a long winding path, which he knew his father and grandmother would never climb. But guilty because this was his wedding morning and the honeymoon had been the night before. Never, he realized, as he looked down upon the city of hills and the beautiful bay, had they been so sexually alive as after she had come home enthralled from the opera. They had risen like Mount Tamalpais across the bay, and had been as wild and uninhibited as its wooded slopes still full of deer and coyote roaming free.

He felt that Tracey was more akin to the Golden Gate itself, a funnel drawing in his winds and mist from the Pacific to cool off the great hot interior of his soul.

And that night of love making was like the city itself, rising and rising toward an ultimate climax in a sequence of hill terraces from the harbor. One terrace rose to Telegraph Hill, with its two-hundred-foot cliff shearing down to the sea; another led to Nob Hill, with the citadel-like Mark Hopkins Mansion at its crown; and the third "tit", as the Barbary Coast girls would laughingly say the city was the only three "titted" broad around, rising up through Vallejo Street to Russian Hill, the highest point of the city.

From his terrace, Mick Lee could clearly distinguish the five peals of the tower bell of Old St. Mary's Church on the edge of Chinatown, from the naked feet paddling up behind him.

"You silly," Tracey giggled, nestling into his arms. "You could get another hour's sleep, you know."

"Hush," he said, hugging her close, "and listen. I think we are standing in an unusual moment in time. I hear not as much as a single bird, a rustle of the wind, or a peep out of the Barbary Coast. For once I think all of San Francisco is asleep."

And, at a few minutes after 5:00 in the morning, Tracey had to agree. Nothing seemed to stir at all in the city.

But at that very moment, one hundred and fifty miles due west of where Tracey stood, Otis Whiteside came onto the bridge of his flagship just as the *Carrie* shuddered. The vessel, ancient by standards of this new century, rose bow out of the water, totally exposing the schooners waterline, remained there for a never-ending second, then with an ear-shattering jolt crashed back into the sea.

The crew were toppled from their bunks, thinking that the slow moving sailboat had been rammed by a faster moving steamcraft.

"Mister Firestone?" Otis barked.

"Sir," the First Mate stammered, "the charts indicate no shipwrecks or reefs in this area, and as you can see there is no other vessel about."

"Damnit, Mister, I can see and I can also feel. Did we, or did we not, just strike and then drag over soft ground?"

"But how, Captain?" the helmsman gaped. "The sea bed is 2400 fathoms below us."

Otis was not aware that a few miles ahead of his vessel was the San Andreas Fault under the sea bed. The "Carrie" had, to a certain degree dragged over soft ground, when with a tectonic jolt one wall of the Fault had slipped in one direction, the other the opposite way, grinding and thrusting and wrenching until the earth split like a gigantic wound. What the "Carrie" had experienced was the kick-back from the great rip—the massive tons of debris sent upward with volcanic thrust, slowed only by its 2400 fathom rise or it would have crushed them like a nut in a cracker. Nor did they know that what they had felt was making seismographs quiver as far away as Cape Town, London, Tokyo, Berlin and Moscow.

Or that the tremor they had experienced was traveling at a speed of two miles a second toward their home port.

Before Otis could get to the wireless room, the operator was receiving a distress signal from the *Argo*. The new class steamer had experienced hull plates buckling, bolts blown out of their riveting and the whole ship breaking up in a calm sea.

And even as Otis listened to this report in dismay the earthquake came out of the sea at seven thousand miles an hour and made the lighthouse on Point Arena sway like a blade of grass, then bore down on San Francisco, ninety miles away.

As though demented in seeking its real target it rolled inland, shifting billions of tons of earth, sending masses of rock rising and falling to form cliffs where only flat land had been before, diving back out to sea only to come in to form a new coastline.

Then it moved on to create terror in a land totally unprepared and unknowing.

Alexander Lee had just stepped from his carriage at the produce market when he felt a deep and terrible rumble. As the horses began to panic he turned to his coachman and gasped.

"Good God, man! Look at Washington Street! It's undulating like the waves of the ocean!"

Before he could say more the shock waves sent him reeling and his coach and screaming horses were dropped into a yawning crack in the street.

High up on Russian Hill, Mick and Tracey lay stunned, ripped from each others arms and smashed to opposite ends of the terrace. For seconds they were held down as if by some gigantic unseen vacuum.

Mindlessly, he was finally able to crawl to Tracey and gather her in his arms. They sat like mutes and looked down on the panoramic vista of force against man.

Man and his structures were no match for this force. Towering buildings were like country folk trying their first jig with too much corn liquor in their bellies. They swayed, rocked back, only to sway again before losing their balance and crashing downward. They danced to the music of the tower bells of Old St. Mary's Church, clanging senselessly one tune, while the city's other churchbells pealed wildly.

"Mick!" Tracey cried, "Look!"

The whole area south of Market Street began to move as though a magician had tried to pull a tablecloth out from under a full table service without disturbing it. The trick had not worked. The earth waves, two and three feet high, shook buildings, rocking some from their foundations, toppled towers and cornices and filled some streets with debris.

"It's heading for . . . and, Oh God, Lillian is alone!"

"But it's . . ." he started lamely.

"Mick," she shouted over the roar of the sound, "We don't need some damn judge spouting words to make us married. Now, let's get dressed and get moving!"

At that moment seven million dollars' worth of stone and brick work was shaken off the building in which they were to have been married, leaving its frame standing among the shattered columns like a monstrous birdcage.

Then, as they struggled to their feet the shaking stopped. Mick took a fleeting glance at Nob Hill and noted that his grandmother's and parent's houses seemed to be standing and unharmed.

Tracey saw the look and could feel his guilt.

"You're thinking of her order to come to breakfast, aren't you?"

He nodded, but couldn't put his thoughts into words.

"Go to her," she said. "I'm not afraid of losing you."

Almost beneath their feet came a sound like nails being pulled by several men at once from a packing crate and then the front of Mick's house sprang outward and dropped to the street.

It seemed to set his mind as to where it should be at that moment in time.

"I'm sorry, Tracey. I can't go to her and I can't see you all the way back to Lillian's. I'm a doctor and doctors will be desperately needed everywhere."

"Yes, Mick, I agree," she answered, knowing that neither she nor Liberty were victors at that moment. Mick Lee had, for perhaps the first real time in his life, made a firm decision without guidance and prodding from the women in his life.

But his grandmother, in little more than a filmy night-gown was prodding another man into action.

"Freddie," she screamed, "I didn't run over here in my bare feet to get a lesson on the Constitution and how you will need Presidential authority and the blessing of Congress. Hell, look at the years it has taken me to get them to move on Panama. We don't have years here, we have minutes and hours before those stunned people turn into a looting mob."

"Of course," he said pompously, "I would find that intolerable."

"And needs not be," she hissed. "You have over two thousand troops at the Presidio. They will obey your orders implicitly."

"As will another I trust," he said, already assuming his role as self-appointed military governor of San Francisco. "I fear the fires worse than this earthquake, Liberty. I will first consult with Fire Chief Sullivan."

That would prove to be an impossibility. The unconscious Dennis Sullivan was at that moment an emergency case at the hospital.

By the time Mick and Tracey had covered a few blocks, amid the chaos and confusion, they were in a different world. The blankness of stony faces not knowing what had hit them was being replaced by looks of stark terror. In panic they were fleeing with whatever their hands had first been able to grasp: a metal washtub, a rug, a favorite rocking chair, a hall portrait of some family member whose name they couldn't even recall.

Ironically, at Mason and Columbus Avenue, they found an old Chinese rickshaw man standing idle, while evacuees with heavy loads on their backs passed him by without seeing him.

"China-boy," Mick barked, pushing Tracey into the rickshaw seat, "do you know the clinic of the half-caste doctor of your people?"

The horribly thin man gave him a demented smile of half understanding.

"Tracey," he admitted, "your quickest route to Lillian is through Chinatown. When he gets you to Eric's clinic scream like hell until Eric comes out and make him drive you the rest of the way. From here I am within walking distance of the Central Emergency Hospital. Tell Eric that's where I shall be until he needs me elsewhere. Are you all right?"

There was a silence during which she could not draw her eyes from his, try as she might. At last she said, with difficulty, while something wept inside, "I will be fine."

And without a proper goodbye kiss, he vanished in one direction as the rickshaw took her in another.

Within a few blocks she was caught up in the babble of a different kind of fear. The streets were packed with coolies, merchants, children, Chinese whores, all trying to make their escape.

Tracey did not understand it and understood it less when the rickshaw man dropped his twin bars with a jolt and fled with a scream of horrible terror. To her left and right the Chinese were screaming and she thought at her. Then, looking down the narrow street, she saw the huge tawny bull, bawling from pain from its already inflicted wounds and the fear of those it feared would still be coming. It eyed her madly, as though she were personally responsible for its pain, and then charged down the street toward the rickshaw.

Then she realized that it was the bull the Chinese were screaming at, pelting it with stones and slashing at him with knives.

It only seemed to anger it more in its charge. An old woman screeched fiercely at Tracey and then shook her fist at the bull. Behind the rickshaw a screaming horde was pouring out of the joss houses and banner-hung bazaars, their arms filled from looting.

Without warning Tracey was yanked from her seat and sent sprawling to the cobblestones. The ricksaw was quickly filled with the loot and pulled away. Now danger came more from being trampled by the horde than the bull.

Strong arms lifted her up, but she did not recognize the man.

"No place for you," he scolded.

"Doctor Larson," she gasped. "I am trying to get to Dr. Larson."

He took her by the arm and pushed and shoved them through the crowd. Ahead a coolie hurled a paper thin machete at the roaring bull. Three-fourths of the steel buried itself in the huge side, sending a geyser of blood into the air. Stumbling, its great head lowered in death, the bull turned and charged in the opposite direction, pursued by the screaming horde.

A few doors down she saw Eric standing on the steps leading up to his clinic.

He paled at the sight of her and let her haltingly explain how she had come to be there.

"He should be shot!" he growled.

"The bull?"

"I was speaking of Mick for leaving you alone," he said angrily. "But the bull possibly as well, although that would cause even more panic."

"I don't understand."

"Of course, I forget you do not speak their tongue. They are screaming for the bull to go back. Go back because his brother needs him under the world. The bull to them, Tracey is their incarnation of their belief that the world is supported on the backs of four bulls. This one, having deserted his post has caused the earth to tremble. Now that they have brought him near to death they tremble and babble that Chinatown is doomed." He sighed. "Perhaps they speak for the whole city. Come, I'll get my bag and take you along to Lillian's."

"What of your patients here?"

"Their families came and took them away," he said in disgust. "One, a little girl, I did not want removed, but in Chinatown the family is a law greater than the doctor."

"Was she very ill?"

"She'll die," he said candidly. "She was bitten by a rat in her crib three days ago. It is very common here, but don't tell that to City Hall. Six years ago this section was hit with bubonic plague, but the Mayor hushed it up. In the last four years I've seen a hundred and thirteen children and adults die from the plague, but Schmitz's health officers will not look upon it as a plague. Come, we'll leave by the back way. It's our shortest route."

Shorter perhaps, but not to Tracey's liking at once. The back streets were like litter filled mazes and the alleys more like tunnels with their overhanging porches that looked ready to fall down on them, earthquake or not.

Human forms they saw not, but another moving, slithering, darting form they saw so frequently that Tracey stopped short.

"Don't stop," Eric commanded. "Rats are cowardly creatures and seldom attack a moving object. But who knows what panic they may be feeling and what courage they may gain by the numbers."

"Numbers?" she gasped, racing to his side.

"Who knows for sure, but they probably number in the tens of thousands."

Tracey clutched his arm and kept her eyes glued to her moving feet. Eric noted and thought it just as well. Three times already he had seen a swarm of the black, brown, red and gray beasts swarm into a collapsed or near collapsed building. He knew, as the rats knew, that a corpse lay in the rubble. But that sickening thought was not what was troubling him. It was the rats of the various species, usually bitter enemies over their territory, running together in a pack, that gave him real fright. If they escaped into the rest of the city it would make the death toll from the earthquake seem minor.

Even as Eric and Tracey made their escape, and the entire population of Chinatown was making its way to Golden Gate Park, fires merged building by building until they were sweeping infernos raging unchecked. But where the fires might have been useful, to burn the rats in the cellars and wall nests, Chinatown refused to cooperate. The tong rooms, paper thin walls, wooden frames older than anyone alive in town, brothels, opium dens and even firecracker factories refused to ignite. What fires the earthquake had started in individual buildings had seemed to smother themselves.

Had Fire Chief Dennis Sullivan not been unconscious in an emergency room he might have laughed. Yearly, Abe Ruef would try to get Chinatown condemned as a fire hazard to the whole city; and, yearly, Dennis would fight him with the facts.

Chinatown, except for the homes of a few rich merchants was a ghetto: living quarters built two, three and four stories above street front businesses.

Sullivan knew these people. Their streets might be the pig-sty of the world, but their flat homes were immaculate. Their food was mainly steamed, which kept the internal wood of their structures constantly damp and resistant to fire to say nothing of the kettle of hot water for tea that always seemed to be bubbling on a charcoal brazier.

And that would have been his next laugh over Chinatown.

It was mainly broken gas lines that were jetting fire through buildings around town and giving a fuel for those fires to feed upon. A grid plan of the gas lines would show that they mainly skirted Chinatown, and although it's major street had been readied for electric lines, very few lines stretched to the buildings.

Except for the rats, it was probably the safest area of the city, and it had been deserted first.

At first Lillian thought she had fallen from her chair in a drunken stupor, but even on the plush carpeting of the dining room the floor shivered and quaked beneath her. Instantly the liquor vapors cleared from her head. She had been through this before, and had only been really frightened the first time. Drawing on experience, she walked quickly to the front door and stood under its frame as the house continued to quake and the crystals of the chandeliers played a musical refrain.

She heard the screams of panic from the girls' rooms and ignored them. The tremor would be over in a few seconds and their screams would have been for nothing.

But this violence she had never seen before. Bricks crashed down from the patio facade, tiles blew from the roof. From the door frame she watched a massive tree jump from the ground like a jack-in-a-box and fall over with more roots exposed than it had branches. And then, in the foyer, the curving staircase ripped from the wall and tilted like a funhouse obstacle.

Despite its precarious tilt, several minutes later, ten amusingly clad creatures came bounding down its swaying steps.

"What are you just standing in that door for?" Margaret demanded. "Get to a window and look out. The whole city is being swallowed up and burning."

"This house seems safe," Lillian shrugged.

"No place is safe," the woman cried. "From the other windows we can see them fleeing to the waterfront. Where is Tracey? We need our money!"

"She's not here."

There was a moment of disconcern. "Then you pay us!"

"Me?" Lillian laughed. "I haven't handled business matters for years in this house. You will just have to wait for Tracey or send word as to where you . . ."

It was then that; the initial wave hit that area. The house seemed to jolt right up out of its foundation, hover and then settle back.

It was so frightening that the ten never said goodbye or left any word. She was about ready to laugh at the oversight on their part, when the gateman broke through their fleeing ranks to get to the door.

Oddly, she thought, this young man has worked here for years and I am just now seeing him face to face, and I really don't want to know the dread on his face.

But as Mark Mathews bounded up, the dread turned to mystery. "You're walking, Miss Lillian?"

"Why, I do believe I am," she gasped. She had been ready to laugh over the fact that the ten who had seen her nightly of late had not noticed her standing without the wheelchair. But here, almost a total stranger had noticed at once. Then she centered on the return of dread to his face. "What is the problem?"

"Bad," he said, fighting back tears. "The gate house collapsed. I . . . fear my sister is dead. And . . . may I use the carriage to get my parents to a doctor? They were crushed in their bed and are bad off."

Lillian bit her lip. Horrible memories and distant words returned when she had lain at the bottom of the steps. Then, as if being out of the wheelchair, had returned other of her reasoning powers, she reacted.

"It will be better to get a doctor to them, Mark. Get the flat wagon and some mattresses and move them up here. I think you and I are alone, so just nab some men off the street. If there is a servant about I'll send them for Dr. Larson or Dr. Lee."

She chuckled to herself, going back through the kitchen and climbing the back stairs to the servants' wing. It was the first time she had acknowledged that Mick Lee was a doctor, even though she had reports that he was a very good one.

"What in the hell is this?" she ranted, coming into the hall. The maids and cooks were huddled down together on the floor as though the roof would cave in on them. "Get up and get moving. It's going to be a day like you've never put in before. You cooks get into the kitchen and get coffee, breakfast and pots of hot water going. You maids, the girls are gone, so I want every bed in this house changed. We already have two patients coming and I've a feeling we will have more.''

''But the earthquake—'' one older maid squealed.

''My dear, from the very conception of this house it was designed to meet the two greatest natural hazards I have known native to San Francisco: earthquake and fire. It may shimmy and shake like the girls on a hot Saturday night, but not even the bouncing of their ten beds at once made to quake. Hell, this is built on massive pillar foundations twelve feet deep. The outer walls are adobe brick eighteen inches thick. The Palace Hotel is still standing, duckies, and the same man built it. Now, let's shag a little ass around here like in the old days.''

Before Eric and Tracey had made their way to the house two other events had taken place there.

A disheveled and distraught Clara came shuffling through the shattered back fence and gate. Seeing her aimless path across the back yard, a kitchen helper went at once for Lillian.

''Oh, Clara!'' Lillian exclaimed, hugging her with the familiar pleasure of the olden days. ''You always are here when I need you the most.''

''Henry's gone,'' Clara said dully.

''You didn't have to tell me,'' Lillian soothed, hugging her tighter. ''I sensed it the minute I saw you. But we have always been realistic women, Clara. Time later for coffin nails, memories and tears. Carl Howard came running through a few moments ago. The city is a mess and Central Emergency Hospital collapsed in this last wave. I told him to pass the word that we could make bed space for thirty or more. What do you think?''

Clara screwed her face with exasperation. ''Bet some of those poor critters on the street ain't even had a morning cup of coffee.''

''Could you see to it?'' Lillian asked gently.

''Better still, I'll get the whole kitchen staff onto it,'' replied Clara imperturbably, ''among other things. Noticed the dirt in this place the moment I walked in, and the fact that you are walking. Glad to see it! Always knew something would fire up your buns again."

Then they heard the gunfire in the street and looked at each other confused. Lillian spun and took off on a run, cursing herself for not grabbing a derringer on the way.

At the main gate she could see a very distraught Mark Mathews, a policeman still holding a smoking pistol and a prone figure on the drive between. And from the look on the policeman's face she horribly sensed his next action.

"Stop!" she bellowed over and over as she ran toward them, even as the pistol came up and was aimed at Mark.

"Keep out of this, lady," Patrolman Curtis barked, "I was just given my orders by General Funston on looting on the public streets."

"But you are on private property," she stormed, coming up next to Mark.

"Then if it is your property, *lady*," he snarled, "they were looting you!"

"Mark?" she said, as cold as she had been able to in the old days to get the truth out of a staff member.

He was near to tears of panic, the shock of his sister and parents the first wave and now this the second wave of his own personal earthquake of the day. "He . . . he helped me with the mattresses and my parents." He looked toward a blanket covered lump. "And with my sister. Then I asked him to help get our personal things out of the gate house. We ain't got much of personal value . . . still. I was inside and heard a shot. When I came out . . . I . . . Why?"

"He's lying, lady," the patrolman sniffed. "They was looting!"

"Imbecile!" she said so forcefully that he jumped back. "A man does not loot from himself and my employees do not lie. Look around, sonny! This is the House of Lily and you may be too young to remember but I shot a man here once. That was self-defense. What you have just done is cold-blooded murder."

"It was orders under martial law," he insisted.

"Nonsense!" she snarled. "Its a good thing I don't

have my derringer or I'd show you my type of martial law. Now get off my property."

Just as he hesitantly started to back out of the gate, Eric and Tracey started to enter, but were stopped by a man calling Eric's name a half block behind them.

In the tableau of such events no one spoke of events past or present while one character left the scene and another arrived.

"I was told I would find you at your clinic or here, doctor," the white clad intern puffed. "Doctor Lee needs you, sir. The first tremor hit Central Emergency dead center. Hospital floor after hospital floor dropped onto each other burying the medical staff, nurses and patients under a mass of brick. I'm afraid St. Luke's Hospital was wrecked in the same way. We have been moving the living to the Mechanics Pavilion. Can you come now, sir."

"We have two patients here waiting for a doctor," Lillian shot in quickly.

"That's beside the point," Tracey said shortly. "Mick needs Eric, didn't you hear."

"And didn't you hear," Lillian shot right back. "The gate house collapsed, as you can see. It killed Mark's sister and crushed his parents. They have been moved to the main house. Now, are they to just lay there and die because your precious Dr. Mick Lee can't function unless Eric is there to guide him."

"Eric," Tracey pleaded, as though she had heard not a word, "Mick needs you."

"I am needed here first."

"And perhaps even longer," Lillian intruded again. "The word has gone out that I am prepared to take thirty patients or more."

"No!" Tracey snapped. "Mick and Eric need to work in proper hospitals, not a place like this."

"The young man just gave you a report on the proper hospitals!" Lillian said sardonically. "What is the condition of the Mechanics Pavilion?"

The intern laughed. "Cavernous with high rafters and still horribly decorated from last nights annual Mardi Gras roller-skating carnival. Ain't a privy in the whole building."

"I fail to see," Eric cut in hotly, "the point of this useless banter. Son, tell Dr. Lee I have patients here. Lily, show me the patients. You, drag that body out of sight and cover it. Tracey, I know the strain you have been under, but don't start acting like a ninny now. It sounds like hospital space will be needed and this place is logical. Help however you can to get it ready."

Chapter 19

Tracey didn't even have time to suffer the sting of his command before a clanging ambulance sped by her and up to the house.

Then, for the first time, she noticed that Lillian was walking briskly ahead of her with Eric. It gave her little joy, for the day was filled with strangeness.

In Duncan Nicol's Bank Exchange Saloon members of the banking community gathered in quick session. For one time in its life, without knowing it had but a few hours before destruction, Nicol's watering hole sounded more like Spider Kelly's on Terrific Street.

"Gentlemen," Robert Duocoming urged, "we have all, on our way here, seen the same scene repeated time and again. The fire crews are seeking, but are failing to find water. The unattended fires will spread and this district is in peril. I recommend that we store all that can be crammed into our vaults and what we cannot, we haul away for storage in Oakland."

The "policy" was accepted by all. No one noticed that one banker was not present, because they paid little attention to him in the first place.

Amadeo Peter Giannini was still struggling to get into the city from his home in San Mateo. It would take him five hours struggling against a tidal mass of humanity fleeing the city before he would reach the Bank of Italy.

Unknown to him, his assistant cashier Armando Pedrini and clerk Ettore Avenali had done that morning what they did every morning. Because the Bank of Italy had no vault of its own, they went through the rubble-filled streets to the Crocker Woolworth National Bank, where they rented vault space, collected the three bags belonging to the Bank of Italy and returned to open for business.

Ironically, one business was not open and functioning—the city government. With Sullivan in the hospital, there was no central control point for the fire crews. Jeremiah Dinan had been appointed Chief of Police barely a year before, the third in six years, and although better than his predecessors, this calamity had him and his men standing by in confusion.

Throughout the morning the city was literally leaderless. Even though Eugene Schmitz had scurried here and there for brief inspections, he had made no command decisions on anything he had seen.

At noon, returning home for lunch, he was again confronted by Langdon. He was smiling and yet not smiling.

"My office has been devastated, which means the carefully gathered evidence, in written form is gone."

"Then the problem is solved!"

"Wrong! It will now be just your word against that of Abe Ruef. I've made up a list of some fifty names. We are in a disaster that is building to a holocaust. I recommend that you name these men to a committee to help you run the government."

"This is a list of my enemies!" Schmitz stated with some degree of exasperation after scanning the list. "Spreckels, Phelan, de Young? You jest? Jimmy Phelan, as a former mayor would like his job back and M.H. de Young, as owner of the *Chronicle* is behind every word Fetterson puts in his editorials. And this has to be a mistake. Johnny Lord? How can you put him in with this list of employers, millionaires and church leaders?"

"Because he is probably the largest employer on the Barbary Coast, could very easily be a quiet millionaire and is the leader of a different form of religion. It's called vice!"

"Still an enemy!"

"Damnit, Mister Mayor, they are the enemies of Abe

Ruef! You don't see his name, do you? That's my whole point. They can't refuse you, because it will be for the salvation of the city that they have helped to create and love. You will be looked upon as astute in selecting them instead of a bunch of Ruef's politcal cronies. If Burns is ever able to bring you and Abe to trial, how is this going to make these fifty men look upon you if asked to testify?''

''I like the thought,'' Schmitz said. ''When the fires are out I shall call them together for ideas on rebuilding the city.''

''No! The running of the city during the disaster,'' he said heatedly. ''The Hall of Justice is still standing, so I have made up these invitations for a meeting at three this afternoon. All they need is your signature.''

''What if I don't sign?'' Schmitz puzzled.

''I said the written evidence had been destroyed,'' he said unsmilingly, perhaps taking some small revenge of his own in what he added: ''But verbal evidence is strong if the source is strong. I am a lawyer. I have never committed perjury in a courtroom and never shall. Still, I know how to answer legal questions evasively without lying. Are you the Mayor of this city or just a puppet on Abe's string?''

''Send the damn invitation!''

At about the moment that Langdon was with the Mayor, A.P. Giannnini had arrived at his bank and nearly went crazy. No customers had entered and between his two employees sat the three heavy canvas bags, which held eighty thousand dollars in gold and silver—every cent that the Bank of Italy had in hard cash.

''Closa da doors,'' he said, regaining his composure. ''The London, Paris, American Bank and Crocker Bank have closed their doors. Give this 'dago banker' a moment's time to think as they must be thinking.''

By noon no one in the House of Lily had time to think. The beds were full, the halls lined with litters, the casino a make-shift operating room and the driveway a line of awaiting ambulances.

By the time the men began to gather for their meeting with the Mayor, the situation at Lillian's was near impossible.

"We can't take anymore," Tracey cried. "Eric has been on his feet for ten hours. Mark has exhausted the places to get medical supplies and we are all bushed, Aunt Lillian."

"Honey," she said, "you don't know the half of it. I've been going through this morning with the most blinding hangover of my life."

Tracey couldn't help but smile. "Then the party was a huge success?"

Lillian laughed with the glee of her former days. "It was a total, horrible failure, Tracey. Not a single soul showed up and I sat and got morosely drunk all alone." Then her laugh turned ribald, as though the point of the joke was yet to come. "About an hour ago they brought old Stephanie in on a litter. Do you know she had been a madam the year I came to San Francisco? But before I could get mad at the old strumpet over last night, she looks up at me with real regret in her eyes. 'Lily, doll,' she said, the tears pouring down over her powdered old cheeks, 'this surely will ruin your party. Ain't a one of us old timers who haven't been looking forward to this with real pleasure. First time the most of us would have had a chance to see the inside of your house.' Oh, Tracey I wanted to scold her and then scold myself and feel pride that they wanted to see the House of Lily. I'm totally at fault. I have it down on your business calendar as Tuesday, April 17, but the invitations do read Wednesday, Wednesday, April 18." Then she smiled wickedly. "Do you think we have time to get the place cleaned back up by tonight?"

Tracey laughed. In that moment, the marvelous aunt-and-niece relationship was warmly renewed. "I'll ask Clara what she can whip up."

"Tracey," Lillian said, a little strongly, "wait just a moment! There's a reason behind why I have used her kitchen staff as litter persons and makeshift maids. The more she has to do on her own in that kitchen, the less time she has to think. Honey . . . it's Henry."

"Oh, no, Aunt Lillian!"

"Would that he were the only intimate friend we're losing. Her face contorted with sorrow. "We've got to save as many as we can who come to us for help."

"It is we who need help," Tracey sighed, "and desperately."

Help would not come until later that night of the first day.

That afternoon the Mayor's committee met and met and met; forming sub-committees that met and met and met. The only thing that adjourned them was that the fires had caught up to the Hall of Justice and they had to move or be burned out.

Perhaps the only effective thing accomplished in San Francisco that day was the dangerous decision made by the President of the Bank of Italy. He loaded his three bags of valuable gold and silver on a wagon and nervously headed towards his home in San Mateo.

Evening came, but not darkness. The world was held in a tawny red of fireglow that was reflected in the smoke balls that rose two miles into the air and hovered.

And with the evening hours came a sound as frightening as the first earthquake rumble. Dynamite had arrived to blast out blocks of the city to stop the fire, but, horribly, in the hands of men unused to its power, they were creating fires that would destroy more than they were trying to save.

Sections of Sutter Street were considered proper to blast out to protect Nob Hill. No one thought to check and see if the gas lines had been turned off. A moment after the explosion of dynamite on Sutter, puffing little explosions went from house to house up Powell like a string of Chinese New Year firecrackers, and then east and west.

It was devilish. The first to start burning was the Mark Hopkins mansion, which incinerated so slowly that art treasures were carried to safety from the gabled Palace. In contrast, the Lee mansion, and those around it burned to the ground within an hour.

One by one they went. The Leland Stanford home blazed

brightly. The Huntington mansion smoldered. A fissure which had not appeared to the surface during the quake was now opened up by the dynamite blast. Beth Duocoming's garden sank ten feet and then her house slowly began to slide into the hole.

Across the street Carol Meeks felt the jolt and thought it another tremor. She reached over to shake Basil to wakefullness and felt cold stiff flesh. It was a moment she had dreaded for years and now that it was there she felt nothing. As a dead husband he could not help her in an earthquake.

She started to scream and wake up her children and suddenly realized they were all married and gone. She sat up in bed and felt a terrible loneliness. Ever after she was never sure when it was that she became aware of the suffocating heat surrounding her.

In little more than a filmy nightdress she mindlessly got herself onto the street and looked back to see the house become a funeral pyre for her husband.

Almost at once, by her side, was a bruised and battered Beth Duocoming.

"Carol, thank God," she gasped. "The house sank and I've been crawling upward forever. At least you and Basil are safe . . ."

"He went quietly in his sleep," Carol said, her voice a little too high pitched. "And Robert?"

"At the bank," Beth said, almost guiltily, "standing guard at the safe."

Then the heat from the fire and her guilt increased her fears. The exodus from Nob Hill was starting to resemble the fleeing horde from Chinatown.

"Amy is just a block over," she soothed. "Let's go to her."

Not having ventured out that day they were amazed to see the street a twisted mass of cable car rails and scattered street bricks. This also seemed to be the dividing line between dawn and dusk. The morning side of the street was a crazy-quilt jumble of buildings twisted and turned. The twilight side had left the houses neatly rowed, but now fire was belching from every window and doorway.

And in the street they found the third member of their long-standing trio. Amy stood, her arms fiercely protecting her son Bobbie, and not wanting to believe what she saw, or what had happened that day. Her home was being destroyed by licking flames. And her husband was missing. At 6 a.m. Daniel Lee had come for Richard Deckler, citing the importance of safeguarding Lee properties as more vital than the care of one's family. Deckler had not been home all day or evening.

"I've spent a good part of the day on the roof," she told her two old friends. "There has been a constant stream of people going to Tracey and Lillian's and I'm sure it wasn't for business."

An hour later, after what seemed like a trip through the bowels of hell itself, they sat at Clara's kitchen table wrapped in blankets and sipping cups of chicken broth.

Suddenly a thousand small ironies exploded and reassembled in Beth's mind. She began to giggle. "It's just like the good old days."

"And what," Clara sniffed, "was so good about them?"

"I think I see her point," Amy remarked with unaccustomed concerned, evidently fearing Beth was suffering from shock reaction. "We went through hell our first night here to get to Charmayne's house and here we are right back in a brothel."

"That's it," Beth continued to giggle. "The Scarlet Sisters together again."

"But changed," Carol said soberly, "just like the house."

Clara's brow darkened. For Carol she could feel compassion, for the day had left them both widows. But work had kept her from properly mourning Henry.

Amy, the sensible, picked up on both of their thoughts, and had a useful suggestion.

"Changed or not," she said, "taking a leaf from the past might help us all. What did we do then? We pitched in and helped."

"And it certainly seems," Beth agreed, "that a few helping hands are needed around here. Clara, what's to be done?"

"A great deal—but perhaps in the morning," she said.

"There is no day or night in this town," Carol said distantly, "and I've already had a couple of hours sleep. When was the last time anyone rested in this house?"

"I'm not tired," Bobbie said. "I'm strong and can help Tracey. May I go find her, mother?"

"Run along," Amy said without reluctance and to the amazement of the others. For the first time in years she was letting the twenty-five year old "boy" loose from her apron strings.

"Well," Lillian said, coming into the kitchen just as Bobbie raced out. "Tracey told me you were here. Looks like we might have to rummage around to find you some clothes."

"We won't require hats or gloves," Beth giggled.

"Oh, Beth!" Amy scolded. "We are here to help, Lillian."

"Bless you," she beamed and launched into countless things they could help with.

Again no one thought to comment on her walking, for they were far more startled by another aspect in her. The long hours had not fatigued Lillian but seemed to have restored her. Her eyes sparkled, her back was ramrod straight and nothing more than coffee had reached her lips. She was needed and felt good about being needed.

The flames, as though to show that they were not snobbish, ran merrily off Nob Hill and advanced on its seamy neighbor district.

As had been the case years before, the firemen made no attempt to save the Barbary Coast. Like Chinatown, in one respect, the area was a maze of private tunnels and narrow alleyways. Unlike Chinatown, except for the relatively newer Johnny Lord buildings, it was a tinder box ready to be devoured in minutes.

The moment the first brothel was consumed in flames, Johnny Lord knew there was no hope for the whole district. But he was already several hours ahead of his competitors. After leaving the Mayor's meeting in disgust, he had smuggled his girls, his money and valuable papers to a wharf on the Embarcadero.

It wasn't just the normal Johnny Lord luck that a boat was waiting. It was a part of a quiet investment program he had undertaken in the past few years. He now owned twenty-seven brothels in Oakland and the boat had been used for the nightly ferry service of his customers.

"Leda," he said, giving a thick envelope to a woman whose makeup was running because of the intense heat, "I'm giving your girls and the Oakland girls a month off with pay. However, I don't want them staying at the houses. Tell the Oakland madams to turn the houses into refugee quarters. This thing is going to get a lot worse before it can get better. In time they will say we were destroyed by an earthquake. Hell, we are being destroyed by stupidity. Also tell the captain that he is to keep coming back to this wharf. If people are here, ferry them across at no charge. I won't be a blood-sucker like many I have heard about. And, Leda, good luck to all of you."

"Why aren't you coming, Johnny? Nothing to keep you here."

"Didn't you know," he smiled ironically, still a powerfully handsome man, even though he had passed fifty. "I'm on the Mayor's Committee of Fifty. I want to make sure they don't destroy more than they already have."

"You don't fool this old whore," she returned cuttingly. "You ain't about to leave until you make sure Miss Lily Fancy Pants is safe."

Johnny swallowed a hurting lump in his throat and stared fixedly back at the burning city. He had moved mountains to get some of the old timers to say they would attend her party, even to the point of wiping out a couple of IOU markers to insure their attendance.

When he had checked on the House of Lily that day he had been amazed to find her not only walking, but making a joke over how she had fouled up the date for the party and had already celebrated it alone. He saw before him the spirit of the Lillian he had loved, hated and now loved again.

And there was his love for the city.

Going by the Fairmont Hotel on his way to the Mayor's early morning meeting, the windows of the hotel cracked from the intense heat surrounding the building. A moment later he saw a flash of red from a ground-floor room. By the time his dray had gone the eight blocks to Van Ness the hotel was an inferno.

Driving down Van Ness to the Justice Building, he was repulsed at what he saw: a goodly two dozen field-artillery pieces manned, loaded and ready to fire destructive charges point blank at the elegant homes not as yet touched by earthquake or fire.

"I'm on the Mayor's Emergency Committee," he called to a group of officers. "When was this action ordered and by whom?"

A major of haughty bearing sauntered over to his dray. "By the only authority there is, sir, General Funston. I really shouldn't let you pass, but do need to get a message to Mayor Schmitz. The General orders the Mayor to evacuate at once."

Johnny learned the Committee had abandoned the Justice Building, then the Plaza and were now in the Police Department. His news of the Fairmont Hotel cast a cloud of gloom over them and there were sheepish grins about General Funston and the field-pieces.

"After you left the meeting," Archbishop Montgomery whispered, "the Mayor gave approval for dynamiting, but only if we were kept informed of each building to be destroyed. The General has informed us of nothing."

"Are we then subservient to the military?"

Angry murmurs came from several Committee members who heard his question.

But at that moment Eugene Schmitz began to run the meeting like a bad dress rehearsal. Again and again he would go over points that the effective sub-committees had agreed upon in their private meetings throughout the night.

Then, with the surprise arrival of General Funston and Abe Ruef, they were brought right back to square one: dynamiting and shelling.

During the night "Fearless Freddie" had won an ally in Abe Ruef, but the General was apolitical and did not see the real Ruef motives.

"This is also my town," Ruef reminded them, "even

though you didn't see fit to include political parties on this committee."

"Din't seem to keep you out," Downey Harvey sneered.

"I am here as a citizen," Ruef shot back, "with faith in General Funston's plan. We have a golden opportunity, gentlemen. The Barbary Coast is ablaze and soon will be no more. But look at the General's map. Dr. Herstein, I believe, has reported to you on the plague that could come out of Chinatown. Why let it? Dynamite those rats all the way back to China."

The members quickly agreed to this.

"And again the map," Ruef went on, acting as though he were the chairman, sweeping his hand down the area from Grant Street to the Embarcadero. "With Chinatown this whole area should go."

Alex Lee gasped. "That is crazy. That area has not been hit by fire."

Ruef smiled. "Vested interests, Mr. Lee, because it includes your produce district?"

"How dare you?" Judge John Hunt gasped. "Vested interests, indeed. That produce area has continued to bring in food stuffs and distribute it free, sir. I demand you withdraw this scheme."

"No, I will not," Ruef blustered. "Most of you have lost millions. How you get them back is of what I speak. With Chinatown, the Barbary Coast and the seamy district that surrounds the produce blocks, we have a chance to rebuild that whole area in a beautiful European style. Mr. Lee would make more profit on that than on his lettuce trade."

"You seem to be overlooking one point," Robert Duocoming said. "There are hundreds, even thousands of property owners in that area. This is hardly the time, even if we could reach them all, to propose such a scheme. Order of business, Mr. Mayor."

"I haven't given up the floor," Ruef barked, "and the property owners mean nothing. We are under martial law and I see that as signifying no property rights. The General is ready to dynamite these areas, even if you are too fearful to do so."

All were uncomfortably aware that through the humid and depressing meeting so far, the sounds of shell fire had increased along Van Ness.

Johnny Lord and Alexander Lee were the only two to see the real thrust of Abe Ruef's finger at the General's map. Each time it came down, it was directly on the block that housed the House of Lily. The man had waited a long time to get his revenge and it would be crushing.

"I'm not fearful," Schmitz said. "Do it!"

Several looked at each other and thought the same. The Mayor was back in Ruef's hip pocket. Opposition came from a strange quarter, considering the area involved.

"I am reminded of a story," The Archbishop said, and they looked at him in puzzlement. "Once one of the Holy Fathers called together the College of Cardinals. At the outset of the meeting he announced exactly what they would decide at the conclusion. 'Then, Pappa,' a Cardinal asked, who had made a long ocean voyage to get to the conclave, 'why call us here in the first place?' To the Holy See it was simple. 'Brother,' he said, 'it is the people who must think I have your blessing on this matter.' Mr. Mayor, I don't want my people thinking I have given you my blessing on anything unless it comes from a vote of this committee."

A motion was quickly made to dynamite only those areas, such as Chinatown, which were a health problem or could serve as an effective fire-break.

"An amendment," Archbishop Montgomery demanded, "That no place offering humanitarian refuge may be destroyed without approval of this committee."

They accepted it as calculated to protect church property and approved it quickly, and then approved the motion.

"You surprise me, Your Eminence," Johnny said, as they left the meeting. "You know that Ruef was out to destroy Lillian McHenry and her brothel."

"Out in the harbor is a ship," the old churchman said, as though he had not heard. "It was donated to us to take the place of St. Luke's Hospital. The majority of its patients are transferred there from another hospital. Quite a remarkable one. It has a single Chinese doctor. I stopped there on my way to this meeting. I was tempted in this meeting, Mr. Lord, to speak to my amendment about this establishment run by an order of Sisters." He smiled. "The Scarlet Sisters, I am told. Well, the heart of Our Lord Jesus was also scarlet and I shall protect the grand work that they are doing for our citizens even if I have to stand before Funston's aimed cannon. And as for the future, my boy, I would like to see what survives before we start building upon its ashes."

But it did not thwart Abe Ruef. He had never bowed to a committee before and he certainly was not about to start. Like Liberty, he saw a great political future for Freddie Funston, but strictly as his replacement for Eugene Schmitz. He was also wise enough to know that as the city burned so did its records and skeletons from the past. Already in his mind, he could see his ownership of the great triangle of land bordered by Market, Powell and the Embarcadero. If it was not devastated soon, he would make sure that Funston's troops put it in a condition that could come under martial law. Then, because he controlled the building permits, he would make millions on what only he would allow to be rebuilt on the ashes.

"But the churchman made a small error," he snickered at the General. "May I point out his error to you on the map."

On the first day and night of a tragedy people run on the energy of the unexpected. This could not be happening to them, so it is a form of nightmare. It is an excitement. Better to be involved than not involved. The death and carnage is a backdrop of the drama, an accepted part of the plot, strangely talked about but not fully accepted at that time.

As the hours of the second day creep along for some, and madly race for others, the toll on mental and physical strength begins to show.

Tempers flare, backs ache, a universal question mark arises. "Will this never end?"

It was thus at the House of Lily. Each moment Lillian

feared Eric could not stand another moment. She cursed the man in his cassock who promised help and in turn prayed that he had not forgotten his promise.

Even with the blessed help of the Scarlet Sisters, it was coming to the time when they'd been on their feet in the house for twelve hours. And still the wounded and dying came.

"From where?" Lillian wondered aloud. "The city didn't have this many people to begin with, did it?"

"Aunt Lillian," Tracey said, ignoring the fact that she had overheard her. "Eric can't go on. Let me go and try to find Mick."

"It would be futile," Lillian said gently. "You heard what Bishop Montgomery said this morning. He would check his staff people and try to find him. When the nurses he promised get here, then we shall have an answer."

At that moment it seemed as though another quake had hit the area. The floor shook beneath their feet, the foyer chandelier danced dangerously and their ears were filled with a shattering boom.

The dying echoes of the explosion were replaced by screams coming from several directions. Confused, thinking it had been her house, Lillian ran through the front door to the driveway.

To the left, at the corner of Kearny and Jackson, and to the right, at the corner of Kearny and Washington, mushroom clouds of smoke and debris appeared. Then they were followed by more explosions and more smoke clouds and screaming.

By the time she got to the gate and the street, she was met by a throng of blood drenched people, pursued by Marines with fixed bayonets. Ironically, in the throng of people were three black clad Nuns.

Lillian looked up and down Kearny. The cannon were being reloaded and reaimed, even though screams still came from the buildings just fired upon.

"Go in! Go in!" Lillian cried. "There is a doctor to help you! Mark! Help me find a sane person among these murdering animals!"

"I'm in charge," said a sergeant, "and lady, I want no

sass. You people were told hours ago to get the hell out of here."

"Look, *sonny*," she said darkly, pulling out the paper Johnny had left with her earlier, "This piece of paper is all I've been told. Now, get an officer over here pronto and if one more cannon goes off, that shot gun my gate keeper is holding will be the last sound you hear."

He blinked and shouted: "Steady on the line! Steady on the line! Officer of the day! Officer of the day!"

A big-boned man with a blistered red face from too long on the firing line came on the run. He started to open his mouth but Lillian silenced him with a single look.

"From the screams I hear," she snapped, "you fired on occupied buildings, and from the aim of your cannon you intend to fire upon more. Stop your fire and order your men to save what lives they have not already taken."

He laughed sarcastically. "They were warned."

"By whom?"

"Don't make a damn bit of difference to me lady," he insisted. "I was ordered here to blow out everything in this area."

"Including me?"

"Big mistake on their part," he said ruefully. "Hard to blast everything out around you on all four blocks and still keep you from being set afire."

"Because I am a hospital?"

"Thought it was because you were a whore house for the later use of my marines."

Lillian shrugged as though the matter were not hers to solve. "You saw the nuns, which you nearly killed on the street enter. What does that suggest to you?"

The man was so bitterly disappointed that he flung his anger at the men nearest him. "Did you ass-wipes give me the wrong location? Get ready to move out!"

"No!" Lillian barked. "Unless you expect to slave away the rest of your life in the lowest ranks of the military you will not leave this area until every living human being has been brought from the shelled buildings to receive aid!"

"What is this? What is this?" Abe Ruef demanded,

riding up on a horse that he could hardly control. "This whole area was to be destroyed by now."

"But . . . but . . ." the Marine officer stammered, looking from Lillian to Abe.

"Soldier," Abe fumed, "I have just been with General Funston and now his orders on this matter. Now, get those cannon barking."

At once Lillian saw his ploy. Destroy every building around her block and the fire-storm was bound to consume her in the middle and force her to flee. But Abe had made one error and the officer another, as she saw it.

Too many years in her profession gave her the knowledge that the Marine officer was attached to the Navy and had instinctively resented being called a 'soldier' by Abe.

"Ensign," she cooed, giving him proper rank and service status with a single utterance, "I request you to read this document out loud to this gentleman. Then, as the proper military authority present, make your own command decision."

The Marine officer and Abe Ruef were a little mystified. Abe, because he had left the meeting before Tirey L. Ford had raised the question of identification that might be needed by members of the committee or people in restricted areas. The officer, because he and his men had been put ashore less than two hours before, their ears filled with stories of looting, murder, rape and a population gone wild.

Ensign Nathan Browning would play a middle ground between them, but accepted the paper from the lady and read:

"The Bearer is a member of the Relief and Restoration Committee of Law and Order, or a sub-committee member thereof, and is invested with the same powers that I possess. You are therefore notified to give him every assistance possible in the prompt performance of his duty and cheerfully comply with any request that he may make, signed: Eugene Schmitz, Mayor."

Abe stormed, seeing only one attack area open, "It does not say *she* and is therefore a false document."

"What document in this land says 'she' and not 'he'? It is as interchangable as 'we the people!' "

Browning now saw no middle ground to stand upon. He turned and ordered his men to help the refugees they had just created.

"Your reprieve is only temporary," Ruef said.

"Abe, you should be gripped by the throat and shaken until you are made to realize that no one is winning anything. I'd feel sorry for you, but I don't have the time."

She turned and left him puzzled. To his way of thinking the situation was quite simple. He would just throw the whole situation back at the General.

With the arrival of the Nuns it gave them an opportunity to break into groups and get some rest periods.

Within a couple of hours the Archbishop had brought about a second miracle, the arrival of another doctor.

Dr. Alfred Spalding was a member of the last medical team forced to flee from the doomed Mechanics Pavilion.

"Dr. Lee," Eric asked. "Where did he go?"

The man blanched, his thin face gray with misery. "During the night a man was brought in who had been shot by a soldier. It was Dr. Lee's father and we could do nothing to save him. Shortly after we got word that Nob Hill was burning. He . . . he went to pieces, Eric. He picked up the blanket wrapped body of his father and said he was taking him home. It was best to let him go and I haven't seen him since."

Eric frowned at Lillian. "We better keep this news from Tracey."

"No need," a sob came from the door of the casino, "I heard. Poor Mick."

"Come along," Lillian said, putting an arm around her shoulder, "you are going upstairs for some rest. You too, Bobbie."

Tracey accepted, her mind and body barely functioning, and oddly feeling no alarm for Mick. She sensed what he had meant by taking Daniel Lee home. It meant home to

Liberty and if Mick was with his grandmother then he was safe. Not even fire would dare to stand up to Liberty Lee.

But even as Tracey fell into a deep sleep her thought was being proven quite incorrect.

"Some one go for Miss Lily!" Clara barked, looking out the back window. Through the broken back gate came a trio in abject misery. Despite her personal feelings, Clara ran to help them inside.

Liberty accepted her strong arm with gratitude.

"Charles will need help also," Liberty said. "He has carried her forever."

Disheveled and unshaven, the old butler looked near collapse.

Lillian came on the run, took one look and barked orders over her shoulder.

But even with help at his side, Charles refused to give up his duty, but did let the two kitchen helpers support him on each arm and lead him directly to the casino.

As though she had to explain, Liberty let Clara put her down in a kitchen chair, but kept her eyes on Lillian.

"That's my daughter-in-law. The poor thing came unravelled when it was apparent we would lose both our houses. Charles had the dray ready to take us to the Southern Pacific Depot. It became a frightening journey for the poor horse and I finally agreed with Charles that we would do better on foot. We had gotten out, but not her. The horse bolted and mindlessly ran right into a burning building. By the time Charles and I could get to her and get her out, she was a torch. We used our own bodies to smother and beat out the flames, but her hair was already gone and pieces of her dress stuck to her flesh. Since then, which has been forever, we have been wandering in search of help for her. Finally a soldier directed us here. Will it be Mick caring for his mother?"

Lillian hesitated. She could not fail to notice the remarkable change in the woman. She seemed so old and shriveled. More than her outward appearance, though, Liberty's voice shocked Lillian. The strong, powerful voice which had forced mighty men to do her bidding—the voice that had always been so confident—had faded to a weak and frightened whisper.

"Mick was on duty at the Mechanics Pavilion," Lillian said at last, knowing that she had to speak the full truth. "His mother will be seen by Dr. Spalding, who just came from there. It has been evacuated, but before it was, Mick left to take his father home. It's bad news about your son, I'm afraid, Liberty."

The woman did not flinch. "I've sensed bad news coming for hours," she said, amazingly with more strength to her voice. "One can always face these things better with a cup of hot tea in their hands. Might I impose?"

Clara was already seeing to it and Lillian had to turn away. Despite everything in the past, the woman had caused her eyes to fill with tears. Here was the true strength that they all would need in the future.

Chapter 20

Friday morning, April 20th, Abe Ruef got his desire, but by no act of his own.

It had been another sleepless night for Eugene Schmitz and at 4 a.m. he was in no mood to be pushed around.

"This monster has had two heads long enough," he roared, the whiplash of his voice infuriating General Funston, but reminding Fire Chief John Dougherty that he had used the same tone on his firemen and the Mayor to bring the meeting about. "Dougherty's men have fought their hearts out and all they have to show for it are a few buildings. And why? Because every time they make a little headway they are defeated by your lunatics. The fire never would have gotten across Van Ness without their cannon fire. I'm glad we are standing on the steps of St. Mary's Cathedral, because I want God as my witness. I am giving you one hour to pass *my* order down the fire lines. The artillery bombardments and dynamiting will cease! And I don't want to hear another word on the subject!"

Funston spun away, like he had just lost an argument with the devil. But the order he issued was slightly twisted. The use of explosives was to be stopped until further orders on his part.

By 5 a.m. the order had reached every commander. Captain Arthur Fung was proud of the zealous crew under him. Like little boys at play they had dynamited some very impressive buildings, but none as impressive as the Viavi Building on Green Street. He had used every last bit of explosives available to him and it was a shame it would now be for naught. He took off his garrison cap and scratched his head. A sudden wind tousled his hair and he looked toward Fort Mason. The flag on the building top was whipping about.

For a moment he had been tempted to ignore the order, but a standing rule he could not. Every time the wind had as much as fluttered the flag they had curtailed their blasting. In disgust he threw his hat to the street.

He was never aware that the "fire" man took that as a signal to push down the plunger to ignite hundreds of explosive caps.

No one had been warned back and the front of the building instantly crashed down on the captain and four of his crew. A firestorm shot two hundred feet into the air, carrying with it massive rafters that were alight like match sticks. As though weightless, they were catapulted over a wide area previously untouched by fire. The force of their downward plunge crashed them right through roofs and ignited interiors. Within seconds the blast was responsible for over eighty fires, some as far away as the House of Lily—a good two-mile distance. Within minutes the whole north side of Green Street was an inferno, driven onward by a gale-force wind.

The rafter, like a flaming arrow, went through the clay tiles as though they were paper thin, spewing flames onto curtains and bed clothes in a maid's third floor room before crashing again through that floor and igniting a cook's room below.

Ironically, no one was on either floor in that wing at the time. At 4 a.m. Johnny Lord had come into Clara's kitchen with a young naval officer. The man and his sailors had been assigned the task of keeping the food supplies moving from the Embarcadero wharfs to the produce district for distribution and to safeguard it against graft and looting. To the amusement of Alex Lee, but not the sailors, the navy had failed to make arrangements to feed them.

Johnny, who had been placed on the Food Distribution sub-committee, saw little that was funny in the matter. The other sailors from the Pacific Squadron could get back to their ships for food and relief. He had nothing but praise for this downy cheeked officer and his fifty men. They were keeping calm and order in what could have been an explosive situation, without one word of complaint. He was going to see to it that they had a hot breakfast that morning. And to his way of thinking, that was fifty more for Clara to feed.

She took the challenge gracefully, but tumbled every one out of bed to help.

They came in groups of ten, starting just a few minutes after five o'clock and a minute after the flaming rafter. They marvelled at their luck in being in such an elegant dining room and eating such great food, but the main talk was the explosion they had seen as they came up Washington Street. It had been heard and seen all over town.

Still, they had little time to do much talking. Each group had been limited to under fifteen minutes to eat before the next group would arrive. This kept sailors in motion at the dock, at the produce district warehouses, moving back and forth from Lily's.

But as they were all approaching the house from the front, no one saw the glow spread from room to room on the second and third floors of the rear wing. The fire was unable to break out of the eighteen inch thick walls or penetrate the clay tiles of the roof. The hole made by the piercing rafter was so near the main kitchen chimney stacks that the smoke that rose from it seemed to be coming from those chimneys.

If the heat in the kitchen seemed to rise, everyone put it down to the added cooking and frantic pace to feed the sailors and get them on their way.

The fire was in no hurry. Nathan Tedder, believing he had built a house completely invulnerable to earthquake and fire, had not fully considered internal fire. It had plenty to feed on in the thick-raftered ceilings, the heavy wood panels that divided the rooms and the parquet floors. The rafters in the second floor rooms were not just for show. Room by room they were part of the grid work that supported a foot thick sub-floor and a two inch thick hardwood floor. Locked together in such a way that they had give and take space during earth tremors. But the air pockets kept renewing the fire's life, whereas had it been solid it might have charred a single side and smothered itself out like an unturned log in a fireplace.

Tracey slept through the night, on Lillian's strict orders that she not be disturbed. But it was not a normal awakening. She lay in a pool of her own perspiration and it oozed from every pore. At first she thought she was ill, but this heat was not from fever. It surrounded her like an airless summer day when no breeze came in off the bay.

Then, from down the hall, she heard a strange sound. The whimpering of a male voice. It took her a second to recall that Lillian had bedded down Bobbie Deckler on the living room sofa.

She jumped from bed, pulled on a wrapper and went to see what was troubling him.

He stood, staring back towards Lillian's office. His poor brain fearful that every horror of the last twenty-four hours was starting again.

Tracey didn't want to frighten him and had to subdue her own fright.

The north wall of Lillian's office, which abutted the eastern end of the back wing, was merrily dancing with little licking flames. Her first thought was that Lillian had left one of her horrible cigarettes burning and it had set the room on fire.

"Come here, Bobbie," she soothed, "The door to the outer hall is this way. We will quietly go downstairs and let them know what is happening."

He obeyed, but once in the outer hall, she looked back at the door that led to the enclosed wing. Even at that distance she could see the paint on the door bubbling and peeling. Quickly, she let her eyes roam along that wall to the start of the balconies of the far wing, along them and back to the main staircase. Nothing seemed out of order, except for the black clad Nuns going in and out of the rooms.

Still, paint didn't bubble like that without something horribly amiss behind the door.

"Bobbie, I think I should dress," she said, hoping he would just see that as a very sensible thing for her to do. "You run down stairs and find Lillian for me."

He smiled brightly, willing to do anything she might ask.

And before he was a step away she was back inside the apartment and tearing along to her room. She sensed what they might be facing and pulled on the most sensible clothes her mind could quickly focus upon. She had seen the oddities that burned out people grabbed in a moment of panic. She was not in a moment of panic, yet, but had only one item that she felt could never, ever be replaced. She tore up a petticoat and tied her daily journal securely to her stomach. Nothing had gone into it for four days, but those were moments she could recapture. It contained things she could never recapture.

She was dressed and back at the top of the stairs by the time Lillian started to run up them.

There was the strangest sound, like the house knew it was in peril. It came from behind the three storied high wall opposite the grand staircase. They both looked toward the source of the sound, just as the last group of sailors came from the dining room and looked up as well.

Then, from the second floor up tons of plaster veneer and burning wall wood came crashing down to the foyer below.

Now the sailors became animated, beating out cinders that fell on them, using their hats, hands or anything they could find to attack the hundred little fires that fell and kept falling.

"The floor is marble," Lillian shouted down.

"It's what?" one called back.

"It won't burn! Put your backs to the real problem. Let's get the patients out of here."

Tracey ran down to her in disbelief. "Surely it won't take the whole house."

A cold fury swept over Lillian. She could now see into two full gutted floors. "We can't take that chance," she snapped. "We've been told that everything is burning from Green Street to the bay and from Green Street back to California. We won't see a fireman coming here."

"Where will we take them?"

As Lillian, they had been moving down to the foyer. As

a sailor ran by, Lillian grabbed him by the arm and hauled him back.

"Are all the produce warehouses in use?" she demanded, and only then noticed that he was the young officer leading the group.

"One's empty," he gasped.

"Then that shall be our new hospital!"

"Impossible!" he yelled. "They are cold as hell at night and drafty throughout the day, even without a wind like we are getting right now."

"Don't you yell at her," a fierce voice barked at his back. He turned to see the little old lady who had helped serve his men breakfast. "She knows that it is better for them to be a little cold than heated to a cinder crisp."

"But lady," he gasped, "I don't have the authority to just move these people onto Mr. Lee's property."

"Look, you young whippersnapper," Liberty hissed. "That Mr. Lee you talk about came right out of my womb and if he doesn't like Lillian moving her patients there, we'll just remind him that he wouldn't have that property without her. But you don't have to say a thing to him. You there," she said, pointing at Tracey, "seem dressed for the outside. Give me a hand. I thought I was strong enough to carry breakfast plates for Clara, but she puts too damn much food on them. I need a strong arm to help me down to see Alexander. Do you have an extra cloak, Lillian? I seem to be reduced to what I have on my back."

"Do you also want a hat and gloves?" Lillian suddenly laughed, running for the foyer closet.

It gave Liberty pause to chuckle. "That is the silliest fad to ever hit this town and by damn I bet it is the only one that is carried on after this turmoil is over."

She turned back, after Lillian had put a cloak around her shoulders. She grabbed Lillian by the shoulders and pulled her into a hug.

"I thank you all, even though I sensed Charles was carrying around a corpse. Because you will need man-power here, I leave him in your charge." Then she turned. "Well, young lady, I thought you were going to give me your arm."

Lillian saw the revolt in Tracey's eyes and felt strange in coming to Liberty's defense. "Tracey, Mrs. Lee was put through another family tragedy while you slept. She and her butler brought Mick's mother to us, but we could not help. Not only has she not been to bed, but she helped Clara serve breakfast."

"Oh, hush!" Liberty said. "Tracey and I are quite aware of where we stand with each other. We've been sparring partners over the same man for years. It will keep us both on our mettle until we find the stupid little whelp Mick. But, Tracey, trust this old woman's feelings. Mick is the image of his grandfather. See a job to do and he would stop to do it, regardless if it was time for him to be home for supper. And Lord knows, there is a job for a doctor in every corner of this town."

Still, Liberty could see the questioning in Tracey's eyes as to Mick's condition the last time he'd been seen. Despite her words, it was a fear for Liberty, as well. Never had she felt so old and rudderless. That was why she had jumped on the sailor. She had clutched onto the news of Alexander's whereabouts with relish. Her first-born was dead, with his wife. She was not even aware if Miranda was in town. It was hard for her to keep up with Miranda and so she didn't bother. Nor had she tried to keep track of Alexander, but she needed him now desperately.

Chapter 21

Even as the last of the patients were moved to the produce warehouses, the inferno had jumped Van Ness again and was rolling up Russian Hill. The wooden buildings on these slopes were particularly vulnerable. Dried out by the hot air blown over them for days and now the gale-force winds.

A young, disoriented man watched from his balcony, not quite aware of how he got there or why he was there. He was somewhat aware that he hated fire, because he was somehow aware that it had taken from him so much of what he had loved. Therefore, when he saw the house just below burst into flame, he did not hesitate to go and join the firefighters.

Throughout the morning and early afternoon he worked with maniacal fury alongside others who lived on the hill and wanted it saved.

He saw a woman who had been hoarding water for days share its precious buckets to save a neighbor's house. He saw an Italian bring from his cellar barrel upon barrel of home made wine to quench fire rather than thirst.

He, as far as he knew, was just another one of them. No different than the prizefighter, the box factory worker or the lumberman. Until one man looked at him a little puzzled.

The man grabbed him by the shoulders and spun him around. "Hey, Doc, it's me, Josh Moody. I got you out of bed to bring my kid into the world, remember? Why the hell are you playing firefighter? Leave that to us stiffs. You should be out taking care of the people who need your talents, Dr. Lee."

"Yes," Mick said dully, "you are right."

He rambled down the hill to Columbus Avenue, experiencing the memory of that same journey with Tracey. But how the landscape had changed! Nothing was familiar in the ravaged Chinatown and no Chinese clinic to be found.

Instinct, rather than memory, drew him toward the House of Lily. He recalled looking at burning structures with something heavy in his arms. He had dropped the weight of his father's body and stepped forward to watch the captain's walk of his grandmother's great mansion collapse to the ground and burn. Behing it, the pile of bright embers had been his parents' home.

Now, came another shocking scene. The House of Lily was a gutted skeleton. The tile roof had collapsed inward, with no more rafters to support it. Tongues of flame still licked from every blackened window. The intense heat had dried the adobe brick walls to such a degree that the straw mixture was burning and causing the eighteen-inch-thick bricks to crumble to dust. Even as he watched, a whole wing slowly folded in upon itself.

He took a deep breath and closed his eyes, trying to recall why he was there in the first place.

"Sir," a hesitant voice said, "This area is not safe."

When he looked at the speaker, his gaze was calm and steady. "I am a doctor."

"This hospital was moved down to the produce district after it caught fire. They will sure be glad to see you, sir. Seems everyone has heard about it. If you don't know the way, might as well follow the litters. Must be hundreds down there by now."

Mick Lee had only heard a portion of what the sentry said. His mind had stopped on the words produce district. He shuddered, his mind oddly mixing a youthful thought with that of his adulthood. His mind could only see the produce district as he recalled it on the day he went for his first long pants, but his doctor's mind was chagrined at that foul place for a hospital. This just couldn't be. He would just have to find Eric Larson and get the location changed. But where? All of San Francisco was like hell on earth.

The arrival of the *Carrie* at its pier next to the produce wharfs, didn't seem to help, even though it was quickly transformed into a hospital ship, its crews pressed into service as nurses and litter carriers, it barely made a dent.

The truth was horrific. This black Friday saw more death, pain and destruction than all the days before.

The growing list of crimes laid at the door of the military were put aside by Funston's aides for later investigation. The General was not to be disturbed by such minor matters. He sat brooding in his Fort Mason office, letting the rest of the city burn, waiting for the Mayor to come and say that he had been right and the Mayor wrong.

By four o'clock that afternoon, with no words from Mayor Schmitz, his determination to be the supreme authority returned.

"All right, Do it!"

Thus began a personal vendetta between two men with strong egos and senseless disregard for the masses. The cannons boomed aimlessly and Schmitz called for a private army until he got his way. But it was a leaderless army without weapons and Funston still had shells for his cannons.

Yet, the rumor of a private army spread. Many soldiers had looked forward to the time when they would be the sole guardians of a deserted city. Fearing they would lose their opportunity to loot, some deserted their posts and began to pick through the rubble for bronze, brass and partly melted jewelry.

Sickened, and frightened for their own safety, those whose Nob Hill homes were untouched by fire were forced out at the point of a bayonet.

Robert Duocoming had been unhappy over his meeting with the other bankers, who wanted a "bank holiday" declared until mid-November. A six months' recovery time he felt was unreasonable. He liked better the simple approach of A.P. Giannini. The Italian banker had eighty thousand dollars in gold and silver hidden in his San Mateo home. Although this represented the only cold cash that bank had against $846,000 in deposits, Duocoming knew the hard facts. A run on the Bank of Italy would do little damage, because he knew the largest depositor was Miranda Lee and the second largest Liberty.

But that cash, coupled with what he had in his home safe, loaned at this point in time, would reap millions in the future.

Because of his sooty condition after digging through the debris of his home to locate the safe, open it, bag the money and come back onto the street, he was immediately challenged by a sentry.

"It is quite all right," he said, reaching for his pass. "I am a member of the committee and this is . . . was my home. I have come here on business vital to the whole community!"

For some reason—whether the soldier was deaf from too many cannon blasts or not wishing to admit he was illiterate and could not read the pass—no one ever knew. He threw the pass to the ground and promptly bayonetted Duocoming through the chest.

Seriously wounded, Duociming threw the money bag over his chest to ward off further attacks, but the soldier was already leaving.

"Just another looter," he growled. "Leave him to die."

The second soldier saw the pleading in the man's eyes as he staggered and then fell. He had believed the man, even though his sergeant had not.

He could read, and did as he squatted down beside the dying man. Twice he had been on sentry duty when the Mayor had had his meetings in various spots in town. This man he had never seen, but knew the manner of men who had been issued these passes.

"You coming?" the sergeant growled, without looking back.

"He's still alive," the private called.

"Damn do-gooder," the sergeant mumbled, moving ahead and rounding the corner.

Duocoming felt he was in reasonable hands when he was lifted by the shoulders. Then puzzlement grew as the hands slipped up to his neck. Within seconds he felt nothing as his body was hauled behind a pile of litter and quickly stripped of its clothing.

The young private, however, was methodical in his desire for escape from that military madness. He carefully dressed Robert Duocoming in his uniform, with his identification papers.

The pass was all that had at first intrigued him. He had seen its magical power to get a man in and out of forbidden areas. He just wanted to use it to get him out of this whole impossible place. Almost as an afterthought he picked up the money satchel to take along. He thought it gave him a certain air of authority and was unaware that he carried away some $20,000 in gold coin.

All through the evening, Liberty kept a close eye on what she thought was a great plan on Alexander's part. The boats that brought the foodstuffs returned empty across the bay. They could return with patients to the comfort of private homes and hospitals in Oakland. It seemed, however, to take forever to get rid of that endless procession of misery.

Time and again she tried to count the litters and the numbers never seemed to end. Then her mind stopped counting as her eyes went back up the row of sufferers. She squinted at the figure in the long green smock. In the overall canvas of misery a long green smock had come to represent in her tired mind a doctor going about his endless task. How long this doctor had been working the rows she didn't know, but she now stood for some time and watched his calm efficiency with growing respect and love.

Slowly she became aware that someone else had noticed him and was coming down the aisle. Their eyes met and held in open challenge.

Never again would Liberty be able to regard Tracey as a girl. She had always been aware of her intelligence and had come to recognize her strengths as a woman. So much of Liberty's world had died or was dying in the flames. The Phoenix bird, if it was to rise from the ashes, had to be in the hands of youth and strength.

Tears glistening her eyes, Liberty smiled and nodded for

Tracey to make the first approach. She was not being gracious in defeat. She was being crafty in victory.

Mick put the blanket over the woman's face. He squatted there, more tired than he could remember every having been before, and then saw the small feet at the head of the litter. He looked up and stared at Tracey's face, so calm, reassuring and loving.

Slowly he rose to put his arms around her and she came to him.

Johnny Lord, watching nearby, put his arm through Lillian's. "Will you step back and let them be together?"

"Do I have a choice?" she said. "I'm going to have enough problems piecing my own world back together. It's not going to be easy on us old broads. Helena told me awhile ago that she would like to go back to teaching. She, at least, has a profession to fall back on. Clara is made of stout stuff. The trio have had each other to lean upon since childhood and will just keep leaning. I have had one invitation. Otis found his house gutted, but his family safe in Mammy Pleasant's old house. He says Carrie would like to offer me the hospitality of her house. It wasn't put in so many words, but I guess I do have family after all."

"I've a proposition to make to you, Lillian," he said. "I want to sell the houses in Oakland to each madam. I don't know if it will ever pay off, but I did have the Barbary Coast property insured. It, too, I want to sell. I'm getting too old for this racket. I need you, Lillian, to talk to and to be with and to help me start something new. Will you have me that way?"

"I don't think I heard right," she laughed.

"Then I will put it this way," he sighed. "Will you have me as a husband?"

"Yes," Lillian said. "I'll have you that way, Johnny."

Saturday morning dawned gray. By 7:15 exactly—seventy-four hours after it had begun—Dougherty's firemen had the burned area narrowed down to the Slot, where the fire had started its destruction. Then came the blessed rain.

Eric Larson sat on the porch of his little house, ironically an untouched island on the fringe of the sea of destruction which had been Chinatown and the Barbary Coast, and let the moisture seep into his parched skin. He would nap, awake with a start and then nap again. His body and mind so accustomed to the ritual that it would not fully relax and sleep.

At one point he fought to keep awake. For a moment he thought his napping mind was playing tricks on him, as the point of his curiosity seemed hardly to change from one waking time to the next.

Then he realized that an old Chinese woman was just inching along the street, just a tiny step at a time so that she wouldn't fall.

"Old grandmother," he called, "may I offer you a chair on my porch?"

She nodded, clinging to one of the last pickets left on his fence. Then his heart broke and he rushed down the four steps to help her up and into a seat beside him. The pain in her feet came from the many years they had been bound as a girl and a young woman. They marked her as quality—a woman who'd never had cause to walk farther than around her own home and courtyard. It was a practice he despised as a doctor and a man.

"Thank you, son of Kai Soong."

He looked at her, a little startled. "You know me as such, Old Grandmother."

"When the earth shook my son, I came to your clinic for our people. Your hands were busy and then they said we must walk across the hills to live in the park. It was said years ago by Kai Soong that the earth would shake and burn." She chuckled. "He did not say that old feet bound in youth would have to walk back and forth over the hills to see his son." Then she sighed. "It is hard to make out the old streets and buildings. This destruction is far greater than the Tong Wars."

"You do not go back that far, Old Woman."

"I do," she smiled. "I was three and the daughter of the cabinet maker to Wang Soong. I sat as a child and saw the beautiful furniture that my father created for Master Wang. And when he was finished with his creations, and learned his tongue would be cut out over them, he quietly sold me as a child bride to Chingwegh, the undertaker. Like you, my name was changed to protect my life."

"Was that necessary?"

"Son of the Old Master," she said quietly, "they cut out my father's tongue by starting at the throat and made sure my two brothers would only speak in pleasant gardens hereafter. I take your words to mean that you have not learned the secret of Wang Soong on your own?"

He laughed drily. "Old Woman, I put it out of my mind years ago. Had the fortune of Wang Soong been more than a myth, my half-brother would never have allowed me to survive. A bargain was struck, as you must know by my being called Dr. Larson."

"Myth," she laughed huskily, "of Kai Soong's design. When last did you sit upon his chair and peer through his great screen?"

"I never did, but recall his doing so as a child. An identical screen was in the House of Peony, for I recall seeing both screens years later in his rooms at the House of Lily."

"Both sets created by my father, as well as the rest of the heavy ornate furniture. Heavy, because of the internal being of each piece. Clever craftmanship to hide within and upon the gold for which they fought. But Old Master Kai Soong ended up with both screens and the House of Soong. The problem of which was which was left up to you."

"And is now a futile point," he laughed. "Fire has taken them both."

"This fire," she said slowly, "has only destroyed the years of painstaking woodwork of my father to conceal its inner framework, or the delicate open-work designs of the many screens. In the heat of these days, Master Soong, that gold could only melt as it was melted before. It was estimated at three million dollars in the days of my father."

"And much more now."

Madam Chingwegh's sigh was one of contentment. "My duty is over. I know that you will use it wisely. I must go now."

"Where?"

She started.

"I will find a place, even if I have to walk back over the hills to the Chinese people in the park."

"Old Grandmother, I sometimes long for the traditions and food of my youth. My house is small and occidental in design, but it longs for the touch of an older generation to grace it. May I offer it's hospitality to one of your class, with the obvious obligation?"

"Which is?" she asked dubious of his half-caste state.

"A man without family has no foundation for marriage. I suddenly desire this, and need an Old Grandmother to guide me to a proper bride. May I count on you?"

The Aftermath

In 1910 the French press gave critical acclaim to "The Gilded Lily." America seemed a little shocked by the frank book about a girl's upbringing in a brothel. San Francisco howled with delight over the T.W. Lee book. Even though designed as a work of fiction, the citizens could see behind the facade of the "fictional" characters. Richly laced with the past and present history of the city, the convicted Mayor and political boss bore a striking resemblance to Eugene Schmitz and Abe Ruef.

The 'Scarlet Sisters' preened at their inclusion. Liberty hid her smiles when Alexander Grace Wells Lee grew indignant over his apparent characterization in the Tracey Whiteside Lee book. He huffed and gruffed, finding it an embarrassment as the President of the Lee Enterprises, but the family knew the source of his grousing. Luann Lee wanted people to forget that he had plucked her out of that brothel for marriage.

Lillian and Johnny Lord had little time to do more than praise Tracey's novel. The day after the fire, they made two major decisions: the house would be rebuilt as a restaurant and home to house four orphans they planned to adopt.

For reasons that Tracey could respect, Eric Soong Larson wished no mention of the Wang Soong gold. It was quietly put into the hands of A.P. Giannini for deposit until it could be used to build the Larson-Lee Hospital.

There were some, like Miranda Lee, who were a little miffed that they were not included. Tracey took it in stride, but Mick suggested that Tracey could do a whole book on the men in Miranda's life.

Then San Francisco put aside "The Gilded Lily." They were eager to look ahead and with a plan that lesser cities might have found too ambitious. The 1905 plan to hold the World's Fair in 1915 was revived and expanded. The San Francisco Exposition would become the Panama Pacific International Exposition.

They were the gateway to the Pacific and through efforts of one of their own, Liberty Lee, the Panama Canal made them a gateway to the Atlantic.

And throughout those years T.W. Lee continued to keep a daily journal. She wanted her children never to forget their priceless heritage.